Sandy is a writer, trav.......................................ngthy bucket list, and many ....homes in her novels. She's a.....................................lover and a coffee snob.

Sandy lives in Mel......................................n, who she met while travelling in Greece. Their real-life love story inspired Sandy's debut novel *One Summer in Santorini*, the first in the five-book Holiday Romance series with One More Chapter, an imprint of HarperCollins.

The series continues in Paris, Sydney, and Bali with Tuscany the final destination in the series. Sandy's novels *The Christmas Swap* and *The Christmas Trip* celebrate her favourite time of the year, and her romcom, *The Dating Game*, is set in the (fascinating) world of Reality TV.

www.sandybarker.com

 twitter.com/sandybarker
 facebook.com/sandybarker-author
instagram.com/sandybarkerauthor

Also by Sandy Barker

The Holiday Romance Series

One Summer in Santorini

That Night in Paris

A Sunset in Sydney

A Sunrise Over Bali

A Wedding in Tuscany

The Christmas Romance Series

The Christmas Swap

The Christmas Trip

Standalone

The Dating Game

THE CHRISTMAS TRIP

SANDY BARKER

One More Chapter
a division of HarperCollins*Publishers* Ltd
1 London Bridge Street
London SE1 9GF
www.harpercollins.co.uk

HarperCollins*Publishers*
1st Floor, Watermarque Building, Ringsend Road
Dublin 4, Ireland

This paperback edition 2022
1
First published in Great Britain in ebook format
by HarperCollins*Publishers* 2022

A catalogue record of this book is available from the British Library

ISBN: 978-0-00-855280-0

Printed and bound in the UK using 100% Renewable Electricity
by CPI Group (UK) Ltd

For my nephew, Alexander, who loves Christmas as much as I do
(one day, you'll be old enough to read this)

Prologue

The May Ladies - Mexico

'Well, isn't this lovely?' said Lucy, her eyes scanning the large, light-filled room.

'Yeah, not too shabby,' added Chloe, dropping her heaving backpack onto the terracotta tile floor. 'And check out this view!' She made her way over to the large glass doors, opening them wide and stepping out onto the balcony. 'Holy crap! Jules, come check this out!'

Lucy joined Chloe on the balcony. 'Oh my goodness.'

'I know, right,' said Chloe.

Lucy's eyes swept over the view, drinking in every detail—the terracotta-tiled roofs of the resort, the *two* pools, both bright blue and beckoning, the broad white-sand beach dotted with beach umbrellas and sun loungers, and the ocean, its waves lining up in perfect rows and crashing at (almost) regular intervals. The last time she'd been to a beachside resort was the trip to Maui with her parents when she was eleven—where she'd met Chloe and Jules at the kids' club.

1

This was simply heaven.

She turned towards the room. 'Jules, you have to see this.' There was no answer, so she went in to investigate, Chloe following closely.

Stepping back into the room, their eyes taking a second to adjust from the bright sunlight, they found Jules rummaging through her suitcase.

'What are you looking for?' asked Chloe.

'My phone charger. Phone's nearly dead.' Chloe and Lucy exchanged a look. 'Where … ah, here.' They watched as Jules plugged the charger into the nearest outlet, then connected her phone. Jules plonked onto the bed—one of two queen-sized beds—and stared at it, chewing on her lower lip.

'Jules, don't you want to come and see the view?' asked Lucy.

'Yeah, it's amazing.' Chloe sat next to Jules and watched her closely.

'Not right now, thanks.' Chloe and Lucy traded looks again, their shared concern evident.

'Are you expecting a phone call?' Lucy asked. It may have been an obvious question but she was at a loss for what else to say. This was the first time the three of them had been together since Maui, eleven years ago. By happenstance, their families had stayed at the same resort and they'd met at kids' club, forming a fast friendship based on little more than all being aged eleven and born in the month of May. The May Ladies, as they'd dubbed themselves back then, had forged their friendship via long email chains and interactions on Facebook. They were close—for online friends who lived in three different countries—but being there with Jules, fresh from a devasting breakup … well, Lucy was feeling a little out of her depth. Especially as she'd never even had a proper boyfriend.

Maybe it wasn't a good idea for them to have come.

'Jules, he's not going to call,' said Chloe.

Lucy's 'gently, gently' approach wasn't making much of a dent in Jules' sorrowful mood, so why not try tough love? Jules shot Chloe an irritated frown.

'What? He's not. You broke up with him and then you brought your girlfriends on your romantic holiday to Mexico. Why would he call?'

Jules' lip quivered, but she clamped her teeth shut, tensing her jaw, and bit back the threatening tears. Yes, she'd broken up with Peter but she'd *had* to. He'd been a prize dick when her parents announced they were getting divorced. 'What's the big deal, Jules? My parents have been divorced for *years*.' When he'd shrugged at her then gone back to watching football, she'd wanted to punch him in the face.

Because it *was* a big deal.

Her mom, her dad, Will, and her—they were a *family*. A tightknit family unit who not only loved each other, but got along. They were *friends*. That, her mom had told her, was part of the problem. Her mom and dad had fallen out of love a while back and were more like brother and sister than husband and wife.

She shook her head, only semi-aware of Chloe's hand on her shoulder. Why did she think Peter would call? Did she *want* Peter to call? Yes. And no.

'Because it's our anniversary,' she said softly. 'Or it would have been. Two years.'

'Right, but it's *not* your anniversary because he was an arsehole to you, so even if he does call, you're not going to talk to him!'

'Um, Chloe?' Lucy thought Chloe had gone too far. Jules needed kindness and support, not someone saying horrible things about the love of her life. Even if they were true.

'It's okay, Luce,' said Jules. 'Chloe's right.'

Chloe nodded, keeping her eyes locked on Jules. She liked being right but, even more so, she was glad Jules was finally seeing sense. She definitely didn't want to spend the next ten days watching Jules sink into depression over some dickhead named Peter. Yes, two years was a long time to be together—*her* longest relationship had lasted four weeks, two days, and three hours—but what sort of guy tells their girlfriend to 'get over it' when she's devastated by her parents' divorce?

'Too right I am,' Chloe agreed. 'Peter's a dickhead.'

'Hey! I still love him, you know.'

'Of course you do,' said Lucy, bobbing down in front of Jules. 'You don't get over someone you loved in a few days.' Lucy's experience in this area consisted of a steady diet of chick-lit, romcoms, and *Cosmopolitan* magazine—but surely everybody knew that?

'Totally,' said Chloe, changing tack. 'And look, one day, you'll meet some cool, handsome, really nice guy and he'll make Peter look like the total di—'

'Chloe!'

'Like a *moron* for leaving you.'

'I left him.'

'Semantics, Jules. You wouldn't have had to if he'd been more supportive.'

Jules nodded solemnly, then lifted her gaze to meet Chloe's. 'You said "handsome". Is that on *your* list?'

'My list?'

'You know, your wish list. For a guy,' Jules replied.

'I read that *men* fall in love with the women they're attracted to and *women* become attracted to the men they fall in love with,' said Lucy, glad she could contribute to the conversation.

'I read that,' said Chloe. 'Wasn't it in *Cosmo*?'

'What the hell does that mean?' asked Jules, talking over her.

'I suppose it means that sometimes, if we meet someone we

like,' said Lucy, 'we may not be attracted to them right away—not until we get to know them and discover how clever they are, or that they're really nice—'

'Or funny,' interjected Chloe.

'Exactly. And then after spending time with them, they become more attractive to us. Or at least, I think that's what it means.'

Jules nodded slowly. 'I didn't like Pete when I first met him.'

'Really?' Chloe and Lucy asked together.

Jules smiled for the first time that day. 'Yeah, he was super arrogant—that guy in class who always has the answer, you know? And even if other people knew it, he'd jump in so he was the first …'

'See? Dickhead,' Chloe asserted.

'Yeah, but when I got to know him, I realised it was probably because he was the youngest of six.'

'*Six*?' asked Lucy, incredulous. She was an only child and the thought of having five siblings was alarming. No wonder his parents had divorced!

Jules chuckled. 'Yeah.' The smile dissipated as she conjured a thought of his family get-togethers. She'd never go to one of those again.

'Hey!' Chloe jostled her with her shoulder. 'Stop that. You loved him— sorry, you *still* love him, despite him not understanding you or giving you any support whatsoever, even though you were at your lowest—'

'Jesus, Chlo …' Jules shook her head.

'Sorry—a bit of a tangent. What I meant to say is that it's gonna hurt …' Chloe may not have been speaking from experience, but it was a reasonable assumption. 'But we're here and we're gonna have fun and drink lots of margaritas and eat a million tacos and sit in the sun and just …'

'Help you get over him,' said Lucy, finishing Chloe's thought.

'Exactly,' said Chloe. 'Okay?'

5

Jules looked at her two friends—her best friends, really, because other than her parents and Will, she wasn't really close to anyone else. That's why it had been a no-brainer to invite them to come to Mexico. The vacation was already paid for—her dad had gifted her a bunch of airmiles to book the all-inclusive resort—and rather than sit at home and wallow about her breakup with Pete …

Pete.

She sucked in a sharp breath, the pain acute. *Breathe, Jules,* she told herself. *It's going to be okay.* She glanced at her phone which lay inert, its screen black. He wasn't going to call.

And, she realised, she didn't want him to. 'Okay,' she said eventually—more to herself than the others.

'Great,' said Chloe jumping up. 'Now, two things: go and look at the view because *oh-my-god* and then we're getting our bathers on and going down to that swim-up bar. First round is on me.'

'I thought the resort was all-inclusive?' asked Lucy, confused.

'Whatever,' said Chloe—more semantics as far as she was concerned. 'Now up,' she said to Jules.

Jules tilted her head, a grateful smile breaking across her face. 'Ohhh-kaaay,' she said, peeling herself off the bed. She trundled off to the balcony door and stepped out into the warm, humid air—a stark contrast to her hometown in Colorado—and inhaled deeply as she took in the view.

The girls were right; it was really pretty. All she needed to do was stop obsessing about why she was there without Pete and enjoy (what she hoped was) the very first May Ladies' vacation.

'Hey,' she said, turning back towards the others. 'Thank you.'

Lucy smiled at her benevolently, reaching out to stroke her arm. 'Of course.'

'You're welcome,' said Chloe. 'Now can we *please* go to the bar before my jetlag hits and I'm as useless as tits on a bull?'

Jules and Lucy shared a look, Jules succumbing—at last—to an all-encompassing laugh. Lucy tittered politely behind her hand.

'What? What did I say?' God, Jules loved that weird little Aussie—*and* Lucy. Yep, she'd definitely done the right thing. This was going to be a great vacation. She just knew it.

'No, seriously, what?' asked Chloe.

Chapter One

CHLOE

Los Angeles

'Chloe! This way!'
'Chloe, over here!'
'Chloe!'
'Chloe, turn to your right!'

Will I ever get used to the red carpet? Chloe wondered. This was her fourth event—no, *fifth*—in as many months and it was no less surreal than the first, that movie premiere in London. This time last year, Chloe had been a single Event Manager living in Melbourne who'd never even *met* the world's biggest film star, Archer Tate. Who would have thought that a plan to swap Christmases with her besties and a trip to England would have led her here?

Archer waited off to the side as she angled her body this way and that so the horde of photographers could get their shots. She caught the eye of the Red Carpet Coordinator—a job title she'd never heard of until this year—and the woman smiled at her politely, then nodded, meaning it was time to move on. Chloe joined her boyfriend, reaching for his outstretched hand and feeling an envelope of safety wrapping around her as soon as their palms touched.

As he led her into the movie theatre, he leant closer and murmured, 'You look absolutely stunning.'

'Thank you, but you've already told me a dozen times,' she teased, peering up at him through her false lashes.

'It's no less true now than it was at home or in the car.'

'I still can't believe they wanted shots of me on my own. *You're* the famous one.'

He smiled at her thoughtfully. 'I think we can safely say that you're *also* famous now.'

'Mmm,' she replied vaguely. There was a time when the name 'Chloe Sims' had referred to a rising star of the Australian event management industry. Now she was 'Archer Tate's girlfriend, Chloe Sims'. Chloe knew it was just part and parcel of being in love with the world's biggest film star, even though, to her, he'd ceased being 'Archer Tate' soon after they'd met. He was just her loving, kind, talented—and yes, unbelievably handsome—boyfriend.

But on occasions such as this, she was reminded just how surreal her life had become.

She'd spent most of that day in the eye of a dreamlike hurricane as a stylist, hairdresser, manicurist, makeup artist, and even the security team from Tiffany's had whirled around her as though she were a sentient mannequin. The results were undeniably impressive. She was sheathed in a black floor-length, bias-cut gown—hand-beaded—and her black hair was styled into a perfect replica of Louise Brooks' bob. Her makeup was, at first glance, fresh and natural-looking—save for the bold orange-red lipstick—but had taken an hour to apply. And she was wearing $200,000 worth of Tiffany diamonds. Borrowed of course, as she was constantly reminded by the two hefty tuxedoed men trailing behind them.

A no-nonsense woman with a tablet in hand approached them in the aisle. 'Mr Tate, Ms Sims, this way, please.' She led them past a packed and milling audience to the front of the auditorium where Archer, as the movie's writer and director, would soon make a short speech. Cate, Tom, and Jen were already there along with Cate's husband, Andrew, and Jen was laughing at something Tom had said, her head thrown back and her laugh throaty, almost wicked.

'Chloe!' As soon as Jen clapped eyes on her, she rushed over. 'Fuck, you look *fantastic*!'

Chloe laughed. 'Um, hello? You look pretty amazing yourself.' Jen looked down and regarded her gown as if seeing it for the first time.

'Thanks. It *is* gorgeous but the boning's killing me,' she said, tugging at the bodice. 'Makes me wish we'd made a shorter movie.' She laughed again.

'At least we get to sit,' quipped Chloe. 'Not sure how much longer I can stand in these.'

They both looked at Chloe's shoes. 'Super pretty though.'

'Jen, you look positively divine.'

'Hey, Archer.' Jen accepted a cheek kiss from Archer and, watching the exchange, Chloe mentally pinched herself. If being primped and preened by Hollywood's best wasn't bizarre enough, here she was chit-chatting with her new gal pal, Jennifer Lawrence.

Last year, when Archer had decided to finally pursue a project he'd had in mind for years, he started tossing around names of actresses to play Eloise Capel—a local legend in his hometown hamlet in Oxfordshire and the subject of his passion project. That was when he'd first mentioned Jen and, embarrassingly, Chloe had imagined the two of them becoming besties. Their friendship wasn't *quite* of that calibre—her *actual* best friends, Lucy and Jules, had nothing to worry about there—but on set, with Chloe cutting her teeth as an Assistant Producer, they'd cemented their friendship over a shared love of trashy reality TV, funny dog videos, and mercilessly teasing Archer. He'd been good-natured about it, as he was about most things.

This was the most surreal aspect of being with Archer. He was genuinely friends with some of the world's most famous people. They'd had lunch with the Obamas a couple of months ago—the *Obamas*!

Cate looked over and gave her a little wave and a warm smile, which Chloe returned. The woman with the tablet, clearly used to bossing around Hollywood's A-list, asked them all to take their seats in the front row, then shepherded Archer to the mic stand. The house lights dimmed and the hum of the audience members' voices quietened.

This was it—the premiere of *An Extraordinary Woman: The Eloise Capel Story*. Chloe had been there at the film's inception, through the whirlwind of bringing a movie to the screen in record time, and now Archer was telling a packed auditorium how it had come to be. Like the thousand other people in the auditorium, Chloe was riveted by his words. She was also proud of Archer's passion, humility, and good humour. When he praised the incredible cast and crew for their limitless talent and hard work, Chloe had to blink away tears.

They'd done it. And in two hours and forty-eight minutes, she'd see her name up there on the big screen. Assistant Producer—Chloe Sims.

Chapter Two

LUCY

London

'Hello, loves,' Lucy called out as she bundled through the front door of her flat. She might be the only person in history who greeted her house plants after a trip abroad but since her promotion and her flatmate, Val, moving out, they were all she had for company.

Lucy left her carry-on and case in the small entry and, kicking off her shoes as she went, beelined for the sofa and plopped onto it, her handbag still looped over her shoulder. She shrugged it off and rummaged for her phone and, seeing the time shouting at her from the home screen, did a series of calculations.

Twelve hours since Will had seen her off at Denver airport. Twenty hours since she'd slept—well, properly, in a *bed*. And two hours before she was due at work. Or she could beg off and work from home. Now that she'd been appointed Division Manager after the departure of (thieving, lying, horrid) Angela, no one would question it.

She glanced around at her 'plant babies', all thriving under her neighbour's care—Anne obviously had a green thumb, as they always looked far spritelier after a trip than when Lucy was their primary carer—and sighed. She could barely muster the energy to peel herself off the sofa—work from home it was!

Her phone pinged in her hand, startling her. A message from Will:

Hey babe. Home safely? Miss you already. W xo

The tension in Lucy's shoulders dissipated as she smiled involuntarily. Lovely, lovely Will. She tapped out a reply:

Just got home. Shattered. I miss you too.

At those last words, her breath caught and tears prickled her eyes.

Last year, she'd wanted to swap Christmases with her best friends to experience a proper white Christmas in Colorado—and to give Chloe her longed-for traditional Christmas in Oxfordshire. What she hadn't accounted for was that Jules' little brother, whom she hadn't seen since he was eight, was now a grown (and very gorgeous) man. She'd fallen for him, despite knowing that loving someone who lived across the world was hard—as documented in excruciating detail by every woman's magazine, lifestyle blog, romance novel, and Hallmark movie that covered the topic. Long-distance relationships rarely worked out.

And this was why—this feeling right here. The feeling of 4799 miles separating her from Will. Lucy knew the exact distance because she'd calculated it one lonely night while devouring an entire packet of bourbon creams.

Besides, since last Christmas, they'd only seen each other in person three times—and all three had been in Colorado. Off the back of Lucy's promotion at the start of the year, she'd been tapped on the shoulder to support the law firm's American office in San Francisco. And after each work trip, she'd managed to tack on a visit to see Will, taking annual leave. It was the perfect set-up if one was going to commit to long-distance love.

Well, perfect for Will, it seemed. He never appeared to be crushed by the emotional hangover of one of their trysts like she was. Or perhaps he was just better at hiding it.

Their arrangement was thus: she'd arrive at Denver airport on a Friday evening, mentally exhausted after an intense week of working with the Americans, and Will would envelop her in one of his wonderful Will hugs, then kiss her passionately right there in the airport. That she didn't mind this kind of public display was testament to how (especially) good those kisses were. Then he'd step back, his eyes roving her face, before he stooped for a second kiss, softer this time, and she'd sink into his embrace as though it were a homecoming of sorts.

Then he'd drive them to his flat—a little faster than he'd usually drive, or so he said—and they'd spend their first night together babbling at each other as though they didn't connect every day, then making love into the night.

By the Saturday morning, Lucy would be well ensconced in the warmth and exhilaration of their relationship, feeling almost like a normal couple as Will bustled about his kitchen making pancakes—his dad's recipe—or bacon and eggs. Then they'd spend eight glorious days together, visiting sights of interest in Boulder and (further afield) Denver, going hiking, or taking a drive up into the mountains.

And on the rare days Will had to work, she'd head to a local coffee shop, sipping (terribly made) tea and catching up on her reading, or she'd stay at Will's and binge the Hallmark channel.

Just knowing he would be home that evening was enough to make her feel—again—like any other couple. 'How was your day, dear?' she'd asked once. The confused, then amused, look on Will's face had been enough for her to shelve the expression indefinitely.

They would also dedicate one evening to dinner at his dad's where Nate would conjure an impressive meal from his equally impressive kitchen, and one with his mum, Steph, and her husband, Joe, at some up-market restaurant that Steph insisted on taking them to.

This was Lucy and Will's 'normal'—these Colorado visits supplemented with daily messages and tri-weekly video calls, always during Lucy's evenings and always on Sundays, Wednesdays, and Fridays. Lucy liked the regularity of their scheduled calls—or, rather, she *needed* it. The days—*weeks* even—after she said goodbye to Will and re-entered her London life were becoming more and more excruciating.

She missed him. She missed his arms around her, how he smelled, how his lips felt on her skin, waking up next to him and watching his gorgeous face while he slept, the way he casually slung an arm around her shoulder or reached for her hand when they were in public.

Lucy missed *Will*. And yes, the funny memes and 'you've got to watch this YouTube vid—it's hilarious' messages and lengthy text exchanges they shared when one of them was having a bad day, helped ease the longing. But there had been *months* in between visits and that was a long time to go without seeing your boyfriend in person.

On this last visit, dread had crept in earlier than previous ones. Last Thursday morning, Lucy had woken up feeling sick and uneasy. *Only three more nights*, she'd thought. By the time Will had woken up, she'd worked herself into a lather and he'd had to hold her and shush away her tears.

As the minutes ticked away, edging her closer to the start of a new work week, Lucy succumbed to sobs. *Oh, Will …*

She looked at her phone, now blurry with the sheen of tears, and pressed 'send'.

Chapter Three

JULES

Melbourne

'You're here!'

Jules was always glad to see Matt but especially after an intense week at work. Her job at an organisation that supported children with special needs made her feel like she was doing something worthwhile, even if she was only the tech lead. But there were times when the heft of the work would fall on everyone's collective shoulders and this past week had been especially brutal.

As soon as she saw Matt's smile—and knowing they had the whole weekend together—the emotional burden of the week dissipated.

'Hey, gorgeous,' he said from across the room, his smiling warming her, even from fifteen feet away.

Dexter wangled his way to the front of the line to greet her. Resting her laptop bag on the floor, she knelt before him as his wagging tail threatened to knock over a tall pot plant. 'Hey, Dex. Hey, shhh ...' Jules pulled him close and he calmed down as she stroked his thick coat, then captured his head in her hands and let him lick her cheek.

'You don't let me do that,' said Matt.

She stood, laughing softly, and wrapped her arms around Matt's waist, falling into his embrace and inhaling his distinct, masculine scent. 'This is nicer than letting you lick my face,' she said.

Eventually, Jules leant back, taking him in. Matt's eyes were right out of one of those romance novels Lucy read. So. Fricking. Sexy. He gently kissed her and she was about to pull him closer for something a little less 'PG' when the bathroom swung door open and Davo walked into the living room wearing only a towel around his waist.

'Hi, guys,' he said, slipping past them.

'Hi, Davo,' Jules replied, a little deflated. It looked like Davo was staying the weekend—contrary to what her roommate, Ash, had told her a couple of days ago.

'Bayabe, where's your robe?' chastised Ash from her bedroom.

'Forgot it,' Davo said before the door closed behind him. There was a thud, giggles from Ash, a booming laugh from Davo and then …

'Uh, should we put some music on or something?' Matt asked, cringing.

'God, yes.' Jules slipped out of his embrace and headed into the kitchen. 'Hey Google, play *anything* on Spotify,' she said.

'Playing "Anything Could Happen" by Ellie Goulding on Spotify,' said their virtual assistant.

'That'll do,' Jules muttered to herself. 'So, what's going?' she asked, scouting the kitchen for an open bottle of wine.

'Chardy. Not opened yet. I put it in the fridge an hour ago, so it should be right to go.' He retrieved two glasses from an overhead cupboard.

'Aww, you waited.'

'It's a bloody nice Chardonnay,' said the hot winemaker. *Well, he'd know,* thought Jules. 'Didn't want to crack it open before you got home ...'

Jules took the bottle out of the fridge door and handed it to Matt. 'Worried you couldn't constrain yourself?'

Matt stopped what he was doing, tossing her a sideways glance that conveyed everything he was thinking before he even said a word. 'The only thing I have trouble constr—'

'Sorry, guys!'

Davo, having changed from a towel into a pair of 'undies' (as the Aussies called them), scurried from Ash's bedroom, across the living room, and into the kitchen, practically pushing Jules aside to reach into the fridge. He smiled sheepishly at Jules before scurrying back to Ash's room—butt crack peeking out from his 'tighty whities' (as Jules called them) and a beer bottle in each hand.

The door closed again and there were more giggles from Ash.

Jules and Matt locked eyes. 'I feel like we're living in a frat house,' she said. 'Any second now, someone will do a keg stand, then accidentally knock over the beer wall.'

'I have no idea what a keg stand is—'

'You're not missing out,' she quipped.

'Fair enough. And those two ... I *love* that they're back together ...'

'Love it. So happy for them,' agreed Jules.

'But ...'

'But ...' she agreed.

'I mean, seriously, I get that analogy—the frat house ... We're in our thirties, right?'

'Last time I checked.'

'Mmm.'

'Wanna go out for dinner?' asked Jules.

'*So* much.'

'Let me just get changed real quick.'

As Jules closed her bedroom door to get changed into something more casual, she heard Matt say, 'Sorry, Dex, but you have to stay here, bud.' Dexter dog-sighed his reply and Jules cracked up. God, she adored those two.

———

Jules woke early Saturday morning with Matt spooning her, his long fingers splayed on her bare thigh, and Dexter snoring softly from his dog bed near the window. She snuggled closer to Matt, hovering between dozing and awake as she pondered the night before.

They'd come back from dinner at a local steak house to find that Ash and Davo had wrapped up their amorous adventures and were on the couch watching a movie—fully dressed, thank god.

It *had* sorta irked Jules to see them curled up on the couch—she'd been hoping that she and Matt could watch something together—which was unfair because it was essentially Ash's apartment. When Jules had moved to Melbourne in April, she'd taken up residence in Chloe's old room, and Ash had been just as welcoming then as she had been during Jules' trip to Melbourne for Christmas last year.

Actually, even *more* welcoming, because there was a big difference between hosting a friend-of-a-friend for ten days and letting them move in with you. Ash had been an awesome friend to Jules over the past five months—helping her get settled in the city, walking her through the logistics of Australian life, putting up with Matt's constant visits …

A couple of months ago, Ash had joked that Matt should 'kick in for rent'. She'd immediately recanted, however, when Matt reminded her how often her boyfriend, Davo, stayed over. This meant there were many weekends when the apartment was jampacked with four adults and a dog. Even though they were all good friends—Ash and Matt had been at college together with Chloe—Jules wanted to get her own place.

It was just that she'd lived alone all of her adult life till now—and she *loved* having her own space. But even though there were several one-bedroom apartments close by that were within her price range, she didn't know how to broach the subject with Ash—*or* Matt. *Especially* as he kept hinting about her moving down to his vineyard. She could make it work professionally—she was only really needed at the office once or twice a week. The other days, she worked from home, or from Matt's if she was down on 'The Peninsula'—wine country to the south-east.

But was she ready for full-on cohabitation?

If she was honest with herself, the answer was 'no'. Things with Matt were perfect as they were. Jules smiled to herself, taking a deep breath and stretching her legs down the bed. That had been the biggest surprise while swapping Christmases with her besties last year. And the best.

Matt.

She'd met him soon after she'd arrived in Melbourne from Colorado and for the first few days, she'd considered having a fling with the hot winemaker. What an awesome way to spice up the holidays! But then he became *Matt*—not just hot, but thoughtful and funny—one of those 'still waters run deep' sort of guys, like her dad … *And* she'd met Dexter. She wasn't sure which one she'd fallen for first, but by the time she and Matt flew to Colorado for New Year's to meet up with the others, she had been head over heels *in like*.

Or at least, that was what she'd told herself. Jules was never one to jump into something heart first—well, she hadn't been for a long time. The only thing was, Matt was easy to fall in love with. She pulled his arm around her and placed his hand on her breast.

He stirred, then shook with laughter. 'Good morning to you too,' he said, his voice in her ear.

Chapter Four

THE MAY LADIES

'Hey, you two,' said Chloe, flashing a wide smile at Lucy and Jules. She'd missed them so much. Their weekly calls—practically a May Ladies institution—had been scaled back recently because they were all flat tack with their busy lives. Still, busy or not, three weeks had gone by and that was far too long without talking to her besties.

'Hi, loves,' said Lucy.

'You didn't cancel on us, Chlo,' teased Jules.

'Ha-ha. It wasn't my fault last time. There was an emergency. We only had a four-hour window to do some last-minute ADR.'

'What the hell is ADR?' asked Jules, just as Lucy said, 'I don't know what that means.'

'Ha! Snap, Luce.'

Chloe shook her head good-naturedly. 'It's just re-recording dialogue. There was an issue with the sound edit.'

'Oh, so was *Jen* there?' asked Jules.

Chloe wasn't sure if Jules was still teasing or actually annoyed that she'd become good friends with Jen Lawrence.

'Uh, no. It was some other actors,' she replied vaguely.

'And how was the premiere the other night?' asked Lucy. 'You looked wonderful, Chloe.'

'Thank you, Lucy,' she replied simply. She didn't want to launch into a conversation about making *In Style*'s 'best dressed' list that week, though she had. 'It was good—nerve-wracking, though. I mean, *I* was nervous and it's not even my film. And I thought Archer had it together but he practically crushed my hand throughout the whole movie. When it ended, he sighed like he'd been holding his breath.'

'Makes sense—first-time director and all that,' said Jules.

'Absolutely,' agreed Lucy. 'But the reviews have been good—five stars from *The Independent* and they hardly like anything!'

'We saw that,' Chloe said with a proud smile. She'd learnt a lot about reviews in the past few days but even more so, she'd learnt a lot about Archer's relationship with reviews. As an actor, he never read them—'What's the point?' he'd say with a shrug. 'I'm proud of the work we did, so …'—but as writer and director, he'd been almost obsessive. Last night, Chloe had come back from the bathroom after getting ready for bed and he'd fallen asleep sitting up, his tablet in one hand and phone in the other.

Fortunately, the film was a hit; audiences and critics alike were singing its praises—*and* Archer's.

'I'm really proud of him,' she added. 'He's worked so hard …' Lucy tilted her head and smiled at her.

'Do you guys get a break now?' asked Jules.

'Yes! A couple of months at least and we're *very* excited about that. This year's been full on. I suppose it has been for all of us, hasn't it?' Chloe asked rhetorically. She had drastically changed careers and taken up a life with Archer, Lucy had been promoted and was dating Jules' brother, Will, long distance, and Jules had packed up her whole life and moved to Australia!

'I'll say,' replied Jules. 'But in a good way. Hey, speaking of breaks … what did you guys decide for Christmas?'

'Oh,' said Lucy, her face contorting pensively. 'Still deciding …'

'That's not like you, Luce,' Chloe chimed in, 'leaving Christmas plans to the last minute. Better hurry up—it's only three weeks away!'

Chloe's right, thought Jules. It *was* weird that Lucy still hadn't decided between Christmas with her parents in Oxfordshire and flying to Colorado to spend another white Christmas with Will and the rest of her family.

Jules had considered a trip home to Colorado a couple of months back, but she felt like she'd only just left—*and* she wasn't sure she wanted to swap a warm, sunny Christmas for a freezing cold, snowy one. Maybe next year.

Instead, she and Matt were hosting the traditional orphans' Christmas at his place—well, 'traditional' because their close circle of Melbourne friends, who'd embraced her as one of their own, held it every year. Though, this was only her second one. She was really looking forward to hosting—even though it was going to be a tight fit with Ash and Davo, and Callie and (heavily pregnant) Thea in Matt's two-bedroom house.

'Which way are you leaning, Luce?' she asked. Jules knew Will really wanted Lucy in Colorado, but maybe it was time to nudge him towards a trip to the UK to finally meet Lucy's parents.

'Er …' Lucy shrugged noncommittally and Jules wondered if something was up between her and Will. She'd interfered in their relationship before—last year when Lucy and Will were just getting together—and it had *not* gone well. She would keep out of it unless she was asked to give her two cents.

'Well, Archer's taking me to Paris for Christmas,' said Chloe. Jules could tell that Chloe had waited as long as she could before bursting with the news. Now that she was jet-setting around the globe and rubbing elbows with the rich and famous, she'd become especially mindful of not coming off like a total diva. It was another reason to love her Aussie friend—a lot of women in her situation would have gone 'Full Kardashian'.

'Oh, how wonderful,' said Lucy, glad the focus had shifted away from her. She wasn't up to talking through her relationship woes—particularly as she'd hate to come off as ungrateful. There were millions of people out there who longed to find someone special. So what if her special someone lived across the world? At least he existed!

'Yeah, I know. But seriously, I don't even know if I have the energy to sightsee. I'll probably spend the whole time holed up in the hotel.' Chloe punctuated her point with a wide yawn.

'But it's Paris, Chloe! What a waste!' The words were out of Lucy's mouth before she'd formed the thought but Chloe's chastised expression made her wish she could take them back. 'Sorry, lovely. Just ... you know, *Paris*.'

'I know,' sighed Chloe. 'Part of me just wants to stay here in LA—sleep in, swim, read. *Not* freeze to death.'

'So LA life suits you, Chlo?' asked Jules.

'Ha!' laughed Chloe. 'The weather does, at least. The rest of it ... I dunno,' she added with a shrug.

'Have you at least found a decent coffee place yet?'

'God, no. But I've got a tip on a café a few suburbs away—it's run by an Aussie couple. Probably worth the drive. But that's LA. Everything is at least a thirty-minute drive away—even coffee.'

'And I just have to go downstairs,' bragged Jules.

'Yeah, yeah.' Lucy knew that Jules had become a coffee afficionado since she'd moved to Melbourne—or 'coffee snob', as Chloe liked to say.

But as she listened to her two best friends chattering away, the gnawing feeling in her stomach intensified. She truly was happy for them both but that didn't mean she wasn't also envious. If only her relationship with Will wasn't so one-sided. Maybe she should press him to come for Christmas instead of her going to Colorado. They'd have to stay at a hotel in the next village or find somewhere else nearby to stay, of course. *She* barely fit in her childhood bed. There was no way both of them would—Will was six-foot-three! At the thought of her and Will squashed into a single bed with a bright-pink duvet, she giggled.

'You right there, Luce?' asked Chloe.

'Oh, er … yes. I just thought of something funny.'

'Cool. Look, I hate to do this, guys, but I need to g—'

'Yeah, we know—life of the bigshot Hollywood producer …' Jules teased.

'Hey!' They smiled at each other, Jules chuckling softy at Chloe's expense.

'Before you go, can we *please* promise to talk next week?' Lucy asked. *Ugh*. She hoped that hadn't come off as whiny.

'I'm good for next week. Chloe?'

'Um … *yesss*?' she replied, posing 'yes' as a question.

Jules shook her head. 'Why don't you have your people get in touch with our people, set something up?' *Jules is in proper teasing mode*, thought Lucy. And here she was feeling bad about her Paris comment.

'Yeah, yeah, hilarious … right—really gotta go. Love you.'

'Love you too.'

'Love y—' Lucy was a second too late and the rest of the word was said to a black screen. At least they'd finally got to chat, she supposed.

Her mind flitted back to Will. She really did love him. And when they were together, it felt wonderful—*perfect*, even. It was just the long weeks and months without him that left her doubting. Was he really as invested in this relationship as she was? And if so, when was *he* going to make the trek across the Atlantic?

'I'll ask him to come for Christmas,' she said to herself out loud. She glanced over at her peace lily, its leaves drooping now that she was back in charge of its care. *Does that mean more water or less?* she wondered. She'd have to ask Anne. 'What do you think, lily? Would you like a visit from a handsome American?'

The lily sat motionless, clearly indifferent to Lucy's (brilliant) idea for reigniting her waning love life. At least, that was what she was telling herself. Deep down, Lucy knew that this was a test. Did Will really love her?

Chapter Five

ARCHER

Los Angeles

'How's the packing going, my love?' Archer stood in the doorway of their walk-in closet and watched, amused, as Chloe sat amongst an explosion of clothes.

'Argh!' Chloe huffed out an upwards sigh that ruffled her fringe. 'Look, I promise I'm not going to become one of those spoiled women who complains about having to pack for Paris but …'

'You don't know what to pack for Paris.'

'Exactly.'

'Should we phone the stylist?' he asked. Archer knew from experience—specifically, with love interests past—that as a woman, packing for the fashion capital of the world was practically a minefield when compared to what he'd be packing—a coat, a pair of jeans, some dress trousers, and a week's worth of dress shirts. Simple. Chloe crinkled her nose at him. 'I know, I know … you don't want to be—'

'One of those women,' she finished. 'Even though I'm totally out of my depth. Maybe I should watch some episodes of *Emily in Paris* for inspiration.'

Archer grinned and was about to reply when he was interrupted by the ringing of his phone. He retrieved it from his pocket, seeing that his assistant was calling from London. 'Hallo, Anya, how are things on your side of the world?'

'Have you seen the news?' she asked cryptically.

'Er, no.' He switched the phone to speaker mode and navigated to a news site.

'It affects your flights,' Anya said. 'Actually, it affects all flights in and out of Europe.'

Chloe stood and came to his side, frowning at his phone just as he tapped on a headline. Mount Eyjafjallajökull in Iceland had erupted—again—and an ash cloud was descending on Europe.

'Bollocks,' he said, right as Chloe said, 'Oh, crap.'

'So, you've seen it?' asked Anya.

'Yes, just now.' He glanced at Chloe. Lips pursed and nose scrunched, she perched on the pouffe in the middle of the closet.

'I've already confirmed it—BA has cancelled all flights. I'm still trying to get hold of the George V,' she said, using the French pronunciation, 'but I'll cancel the room when I get through.'

'Thank you, Anya,' he replied. 'And happy Christmas.'

'Happy Christmas,' she said. 'Oh, and Archer?'

'Yes.'

'Thank you again—it's beautiful and you really shouldn't have.' She was referring to her Christmas gift, a snow-white Prada handbag she had not-so-subtly hinted at being on the top of her wish list.

'I should have and you're welcome.'

She giggled. 'Bye-eee,' she said, ringing off.

Archer slid the phone back into his jeans pocket and looked at Chloe. She was clearly disappointed, but it wasn't lost on him that his previous girlfriend—Madison Strumpet—would have launched into a full-blown tantrum at this news.

'So!' said Chloe brightly. 'I guess that solves my packing dilemma.' She smiled up at him and he stepped forward and reached for her hands, pulling her up. He slipped his arms around her waist and hers slid up his chest and came to rest.

'How do you feel about Christmas in LA instead?' he asked.

'Honestly?' He nodded. 'It's fine. We can go to Paris another time. It'll always be there—unless there's an alien invasion or the Zombie Apocalypse, or something ...'

'Mmm, it is good to consider every contingency,' he agreed, winking.

'Exactly. Actually, now that I think of it, if you're going to invade another planet, you're not going to destroy its prettiest cities, are you? You'd keep those intact. Even aliens would want somewhere nice to go on holiday.'

'Flawless logic,' he said smiling.

'I think so.'

God, he loved this woman—she was clever, beautiful, *funny* ... but most of all, he loved that she was a genuinely beautiful person. As he'd known for some time now, this was the first time in his life he'd truly been in love.

It hadn't all been smooth sailing over the past year, either, which had deepened his feelings for Chloe. First, there had been the incredibly tight schedule to get *An Extraordinary Woman* into cinemas in time for Christmas—the fastest film production he'd ever been part of—but there had also been the 'Madison Factor', as he thought of it.

Madison had been a looming presence in their lives since she'd shown up at the Ritz London, where Archer and Chloe had been staying after Christmas last year. Immediately afterwards, Madison has gone to the press accusing Chloe of stealing Archer away from her, even referring to Chloe as a 'skank'—a horrid and grossly unfitting word for his darling.

Since then, Madison had tried to paint herself as the poor abandoned girlfriend and Chloe as a 'homewrecker'—even likening herself to Jennifer Aniston. It was all a fabrication, of course—Archer had ended their relationship *long* before he'd met Chloe. *But why let the truth get in the way of a good story?* he often thought wryly. Madison's efforts to keep the story alive had led to multiple instances of her face filling the front pages of the tabloids and Chloe's name being dragged—once again—through the mud.

He knew that it hurt Chloe—and he and his publicity team tried their best to shield her from it each time it occurred—but, impressively, she had always taken the high road, refusing to publicly respond, refusing to be dragged into the mire, and refusing—even to Archer—to say anything bad about his ex-girlfriend. *Chloe* was the extraordinary woman.

And she may have taken the news about their cancelled plans with the grace and maturity he'd come to expect from her, but Archer still wanted to find a way to make this Christmas special. *And*, he quickly realised, Christmas in LA was not the answer. Yes, it had been their home for the past few months, but he'd been eager to get back to somewhere more ... well, *more*. Besides, he was hardly going to propose to Chloe on the beach, surrounded by volleyballers, rollerbladers, and surfing Santas.

No. If his plans to propose atop the Eiffel Tower on New Year's Eve—a cliché, he knew, but was there any better place in Paris for a marriage proposal?—were now an impossibility, he'd have to come up with something equally as romantic. And just as special.

He had an idea.

'Hey, Archer!' said Jules. 'Ah!' she shrieked. Dexter, Matt's dog, was clearly oblivious to the fact that his mistress was trying to take a video call, licking her all over her face and making her laugh. 'Dex, go to your bed.'

Dexter disappeared from the screen and Jules wiped her cheek. 'Sorry, Archer. He's going through this phase—if one of us is on a call, he wants our attention.'

Archer's mouth quirked. 'Sounds like a toddler.'

'Yeah, except he's seven, so ... like, fifty in human years.'

He grinned. 'I know quite a few fifty-year-olds who act like toddlers.'

'Oh, really? Spill!'

He tapped the side of his nose. 'Sworn to secrecy.' He added an eyebrow raise and Jules smirked.

Archer considered himself very fortunate. Not only had he met and fallen in love with the perfect woman for him, he'd become quite friendly with her dearest friends. Jules, with her dry sense of humour, was brilliant fun and her boyfriend, Matt, was a quiet, thoughtful bloke—a gentle soul who also happened to make an exceptional Pinot Noir.

'So, have you seen the news?' he asked.

'About Europe? Yeah,' she replied. 'Chloe must be bummed.'

He checked over his shoulder in case she'd snuck up behind him and could hear the conversation, but she was still inside. 'Actually, that's why I'm calling ...' he said as he stared out over the Pacific.

'Oh-kay ...'

'What are your plans for Christmas?'

'We were supposed to be hosting an orphans' Christmas, but that sorta fell apart, so it's just me, Matt, and Dex. Why do you ask?'

Archer was not able to get through to Lucy—she was mid-flight on her way to Colorado—but he did speak to her boyfriend, Will—also a nice bloke but much more outgoing than Matt. Will loved Archer's idea and promised to talk to Lucy about it as soon as she landed, then get back to him.

That left one more call …

'Hello, stranger,' said Sean. Archer chuckled at the gentle ribbing—he was terrible at staying in touch. 'To what do I owe the pleasure?'

'I was just calling to say happy Christmas.'

'Liar.' A husky laugh emitted from his phone and Archer grinned.

'You've got me.'

'So, why *are* you calling? You finally decide to throw in the acting gig and join me at the helm?' Sean was referring to her charity whose sole purpose was to ensure every child in the world had access to clean water, decent food, and healthcare. Archer had contributed large sums—it was a critical cause—but it wasn't the first mention of him joining its Board of Directors. 'You know you want to, and no one can say you didn't give acting the good ol' college try.'

At this, he laughed loudly. 'I'll think about it, but why I'm really calling is to see if you still have that place on Kauai?'

'Oh, yeah. I'd never sell that place—divorce or no divorce.'

'And are you—?'

'There? Nah. I'm in San Fran for the holidays—I barely even get time off. I think my assistant's scheduled forty-five minutes when I can open Christmas presents and chug some eggnog. You want to use it?'

'Only if it's not an imposition.'

Sean laughed. 'Archer, the President could be in residence and I'd kick him out for you.'

'Brilliant. Thank you.'

'But not just you, right?'

'No, I'll be bringing Chloe—'

'I want to meet her, Archer. In the New Year. Promise me.'

'I promise. You'll adore her.'

'I have no doubt. Anyway, bring as many people as you like—it sleeps about twenty. And Leilani's there—remember her, our housekeeper?'

'Oh, yes, of course.' Leilani was a big-hearted, vivacious woman who was just bossy enough to keep the home running smoothly and Sean's guests in line.

'I should change her job title, though,' said Sean. 'After fourteen years, she's practically family. Anyway, I'll let her know you're coming and give her your number. Coordinate with her, okay?'

'You're really sure? It's not an imposition?'

'Not at all. Take it. At least someone will get to use it this Christmas.'

'Thank you, Sean. I'll make it up to you.'

That deep laugh came back down the line. 'I'm holding you to that.'

They ended the phone call and Archer was relieved that his plan was coming together. He had other options if they hadn't been able to stay at Sean's—there were lots of places to rent on Kauai—but it really was the perfect location for what he had in mind. He'd only stayed there once before but it was a beautiful home in a stunning, secluded location and had just the right mix of luxuriousness and homeyness.

Chloe would love it.

Now he just needed to tell her to pack for warmer climes and wait to hear back from the others.

Chapter Six

CHLOE

Hawaii

'I still can't believe we're spending Christmas in Hawaii,' said Chloe, her eyes riveted to the view as the small aeroplane arced over the blue waters of the Pacific. They'd just taken off from Honolulu and in less than thirty minutes, they'd land at Lihue Airport on the island of Kauai.

'I'm just glad you're happy with my contingency plan.'

Chloe turned back towards him. 'Of course! It's so thoughtful, Arch. If Europe's a no-go, this is the next best thing. Besides, I've only ever been to Maui—and that was more than twenty years ago.'

'I remember you telling me,' he said, his blue eyes twinkling. 'That's when you met Lucy and Jules and became the May Ladies. I'm surprised the three of you have never been back.'

'It's on the list,' she said, feeling the pull—and, yes, the sting—of nostalgia. She looked back out the window, watching the lush green mountainous island get closer as she indulged her sentimental feelings.

It had been an incredible year but she really missed everyone—her parents, her brother, her friends in Melbourne … But most of all she missed her besties.

She hadn't seen Lucy since she and Archer moved from London to LA after filming had wrapped up. It had been amazing living so close to one of her best friends and getting to see Lucy most weekends. They'd become closer than ever, with Chloe often playing agony aunt to help Lucy cope with the trials of a long-distance relationship.

She knew Lucy didn't want to burden Jules with her woes, not wanting to come off as resentful of Will. Being in love when you lived across the world was hard enough—Chloe had done that for three months before her move to London to be with Archer and start her new job—but Lucy's boyfriend was also her best friend's brother. Talk about an emotional obstacle course—especially when you were Lucy, who always wanted to make everyone happy.

And Chloe hadn't seen Jules since *forever*, not since early January when they were all in Colorado together. Jules may have taken over her part of the lease on the rental flat in Melbourne, but Chloe was already in London by the time Jules made the move to Australia.

Hopefully, sometime next year, they'd all be together again.

She felt Archer's hand on hers and met his eye. 'You seem a little …' He didn't finish the thought, leaving her emotional state unnamed, but Chloe didn't want him thinking that she was unhappy or ungrateful, so she leant over and kissed him.

'Just thinking about the girls.'

'You miss them,' he said simply.

'Always,' she replied.

'Understandable, my love.'

He pressed a kiss to the side of her head and she nestled against him as they began their descent.

'Oh my god, I can't get over how *green* it is—it's even more vibrant than it is from the sky!' said Chloe, gawking at the scenery, her mouth agape, as Archer navigated the Jeep along narrow, winding roads.

'Incredible, isn't it?' he replied. 'It's only been a couple of years since I was here but my memory is dull compared to the reality.'

'I can't believe we get to spend Christmas surrounded by all this. Hey,' she said, turning to him. 'What are you thinking we'll do while we're here?'

'How do you mean?'

'Well, we've got twelve days and I didn't really have time to research …' She'd had exactly one day between the news about the volcano and getting on a flight to Hawaii, so her usual 'planning to the nth degree' mode of travel had been obliterated. 'What's there to do?'

Archer smiled. 'Right. Well, there are beaches, of course, and we could go sailing or hiking, perhaps drive up into the mountains, take in the scenery—there's a veritable plethora of outdoor adventures on offer.' Obviously, the natural beauty of Kauai—and getting out amongst it—were huge drawcards for the island, but when Chloe heard all those activities listed off like that, she was a little overwhelmed.

'Or we could just hole up at the house,' she offered, making him laugh. 'Sorry—I don't mean the whole time and of course, there's Christmas …' though Chloe had no idea how they'd be celebrating.

'We can definitely "hole up" as you say. At least for some of the time.'

'I hope that doesn't sound ungrateful—or boring. It's just … now that we'll be stopping still for more than a few days, I think it's finally hitting me how exhausted I am.'

He reached across for her hand. 'I completely understand, my love. Filmmaking *is* an exhausting endeavour—constantly at a cracking pace for months on end.'

'Yeah.'

'That's why I rarely do them back-to-back. I try to take off at least a month in between, if I can.'

Chloe was hoping for at least *two* months away from movie-making. She *loved* her new job, sure, but Archer wasn't exaggerating about the pace. Once he'd had a yes from a major studio back in January, he'd locked himself away to write the script, and his producer friend, Fiona, had started pre-production, including hiring the crew, scouting for locations, and casting. By the time Chloe had squared away her move to the UK, they'd been ready to start shooting. She'd then endured an extremely steep learning curve as a first-time Assistant Producer under Fiona's tutelage. Then a fourteen-week shoot in the UK and a move to LA for post-production. That had been followed by the never-ending round of media interviews and PR events. After the premiere last week, Chloe and Archer had slept for fourteen hours straight.

As an afterthought, Chloe added, 'It is incredible, though, *and* fun—well, most of the time.'

'Yes, most of the time.' They swapped smiles across the car, then Archer's eyes returned to the road just as Google announced that in 300 yards, they would arrive at their destination. Archer slowed the Jeep and approached a gated driveway, pulling close to the intercom which stood atop a metre-high pole. He opened the window and the car filled with warm, humid, fragrant air. He pressed the button on the intercom and they waited.

'Aloha,' sung out a melodic voice.

'Aloha, Leilani, it's Archer and Chloe here.'

'Hello, Mr Archer. Please make your way up to the house.'

The wrought-iron gate began rolling back, its menacing spikes glinting in the sun as it disappeared behind an enormous hedge of glossy green leaves. When they had enough room to pass by, Archer drove slowly up the steep curved driveway. The 'house' was revealed as they rounded a bend and Chloe gasped. It looked more like a hotel—it was huge!

'Didn't you say that Leilani is the only one here?'

'Er, yes,' he replied.

'Must get lonely when no one's visiting,' she said to herself.

They pulled to a stop outside the front door and as Chloe got out of the Jeep, she was startled by a loud shriek.

'What the—?' She registered a shock of red curls right as she was enveloped in a tight hug and Lucy's signature floral fragrance. As she wrapped her arms around Lucy, she saw Jules standing close by, grinning at her.

'Oh my god! Jules, get in here!'

Jules joined the hug and Chloe squealed with delight then succumbed to happy tears, shaking with sobs and laughing with glee. She couldn't believe it—the May Ladies were reunited.

It was already the best Christmas present Chloe had ever had.

Chapter Seven

LUCY

Hawaii

Lucy wiped away tears and grinned down at her two best friends. She'd already had a couple of hours catching up with Jules, but to see them both together, being able to hug them both at the same time … it made her heart sing.

'Chlo, you've got to see this place. It's incredible,' said Jules, stepping back. 'There's an infinity pool—'

'And a cinema!' interjected Lucy.

'A cinema?' asked Chloe, incredulous. Lucy nodded—she'd already begun compiling a mental list of Christmas films she wanted to watch with her best friends. Chloe laughed. 'To be honest, the last thing I want to do now is watch a movie, but I'm all for chilling out in that infinity pool.' Lucy deflated but Chloe didn't seem to notice.

Jules slung an arm around Chloe's shoulder the way that Will would with Lucy—the genes rang strong in their family—and led her into the house, both chatting excitedly. Lucy, somewhat detached from the hubbub, was about to offer to help with the bags but realised that the men had them in hand—literally—and she quietly followed everyone inside.

It was only when Leilani, a lovely woman she'd met just hours before, patted her on the arm as she passed and gave her an understanding smile, that Lucy realised how out of sorts she was.

She'd been so caught up in catching up with Jules and the excitement over seeing Chloe again—not to mention being struck with awe as each hallway, walkway, and doorway of the enormous property revealed something even more spectacular—that she'd pushed aside what she was truly feeling.

She'd also completely lost track of time and had no sense of what day it was, what time it was back in London, or how much sleep she'd had in the past forty-eight hours. Calculating and keeping track of these details was how she typically managed to wrangle the feeling of displacement—and jetlag—that came with international travel.

But this time was different.

As she silently followed the others around while they played tour guide for Chloe—Archer knew the property very well, it seemed, so occasionally contributed to the commentary—Lucy watched with detachment, unable to pinpoint the odd mix of emotions swirling through her.

Yes, she was now with her two best friends, but this wasn't at all what she'd wanted for Christmas—what she'd hoped for and mentally planned for.

A couple of weeks ago, she'd finally got the nerve to ask Will to come to Oxfordshire for Christmas—to meet her parents and see where she grew up. But he'd said he wasn't able to get away from his company for long enough to make the trip 'worthwhile', something about not taking more time off than he gave his employees. It had stung, but Lucy had agreed that it didn't 'make sense' for Will to fly all the way to the UK, only to have to turn around again a few days later.

So, she'd had an early Christmas celebration with her mum and dad last weekend—her mum had gone all out and cooked a full Christmas lunch, even though it was only the 17th of December—then got on a plane to Colorado a few days later.

On arrival, Will had seemed even more excited than usual to see her. Lucy had wondered if he felt bad that, once again, *she* had made the long trek across the Atlantic so they could be together—and at *Christmas*. Lucy had fallen into his arms as she always did, the stress of travelling and any modicum of resentment washing away as soon as she felt those strong arms around her and his soft, pillowy lips pressed against hers.

And then he'd sprung the news on her.

They weren't staying in Colorado. In six hours, they were getting on a flight to Honolulu.

'I'm sorry, what do you mean?' she'd asked, confused.

And the whole plan—Archer's plan—came tumbling out. For a moment, Lucy had been too shocked to fully absorb what this meant for her—good and bad—but on the drive to Steph and Joe's house, so Lucy could 'raid Mom's summer closet'—she had recognised that her prevailing feeling was being properly cheesed off.

She'd packed for a Colorado Christmas—a *white* Christmas—and unlike last year, she'd been prepared. She'd even bought a snowsuit! And now she was supposed to forage about in her boyfriend's mother's cupboard unsupervised—because of *course* Steph was already up at the family cabin in the mountains—and collate suitable attire for a tropical holiday? How mortifying!

And not to mention that Will had been unable to step away for work long enough to justify a trip to the UK, but now they were going to spend twelve days in Hawaii? He'd explained that he would need to work remotely in the week between Christmas and New Year, but still. If that had been a possibility, then why couldn't he have worked from her London flat? She had excellent WiFi!

She'd seethed her way through the harried cupboard-foraging and repacking and all the way back to the airport—this time with Will's luggage, including a *surfboard*—but by the time they'd settled into their Business Class seats on the flight to Honolulu—a gift from Archer for scuppering their plans—she'd run out of steam.

'Excited?' Will had asked.

Well, no. She wasn't excited. She was exhausted—both physically and emotionally—but she'd nodded and smiled. That's when a frown had nestled on his face.

'It's a lot, isn't it?' She'd nodded again, this one lacking any pretence of joy or excitement or enthusiasm. 'Hey, did I screw up?'

'What do you mean?' She'd known full well what he meant but was stalling—she wasn't sure if she should answer truthfully, if she was prepared to have it out in the forward cabin of an aeroplane.

'Saying yes to this trip without asking you.'

'Oh, I …' *Should I say something?* she'd wondered.

'It's just that I haven't seen Jules in eight months—and it's been even longer for you, almost a whole year. *And* the three of you haven't been together since New Year's and *Dad's* joining us tomorrow and Archer says the place we're staying at is incredible … I told him I'd ask you first but then I thought … well, that you'd *love* it—that it was an awesome surprise—and I called him right back.' Lucy had watched his brilliant blue eyes dancing with excitement as he explained all the reasons—*good* reasons—he'd made the decision without her, and caught the moment he realised. 'But I should have waited, shouldn't I? Until you landed? Asked you if it was what you wanted.'

Lucy had reached for his hand. 'Yes, you should have. And I would have said yes—of *course*—for all the reasons you've just mentioned but it would have been *our* decision. We could have taken the same flight as your dad. *And* I wouldn't have been running around for the past few hours like a proverbial chicken with its head cut off trying to assemble enough clothes to get me through to New Year's.'

'I told you, my mom didn't mind.'

'Yes, but *I* did! It was embarrassing, Will.'

'I'm sorry. I figured it was better than trying to find summer clothes in the middle of winter at the mall. Especially three days before Christmas.'

'Well, yes, I suppose it was the better of the two options, but still—it's your *mother*, Will. Yes, she has good taste and sure, we're similar sizes, but … ugh. Thank god Jules is bringing me one of her swimsuits—and thank you for teeing that up, by the way.'

He'd conceded a smile at that, then got serious again. 'So, do you accept my apology? You're totally right about the "our decision" thing. We should have made it together. I shouldn't have sprung it on you the second you landed.'

She'd stretched across the chasm between their seats and given him a kiss. 'Forgiven,' she'd said. Only she hadn't even raised the matter of Will's working arrangements. Instead, she'd swallowed her resentment along with her worries that she was far more committed to this relationship than Will was. When the flight attendant came around to offer sparkling wine, Lucy had replied with an enthusiastic 'Yes, please,' then decided to spend the flight getting (happily) tipsy and looking forward to seeing her two best friends.

Now, as she watched them explore the enormous property, boyfriends in tow, she wondered how they were going to make the tropics feel even *remotely* Christmassy. Her mum had sent her away with one of her famous Christmas cakes but she'd stupidly left it at Steph and Joe's when she was repacking her carry-on to come to Hawaii. And, yes, she'd packed her Christmas stocking and one she'd bought for Will at Harrod's, but they were such minor contributions—they hardly made for a proper Christmas on their own.

Not to mention that in her own explorations earlier, she hadn't seen a Christmas tree (!) and with everything being last-minute, she didn't even have gifts for the others. At least they could watch Christmas films in a proper cinema, she supposed. Only Chloe wasn't up for that, apparently.

Lucy was being ridiculous, she knew. A grown woman of thirty-four should not have this much attachment to Christmas traditions but Lucy had mentally prepared for one experience and she'd had no time to recalibrate.

'Can you believe it, Luce?' asked Chloe as they stepped onto the ocean-facing terrace. Her face was lit up with an enormous smile and she reached out to squeeze Lucy's arm. 'I mean, *look!*' Chloe swept her arms wide, indicating the incredible view, then turned back to Lucy and Jules, who stood close by. 'And we're all here together.'

Chloe teared up and pulled Lucy and Jules into another three-way hug. 'I love you, girls,' she said. 'I've missed you so much.'

Lucy felt Jules' arm squeeze her tightly and heard a muffled, 'Love you too,' then felt the prickle of tears in her own eyes. *This.* This was why Will's decision—as much as it had initially irked her—had been the right one. If he'd waited, they wouldn't have had such a brilliant reunion and Archer's surprise for Chloe would have been spoiled.

Chloe stepped back, fully crying now but wearing an enormous smile. 'This is going to be the best Christmas ever,' she said.

'Hell, yeah,' replied Jules.

Lucy could only nod, not trusting her voice for the huge lump in her throat. All her anger and doubts fell away with the realisation that the May Ladies were about to share their first Christmas together.

Maybe Chloe was right. This might just be the best Christmas ever.

Chapter Eight

JULES

Hawaii

Jules leant against the railing and watched the rise and fall of the ocean swell far below the clifftop mansion. She inhaled deeply, detecting a floral scent in the air—frangipani, maybe—and smiled to herself. She loved her home state of Colorado—well, *mostly*, as the brutal winters were to be endured rather than enjoyed—but it was a cosmic irony of sorts that she'd been born and raised in a landlocked state when she felt more at home on the coast. Salty sea spray would forever lift her spirits and that afternoon, it was enough to help her shake off the last of her jetlag.

They'd arrived in Honolulu late that morning and had waited at the airport for Will and Lucy's flight to land, then all flown to Kauai together. Archer had arranged a car to meet them—the first time Jules had ever walked out of an airport to see a chauffeur holding a placard with her name on it—and they'd arrived at the mansion several hours ago.

That had been enough time to unpack—which for Jules meant

unzipping her suitcase, then lying on the bed watching, amused, as Matt emptied the entire contents of his into the huge walk-in closet—hangers *and* drawers—having a quick shower, fooling around on that enormous bed, eating a light lunch Leilani had prepared for them, then touring the entire property.

It *was* incredible—like something out of a movie, which Jules supposed was apt considering one of Archer's bazillionaire friends owned it, someone called Sean. They must be pretty good friends if this Sean guy was letting them all stay there, especially during the holidays and especially with Leilani on hand to look after them. There was even an SUV they could use.

On arrival, Leilani had greeted them at the front door—just like she'd greeted Chloe and Archer—and when she introduced herself, she'd said, 'I'm a little bit butler, a little bit chef, but mostly I'm a mama.' Then she'd laughed heartily, instantly endearing herself to Jules—and likely the others.

When Leilani had shown them to their rooms—suites, really—she'd apologised. Because she was the only one there, they'd have to make their own beds each morning. At that, *Jules* had laughed heartily. She *never* made her bed and she wasn't going to start with that behemoth.

Matt appeared at Jules' side and snaked an arm around her waist, and she nestled close to him. 'Not bad, eh?' he asked rhetorically. She turned her head for a kiss, luxuriating in the softness of Matt's lips. Maybe they could slip away for some more fooling around before dinner.

'Geez, you two. We've only been here five minutes and you're already at it,' teased Chloe.

Jules sniggered, pulling away from Matt who tutted his disappointment as he threw a look over Jules' shoulder.

'Nice one, Chlo—cutting my grass like that.' Jules wondered if there would ever come a time when she'd master the full glossary of Australian idioms.

'Ha!' laughed Chloe, taking up a spot at the railing on the other side of Jules. 'Wow,' she exclaimed as she looked out over the Pacific. Jules nodded in agreement.

Matt stepped away, joining Archer and Will—probably to talk about surf beaches. Like Will, he'd brought his board to Hawaii and Jules knew he was keen to get out there. This gave Jules an opportunity she might not have again any time soon.

She leant closer to Chloe and whispered, 'Something's up with Lucy.' Chloe peered up at her, then swung her head in Lucy's direction. She was further down the terrace watching the view like they were but, unlike her friends, Lucy was slumped against the railing, her shoulders drooping. 'See what I mean?'

'Hmm, she does look a bit tired.'

'Well, yeah, two long haul flights back to back, but I think there's something else going on. She had the energy of a puppy when we first got here—exclaiming about practically everything, *literally* bouncing up and down the closer it got to your arrival but now *look*. It's like someone stuck a pin in her, letting all the air out. I'm not sure it's just jetlag we're dealing with here.'

Chloe frowned. 'Yeah, you might be right. Quick May Ladies catchup once everyone's settled in?'

'Yeah, good call.'

'I still can't believe you're all here,' Chloe said, shaking her head and smiling. 'Best. Surprise. Ever.'

Jules laughed then squeezed her friend's shoulder in a side hug. 'Wouldn't have missed it for the world. And did you hear? My dad's coming tomorrow.'

'No!' Chloe swatted Jules' arm, incredulous. 'Seriously?'

'Yes, seriously,' Jules replied, rubbing her arm. Her Aussie friend may be tiny, but she packed a punch.

'I haven't seen him since …' Chloe frowned again, this time in concentration.

'Since we were kids.'

'Oh yeah, you're right.'

'You'll love him. He's a total sweetheart.'

'Of course I will!'

'Once I knew we were all coming here, I couldn't bear the thought of him up at the cabin with Mom and her whole side of the family—*alone*. It's different when Will's there as a buffer—or I am, but …' Her voice caught. She had a soft spot for her dad and she couldn't wait to see him. It had been the hardest part about her decision to move across the world to Melbourne—leaving her family behind, especially her dad.

Chloe leapt in. 'I get it. But now you get to have Chrissie together.'

'Yeah.' Jules smiled.

'Righty ho, everybody,' Archer called out. 'By my calculations, it must be time for some celebratory fizz!'

'Or beer?' asked Will hopefully.

'Or beer. Absolutely.'

Jules observed how Archer corralled them off the terrace and into the expanse of the living room—a bit like a sheepdog mustering a wayward flock. The thought sent a small pang of sadness through her as she thought of Matt's dog, Dexter, but no doubt he was having fun with Twoey—Matt's partner in the winery—and his family. Twoey's kids loved Dexter.

Jules hoped he was, in any case.

———

Jules and Chloe stood at the door to Lucy and Will's room, silently asking the other if they were ready. On Jules' signal, Chloe knocked three times, paused, then added another two knocks in quick succession.

As far as secret knocks went, it was hardly 'covert operation' level but it had served them well enough when they'd stayed at that two-star hostel in their twenties. There'd been no lock on the door and the bathroom was down the hall—hence the knock. Then the two May Ladies who were inside the room would remove a barricade they'd fashioned out of their backpacks and the battered dresser to let the third slip into the room. None of them had slept that night, and the next day, Jules had insisted they move to a three-star hostel and wear the exorbitant cost of an extra $15 a night.

'Maybe she's asleep,' whispered Chloe right as the door swung open. 'Oh, hey, Luce! We're just wondering if you wanted to join us for a swim.'

Jules held up the modest one-piece she'd brought for Lucy—what she wore when she swam laps at the public pool—and plastered a smile on her face.

Neither Chloe's enthusiastic invitation nor the loan of a swimsuit seemed to appeal to Lucy, who plodded back into her room and plopped on the end of the bed without saying a word.

'Luce, what's going on?' asked Jules, crossing the expanse of the room—a twin to hers and Matt's but in mirror-image. She sat next to Lucy and looked up at Chloe, who was still standing, and they shared an 'I have no idea' look.

'Oh, nothing. Just tired is all.'

'Well, yeah, totally understandable,' Jules said, right as Chloe said, 'Bollocks.'

Lucy's head snapped up, her smile seeming to surprise even her. 'Are you swearing like a Brit now, Chloe?'

'When in Rome ...' Chloe replied vaguely.

'Only we're in the US. *And* you've been living here for months, so I think the word you're looking for is "bullshit",' retorted Jules.

'Good call,' said Chloe, switching seamlessly to American slang. 'Bullshit, Luce. What's really going on?'

Lucy looked at them in turn, then flopped back onto the bed dramatically, her arms flung over her head and her masses of long red curls splaying out around her face. 'It doesn't feel at *all* like Christmas!' she declared.

'*Ohhh*,' said Chloe and Jules together.

'It's all *hot* and *tropical* and there are bloody palm trees everywhere ...' Lucy must have been really upset, Jules realised—she hardly ever swore. Lucy sat up as abruptly as she'd lain down and pinned them both with an incredulous look. 'The guys are *surfing* right now. Surfing! How is that even remotely Christmassy?'

Jules bit her tongue, even though she'd *loved* her first hot Christmas the year before. For Jules, Christmas wasn't tied to the weather, it was about the people you shared it with. But she knew Lucy felt differently—*very* differently—and she should have known what was bugging her.

'And I was *so* looking forward to another white Christmas—even that odd thing with the Christmas tree your family does,' she said to Jules. Lucy meant when the 'menfolk', as her dad called them, would go out into the forest outside the family's cabin, choose the ugliest, scrawniest tree—one that no one would *ever* want for their Christmas tree—then chop it down and drag it inside where it would be decorated with homemade paper chains and popcorn strings. It had been a tradition since the year there had been a mix-up about who was supposed to bring the tree—her parents or her aunt and uncle—and no one had.

'And going back to the hunting cabin ...' Lucy added with a breath sigh. Ugh—Jules did *not* want to think about her best friend and her brother's romantic getaway to the hunting cabin. It was bad enough that she'd *called* Lucy when they were there last year. So humiliating—for *everyone*. '*And* your dad's famous Christmas breakfast!'

'All excellent points, Luce,' said Chloe. Jules glanced at her. *Spoken like a producer*, she thought. Chloe had mentioned a few times that the biggest part of producing was diplomatically managing people's expectations. Not a bad skill to have under your belt, especially when your best friend seemed on the verge of losing it, and it did seem to calm her down a bit.

'And don't forget, Dad's arriving tomorrow. We can still do the big, traditional Christmas breakfast—pancakes, cinnamon rolls, all of it,' added Jules, glad she could finally be of use.

Lucy pursed her lips in acknowledgement, but it was obviously a small dent in an enormous set of shattered expectations. 'Look,' said Chloe, 'how 'bout we blame the volcano? If the bloody thing hadn't erupted, I'd be in Paris right now, you'd be getting your white Christmas and Jules—'

She stopped and looked at Jules, who leapt in with, 'And Matt and I would be having a quiet Christmas on our own at the vineyard.' Their Christmas plans had whittled down to just the two of them when the others had accepted invitations to 'go home'. Jules had been fine with that but Christmas in Hawaii with her best friends and her dad and her brother was a huge step up.

'Right—that. But the volcano *did* erupt and now look! We're all here together—the first time the May Ladies have had Christmas together. We can make our own traditions!' Chloe enthused.

Lucy's mouth flattened into a capitulating smile.

'Luce, come on,' said Jules. 'You've been up and down since we got here. *Please*, let's just have a great time and like Chloe said, we can create our own traditions. Leilani will help, surely.' She jostled Lucy with her elbow. 'How does that sound?' Lucy nodded, albeit not very enthusiastically. 'Great! Now put this on.' She placed the swimsuit in Lucy's hands. 'We're going swimming in that incredible infinity pool and that's final, young lady.'

Lucy smiled for real at that and Jules expelled a sigh. She knew from experience that if just one of them wasn't feeling it, then the whole trip could fall apart.

'And hurry up,' said Chloe. 'Leilani's mixing up mai tais as we speak.'

'Yes, ma'am,' replied Lucy.

'Oh, god, Luce, your American accent is worse than mine.' Chloe cracked herself up and made for the door.

'You really okay, now, Luce?' asked Jules.

Lucy nodded at her. 'Yes, I think so.' There was a flicker of something across Lucy's face that Jules couldn't quite put her finger on, but she let it go. 'Now shoo, so I can change.'

'Yes, ma'am,' Jules replied and she left to the welcome sound of Lucy's laughter.

Chapter Nine

CHLOE

'Oh, this is the life!' said Chloe as she bobbed about on a giant pineapple sipping a mai tai.

Jules' laughter carried from her spot on one of the six sun loungers lined up along the non-infinity edge of the pool. 'Isn't this just a typical day for you, Chlo?'

'Oh, yeah, totally. Every day on set was exactly like this, only you would have been Jen and Lucy would have been Cate. Especially with that sunhat, Luce.'

Lucy looked up from her book, her face barely visible under the wide-brimmed hat. 'Sorry?' she asked.

'Never mind,' said Chloe.

'I guess we're lucky to have made the cut then,' said Jules.

'Cate and Jen had plans—Christmas with their families.'

'Ha-ha, very funny.' Chloe giggled to herself, trailing a hand in the water and tipping her head to the sun. Growing up in Australia, she'd had 'sun sense' drilled into her since she was old enough to say the words, so she was slathered in SPF50 but at the same time, the sun felt *so good* on her skin.

'Another round, ladies?' The quality of Leilani's voice sounded almost like a song to Chloe—and not just because she was offering more cocktails.

'Ooh, yes please,' said Lucy. 'Can I help?' She swung her long legs off the sun lounger and stood, towering over the Hawaiian woman.

Leilani waved her off. 'No, no, I don't need any help but you can keep me company if you like.' She padded over to the poolside bar—of course there was a fully stocked bar next to the infinity pool—and took up her spot behind it as Lucy slid onto one of the tall barstools. The two women started chatting but Chloe could only make out every other word, so tuned out, closing her eyes behind her large round-framed sunglasses.

'Hey, Chlo.' Jules had slipped into the pool and sidled up to Chloe so stealthily that she scared the crap out of her, almost making her tumble off the pineapple.

'Geez!'

Jules cracked up as she helped stabilise the large piece of floating fruit. 'Sorry. I just wanted to talk to you about Lucy,' she said quietly.

'What do you mean? We talked about Lucy and then we talked *to* Lucy. It's all good, Jules.'

'I don't know. I mean, we know what gives but we still need to figure out the Christmas stuff.' Jules glanced towards the bar then back at Chloe. 'I'm guessing that as soon as the mai tais wear off, Ms White Christmas over there is gonna turn all morose again. I think we need a plan.'

'Now I *am* going to fall off my pineapple. You never want to make a plan.'

'Ha!'

'Well maybe we can ask Leilani to help—when the guys get back. Will can distract Lucy and you and I can sort everything out with Leilani. How's that for a plan? What? What's that face? You don't like it?' Chloe asked.

'Nothing, never mind.'

'Say it.'

'I just ... I don't want to think about Will "distracting Lucy", that's all.'

'Oh god. Jules, get over it. Your brother is bonking our best friend!'

'Ewww, *god*, Chloe!' Jules punctuated her (prudish, Chloe thought) reaction by splashing Chloe with a huge sweep of one arm, drenching her from top to toe and leaving her gawping like a fish out of water.

'Oh you are dead, you are!' Chloe rolled off the pineapple, holding it as a shield with one hand while flicking water at Jules with the other.

'Lame!' taunted Jules, dousing her with water again. She had much longer limbs than Chloe, an unfair advantage in a water fight.

'Oi!' The shout came from the side of the pool and both Chloe and Jules stopped long enough to see Lucy holding aloft two freshly made mai tais. A good thing too, as Chloe's previous one—only half-finished before Jules' assault—was now mixed in with the pool water, the plastic cocktail glass bobbing nearby, inverted.

'You're lucky I like cocktails more than I like winning,' teased Jules and she waded through the waist-deep water to the side of the pool.

'Just watch it, Jules. I know where you live.' Jules' husky laugh shook her shoulders as she reached up for one of the glasses, then threw a look back to Chloe. Chloe completely adored her—*both* of them. As she often thought, that had been the hardest part of the past year—being away from her closest friends and her family, and not having as much time for video calls and proper catchups as she'd have liked.

There were also times when she'd missed Ash and their flat in

Melbourne so intensely, she'd become nostalgic for weird things, like the dodgy hot water system which meant one only of them could shower at a time despite having two bathrooms. She'd also missed Melbourne—her friends, the city, the atmosphere, the *coffee*. LA was just a whole different universe to the city she'd grown up in and had called home for thirty-three years. She hadn't even owned a car in Melbourne, something that anyone from LA would find mind-blowing and very, *very* weird.

But the way she'd missed Jules and Lucy ... it was a longing made even more acute by their remarkable trip to Colorado over New Year's last year. What a special time that had been, imprinting an already unbreakable bond of friendship with something profoundly beautiful and intense. Maybe it was as simple as the three of them being together on the cusp of falling in love.

Chloe still couldn't believe they had the next twelve days together. She only hoped that her Christmas gift for Archer was special enough to show her appreciation. He'd been so thoughtful in bringing them all together and not just any gift would live up to that.

———

'Leilani! Just the woman we wanted to see,' said Chloe as they walked into the kitchen.

'Clever of you to find my hiding spot,' Leilani teased with a wink.

'Wow, it smells incredible in here!' said Jules, sneaking a slice of capsicum from one of the cutting boards.

'Thank you! It's my spice mix for the fajitas,' Leilani replied, flicking her wrist. The spices danced in the air for a sec before landing back in the hot pan. 'Not exactly a traditional Hawaiian dish, but I *love* Mexican food.'

'Oh, me too! And ever since I moved to Australia, I've been craving it—big time.'

'We have good Mexican food in Melbourne,' said Chloe, a little defensive at even a minor smirch on the good name of her hometown.

'Uhhh …' Jules trailed off with a smirk.

'Hey!'

'Well, hopefully I can live up to your expectations,' Leilani threw over her shoulder as she tossed the spices again.

'I think we're well beyond decent fast food,' said Jules looking around the kitchen.

'What can I help you with?' asked Leilani, turning off the heat under the pan and giving them her full attention.

'First off, you don't happen to have a Christmas tree lying around here anywhere, do you? Or maybe a potted ficus or something that we can drag inside and decorate?' asked Chloe.

'Ficuses, yes—there are dozens on the property but they're native, so none are in pots.' Leilani paused, saying 'hmm' quietly to herself. 'There are the topiaries,' she offered.

Chloe had noticed them standing either side of the impressive front door, but they were a little *austere* for a Christmas tree. Besides, they were enormous and she was doubtful they could be moved. 'Mmm, maybe.' She shrugged noncommittally. They might have to go into town and hit up the nearest Walmart. Nothing could feel *less* Christmassy, but desperate times and all that.

'Wait a minute!' said Leilani, her face glowing with an idea. She checked all the burners on the stove to ensure they were off, then untied her apron and set it on the counter. 'Come with me,' she said with a waggle of her eyebrows. As they were leaving the kitchen, Jules snuck another piece of capsicum. 'I saw that!' Leilani's chortle echoed against the marble floors as Jules and Chloe followed closely.

'Leilani, you're a lifesaver!' said Chloe, brushing dust off a large rectangular box. Leilani had her back to her, systematically checking the contents of plastic tubs.

'I'd forgotten because the family hasn't had Christmas here since Audrey was a little girl.'

'Audrey?' asked Jules.

'Sean's stepdaughter. She's twenty-two now, so we're going back a while. I think this is the one. Can you help me, please?' Jules effortlessly lifted the large plastic tub off the shelf and placed it on the garage floor. 'Thank you. Now, let's see ...' Leilani lifted off the lid and the three of them peered inside. 'Hmm.'

'That's ...' said Jules.

'Slim pickings,' finished Chloe diplomatically, screwing up her nose at the ratty-looking Christmas decorations. She looked at the others. 'We're going to have to go shopping.'

'And I'm going to have to clean out these shelving units. There's a lot of junk in here,' said Leilani. 'In the New Year, though. That's a task for another day.'

'Or another year,' said Jules.

'Hee-hee, yes.'

'Let's get the tree inside, then find Lucy,' said Jules. 'If we're shopping for Christmas decorations, she's gonna wanna come.'

'Yeah, good point. But at least we have a tree! Operation "Best Christmas Ever" has now begun!' Chloe declared.

'Yeah, no pressure or anything, Chlo,' huffed Jules. Chloe pointedly ignored her—this wasn't a time for pessimism. On her instruction, they hoisted the large box into the air and commenced a duck-waddle towards the house, Jules carrying one end on her own.

'So, Leilani, what do *you* do for Christmas?' asked Chloe middle waddle.

'Oh, I usually give myself the day off—no chores, no planning or preparation. I don't even respond to emails,' she said, her eyebrows waggling cheekily. 'Then I make myself a delicious meal and watch something on Netflix.'

Chloe stopped walking and nearly dropped her corner of the box. 'What? You don't see your family? You don't go home?'

'No family on the island. Besides, this *is* my home,' she replied simply.

Chloe and Jules shared a baffled look. 'Well, you'll have Christmas with us this year,' said Chloe.

'Oh, no, I don't want to get in the way. Christmas is not such a big thing for me. That's why there's so much dust on this box,' she added, laughter in her voice.

Chloe was stunned to the core—someone who didn't celebrate Christmas. And it wasn't because Leilani observed a different holiday—say, Hanukkah or Kwanzaa—she just seemed indifferent. To *Christmas.*

They resumed walking while thoughts zipped through Chloe's mind. She knew that Jules wasn't as much of a Christmas enthusiast as she and Lucy were but she still celebrated. But a person who just 'took the day off and watched Netflix'?!

'*Please* say you'll have Christmas with us,' Chloe pleaded as they stepped inside and dropped the box in the tiled entry.

'Mmm. I will think about it,' Leilani replied, pursing her lips.

Chloe narrowed her eyes as Leilani unwaveringly met her eye. She had an air of stubbornness about her but Leilani didn't know how convincing Chloe could be. She decided to take Leilani's response as a 'definitely maybe' and, sometime in the next couple of days, she'd convince her to join them.

First things first though—shopping for Christmas decorations.

'Lucy! Luce, get your bum down here!'

Chapter Ten

LUCY

'Mmm, your skin tastes salty,' Lucy murmured, her lips pressed softly to Will's shoulder.

He lifted his head and pinned her with a look that shot a surge of lust right through her—*another* one. There may have been an undercurrent of emotional discord between them—well, in her mind, anyway—but physically they were still very much in sync. 'Should I have taken a shower when I got back?' he asked, smiling cockily.

She shook her head against the pillow. 'I *like* you tasting of the ocean.' He dipped his head and captured her mouth in a lingering kiss. She liked that too. Will's kisses were the stuff of dreams—*literally*. There were many nights she had woken to the stark realisation that she was alone in her bed having dreamt of Will kissing her.

She was just about to pull him closer—long-distance lovers *re-reuniting*—when Chloe's voice rang out from downstairs.

'Lucy! Luce, get your bum down here!'

Will sniggered, the vibration of lips tickling hers which set Lucy off. 'Awful timing, your friend,' he said, rolling off her.

Lucy missed the weight of his considerable physique the second he was gone and sighed up at the ceiling where light, reflecting off the whitecaps below, danced like fairy lights. 'I'd best go see what she's bellowing about,' said Lucy.

She got off the bed and padded naked to the bedroom door, something she had never done with any of her previous boyfriends. She'd always been coy about her body, reluctant to let it be seen at all, let alone in broad daylight. But over the past year, Will had—with appreciative glances, gentle caresses, and lust-filled words—*finally* got her to believe that she was just as beautiful as he said she was.

She opened the door a crack. 'Coming!' she bellowed back, closing it again.

'Not quite, but if we're quick we can rectify that,' said a very naked, utterly gorgeous man from their bed.

Lucy giggled. 'She can wait.' She ran over and launched herself on top of Will.

'Oof.'

'Sorry, did I wind you?'

'Just a little,' he croaked. He wrapped her up in his arms and rolled her over, then peered down at her, his eyes not only glazed with lust but filled with love. It was moments like these that made all the loneliness and misery of being in a long-distance relationship simply vanish. She was loved.

Lucy reached up, touching her lips to Will's and, almost instantly, the sweet kiss became so much more as Will slid one strong hand down her body and made good on his promise.

'Finally,' said Chloe. 'What took you so long?'

'Oh, er ...' Lucy threw a glance over her shoulder at Will, a giggle escaping.

'Oh, brother,' said Jules rolling her eyes.

'Ha—*literally*,' responded Chloe.

'Bleurgh.' Jules began busying herself with a large box, picking at the edges of the packing tape with her nails.

'Ooh, is that what I think it is?' asked Lucy.

'It is! Surprise!' said Chloe, clearly well chuffed with herself.

Lucy crossed the expansive lounge and watched as Jules peeled off the last of the packing tape from the box. 'Let me see,' she said, reaching for the cardboard flaps. She threw open the box releasing a small cloud of dust which she swatted away. 'It looks all right,' she said, removing branches and laying them on the floor.

'Not what you're used to, Luce,' said Chloe.

'Or you,' added Jules. 'Your tree back in Melbourne was *blue*.'

'Blue?' asked Lucy, looking up at Chloe. 'As in *blue* blue?'

'As in the entire tree is made of powder-blue tinsel,' said Jules.

'Hey, I didn't pick it out—Ash did. Besides, it was pretty.'

'Hmm,' muttered Lucy unconvinced. She resumed unpacking the tree.

Will had joined her on the floor and was rummaging through the box. 'Instructions?' he asked, looking up at Chloe.

'It's a Christmas tree,' teased Chloe, 'not flatpack furniture.'

'I think you're up, Chlo,' said Jules. 'You're the only one with experience putting together a fake tree.'

'What's this about a fake tree?' asked Matt, entering the room, Archer in tow. Unlike Will, they both looked freshly showered.

'Oh, do we have a Christmas tree?' asked Archer.

'We do,' said Lucy, grinning from her spot on the floor and holding up a branch.

'Brilliant. And ornaments?' Archer asked, looking about.

'No ornaments,' said Chloe. 'But Leilani says we can get some in town.'

'Right, so …'

'But not from Walmart,' she added quickly.

'What's wrong with Walmart?' asked Will.

Several pairs of eyes landed on him incredulously. 'Uh, mate,' said Matt, 'pretty sure the girls want to go in a different direction.'

'Absolutely!' declared Lucy. 'No plastic baubles for the May Ladies' tree!'

'Ahem … the *ladies'* tree?' asked Will, his eyebrows raised. Lucy shot him a somewhat contrite smile. If she, Jules, and Chloe were the May Ladies, what did that make their boyfriends? The May Gentlemen? The thought made her giggle again.

'I'm thinking, local artisans, maybe a Hawaiian theme …' said Chloe, seemingly ignoring Will and Lucy's exchange.

'Sounds like a perfect plan,' replied Lucy, sitting back on her heels. It was also a perfect deflection from her minor faux pas. Lucy noticed a shrug from Jules but she knew Jules wasn't as fussed about Christmas trees as she was—*or* Chloe. Jules had grown up with a scraggly tree dragged in from the forest on Christmas Eve, draped in nursery-school decorations.

When Lucy and Will had successfully unpacked the box and laid out the branches in piles, longest to shortest, he began putting the stand together—*without* instructions. Chloe was right—it did seem fairly simple once they'd unpacked everything.

Matt eyed the box. 'Uh, looks like we're gonna need a step ladder. It's twelve feet tall. I'll just go ask Leilani,' he said, heading off towards the kitchen. At the mention of Leilani, Lucy noted the spicy smells of Mexican food and her mouth watered. Hopefully it wasn't too long till dinner, as she'd worked up quite an appetite since Will had returned from surfing.

'How about some Christmas music?' asked Archer.

'Ooh, perfect, babe, thanks,' said Chloe from her spot on a long sofa.

'I think I can make sense of this,' said Archer, frowning at the components of an extensive stereo system. He pressed a few buttons and took out his phone, tapping on it then looking back at the stereo. Not long after, the sound of Bing Crosby's voice filled the large room and Lucy felt a wave of contentment wash over her.

Matt came back into the room, a metal step ladder hoisted over one shoulder. 'Hey, that's looking great already,' he said indicating the half-built tree, 'but it needs a bit of fluffing.'

'Fluffing?' asked Will and Jules at the same time.

'Yeah, you know …' Matt put down the ladder and began bending the smaller branches of the tree to separate them from each other. 'See? Fluffing.'

'Right, so does that make you the official tree fluffer?' asked Will with a smirk. Jules sniggered, flashing Will a look.

Matt seemed confused, obviously not getting the joke. To be honest, Lucy didn't get it either. 'What happens if I say yes?' he asked. At that, Jules and Will began full-on laughing. 'What? What am I missing?' Matt looked at the others, his confusion evident. 'Why's that funny?'

'Does it have anything to do with the adult film industry, by chance?' asked Archer, his mouth quirking in a lop-sided smile.

'Got it in one,' said Will, slotting another branch into place.

Matt held up his hands, seeming more confused than ever. 'Hun,' said Jules, 'a "fluffer" is the person on set who … you know … keeps the male actors … um … *ready*.'

'In between takes,' added Will.

'Ah, yeah okay, that's pretty funny,' Matt conceded, laughing at his own expense. 'But hang about, how do you two know that? Wait,' he added, side-eyeing Archer, 'more to the point, how do *you* know that?'

Archer threw his head back and laughed. 'It's not from personal experience, I promise.'

'Yeah, yeah, sure, mate,' Matt teased with a broad grin.

'Though I do have a funny story I can tell you later,' said Archer.

'I'm holding you to that, Arch.' The two men traded amused looks. 'And don't think you're off the hook either, young lady,' Matt said, jokingly waggling a finger at Jules.

'Is it wine o'clock yet?' asked Jules brightly.

'Excellent diversionary tactic, Jules,' quipped Chloe.

While Archer took Matt off to 'raid Sean's cellar'—with permission, he hastened to add—Lucy couldn't help smiling to herself. It really was brilliant fun being there with everybody—the easy banter, the silliness and laughter.

And as she watched Will climb the ladder to slide the top branches of the tree into place and a new song started playing, Lucy couldn't help but agree with Mr Crosby. It *was* beginning to look a lot like Christmas.

They were seated around a dining table out on the terrace, plates scraped clean. Leilani's meal of fajitas, roasted corn on the cob, fresh salsa and guacamole, and Mexican-style rice had been a triumph, and Lucy was feeling more than a little full. *Just one more bite*, she'd thought, only it hadn't been just one more, it had been a few—it was such a delicious meal!

The sun had set but the fragrant air was still warm and the faces of Will and her friends glowed from the subtle outdoor lighting.

'And so …' said Archer, master storyteller in full swing and at the climax of a tale about (Dame) Helen Mirren, 'she walks onto set in the most *extraordinary* costume. I mean, nipped in here,' he said, indicating his waist, 'and cut *rather low* here …' He waved a hand in front of his chest. 'And there's this stunned silence—I mean, practically everybody on set is completely still—*gobsmacked* because she looks absolutely stunning, so incredibly sexy—and she casts her eyes about the set, raises one eyebrow, then shouts out, "Cancel the fluffer!"'

Like everybody else, Lucy dissolved into laughter.

'And that is *exactly* what happened,' said Archer, wiping tears from under his eyes. 'That exact reaction. There was this beat and then we're all falling about laughing. The poor director had to call lunch early because everybody kept corpsing throughout the entire scene—even Helen! This very serious scene and we can't stop laughing!'

That set them all off again and Lucy pressed a hand to her chest, trying to catch her breath. Every time she thought she had it under control, the laughter bubbled back up. 'Phoo,' she sighed eventually, reaching for her water glass.

'Hi.'

The voice came from the shadows near one of the two guest bungalows and Chloe nearly leapt out of her chair. All six heads turned in the direction of the voice as a young woman stepped into the light, like a waif emerging from the mist.

'Hi, sorry. Didn't mean to scare you,' she said. 'I just … I'm Audrey.'

'Oh!' Archer leapt out of his chair as though he'd just remembered something. 'You're Sean's stepdaughter.'

'Ah, yeah. Sorry, I don't want to interrupt or anything …'

'No, not at all. Sean texted to say you might be coming. Sorry, everybody,' he said to the others. 'It completely slipped my mind. This is Audrey, Sean's stepdaughter. Audrey this is my girlfriend, Chloe, and our friends, Matt, Lucy, Jules, and Will,' he said, indicating the others in turn.

'Hey,' said Audrey, looking around the table as Archer said their names. Lucy lifted her hand in a wave but, though Audrey was smiling, it didn't reach her eyes and she wore an expression that Lucy was far too familiar with. *She's sad—heartbroken even*, thought Lucy, instantly empathising with her.

That is until Audrey's eyes landed on Will and noticeably brightened.

'Hey, Will,' said Audrey.

'How's it going?' Lucy watched Will closely, dismissing the minor jolt of jealousy as soon as she saw how indifferent he was to Audrey.

'Much better now, thanks.' Audrey sat in the chair that Archer had commandeered from somewhere and leant against the table, her chin propped up by one hand and her eyes firmly—and obviously—locked on Will.

Any empathy Lucy had felt dissipated into the night air. *Oh, she can sod right off.*

Chapter Eleven

JULES

J ules watched curiously as Audrey made an obvious play for her brother—not the objectively handsome and (very) famous movie star, which told Jules that Audrey was used to being around famous people. If you were blasé when Archer Tate stood to introduce you around a table, that said something. Still, her play for Will was gutsy considering the math—three women and three men. Wasn't it obvious they were all paired up?

Will reacted exactly how Jules knew he would—that is, no reaction as he was completely oblivious. He'd had two serious girlfriends in his twenty-nine years—Tiffany, who broke his heart right after college, and Lucy. And in between the two, Jules had witnessed dozens of women throw themselves at Will but, like Audrey, they didn't know what she knew. He had no *idea* that the hair twirling and lip biting, the leaning in and laughing at everything he said (even when it wasn't remotely funny) was flirting.

He was a straightforward, what-you-see-is-what-you-get sort of guy—a lot like her dad, though Will was extroverted and her dad was an introvert like her. But even if Will hadn't been in love with Lucy—which he was, Jules was sure—Audrey wouldn't have stood a chance.

Speaking of Lucy … Jules looked further down the table to discover that Lucy was also watching Audrey. Only she wasn't oblivious to the girl's overtures. Nope, Lucy was wearing a murderous expression and looked like she might start a catfight any second now.

Jules stood abruptly, causing the others to look at her. 'The table,' she declared, 'just clearing the table.' She reached for plates and cutlery, stacking them haphazardly while throwing Chloe a pointed look. *Finally*, she got the hint.

'I'll help you,' said Chloe, leaping to her feet.

'I can do it, darling,' offered Archer right as Matt stood and said, 'I'll help.'

'Nope—all good,' replied Jules. 'You two sit,' she said to the guys. 'Lucy? Wanna help?' Matt caught her eye, giving her a quizzical look. With a tilt of her head, she conveyed that she'd explain later.

'I'm not exactly thrilled about leaving Will out there with that girl,' Lucy hissed when they got into the kitchen laden with dirty dishes.

'Nothing's going to happen, Lucy. Not with Archer and Matt there,' assured Jules.

'Wonderful, so for the next twelve days I just have to make sure Will's never left alone.'

'Ha!' laughed Chloe. 'Will would never do anything, Lucy.'

'Definitely not,' said Jules as she began rinsing dishes at the sink.

'Well, I know that,' said Lucy tartly but Jules wasn't so sure Lucy did.

'Trust me, he doesn't even know she's flirting with him.'

Chloe laughed again, then stopped. 'Oh, you're serious.'

Jules nodded, then handed over a stack of rinsed plates so Chloe could load them into the dishwasher.

'Even if he doesn't,' said Lucy, 'it's just so *rude*. What type of person suddenly appears out of the shadows, coming upon what is obviously three couples, then starts making goo-goo eyes at one of the men? The nerve!'

'I like this side of you, Luce,' said Chloe. 'What should we do? Wait till she's asleep and put gum in her hair?'

'You seem very blasé about all this,' said Lucy accusatorily.

Chloe shrugged. 'I've had to become impervious. When you're dating someone like Archer ... do you know I've *literally* been pushed aside?'

'Oh, right, of course—soz,' said Lucy, reaching for Chloe's arm and patting it.

'Eh, what are you gonna do?' said Chloe with a half-smile.

'Look,' said Jules as she wiped down the benchtop. 'You know there's nothing to worry about where Will's concerned, but I haven't exactly warmed to her—and neither have you,' she added, pointing at Lucy, who shook her head. 'So what do we do? Just avoid her?' Lucy shrugged. 'Hey,' Jules said, turning to Chloe, 'is Audrey staying through Christmas and New Year?'

Chloe held up her hands. 'Hey, I have no idea. I didn't even know she existed till she emerged from the shadows.'

'That was weird, right?' asked Jules.

'Yes!' agreed Lucy.

'I mean, how long was she standing there watching all of us?' added Jules.

'Exactly!' Lucy agreed even more emphatically.

'Yeah,' said Chloe. 'It was a little weird. I'll ask Archer—see if we need to think about including her in our Christmas plans.' Lucy groaned. 'I know, but if she's going to be here, we can't exactly leave her out. What are we supposed to say? "Hey, you totally freaked us out so can you *not* join us for Christmas—even though this is essentially your house?"' Now, Jules laughed.

'Mmm, good point, I suppose,' said Lucy, her expression teetering between annoyance and compassion.

'You going to be okay, Luce?' asked Jules.

Lucy sighed. 'Of course. I was probably just overreacting. Besides, the whole thing with Will aside, I got the sense that …' Lucy's voice trailed off and a frown appeared.

'The sense that what?' nudged Chloe.

'She just seems sad is all.'

'Audrey?' asked Chloe. She didn't seem convinced.

'Perhaps not,' replied Lucy, 'but I thought I saw something in her eyes when Archer was introducing her.'

'Hmm.' Chloe pursed her lips.

'Come on, we'd better get back out there,' said Jules. Chloe closed the dishwasher and as they walked back to the terrace to join the guys, Jules grasped Lucy by the shoulder. 'It'll be okay, Luce.'

Lucy nodded, her jaw set.

'You sure you don't want me to come?' asked Matt.

'I'm not even sure if I want to go,' retorted Jules. She scooped her honey-coloured hair into a neat ponytail and wrapped the hair tie around it three times.

'So don't. Stay here.'

Jules looked over at the bed where he was watching her, his hands behind his head. Matt wasn't one to typically sleep in, especially as he had a winery to run, but with jetlag and the time difference, they'd slept in till 9:30 that morning. This meant Jules was running late for her excursion into Lihue to find Christmas decorations with Chloe and Lucy.

'Tempting.' It really was but the girls would 'have her guts for garters' (one of Chloe's favourite expressions). Apparently, they couldn't plan for a May Ladies' Christmas without all of the May Ladies.

At that thought, Jules smiled to herself. Part of her *still* couldn't believe that Archer had pulled it off—getting all six of them here for Christmas? It was a minor miracle—some might say, a Christmas miracle—so she'd play along. *And* her dad was arriving today—something extra special to look forward to.

She spread a dollop of SPF50 tinted moisturiser over her face and neck—her go-to now that she lived in Australia—slicked on some lip balm and called it good. She crossed the room and sat on the edge of the bed to say goodbye to Matt. Argh, he looked so sexy with his mussed-up curls and the way his biceps popped like that. She wished she could stay. She flicked her wrist to check her Fitbit. It told her she did *not* have time to indulge her lusty thoughts; she barely had enough time to grab a granola bar from the kitchen without keeping the girls waiting. She kissed him quickly, then wriggled in his embrace when he captured her in his arms.

'Ma-att, I've gotta go. You *know* Chloe.' The low rumble of his laughter vibrated through her. She could buy a minute or two by skipping the granola bar but she still wasn't keen to incite the wrath of Chloe, master organiser and 'bossy little thing'.

She pushed herself away and looked down at him. 'You guys going surfing again today?' she asked.

'Not sure. I s'ppose I'll drag myself out of bed then check in with the guys, eh?'

'Well, have fun.'

'You too!' he called after her.

She paused at the door to their room. 'And be careful. No trips to the emergency room this year,' she said. He'd fallen off a horse last December—just a sprain, thank god.

'Yeah, yeah.'

'Love you.'

'Love you, too, hun.' He added a dimpled grin and Jules closed the door and headed downstairs, smiling to herself the whole way. It had taken a few months of dating after she'd first moved to Australia for her to say those words but the first time they came out of her mouth, they'd felt *so good*. Just like they had every time since.

Jules had no doubt that Matt was who she'd spend the rest of her life with.

She'd geared herself up for a morning of 'Christmassy fun' with her best friends. What Jules hadn't planned for was including Audrey. But there they were, Chloe sitting beside her clutching one of her famous lists and Lucy and Audrey in the backseat—and all four of them silent. She watched Audrey in the rear-view mirror trying to figure out what her deal was. Had she asked to come along or had Chloe suggested it?

Chloe was one of those people who liked to include others, a trait that Jules had long admired in her—it was essentially the reason they'd all become friends when they met aged eleven. Lucy had been (even more) painfully shy back then, but Chloe had drawn her into the activities—well, coerced is probably a better word. You didn't say no to Chloe back then either. Jules, mature for her age and resentful she even had to *be* at kids' club at all, had tried to play cool, watching most activities from the side lines, arms folded across her chest. Chloe had responded to that challenge by (literally) dragging her across the room, saying, 'Come on, we need a third person for our team.' For some reason, Jules, who was much taller and stronger than the strange little Australian girl, had gone along with it.

Twenty-three years later, they were spending Christmas in Hawaii—with a stranger. But even if Audrey turned out to be born in May, she was *not* becoming a May Lady. Not if Jules had anything to say about it.

'Want to try the radio, Chlo?' she asked.

'I have a better idea.' Chloe fiddled with the controls, linking the car's Bluetooth to her phone and hitting 'play' on a Spotify playlist. Seconds later, Michael Bublé's warm, resonant voice filled the car and Jules felt her shoulders fall an inch. She looked in the rear-view mirror again and noticed that Lucy, her eyes glued to the passing view, now wore a small smile.

***

'Are we done yet?' whined Audrey.

Jules didn't want to admit that she was on Audrey's side, but she also felt shopped out. They'd driven the length and breadth of Lihue and the trunk was packed with what would, according to Chloe, pass for Christmas ornaments. At one point, even Lucy had asked if they could stop at Walmart considering how scant the options were in the souvenir stores. They'd found a handful of actual Christmas ornaments but had mostly stocked up on leis made with silk flowers, fabric pineapples, and pendants made from paua shells.

'Just one more stop!' said Chloe.

'Thank god,' Jules muttered to herself. In her peripheral vision, Chloe's head snapped in her direction, but she pretended not to see.

'It's one of the local spas,' continued Chloe. 'I figured we could treat Leilani to a spa day for her Christmas gift.'

'She'll like that,' said Audrey and Jules noticed that she visibly perked up.

'You've known Leilani for a long time, haven't you?' asked Jules.

'Yeah, since I was eight.'

'Do you only come here during Christmastime?' asked Lucy—the first time she'd spoken directly to Audrey all day.

'Sometimes during the year. Depends.'

'Where do you live normally?' asked Jules.

'In LA.'

'But you're still close to Sean?' asked Chloe. 'Archer said that you sometimes come here together.'

'Yeah, we're still pretty close, I guess.'

Jules noted that even though she was answering their questions, Audrey was playing things close to her chest. 'So, what made you decide to come this time?' she asked, her curiosity getting the better of her.

She watched Audrey in the rear-view mirror and thought she saw her lower lip quiver a little. Audrey sniffed then lifted her chin and stared out the window. 'My boyfriend broke up with me,' she replied, her voice sounding even more childlike now than when she was whining earlier.

'*Oh*,' said Chloe and Lucy at once. Chloe turned around in her seat. 'When?'

'Three days ago.'

'He broke up with you right before Christmas?' asked Lucy incredulously.

Audrey snorted out a wry laugh. 'Yep. He said he didn't want to buy me a Christmas present when he already knew it was over.' Jules caught her shrug in the rear-view mirror, understanding immediately. There was a lot of hurt and a lot Audrey wasn't saying in that one simple gesture.

'What a dick,' stated Chloe, cutting through the gloomy mood in the car. It was the first time Jules had seen Audrey smile. Then she remembered what Lucy had said about Audrey seeming sad; she'd been right.

'How long were you together?' asked Lucy. Jules could tell Lucy's empathy chip had been activated—generous, considering Audrey's behaviour towards Will the night before.

'Four months,' Audrey replied, her tone indicating that, for her, four months was a significant length of time.

Lucy nodded solemnly and reached across the car to pat Audrey on the arm and Audrey smiled at her weakly. Jules guessed that answered the question of whether they'd include Audrey in their Christmas celebrations.

'And what is the dick's name?' asked Chloe.

'Bugs,' replied Audrey.

'Bugs?' asked Lucy. 'As in Bugs Bunny?'

Audrey laughed. 'No … it's his YouTube name. He's a YouTuber.'

'Did you call him Bugs?' asked Lucy, her eyes wide with curiosity.

'Yeah. I mean, his real name is *Marvin*.' Audrey screwed up her face.

'Oh my god, like Marvin the Martian! Ha!' laughed Chloe. 'Bugs Bunny and Marvin the Martian.' She was so tickled, she barely got the last word out.

'You okay there, Chlo?' asked Jules, flicking her a glance sideways. Granted, it was funny but hardly laugh-out-loud hilarious.

Chloe continued laughing but nodded.

'Well, I think we should just call him Roach,' said Lucy, being uncharacteristically dry.

At that, even Jules laughed but mostly because it was Lucy's suggestion and she rarely had a bad word to say about anyone. By the time Google told them that their destination was coming up on the right, everyone in the car was laughing, including Audrey.

Chapter Twelve

CHLOE

They pulled up at the house just after one and even though the outing had been her idea and she'd planned the entire itinerary, Chloe was shattered. She needed lunch and a lie-down—something her mum would say, she realised. God, she was only thirty-four! Besides, a nap would have to wait as she had another outing planned after lunch—and she was roping in Audrey.

As they were unloading the boot, a large man—tall and solid—burst out of the front door and made a beeline for Jules. 'Hello, sweetheart,' he said, wrapping Jules up in a hug.

'Dad! You're early,' said Jules from the circle of his beefy arms. 'I was going to come get you from the airport.'

'I managed to get an earlier flight and your brother picked me up.' Jules, clearly overcome, clung tightly to her dad before they eventually let go. Chloe noticed that Jules swiped her hand under her nose, then blinked back tears as her dad turned towards Lucy, 'Hello, sweetheart,' he said, also giving her a big hug. 'How are you?'

'Good, thank you. Happy Christmas!' Lucy looked almost as

delighted to see Jules' dad as Jules had and Chloe felt a slight twinge. She hadn't seen her own parents in what felt like forever.

'Merry Christmas to you too,' he replied. Then he turned towards her. 'Now I know you're Chloe. Come here, I'm a hugger.' He wrapped Chloe in a hug—just like the ones he'd given Jules and Lucy—and Chloe had to fight back her own tears. How had it not occurred to her till now how much she needed a fatherly hug?

'Hello, Mr Reinhardt.'

'It's Nate, sweetheart.' His blue eyes creased at the corners as he smiled down at her.

'Nate,' she said quietly, adding a nod. 'Hi.' The creases around his eyes deepened.

'And you must be Audrey,' said Nate. 'I hear you're joining us for Christmas.' She looked surprised as he ensconced *her* in a hug but Chloe noticed how she practically melted into it. Perhaps she missed fatherly hugs too.

Nate stepped back and regarded them warmly before turning his attention to the boot. 'Wow. This is going to be quite the tree.' He scooped up most of the shopping bags and headed back inside and they followed with what remained.

Somehow, just having Jules' dad here made Christmas feel even more Christmassy. But it also left Chloe feeling a little hollow. When her parents had announced last year that they were going on a cruise for Christmas, it had hit Chloe harder than she could have imagined—even more so when her brother, Drew, took off to go skiing in Canada.

Of course her subsequent decision to spend Christmas in Oxfordshire where she'd met Archer had been one of the best decisions she'd ever made. But this year, she'd been hoping to take Archer home to Melbourne for Christmas to meet the family. Video calls only went so far and she wanted to show him around her hometown, introduce him to her family and close friends and all her favourite places. But for the second Christmas in a row, her parents were cruising and her brother was skiing. She was sure her disappointment had been the main impetus for Archer suggesting they spend Christmas in Paris.

Chloe decided right then, as they deposited their spoils in the living room next to the enormous fake tree—perfectly fluffed by Matt—that she'd talk to Archer about going to Australia early in the New Year. She'd pin down her parents and brother and they'd have a proper family get-together at last.

Chloe rapped on the door to the bungalow and waited. When she'd waited what she considered enough time for someone to come to the door—even if they'd been in the shower and had to wrap themselves in a towel—she rapped again, harder this time.

The door opened and there was Audrey, looking pale-faced and blinking at her like a marsupial in daylight.

'Sorry, did I wake you up?' She was envious that Audrey had been able to sneak away for a nap while she'd been in full Event Manager mode making lists.

'Um, yeah. What do you need?'

Chloe noticed that Audrey had said 'need' and not 'want'—a distinction she found encouraging. 'I need your help.'

Audrey blinked again, clearly confused, then rubbed her eyes. 'Come in.' She pulled open the door and stepped aside and Chloe entered the darkened bungalow. Once her eyes adjusted, she saw that it was essentially studio-style accommodation with everything but the bathroom in one room. There was a sitting area with two couches facing each other, a kitchenette that looked (as yet) unused, a small dining table with two chairs, and a California king like the one in the suite she was sharing with Archer. Audrey had not availed herself of the two dressing tables or the closet—her clothes were strewn over everything, like Marie Kondo's nemesis had decorated.

'Um, sorry.' Audrey quickly gathered up a handful of clothes from one of the couches and Chloe sat. Audrey just stood there, holding an armful of clothes and looking at her expectantly.

'So, you probably don't know this about me' —she wasn't sure why she'd begun that way. Audrey knew next to nothing about Chloe, *or* the others. She forged ahead— 'but in a former life, I was an Event Manager.' *No reaction. Hmm.* 'And with Jules not really being a Christmassy person and Lucy feeling out of sorts at not having the white Christmas she'd hoped for …' Audrey's face still drew a blank. 'Do you see where I'm going with this?'

Audrey shook her head. Was she dim, or did Chloe just suck at explaining things? 'It means that organising Christmas is pretty much up to me. A full-on, proper Christmas, I mean. This was all really last-minute and I had no idea the girls would be here with their boyfriends, or Nate, or *you* for that matter, so …' Audrey *still* didn't seem to twig. Chloe reached into her cross-body satchel and retrieved a notebook, then held it up. 'This is a long bloody to-do list and I need your help.'

'*Oh!* Okay.'

'You'll help?'

'No, I just meant … okay, I get it now.'

'So you won't help?'

'No, I will.' God, this was like having a conversation underwater. With a turtle.

'Great! So, first things first, we need to go shopping,' said Chloe.

'Oh.'

'I know. We spent the morning shopping, but that was for decorations and this is for presents—for the others.'

Audrey visibly perked up. 'Well I can definitely help with gifts. That's my job.'

'Buying gifts?'

'Well, sorta, yeah. I'm a personal shopper.'

'Wow. That's … brilliant. Like I said, I didn't know Jules and Lucy would be here and I hate the thought of not having anything for them to open on Christmas morning—or Will or Matt.' Chloe didn't mention that she'd already sorted out Audrey's gift when they'd stopped by the spa earlier. One full spa day for Leilani to thank her for making them so welcome—regardless of whether she agreed to be part of the Christmas celebrations—and one for Audrey to help her get over Bugs. It was an inspired gift, if Chloe did say so herself.

'So,' said Audrey, 'see any souvenirs you liked while we were out today?'

'Ha!' It was the first time Audrey had said deliberately something funny—well, as far as Chloe could tell. God, she *hoped* that was meant to be funny and she hadn't just laughed at the poor girl. But Audrey smiled and Chloe felt a rush of relief. 'I'm thinking experiences might be nice, rather than things. What do you think?'

She could tell that Audrey mustn't be asked that question very often because she seemed surprised. But after thoughtful consideration, which seemed to take an aeon, Audrey nodded her agreement. 'I like that idea.'

'Good, and we'll need to find Christmas stockings too. Lucy is all about those. Though, she said she brought hers and one for Will, so we only need them for the rest of us.' Chloe may have imagined it but she thought Audrey's eyes had lit up when she mentioned Will. Maybe Lucy was right—they'd have to keep an eye on the Audrey–Will situation.

'We could just make them,' said Audrey, surprising her.

'What? The Christmas stockings.'

'Yeah.'

'Do you know how to make Christmas stockings?' she asked.

'Um, hello. Easiest pattern in the world.' Audrey punctuated her point by drawing the outline of a stocking in the air with her finger.

'Okay, good point.'

'What about a sewing machine?'

'There's one in the studio.'

'The studio?'

'The art studio—not the yoga studio and definitely not the recording studio.' Audrey's tone said 'duh' but Chloe let it slide. She was stuck on there being *three studios* on the property—art, yoga, or otherwise.

'Right. Makes sense that no one's sewing anything in the recording studio.'

Apparently, Audrey thought that was hilarious. 'As if! Ha! Can you imagine Supie Boo La making a dress instead of laying a track?' She cracked herself up and laughed some more.

Chloe smiled. Even though she'd craved a nap that afternoon, she really *wasn't* that old—but being with Audrey made her feel ancient. Who the hell was Supie Boo La when she-him-they were at home?

'Okay, so fabric for the stockings ...' Chloe made a notation on her list. 'I think we can work on the rest of this on the drive into town. How long do you need to get ready?' Chloe regarded Audrey's outfit, unclear if it was 'leaving the house' attire or her pyjamas.

'Ten minutes?' Audrey replied as though she were asking a question.

'Great. I'll meet you out front. I just need to grab the car keys from Archer and tell him we're heading out.'

'It's really cool that you're with Archer Tate.'

Chloe steeled herself at the use of Archer's full name—it usually indicated that the person was a fan and since they'd been in Hawaii, it had felt liked they'd escaped all that. 'Uh, yeah, I think so too,' she replied, hoping it was an innocuous way to shut down the conversation.

'He's, like, really hot for an older guy.'

Wait, what? 'An older guy?'

'Yeah, isn't he like, forty or something?'

'He's thirty-six,' Chloe replied incredulously. Their underwater conversation had entered white water rafting territory—all ups and downs and navigating perils. Was Chloe supposed to be flattered on Archer's behalf or appalled that Audrey thought of him as 'old'?

'Oh, I thought he was older. Same diff, I guess.' Audrey shrugged and turned her back on Chloe, who took that as her cue to leave and go and find her *old* boyfriend.

'Hey, there you are.'

'Hello, darling heart. Care to play the next round?' She found Archer in the billiards room playing pool with Nate. Of *course* there was a billiards room. If they remade the game of Cluedo and set it at Sean's house, there would be a million permutations that could win the game. It was Mrs White in the Yoga Studio with the Chia Pudding!

'Um, no thanks. Just wanted to let you know I'm heading back into town with Audrey.'

'Back? Didn't you get everything you needed this morning?'

'That was for decorations,' she said simply.

'Ah, and this excursion is for …?'

'Fabric for the Christmas stockings and presents.'

'Right.' There was a twinkle of amusement in Archer's eye but Chloe didn't mind. He often found her amusing but he was never condescending.

'I hope you don't think you need to get anything for me,

sweetheart,' said Nate. 'The invitation alone was the best gift I could have had.'

'Well, you are most welcome for the invitation,' said Archer and Chloe beamed with pride. She loved how he always wanted others to feel included, a trait they shared. 'But if you can stop my darling Chloe from procuring what I imagine will be the perfect gift, then you are a better man than I.'

Chloe rolled her eyes. 'Hey, Arch, this isn't an audition for the RSC.' At that, Archer threw his head back and laughed. Nate just looked confused but smiled politely. 'Do you have the car keys, please?'

'On the hallstand, darling.'

'Cool, thanks.'

She made to leave. 'Wait. Goodbye kiss?' he asked. Chloe looked over at Nate who busied himself by chalking his cue while Chloe kissed Archer (rather chastely) goodbye. 'And are you sure you don't mind Audrey tagging along with you? Again, I'm so sorry I forgot to tell you that she might be here.'

'I don't mind. Besides, she's not tagging along. I'm putting her to work. She's my assistant for the day.'

'Does she know that?' he asked, a smile tugging at the left corner of his mouth.

'Well, if she doesn't, she's about to find out!' Chloe left the billiards room to the sound of two men chuckling.

Chapter Thirteen

LUCY

B arely two days into their Hawaiian Christmas holiday and Lucy was absolutely knackered. She supposed it could be jetlag—actually, who was she fooling? While there were only seven hours' difference between Colorado and London, something she'd become acclimated to, those additional (pesky) three hours meant her body had no idea what time it was.

She stretched her arms over her head and yawned loudly before falling onto the bed face first. If this were a film, she'd start snoring loudly having fallen asleep immediately but it turned out you couldn't sleep if you couldn't breathe. She rolled over and stared at the ceiling. Those whitecaps were at it again, projecting light from the tips of their crests onto the ceiling—like a silvery kaleidoscope. Damn them. She wanted to wallow in her grumpiness, not be cheered by something so beautiful.

She reached for her phone. Hmm, too late now to call her mum and dad. She'd have to wait till tomorrow, though her mum would probably be busy with the Christmas Fair all day and her dad wasn't what one would call a 'talker'. If he answered the phone when she called, their conversation almost always went like this: 'How are you, love?' to which she'd reply, 'I'm well, Dad, and you?' 'Very well, thank you. I'll just put your mother on.' At the thought, Lucy smiled, but it soon disappeared. She really missed her parents. She made a vow right then and there that no matter what, next Christmas would be spent with them in Oxfordshire.

No matter what …

At that, she burst into tears. What if that meant she was there alone, having lost Will to the pressures of a long-distance relationship? Or worse! To a twenty-two-year-old waif-like blonde from Los Angeles.

Oh, she could really catastrophise with the best of them, couldn't she?

'Stop it, Lucy,' she said aloud. 'There's no way Will would leave you for Audrey!' She sat up and went to the window. Their suite not only looked out over the ocean view, but also that infinity pool! She may have had to borrow a swimsuit, but she looked fabulous in it and she was going to lounge by the pool, damn it! She changed quickly and scouted about for her Kindle which was brimming with Christmas romances, most of which were set in the snow—the closest she'd get to a white Christmas this year. She grabbed her enormous sunhat (borrowed from Steph) and headed downstairs, stopping by the kitchen to see about a snack to take with her to the pool.

When Lucy walked in, Nate was there and he seemed to be trying to coax Leilani into letting him cook. Leilani was shaking her head. 'Oh no, no, please, it is not necessary,' she said to Nate. On seeing Lucy, she added, 'Aloha, Lucy.'

'Aloha. Umm …' Lucy wasn't sure if Leilani's reticence was to do with Nate's abilities or relinquishing her place as 'head chef' but Lucy could attest to the former. 'Just so you know, Nate's a wonderful cook if that's what you're worried about, Leilani,' she said, sliding onto a stool.

Leilani waved her hand in the air. 'I'm sure he is, but' —she put her hand on her heart— 'I am like a mama and you are all my chicks. If I'm not cooking for you ...' She shook her head and shrugged. 'I feel *lost* if I'm shooed out of my kitchen.'

Lucy and Nate exchanged a look. 'I would never want to do that,' Nate told Leilani, his hands raised in surrender. 'This is your domain, but you've already been so welcoming and I just want to contribute and ...'

He trailed off and Lucy leapt in with, 'And if Nate cooks us dinner, then you'll have more time to help me!' She had no idea where that had come from. What did *she* need help with—other than relationship advice?

'What can I help you with, Lucy?' Leilani predictably asked.

'Er ...'

'Hey, everyone,' said Jules. 'Leilani, I need your help.'

Leilani smiled. 'This is why I'm here. I'll help Lucy. I'll help you ...' She turned to Nate. 'And I'll think about you in my kitchen,' she said with a pointed finger.

Nate laughed cheerfully, conceding with his usual good nature. 'Okay, okay, but I want to cook my famous pasta sauce and that needs at least four hours on the stove—*minimum*—so think fast.' Leilani tutted at him and Lucy giggled at their friendly banter.

'Hold on, you're making your pasta sauce?' Jules asked her dad. 'Don't tease me 'cause I've been *craving* that for months.'

'Leilani's still deciding whether to relinquish her kitchen,' said Lucy.

Jules turned to Leilani. 'Oh, *please*. Like, seriously, *please*. I've been living in Australia and haven't had my dad's cooking for eight months.'

Leilani tutted again, hands on hips and tossed in an eyeroll. She was almost as dramatic as Chloe. 'Okay. This *one* time.'

'You got it,' said Nate, grinning. 'You wanna show me around?'

Leilani led Nate over to the enormous pantry, then turned around. 'Sorry, I forgot. You wanted my help?' she asked Jules.

'I was just gonna ask if I could make my famous Christmas cookies.'

Leilani's eyes widened. 'Oh, you're a very famous family with all your recipes, huh?'

'It's literally the only thing I can make,' said Jules.

Leilani laughed. 'Okay, you come on the tour too. Oh! Lucy, what did *you* need?'

'Er, never mind.'

'You sure?'

'Absolutely. I'll be out by the pool if anybody needs me.'

Leilani regarded her suspiciously, so Lucy leapt off the stool and departed before she had to lie again. It was only when she was poolside that she realised she'd forgotten to get something to munch on.

'There you are.' Lucy had dozed off and jumped at the sound of Chloe's voice. As Chloe settled on the end of her sun lounger, Lucy wiped a thin line of dribble from the side of her mouth. 'You okay?' Chloe was wearing a concerned frown, so Lucy was quick to reassure her.

'Absolutely. Just getting some sun.' Chloe raised her eyes to the enormous umbrella overhead. 'Er, fresh sea air, I mean.' Lucy inhaled loudly through her nose to really sell it.

'Are you sure you're okay? I know this isn't the Christmas you imagined.'

'It's not but we're all here together, so that's what matters.'

'Are you trying to convince me or you?'

92

Lucy dropped the pretence. 'I don't mean to be a party pooper …'

'Luce, I don't think anyone's used that term since the 1920s.'

Lucy snorted out a laugh. 'Good point.'

'Look, you're not pooping the party or whatever. Just … come with me. I want to show you something.'

Lucy nodded. 'All right.' They stood and Lucy gathered her belongings.

'I sometimes forget what a short-arse I am till I stand next to you, Luce.' She hooked her arm through Lucy's and led her away from the pool towards the garage. *Intriguing*, Lucy thought as Chloe pointed the way up a narrow staircase. At the top, she emerged into a light-filled loft with windows on three sides. Audrey sat in front of a sewing machine.

'Oh, great, you're here. I'm just finishing the last one,' Audrey said.

'Last one …?' Lucy crossed the expansive space, barely noticing that there were easels and art supplies along one wall and in the far corner, a potter's wheel. She headed straight for the sewing area, replete with a pattern-cutting table, an overlocker, and a dressmaker's mannequin. Her mum would have loved it!

On the long workbench next to the sewing machine were Christmas stockings—each made from a different Hawaiian print. And not the sort that Hawaiian shirts were made from, but beautiful—and seemingly genuine—indigenous prints. She picked up a teal stocking, the print depicting circular fishing baskets, and traced the outline of one with her fingers.

'What do you think?' asked Audrey.

What did she think? Lucy came to her senses, having been lost in both the beauty of the fabrics and the thoughtfulness of the gesture. She looked at Audrey, whose expression was a mix of pride and nervousness.

'They're absolutely beautiful. Was this your idea?' she asked Chloe.

'Kind of. I wanted to get everyone Christmas stockings but it was Audrey's idea to make them.'

Lucy turned back to Audrey. 'You're very clever.'

Audrey shrugged modestly. 'They're easy.'

'Well, even if they are, the fabric choices!'

'Yeah, there's this little store I used to go to with Sean when I was younger ...' Audrey's words trailed off to a whisper, the rest of her thought left unsaid.

'So, this space ... it's yours?' Lucy asked, regarding the loft.

'Just this part. Sean set it up for me, like seven or eight years ago—when I said I wanted to be a fashion designer. I even had a tutor—for making patterns and sewing and stuff. You know ...?' She seemed uncomfortable under Lucy's gaze, a feeling Lucy recognised immediately. She didn't like being the centre of attention either. Lucy also sensed that the fact that Audrey *wasn't* currently a fashion designer was something she regretted. Perhaps a conversation for another day, as the poor girl clearly wanted to stop talking about it.

'Well, you've done a brilliant job,' she said, turning her attention back to the stockings. 'And it means a lot that you've done this, so thank you.'

'And look, Luce ...' Chloe picked up two stockings, one in orange and one in yellow. 'I know you brought your stocking from home—and one for Will—but we made these anyway. So you'd have a Hawaiian one.'

'Like a souvenir!' said Audrey. Lucy took the stockings from Chloe and admired them.

'Oh,' she said, noting the embroidered 'L' on the cuff of the orange stocking. She looked at the yellow one and there it was, a 'W'. She regarded the others spread out across the large table, only then noticing that they each had an initial embroidered on the cuff.

'There's two "A"s and two "L"s so we'll just have to remember whose is whose,' said Audrey.

Lucy grinned. 'Thank you!' she said, patting Audrey's on the shoulder. She had *so* misjudged this girl, but then she realised something. 'Oh no, stocking fillers!'

'Already on it, Luce,' said Chloe. 'Come on, Audrey—time to head back out.'

She made to leave but Lucy called out. 'Could I come too?'

'Sure, as long as you're not already sick of "Mele Kalikimaka",' Chloe replied, referring to the Hawaiian Christmas song—the only one, as far as Lucy knew.

'Oh, no, not at all.'

'Even though they're playing it on repeat in every shop?' Chloe retorted dryly.

'I don't mind,' said Lucy with a grin. 'Give me a minute and I'll just get changed.'

'You could just go like that, you know,' said Audrey. 'We *are* in Hawaii.'

Lucy looked down at her outfit—a swimsuit, a sarong and flipflops. No, she was definitely changing outfits. 'I won't be long. I'll meet you out front in a few minutes.' She crossed the loft and at the top of the stairs turned back. 'Oh, do you think we should ask Leilani if she needs anything from the shop? Tomorrow is Christmas Eve.'

'Good call, Luce.' Lucy grinned and headed down the stairs.

'I told you she'd love them,' she heard Chloe say.

Chapter Fourteen

JULES

'Dad, that smells amazing.'

'Thank you, sweetheart. Just about done and then we leave it to simmer.'

Jules was at one end of the huge kitchen rolling out sugar cookie dough and her dad had commandeered the stove and its surrounds for his famous pasta sauce. The room smelled of herbs, tomatoes, and garlic. Leilani had fussed over them for a good half-hour before trusting them enough to leave them on their own. And even though Jules was an introvert and loved having time alone, she couldn't imagine living in that huge house by herself like Leilani did most of the year. Surely, she got lonely—at least sometimes?

Leilani had only been able to find one Christmas cookie cutter—a gingerbread man—but Jules could also use it to make reindeer by turning them upside down. The legs would be antlers, the arms would be the ears, and the heads would become the reindeers' noses. Leilani had also found a circle, which Jules would make into Christmas ornaments and a heart, which would … well, just be hearts.

With her dough rolled out, Jules got to work cutting out the cookies and laying them on the baking sheets. The commercial oven was big enough for all four at once, but Jules always liked to do a test bake first, especially when she was learning the nuances of a new oven. She popped the first sheet in with only three doughy shapes on it—one of each—and set a timer for nine minutes.

Her dad was a 'clean as you go' cook but Jules had inherited her mom's predilection for making a huge mess then cleaning it up at the end. But when Jules cast her eyes around the damage she'd done to Leilani's kitchen, she felt a pang of guilt and began wiping down the benchtop.

'So what are you up to the for the rest of the day?' Jules asked her dad.

'Your brother is determined to get me out on a surfboard.'

Jules laughed. 'Sorry, Dad—not laughing *at* you. Just ...' She shrugged.

'No, that was exactly my reaction.' They shared a smile.

'Can you get out of it? I mean, aren't the best waves for surfing first thing in the morning, anyway? That's what Matt says.'

'Apparently that doesn't matter, as my first lesson is on dry land.'

'What?'

Her dad shook his head. 'Doesn't make much sense to me either, but Will seems pretty convinced. Apparently, I need to master "popping up onto the board" before we take it out into actual water.'

'You could just say no.' But Jules knew that her dad would never do that—if Will wanted to teach her dad to surf, he'd go along with it and be riding the waves by the time New Year's rolled around.

Confirming her assumption, he looked up from his sauce and smiled, adding a one-shoulder shrug. 'It could be fun.' He reached for the sponge she was holding and she handed it over, watching as he rinsed it out and methodically wiped down the already clean benchtops on 'his' end of the kitchen. She'd missed her dad so much, it made her heart swell just watching him do something so ordinary. 'Hey, Dad?'

'Mmm?'

'While we're all here … it's just that I'd really like you to get to know Matt.'

Her dad stopped what he was doing and looked up at her. 'Of course, sweetheart. I do too. That's why I asked him to come to my surfing lesson today.'

'Really?'

'Absolutely. If I'm going to make a fool of myself, what better audience than my daughter's boyfriend?'

'Ha-ha. You won't make a fool of yourself.'

He finished his chore and set the sponge by the sink, then rinsed his hands. Wiping them dry on a dish towel, he crossed to her. 'He's a keeper, huh?'

Jules nodded. 'He's a keeper, Dad.' Before meeting Matt, Jules had only had two important men in her life: her brother and her dad. That she'd found someone to love who was as careful with her heart as they were, was a minor miracle.

'Then that's all I need to know. Well, that and I've seen the way he looks at you.' He reached up and cupped her cheek with his hand, like he used to when she was a little girl, then pulled her in for a hug. Jules realised she'd missed his hugs most of all.

'And what about you, Dad?' she asked.

He stepped back and look at her inquisitively. 'What about me what?'

'Are *you* dating? It's been a while …'

'Oh, god.' He looked down at the floor and shook his head.

'What? Will's with Lucy, I'm with Matt … you deserve to find someone who makes you happy, Dad.'

He lifted his eyes, meeting hers. 'Well, thank you, sweetheart, and it's not like I've completely cut myself off from all that ...'

'So, you're dating?'

'Jules ... I ... yes.' Jules could tell that he was uncomfortable with this conversation—understatement of the year—but she wanted her dad to be happy. He deserved to find someone who made him feel loved and appreciated.

'But no keepers,' she stated.

'No keepers.'

'But you're at least ... you know ...?'

'Oh god, are you asking if I'm getting laid?'

'Yeah, pretty much,' Jules replied.

'*Aaand* we're done.'

'What? It's a legit question, Dad. You're only fifty-seven, for crying out loud—*and* you're a total catch!'

Her dad groaned, stirred the sauce once more, then left the kitchen shaking his head.

'You did not,' said Matt.

Jules bit her lip, then cringed. 'I did.'

He laughed. 'You asked your *dad* about his sex life?' He laughed even harder.

'I hadn't meant to ... I just ... I just asked if he was dating.'

'Jules ...' Like her dad had earlier, Matt shook his head at her.

'Yeah. I guess it sorta came out of nowhere. We don't usually talk about those things. It's just that we were talking about you and—' She stopped as soon as she clocked Matt's raised eyebrows.

'*That's* why my ears were burning,' he teased.

'Ha-ha.'

'So what did you say?'

'Nothing much—just that you were a keeper.'

'Oh, wow, thank you. That's high praise.'

'Hey!' His dimples made an appearance, then he came around her side of the kitchen bench and slipped his arms around her waist.

'I think you're a keeper too,' he said quietly, his dark eyes narrowing sexily. She tipped her head and pressed her lips to his. Matt's grip on her waist tightened and what began as a chaste kiss, turned into much more in seconds—his tongue lightly touching hers, his full lips moving against her mouth. She wrapped her arms around his neck.

'God, you two, you're like rabbits.'

Jules *felt* Matt's growl as much as heard it and he tipped his head back, breaking the kiss with a frustrated sigh. 'And *you* have shitty timing, Chlo.'

Chloe, followed closely by Audrey, seemed unaffected by the rebuke, cackling as she set a half-dozen shopping bags on the benchtop.

'What in god's name is all that?' Jules asked, reluctantly stepping out of Matt's embrace.

'Stocking stuffers,' replied Audrey.

Jules laughed. 'God, this Christmas is going to be bigger than *Ben Hur*.'

'You have no idea,' replied Chloe. The timer went off and Chloe perked up like a Pavlovian dog. 'Are the cookies ready?' she asked, sniffing the air.

'They may be *baked*—I'll check—but I can't frost them till they're cool.' Jules donned an oven mitt then opened the oven, turning her head at the wall of heat that emerged, then slid out the baking sheet and placed it on the stone benchtop. With a spatula she lifted one cookie to check the underside. 'Perfect,' she said quietly. A small hand reached across and she smacked it.

'Hey.'

'Hey yourself. These are for Christmas. And I told you, I still have to frost them.' Chloe made puppy dog eyes and they blinked at her above a sizeable pout. 'Oh, don't give me that look.'

'Fine. We're going to the studio to stuff stockings.' She looked around. 'Where did Lucy go?' she asked, like she'd just realised Lucy was missing.

'Don't know,' said Audrey.

'Never mind. We'll just do it ourselves. Come on, Audrey.' Chloe waved over her shoulder and Audrey followed obediently behind.

Jules really didn't get that girl. In less than twenty-four hours, she'd made a surprise appearance, flirted with Will, revealed that she was nursing a broken heart, and now she was spending the afternoon being Chloe's lackey. Jules had no idea if she was a sweet, messed up kid, or a little brat who was playing nice to get what she wanted. At least Chloe seemed to have her in check—for now, anyway.

'So …' said Jules, turning towards her handsome boyfriend and making those dimples reappear.

'Pssst, Jules.' Archer's appearance was borderline comical. If saying 'pssst' wasn't ridiculous enough, he was also peering around the corner, eyes trained on the door that Chloe had just left through. And even more comical was that Lucy and Will were huddled behind him.

'If you're worried about Chloe, Archer, the coast is clear.'

'Thank god.' He sighed noisily. 'Trying to get everybody *but* Chloe in one room has been a nightmare.'

'Uh-huh,' replied Jules. She slid the remaining three sheets of unbaked cookies into the oven and set the time for ten minutes—more sheets meant a slightly longer baking time. By the time she'd done that, the others had foregone their clandestine adventures and were hovering near the breakfast bar. While Archer kept an eye on the door that led outside, Jules shot a questioning look at Lucy, who shrugged.

'Ah, everything okay, mate?' Matt asked Archer, who was bouncing on the balls of his feet.

Jules didn't think she'd ever seen the super-composed, ever-cool Archer Tate this excited. Just then, her dad entered the kitchen. 'Hey Jules—' He stopped short at the sight of the others. 'Oh, sorry, am I interrupting something?'

'No, it's perfect,' said Archer, signalling that he should join them. 'Come, come quickly.' He cast his eyes towards the door again, visibly relieved when Chloe hadn't miraculously appeared in the last five seconds. Nate joined the others and they all looked at Archer expectantly.

'All right, I'll be brief, as I don't know when I can get us all together again without Chloe about.' Jules thought it was a particularly long preamble for someone trying to be succinct and stifled a snigger. 'As you know, the original plan for the holidays was to take Chloe to Paris for Christmas and New Year. But, as the fates would have it, all that had to change—*including* my plan to propose to Chloe on New Year's Eve atop the Eiffel Tower.'

Lucy gasped, then there was a beat of silence before the others erupted into excited congratulations, including a back slap from Nate. 'Wait!' said Archer, emphatically. He glanced nervously at the door again, then back at the others. 'Obviously, it's meant to be a surprise, so we must keep this hush-hush.' Jules smothered another laugh—Archer was so earnest but his acutely English way of saying things was really funny.

Lucy crossed her heart with her fingertips. 'Mum's the word,' she said.

God, thought Jules, *this is like an episode of a British comedy*. 'We promise,' she said.

'Wonderful. I'm still thinking New Year's Eve, so …'

'We'll help,' said Lucy.

'Absolutely—whatever you need,' replied Jules.

Archer seemed relieved. 'Thank you. I knew I could count on

you all. And it's a funny thing when you want to propose to a professional Event Planner … you want everything to go perfectly but of course the one person who *could* help is the one who can't know about it ahead of time. And with my assistant, Anya, on leave …'

'Don't worry, man,' said Will. 'We've got your back.'

'Brilliant. And now that you all know, we can work out everything surreptitiously. Like the dance.'

'Sorry?' asked Matt. 'The dance?'

'Yes! I was thinking that we blokes could do one of those boy-band flash-mob kind of things.' Her dad, Will, and Matt all stared open-mouthed at Archer while he looked around encouragingly. 'Won't that be brilliant?'

'What's going on with you lot?' Chloe had—once again—snuck up on them, Audrey in tow, and the group started as one. 'Well?' she asked.

'Ahh,' said Jules, quickly searching for a quick response that wouldn't ruin Archer's plan, 'we were just discussing how to get Leilani to join us for Christmas.'

'Oh, right, yeah, that's a tough one,' said Chloe.

'I can ask her!' said Audrey, brightly. 'She's practically family, so she'll probably say yes.'

'Oh, good call,' said Chloe, 'go with the whole "family Christmas" angle—lay it on thick.' Audrey smiled, seeming happy that she could help. 'Now, Luce, we need you,' said Chloe, beckoning Lucy with a flapping hand.

'Oh, right, yes.' As the three women left the kitchen, Lucy threw a look over her shoulder—teeth bared and eyes wide, silently communicating, 'That was bloody close!' Jules glanced at Archer who sighed out a slow, steady breath and accepted a pat on the back from her dad.

'Well done, son,' he said quietly. 'Now, can we talk about this dance number?'

Chapter Fifteen

CHLOE

B etween organising a proper Christmas and taking Audrey under her wing, Chloe was busier than a beaver crossed with a bee.

She was in heaven.

Despite her original plans to 'hole up at the house', as she'd suggested to Archer, she'd quickly realised that in lieu of a romantic Parisian escape, where (no doubt) she and Archer would have spent the days wandering the streets of Paris and exploring museums and galleries, this was actually the perfect holiday. Her best friends were here, Kauai was absolutely beautiful (and a stark contrast to the urban sprawl of LA, which she'd begun to tire of), and she *loved* being in charge of making this the best Christmas ever for everyone, especially Lucy.

With Lucy and Audrey following (as instructed), she jogged up the stairs to the studio and made her way to the large workbench where she and Audrey had set up an assembly line. 'Right, so Luce, we've already stuffed your stocking, so no peeking, but we thought you might like to do the rest.' As she'd hoped, Lucy's eyes lit up at the array of goodies that she and Audrey had sourced on the third shopping trip of the day. There were puzzle books, card games, and nano block toys (assembly required), some (not-too-tacky) souvenirs, and a variety of consumable treats, including chocolate-covered coffee beans and dried pineapple—she'd drawn the line at store-bought lollies.

'Oh my …' said Lucy in almost a whisper, 'this is brilliant.' She looked up, her eyes glistening, and Chloe refrained from doing a self-satisfied shoulder shimmy. 'Thank you—both of you.' Lucy reached down to give Chloe a quick, tight hug but seemed a little hesitant when it came to hugging Audrey. Chloe wondered if she was still wary of Audrey over the whole 'flirting with Will' thing—probably.

'That's okay,' said the younger woman, catching on, 'I'm not much of a hugger anyway.' Chloe suspected she was fibbing, but the awkward moment passed with a warm smile from Lucy, who then turned her attention back to the business of stuffing stockings.

'Right so, Luce, you all good here? We've got to track down Leilani and get her to come to the tree decorating party tonight.'

'It's a party now?' asked Audrey.

'It was *always* a party,' replied Chloe matter-of-factly.

'Oh-kay,' said Audrey and Chloe threw her a look. If Audrey was going to be her assistant, she needed to be a bit more on the ball and a lot less sarcastic.

'Please, please go ahead,' said Lucy. 'And don't worry about me. I'm as happy as Larry,' she said, grinning broadly.

'Okay, cool. Aud, let's go.'

Chloe made for the stairs, hearing, 'Um, can you please not call me that?'

'Sorry!' Chloe called over her shoulder. 'Aud-reee.' She was halfway down the stairs when she asked, 'Now, where do you reckon we'll find Leilani?'

'Leilani, *please*,' said Audrey.

'No, no, I don't want to intrude.' Chloe and Audrey exchanged a frustrated look. If they couldn't get her to the tree decorating party, how were they going to get her to join them for *Christmas*?

They'd found Leilani in the linen cupboard. Well, it was more of a linen *room*—a king-sized bed would *easily* fit. And despite their repeated requests that she stop work and join in on the festivities, she kept declining. Apparently, it was 'very important' that Leilani rotate the linens and towels that had just arrived from the laundering company to ensure even wear. That made sense, of course—when you were running a multi-million-dollar estate, you needed to be on top of the details—but it was Christmas Eve Eve! The sheets could stay put for another few days.

'Leilani,' said Chloe, using her best 'negotiator' voice, 'Audrey tells me that you are family to her …' She deliberately left out the word 'like'—'family' on its own was far more potent. And, it seemed, it was also the magic word. Leilani stopped scrutinising a stack of perfectly folded fitted sheets and met Chloe's eye. 'And as you are Audrey's *only* family here, you would hardly be intruding. In fact, it would be *devastating* for Audrey if you didn't join us. Right, Audrey?'

'Oh, yeah, like totally. Devastating.'

Leilani looked from one to the other, her mind visibly chewing on the conundrum behind her brown eyes. She pursed her lips and sighed. 'But if I come to this party, who will …' She circled her hands in the air.

'Who will take care of everything?' Chloe responded.

'Yes!' Leilani punctuated her point with a sharp nod.

'Leilani, I promise you, we'll do everything. Nate's already cooking dinner and we can serve up family-style. Matt and Archer can organise drinks and we can set the table. There really is nothing for you to do tonight besides show up and enjoy yourself. Okay?'

The pursed lips relaxed but they were replaced with a frown of concentration and it occurred to Chloe that Leilani might be one of those people who defined their self-worth by how much they did for others. She had an idea. 'Oh, and I meant to ask you—for Christmas Day, I'm going to need your help.' She could tell she had Leilani's full attention now. 'You see, Lucy's mum sent her to the States with one of her amazing Christmas cakes—I mean, seriously, I practically lived off the stuff last year when I was in England. Anyway, Lucy accidentally left it in Colorado and sure, you're supposed to drizzle them with sherry for months in advance, but I'm thinking that if I called her mum and got the recipe …?'

Leilani's eyes danced with delight. 'Oh, *I* could make one! For sure. I could even take her mom's recipe and, you know, add a touch of Hawaii.' She lifted her chin in pride.

'That would be *awesome*,' encouraged Audrey.

'But you have to promise to join us tonight—for the tree trimming party,' added Chloe.

'*And* Christmas Eve.'

'Right!' Chloe agreed. 'And Christmas Day.' *Why not up the ante?* she thought.

Those pursed lips made another appearance but this time, a smile tugged at the left corner. 'You are …' she said, narrowing her eyes at Chloe.

'Persuasive?' asked Chloe brightly.

'I was going to say, "a bossy little thing".'

'Oh, that. Yeah, I am the original BLT,' said Chloe with a laugh.

'Maybe second edition,' replied Leilani, her mouth stretching to a broad smile.

'Oh, you get called that too?'

Leilani tipped her head to the side. 'A long time ago, but that's why I'm still the mama around here.'

In an obvious burst of affection, Audrey reached for Leilani and wrapped her arms around her shoulders—Chloe had been right about Audrey being a hugger (and fibbing to Lucy). 'Yes, you are,' said Audrey.

Leilani patted her arm. 'All right. I will come to the tree party. But only if you let me finish up what I'm doing.'

Chloe lifted both hands, conceding. 'Absolutely. How about you wrap up here and I'll call Mrs Browning and get the recipe for you. And let me know if you need me to keep Lucy busy and out of the kitchen.'

'Okay, Little BLT,' replied Leilani, her amused eyes trained on Chloe.

'Ha!' Sparring with Leilani was so much fun. 'So, now I'm "Little Bossy Little Thing"?'

'Uh-huh, because *I'm* Big BLT.'

'Gotcha.' They traded warm smiles—birds of a feather and all that—then Chloe tugged on Audrey's arm so they could leave Leilani to her sheets and towels. Once they were out of earshot, Audrey tried on Chloe's new moniker. 'So, what's next, Little BLT?'

'Yeah, *never* call me that, *Aud*.'

'Chloe, darling?' Archer called as he entered their room.

She quickly tucked the half-written card back into her underwear drawer and greeted him from the closet door. 'Hi, babe. What's up?'

He crossed the room in four long strides and swept her up into his arms. As he kissed her—and really, during all those years of kissing the world's most beautiful actresses on screen he'd *perfected* the art—she realised that other than sleeping next to each other, they hadn't had much time alone. She wrapped her arms even tighter around his neck and rose onto the balls of her feet for better kissing leverage.

Archer's lips—as movie goers around the world could attest—were swoon-worthy even just to look at, but under their spell, the (otherwise welcomed) weight of her lists, and her hopes that everyone would have the best Christmas ever, fell away. It was just her and the man she loved.

He lifted her easily, still within his embrace, and with her legs dangling, walked her to the bed where he gently put her down and finally broke the kiss. 'I've missed you,' he said quietly, his eyes drinking in the length of her body, then meeting hers.

'I was just thinking the same thing,' she said, capturing an errant lock of his dark brown hair. She twisted it between her finger and thumb, then raked it back into place with her fingertips.

'You've been very busy since we arrived,' he said.

'And you—chauffeuring the guys all over the island to surf ...' Archer could surf pretty well—he just wasn't obsessed with it like Matt and Will.

'Are you at least having a good time?' he asked.

She smiled. 'I'm having a brilliant time.'

'Good. But do promise me this: after you've organised the greatest Christmas ever—'

'It's "best" Christmas ever,' she corrected.

'Apologies—the *best* Christmas ever ... promise me you will have a proper holiday. We'll relax, read, explore, make love for half the day ...'

She tilted her head, smiling. 'Only *half* the day?'

'For as long as you like. I just worry that you've been in this intense work mode for so long, you've forgotten how to switch off.'

'How do you do it?'

His eyes narrowed, thoughts dancing behind his eyes as he considered her question. 'I wasn't always good at it. After I finished filming *Sharpshooter* in Oman, it took me ages to shake off that character—*and* the intensity of the shoot. I went back home to Mum and Dad's and it was my dad who pulled me aside. He said something like, "Son, you've been moping about like you've actually been to war. Remember, it's all just make-believe—something to entertain people. You need to get out of your head. Now come help me in the garden."'

'Wow.'

Archer chuckled. 'Yes, exactly. And he was right. I needed to get out of my head and get my head out of my arse.'

'Did he actually say that part? About the arse?'

'Just my interpretation.' Chloe smirked. 'And then he put me to work. We built a raised garden bed for Mum's herbs—proper sides made of planks, irrigation, everything. We didn't talk much, but that's just my dad. He's a "still waters run deep" kind of fellow. But just working with him at his elbow for the better part of a week … well, it did the trick.'

'So, working on something physical, something other than a role—that was you *resting*,' stated Chloe. She blinked her large brown eyes at him and his narrowed again, his own smirk appearing.

'Are you saying that slipping into work mode is you resting?' he asked.

'Maybe. It's definitely less challenging than getting parking permits from that village council in Oxfordshire. Our ten trailers nearly doubled the size of the town.'

'Hmm, quite.'

Chloe snuggled in, placing her cheek against Archer's chest. 'But I do like your idea of a proper holiday. After Christmas, I promise.'

He stroked her back, one hand lazily trailing back and forth. 'Excellent,' he said. He pulled back from their embrace and his expression shifted. 'Now, before we go downstairs for dinner, what do you say to making a mess of your perfectly made bed.'

Chloe glanced left and right at the enormous bed—a California king, it was even bigger than their bed in LA. That morning, she'd had to recruit Archer's help to make it—the only way to get the covers smooth and tight, the way she liked them.

'Oh, you're on, Mr Tate.' She snatched a quick kiss before tearing back the covers. 'And you know the best part of us having such a huge bed?' she asked, kicking the covers aside.

'What's that?' he asked, amusement in his eyes, as he slipped his T-shirt over his head.

Chloe eyed his beautiful torso hungrily before responding, 'Its *girth*.'

At that, Archer laughed heartily, then tugged at Chloe's feet, pulling her towards him and silencing her giggles with a kiss.

Chapter Sixteen

LUCY

Lucy's eyes scanned the long mantelpiece and she smiled broadly at the sight of her handiwork, the Christmas spirit enveloping her. Her dad always said that a man would take an hour to complete a job, then two hours to admire it—and for the first time, she truly understood that sentiment.

She'd spent the afternoon in absolute bliss, beavering away in the loft. First, she'd laid out all the beautiful stockings Audrey had made, again admiring both the choice of fabric and the craftsmanship. Then, she'd pored over the stocking fillers Chloe and Audrey had bought, mentally curating a bespoke array for each stocking.

Nearly two hours later—as sometimes, she got the combination of fillers all wrong and had to undo what she'd just done—she felt satisfied that she'd assembled the perfect stocking for each person. Then she'd ferried them down to the lounge in careful armfuls. Someone had left a pile of S-shaped hooks on the coffee table—probably Chloe, as she always thought of everything—and they were perfect for hanging stockings.

Now, there they all were, lined up and spaced exactly, and

Lucy could have cried. She may not have *loved* the cold, dreary weather in Oxfordshire this time of year, but it felt like she had a little bit of home right here. She'd ask Archer to sort out some Christmas music—there was no way she was going to figure out that stereo—and then the room would be perfect.

Well, almost …

She glanced down at the fireplace; it was one of those fancy gas ones with no actual logs, just a row of steel jets behind a pristine glass front. She'd been surprised that a mansion in Hawaii even *had* a fireplace but perhaps to people who lived on Kauai, anything under 25C was considered 'chilly'. Regardless, it had been a lovely surprise and, wouldn't it be wonderful if the fire were roaring when everybody came downstairs? *But then, won't it be boiling in here?* she pondered.

'Not if we turn up the air conditioning!' she said to herself cheerfully. She went off to find Leilani.

The shower was on in the en suite when Lucy got back to their room. She was running a little later than she'd hoped and would either have to settle for a quick rinse to wash away the day or join Will. In less than three seconds she decided on the latter, even though there was every chance it would make them even later for the evening's festivities.

'Hello there,' she said stepping into the two-person shower.

Will spun around, his eyebrows raised and his mouth stretched to a rather delectable grin. 'Wow, what a nice surprise.' He slipped his arms around her and pulled her towards him and she playfully pushed him away. 'Unfair,' he teased.

'First, I can't get my hair wet. You know it takes ages to dry—'

'Lame.'

She lifted her chin at him, feigning primness. 'And second, I'm already running late.' She reached past him to pump some body wash into her palm.

'It's drinks before dinner,' he said, his hands roaming her now-slick body freely. He pulled her against him and she let him, even though the ends of her long red curls were now getting wet. 'Everyone will understand if we're a little late.' His hand swept her hair aside and his lips found the curve of her neck.

Lucy groaned—partly from what Will was doing to her, but mostly because the thought of everybody knowing *why* they were late for drinks was mortifying. When his lips moved lower to her collar bone, she nearly succumbed to the wonderful sensation but a horrifying and very unwelcome thought interrupted her bliss—Will's lips on the birdlike collarbone of a willowy blonde. She shook her head to exorcise the image, her chin colliding with Will's ear.

'Ow.' Will lifted his head and looked down at her, his confusion evident. Hopefully the steamy shower was enough to cloak her embarrassment—her cheeks were no doubt flaming. *Why* had she thought about Will and Audrey together? She'd seen a very different side to Audrey that day—she was just a young woman nursing a broken heart, not some man-eating harpy.

'Everything okay?' Will asked, concern imprinted on his boyish good looks.

She shook her head again. 'Sorry, just had a twinge in my neck.' She lifted her hand and pinched the meat of her shoulder to sell the lie.

'Oh, poor baby,' he said, slipping back into flirtatious mode. 'How 'bout I kiss it better?'

Lucy inhaled deeply, finally losing herself in the here and now. 'Oh, what the hell,' she said softly, spinning within the confines of his arms and touching her lips to his. They could be late.

When Lucy and Will entered the lounge twenty minutes later than planned, Lucy steeled herself for the inevitable teasing. Only there was none. Instead, her friends were zinging around the room, calling out to each other.

'It's not any of these,' said Matt, poking around a panel of light switches.

'Um, what's going on?' asked Lucy. The frenzy ceased, everybody looking at her with a mix of expressions.

'We're trying to figure out the AC. It's gone bananas,' said Jules.

'Yeah, it's like Antarctica in here,' added Chloe.

'Do either of you know where the controls are?' asked Archer.

Lucy could feel her cheeks flaming again. She'd intended for the fireplace to neutralise the cold air from the air conditioner, but perhaps she had been a little heavy-handed in setting the temperature to fifteen. 'Oh, er …' She looked up at Will, who commiserated with a smile.

'Hang on,' said Chloe, 'you're wearing a Christmas jumper.' It wasn't an accusation per se—more of an observation, but Lucy's cheeks got even hotter. What an idiot she was. It wouldn't have been so bad if she'd been able to convince Will to don a Christmas jumper for the tree-trimming party—only he hadn't brought one. It seemed she was the only odd bod who'd thought to bring a jumper—to *Hawaii*.

'Oh, Luce, did you *plan* this?' asked Jules, her mouth tugging into a smile.

'Er … well, yes.' Lucy gestured towards the fireplace. 'Stockings just didn't seem the same above a fireplace without a fire.'

'Good point,' said Archer, coming to her rescue.

'And the stockings look great, babe,' said Will.

'For sure,' added Nate.

Matt piped in with, 'Totally.'

115

Lucy looked about at her friends. Chloe was rubbing her bare arms, Audrey was curled up on a sofa under three throw pillows, and Jules was warming her hands in front of the ineffective fire. Suddenly, the absurdity of her friends freezing while a fire was (supposedly) roaring hit her hard and she started giggling.

'I'm so sorry!' she said, pursing her lips. 'I just thought ...'

'We get it, Luce,' said Chloe, crossing the room to give her a hug, 'you wanted to make it extra festive.'

'Exactly. Silly, really.'

'Not silly—not at all,' said Archer, 'but we can probably sort out more of an equilibrium.'

'Yes,' agreed Lucy, 'absolutely.'

Just then, Leilani entered the room bearing an enormous cheese platter. 'Oh!' she exclaimed. 'It feels like Mauna Kea has blessed us with her presence,' she said. At the confused faces, she added, 'Goddess of ice, snow, and the cold.' A chorus of 'oh' and 'ahh' echoed around the room as she placed the platter on the coffee table. 'I'll be right back,' she said, winking at Lucy on her way out.

'I am very sorry,' said Lucy, stifling another giggle.

'No harm done,' said Archer. Lucy truly did adore him for being so gracious. After growing up across the road from each other, her crushing on her slightly older neighbour all through her awkward teens, there had been two decades of not seeing much of Archer and now he was going to propose to one of her best friends. She couldn't be happier for Chloe.

And the others had been gracious too—even Audrey, who'd come out from her pillow cave to carve off a slice of cheese. 'Luce, it's a good thing we love you,' said Chloe. 'Even though you're a total dag.' Lucy shook her head—she should have known that Chloe would want the last word, having spent twenty-three years on the receiving end of her gentle but loving teasing.

'Hun,' said Jules to Matt, 'we forgot the wine.'

'Oh, right,' he said leaping up, 'sorry, everyone. Be right back!'

'I'll help,' Jules said, following him out of the room as Archer made his way to the stereo.

'Can we do Mariah?' asked Chloe, also helping herself to some cheese.

'Sure, darling.'

Audrey groaned. 'Really, Mariah Carey?'

'Hey!' said Chloe pointing a finger at her. 'You will not disparage the Queen of Christmas.'

Audrey rolled her eyes and muttered, 'Whatever,' under her breath just as Mariah Carey's voice rang out into the large room.

This is more like it, thought Lucy, relieved to be out of the spotlight. Jules and Matt returned with a tray of glasses and two bottles of fizz and Nate helped pour. He handed her a glass. 'You've done a beautiful job, sweetheart,' he said softly and Lucy felt her eyes slick with tears. Will's family had embraced her as one of them and having Nate there was almost like being with her parents.

Almost …

Chapter Seventeen

JULES

'So,' said her dad, clapping his hands, 'dinner first or trimming the tree?'

'Dinner,' responded everyone except Lucy, who replied, 'The tree, definitely!' Lucy looked around the room, her disappointment evident, before yielding to the rest of them. 'Or we can wait till after dinner.'

'Do you mind?' Will asked Lucy. 'I'm sorta starving.'

'No, no, that's fine.' Jules watched Lucy closely, sensing that things were *not* fine with her.

'Awesome,' said Will, planting a kiss on Lucy's head. Lucy's lips flattened into one of those 'I'm not really smiling' smiles but Jules' brother didn't seem to notice.

'You won't regret it, Luce,' said Jules. 'Dad's pasta sauce is killer,' she offered in consolation.

'Speaking of … If we're going to eat first, I'll stir the sauce and get the pasta on.' Her dad left the room, Leilani leaping up to follow closely behind. Even though Jules and her dad had left the kitchen immaculate that afternoon, it was obvious Leilani still had trust issues about anyone else using 'her' kitchen.

It *had* been fun making the Christmas cookies. And after her dad went to his dry-land surfing lesson—seriously, she would have *loved* to have seen that—Matt had wandered in to see if she needed any help. She'd declined, asking him to keep her company instead, and he'd offered to play bartender and DJ while she decorated the cookies.

Within minutes, she had a cold beer in hand and her 'Australian 80s Rock' playlist playing through the Bluetooth speaker that sat on the benchtop. Matt had got her onto INXS and Midnight Oil and a bunch of other 'classic Aussie bands' and now this playlist was her go-to when she was baking or doing chores. Not very Christmassy but she knew she'd hear enough Christmas music in the next few days to last her a lifetime. Having best friends who personified 'the Christmas spirit' was mostly okay but Jules had her limits.

'What d'ya reckon?' asked Matt, one hand resting on her hip and the other raising his glass.

'The sparkling?' she asked.

'Yeah.' Matt took another sip and held his glass up to the light. Jules did the same, noting how fine the beads were. She sniffed the wine, inhaling its honeyed, yeasty aroma. That was another thing about being with Matt—her knowledge of wine had expanded a hundred-fold. 'Pretty good, eh?' he asked.

She took a sip, this time mindfully so she could appreciate its toasty flavour and silky texture on her tongue. 'They definitely know what they're doing in Napa,' she replied.

'Will you ever make a sparkling wine, Matt?' asked Archer, joining their conversation.

Matt's hand left her hip so he could rub the back of his neck—his tell when he felt like he was in the hotseat. Only Jules knew it had nothing to do with Archer's otherwise innocuous question. Matt's partner in the winery, Twoey, had been pressing for them to plant Chardonnay so they could get in on the sparkling wine market. Matt wasn't convinced, especially as they'd only just opened the tasting room in the spring. He thought they should focus on that for the foreseeable future, make sure it really took off.

'Uh, yeah, maybe. My partner and I have talked about it,' he replied diplomatically. When he dropped his hand from his neck, Jules laced her fingers with his and squeezed. He squeezed back.

'Well, I'm very much looking forward to trying the Pinot Noir you brought. Chloe raves about it.'

'I wouldn't say "raves",' said Chloe from her spot on the couch, 'I mean, it's *all right*.'

'*Hey!*' said Matt.

'Bahahaha,' laughed Chloe.

'You crack yourself up, don't you, Chlo?' asked Jules, smiling at her.

'Well, yeah. I'm hilarious.'

'Says you,' muttered Audrey.

'Damned straight,' said Chloe. 'If you don't toot your own horn, you can't expect anyone else to.'

'I'll toot your horn, darling—anytime,' said Archer.

'Ewww, that's gross,' said Audrey.

Jules shared a look with Matt, both sniggering quietly.

'What?' asked Archer, clearly aghast. 'No, I just mean that I'll sing her praises is all.' Another rare moment of Archer being flustered; it was sweet.

'Just wear it, dude,' said Will. Archer dropped his shaking head, chin to chest.

'Ignore them, babe,' said Chloe.

'I'm going to see about the wine for dinner,' he said, his complexion slightly flushed. 'Matt, care to join me?'

'You don't have to ask twice, mate—that cellar ...'

Jules watched them go, her gaze landing on Matt's ass—damn, he looked good in jeans. How long till they could steal away and get some more alone time? She figured maybe an hour for dinner, then another for trimming the tree.

But Lucy ... this was sorta her night. Jules looked over at her and, thankfully, she was smiling as she sipped her wine and chatted to Chloe. Even so, Jules could still sense the undercurrent of discord. It couldn't be the Christmas stuff, not with the stockings hung by the chimney with care—or in this case, above the gas fireplace—*and* they were planning to spend most of the evening trimming the tree.

Jules glanced at Audrey—was she the source? Possibly—Lucy had been pretty pissed at her last night. And although Chloe had seemed to have taken a liking to Audrey, Jules was content with keeping her distance—mostly out of solidarity with Lucy but also because she had limited patience for drama.

'You may have outdone yourself, Dad,' said Jules, sitting back from the table. She'd cleaned her plate—twice. She loved her dad's pasta but she rarely ate this much; 'holiday eating mode' had definitely been activated since she'd landed in Hawaii.

'Thanks, sweetheart.' Her dad shot her a modest smile from his position at head of the table.

'Outstanding dinner, Nate,' said Archer.

'And that's high praise,' added Chloe. 'Archer is practically a professional chef.'

'Hardly, darling. A few months' training a million years ago doesn't make up for years and years in the kitchen. I certainly don't have anything like your pasta sauce in my repertoire, Nate.'

'Can you give him the recipe?' asked Chloe hopefully.

'Ah, no recipe, I'm afraid,' said Nate. 'I just sorta ... you know, intuit it. It turns out slightly different every time.'

Chloe huffed in disappointment and Archer patted her hand as they exchanged an amused look. At least one of them could cook a half-decent meal; Chloe considered making ramen from a packet a culinary accomplishment.

'Hey, Archer,' said Will from the other end of the table. He played with the neck of his beer bottle as though he was gearing himself for something.

'What's up, Will?'

'Nah, never mind.'

Archer laughed. 'Go on.'

Will placed his elbows on the table and steepled his hands. 'Just ...'

'Spit it out,' said Chloe.

'*Okay*. So, I read online that you're in consideration to be the next James Bond.'

'Ah,' said Archer, smiling to himself. Jules had read that too and she swapped another excited glance with Matt. When they *weren't* with Archer and he came up, one or both of them would say (again) how surreal it was that they were friends with him. If she subscribed to that 'six degrees of separation' thing, she'd only be two degrees from half of Hollywood. But she didn't.

Archer was holding court—meaning to or not—as all eyes, including Leilani's, were trained on his face while he visibly contemplated how much he could reveal. Jules clocked Chloe's tight-lipped expression—she definitely knew something, but probably felt it wasn't her news to share.

'I can say this,' Archer began. Jules watched her brother lean in closer. 'I've had some discussions.' He quickly raised a hand. 'Nothing concrete and they're also talking to several other actors.'

'I read that it's down to you, Hiddleston, Heughan, and Cavill,' said Will.

'Well, then you've got better sources than me,' retorted Archer with a chuckle.

'Do you *want* to be James Bond?' Jules asked.

'Ah-ha! There's the rub. Do I want to play one of the most iconic characters ever to appear on screen, setting myself up for comparisons and locking myself into a franchise for at least a decade or ...?'

'You make it sound like a bad thing, mate,' said Matt, teasing.

Archer shrugged. 'There are definitely worse roles.' He added a wink and Chloe sniggered. Maybe if Jules promised not to say a word, Chloe would dish.

'Right. Well, keep us posted,' said Lucy, springing out of her chair. 'Should we start on the tree now?'

Jules stifled a laugh. She could tell that Lucy had waited as long as she possibly could—even talk of Archer as the next James Bond wasn't enough to distract her from trimming the tree. 'Let's do it, Luce,' she said, earning an excited grin from Lucy.

'Menfolk,' said her dad, 'we're on clean up.'

'Oh no, no,' said Leilani, standing abruptly.

'Leilani, please. It's the least we can do. *Please* ... Why don't you head into the living room with the others?' She gave him a weighty side-eye—seriously, this woman was *not* keen on relinquishing her domain—but nodded in resignation, dropping her napkin on the table.

'Hey, wait,' said Will, a stack of plates in his hands. 'You shouldn't be on clean up, Dad. You cooked.'

'Oh, yeah, so I guess it's just you guys then,' he said, grinning at the others.

'Nicely played, Nate,' said Archer, picking up the near-empty platter of pasta.

Jules downed her last sip of wine, then followed Lucy, Leilani, her dad, and Chloe out of the dining room. She paused at the door to ask Matt to bring another couple of bottles when he was done, just in time to clock Audrey sidling up to Will and making eyes at him. Right, so Audrey still had her sights set on Will—despite it being *super* obvious that he was with Lucy. 'I can help if you like,' she said to him, her eyelashes batting so intensely Jules could practically feel a breeze.

Oh, no you don't, thought Jules, any sympathy she'd felt for Audrey falling away. 'Hey, Audrey, I think Chloe wants you,' she said.

Audrey's (sickly) sweet expression soured as she turned towards Jules. 'I'll be there in a minute.'

Will just shrugged, seemingly oblivious to Audrey's flirtations—typical Will. Jules sighed. Unless she wanted to make a thing of it—and with Will, any flirtation would only ever be one-sided—she had to let it go. She was about to join the others right as Chloe called out from the living room. 'Hey, Jules! Bring more wine!'

Jules did an about-face, nearly colliding with Matt, who held out two unopened bottles of his Pinot. 'Oh, thanks, hun.'

He landed a quick kiss. 'Save me a glass,' he said.

'Chloe's in there. You want a glass, you're gonna have to be quick.'

'Yeah, good call.'

'Jules!'

'Coming, *geez*!'

'Oh, hey,' said Matt, capturing Jules' arm with his hand. She turned back again. 'You think maybe we can go somewhere tomorrow? Just us?'

God, that sounded like heaven. 'Sure, what did you have in mind?'

'I don't know. A hike maybe? I just …' He cast his eyes around and came closer. 'I need some quiet time—with you.'

'I hear ya. I'm in.'

'Jules!'

'Oh for the love of …' she muttered. 'I'll be right there!' To Matt, she said, 'Quiet time you said?' He kissed her again, this kiss lingering a bit longer than the last, and she left. By the time she

124

got to the living room, Lucy and Chloe had already laid out the ornaments and were chatting excitedly about the array. Jules wasn't about to shout, 'Bah humbug!' or anything, but she definitely wasn't as excited about trimming the tree as the others.

'Popcorn!' exclaimed her dad.

'Seriously?' Jules asked him. 'I couldn't eat another thing.'

She placed the wine on the coffee table, ignoring Chloe's cry of, 'Finally!' and the sound of a screw cap opening.

'No, I meant, for stringing. I know it's silly being nostalgic for something so minor ...' Her dad shrugged, but now he had Lucy's attention.

'Of course! We *must* have popcorn strings!' declared Lucy. 'That's what this Christmas is all about, isn't it? Including everyone's favourite traditions.' Jules was glad Lucy seemed to have turned a corner on the whole 'not having a white Christmas' thing.

'Though, *please* don't look at me,' continued Lucy, holding out her hands in surrender. 'I was atrocious at it and I blame your boozy hot chocolate for that,' she added, pointing an accusatory finger at Jules' dad. He guffawed and Lucy joined in, grinning.

Lucy was right. His hot chocolate *was* killer—mostly in a good way, but it could also give you a killer hangover if you had too much of it. When the May Ladies had spoken on Christmas Day last year, Lucy had been paying that price.

'Well, I've got popcorn!' declared Leilani. Jules noticed again that Leilani seemed liveliest when she was needed.

'Just plain?' asked Jules. "I mean, we *could* do microwave popcorn ...'

'Nooo,' replied Leilani. 'Too messy—I've got kernels, and air popping is best if you're stringing it. Isn't that right, Mr Nate?' she asked.

Leilani and her dad started talking about the logistics of popcorn stringing—him tossing in another reminder to just call him 'Nate'—and headed to the kitchen, leaving the May Ladies alone. 'Hey, look,' said Jules, 'it's just the three of us.'

Lucy looked up from where she was sorting silk leis by colour and Chloe stopped pouring wine and looked around. 'You're right. A rare moment alone. This calls for a toast.'

Jules shook her head, smiling. Chloe thought any occasion was worth a toast. She'd actually toasted *toast* once. 'Here,' said Chloe, handing around generous pours of Matt's Pinot—as she thought, he'd be lucky to get a glass. 'To us, to the May Ladies.'

'To us,' echoed Lucy.

'To my girls,' said Jules, suddenly choked with emotion.

'Aww,' said Chloe, cocking her head.

'Seriously, I love you two. I don't say it much, but I do,' said Jules.

Lucy draped her long arm around Jules' neck and planted a kiss on her cheek. 'I love you too—both of you.'

Chloe completed the group hug by wrapping her much shorter arms around Jules' waist. 'Love you right back, you big dag,' she said, her voice muffled by Jules' shoulder. The awkward but love-filled hug soon shook from laughter—first Jules', then Lucy's. As they stood back, Chloe was totally nonplussed. '*What?*'

And that made Jules and Lucy laugh even harder.

Chapter Eighteen

CHLOE

Chloe appraised the Christmas tree. For a design they'd cobbled together in a day—and one that included hand-strung popcorn, something she'd permitted even though it was a last-minute addition and it *really* didn't go with the aesthetic she'd planned—it was a very pretty tree. They'd connected the leis to form an ombre garland of silk flowers. The small fabric pineapples punctuated the tree much in the same way pinecones might. And the few ornaments they *had* found in the shops were a pretty and colourful addition.

'What do you reckon, Lucy?' she asked.

Lucy's eyes were alive with delight as she admired the tree, wearing a broad smile and with her palms pressed to her chest. 'It's perfect,' she replied.

Chloe breathed a little sigh of relief which quickly morphed into low-level self-satisfaction. If 'Ms White Christmas', as Jules had called Lucy, was happy, then she'd pulled it off. The others added their approval and Jules piped in with, 'Yeah, it looks really good,' from the couch right before stuffing a handful of popcorn into her mouth.

'I thought you said you couldn't eat another thing,' said Chloe.

Jules' hand hovered above the popcorn bowl, then she retracted it. 'Good call—thanks. It doesn't even have salt.' She brushed her hands together.

'So now the tree's done, can we play games?' asked Audrey.

All eyes settled on Audrey and she stared at the others expectantly. Chloe hadn't been aware that games were on the schedule. She'd thought they would all relax now, spending the rest of the evening chatting and admiring the tree—and *maybe* sneaking a few of Jules' Christmas cookies.

'What do you mean?' she asked.

Audrey retrieved a notebook from its hiding place amongst the couch cushions and opened it to where a pen marked the page. 'So, I've put us into teams and I've planned some fun games for us.'

On the one hand, Chloe admired Audrey's initiative—she was certainly coming out of her post-breakup shell—but on the other hand ... She surveyed the room, catching a mix of expressions. Nate ran a hand over his face as if he were trying to wake himself up. It *was* three hours ahead in Colorado and already quite late where they were. 'Um, what sort of games?' Did Chloe need to shut this down or acquiesce, then cajole the others to join in?

'Um, you know, like old-school games—charades, Win, Lose or Draw ... I thought it could be fun.'

'That does sound fun, sweetheart, but I'm afraid I'm going to have to call it a night,' said Nate.

'Oh, but you're already in a team! With Chloe. And I've mixed us all up so couples aren't together and, Leilani, I thought you could be the judge and maybe keep score.' She looked at them hopefully. *Wow, she's really gone to a lot of trouble*, thought Chloe.

'How about tomorrow night? For Christmas Eve?' Nate asked.

There were mumblings from the others, Archer adding, 'That

could be fun! A real occasion.' Chloe's heart twanged at how kind he was being to Audrey.

'Hang on,' said Lucy, her face contorted by a scowl, 'what are the other teams?'

Uh-oh, thought Chloe with a jolt. *Abort, abort!* 'Um,' began Audrey, consulting her list. 'So there's Nate and Chloe, then you and Matt, and Archer and Jules' —*Please stop talking!* Chloe shouted inside her head— 'and me and Will.' *Nooo!*

Audrey had walked straight into Lucy's snare. Lucy, who was perhaps the gentlest person Chloe knew—thoughtful, kind, generous to a fault, a true empath—*did* have a dark side. Chloe had seen it once—*only* once—and she could either throw herself into its pathway and attempt to save Audrey or she could join Jules on the couch and reach for the popcorn. It was a split-second decision to make, but Jules made it for her.

'Audrey, we should change those teams.' There was no 'maybe we should', just an outright 'this is what we should do'.

'Why?' *Is she really that dim or just playing dumb?*

Chloe looked over at Lucy in time to see the rising colour darken her cheeks. 'Luce, I need to see you in the kitchen,' she said, grabbing Lucy's arm in a desperate attempt to defuse the situation, but Lucy pulled it free, her eyes locked onto Audrey. Chloe followed her gaze—yep, Audrey was playing dumb.

'You know *exactly* why,' said Lucy, her voice low.

'Babe?' said Will, his tone suggesting that he may just be twigging to what was really going on.

'Just a moment,' Lucy said to Will, her eyes not leaving Audrey. 'Don't you?' Chloe's head snapped towards Audrey—this was like watching a tennis match, only down one end there was a powder keg with its fuse lit and it was nearing explosion.

'I don't see what the big deal is,' said Audrey.

'Audrey, I need to see you in the kitchen.' If Chloe couldn't remove Lucy from the situation, she'd settle for Audrey.

'Good idea,' said Leilani, standing and reaching for Audrey.

'I'm not going anywhere. I'm staying right here.' Chloe looked over at Jules who seemed both furious and perplexed. 'It's not fair. I planned this really fun activity ...' continued Audrey. God, this girl *really* couldn't read the room—or, more likely, she could read it perfectly.

'You planned it so you could play with Will,' interjected Lucy. Chloe pressed her lips together to swallow a laugh—this wasn't the time to point out Lucy's unintentional innuendo. She locked eyes with Jules and it was obvious—Jules was thinking the same thing. The snigger burst forth despite her best efforts and Lucy threw her a cross look. 'Sorry,' she muttered.

'So wha—'

'Maybe we should all call it a night,' said Nate, talking over Audrey. Chloe admired him for wading into the fracas but neither Lucy nor Audrey even looked his way.

'Screw this!' said Audrey, throwing her hands up in the air. 'Why'd I even bother? You people are a bunch of assholes anyway. Not you, Leilani, but the rest of you. I mean, who gives a fuck about the stupid tree or stockings or presents! Who gives a fuck about Christmas?!' In an instant, her fury morphed into desolation, her angry expression giving way to tears. She swiped at them. 'Screw this. I'm outta here.' She carelessly tossed the notebook across the room like a frisbee and it struck the Christmas tree, knocking off a couple of ornaments.

'Sweetheart—'

'I'm not your fricking sweetheart,' she spat at Nate. She banged into the edge of the large coffee table with her knee as she pushed past him and winced. Leilani reached for her, but she batted away Leilani's hand. 'I'm fine. Just leave me alone.'

Audrey left by the side door that led to the terrace, leaving it open like a gaping mouth. When Chloe gathered her senses enough to look around at the others, most of their mouths were gaping too.

———————

'I don't think that could have gone worse,' said Chloe as she and Archer made a trip to the kitchen. Chloe was carrying a tray filled with wine glasses—some empty, a couple nearly full—and Archer was carrying the remnants of the picked-over cheese board.

After Audrey's outburst, Leilani had apologised for her then hurried after her, Jules and Matt had made their excuses, along with Nate, and Lucy and Will were having a quiet but somewhat tense conversation in the living room.

'It's not your fault, darling. Audrey clearly has a lot on her mind and I doubt that much of it has to do with us.'

'Mmm, maybe.' Chloe wanted to go back for everything else but she held off, thinking she should give Will and Lucy some privacy.

'Sean *has* mentioned a few times that Audrey doesn't get along very well with her parents.'

'That's not an excuse to behave like that.'

'No, no of course not—but it may be part of the reason.'

'I seriously can't believe she chucked a massive tanty tonight. She was great today—really helpful, *nice* even. I mean, what the hell?'

'Indeed,' he said, his frown becoming a sneer.

'What? What's that about?'

'Sorry … I was just thinking about Madison.'

'Oh.'

He crossed to her. 'No, not like that. Sorry, darling. And now I'm apologising on replay. Sor—'

He stopped short and Chloe pushed him lightly on his chest. 'Dag.'

'Yes, I am very much being a dag.'

'So, why were you thinking about *her*?' Archer's ex-girlfriend, Madison Strumpet, was a moderately talented actress with stunning good looks who had an addiction to drama and, therefore, was a total nightmare. When Archer had dated her, he'd been the mayor of Tanty Town.

'Just the tantrums …' he replied, confirming Chloe's suspicion.

'Oh, right. Still …'

'I know. I shouldn't think of her at all and I'm sor—' Chloe smirked, rolling her eyes at him. 'Have I told you how much I love you?' he asked, his arm encircling her waist.

'Not in the past hour,' she replied, letting him off the hook.

'I love you.'

'I know.'

He grinned for a moment, then it fell away. 'Seriously, though, thank you for being you, wonderful you—and for not throwing tantrums or being unreasonable or …'

'An immature brat?'

'Yes, all those things.' His eyes bored into her and the mood intensified—*stilled* even. 'Chloe, my darling, will you—'

'Excuse me, Mr Archer,' said Leilani, barrelling into the kitchen.

'Yes?'

'Leilani, what's wrong?' Chloe had only known Leilani a couple of days but the woman was clearly distraught.

She frowned, her tense fingers tugging at her top. 'It's just … I went after Audrey, as you know, but she wasn't in her bungalow. And I've already checked the art studio, the gym, the yoga studio. *And* the movie theatre …'

'And you can't find her?' affirmed Archer.

'No and I'm worried.'

'Has she done this before?' asked Chloe.

'Run out?'

'Well, you know, made a big scene and then run out,' said Chloe.

Leilani nodded. 'Once, a few years ago.'

'And?'

'We couldn't find her—not until morning.'

'Oh god,' said Archer and Chloe at once.

'Yes, and with her breakup and everything ...'

Archer walked over to Leilani and patted her arm, then gave it a squeeze. 'No wonder you're worried. We'll help find her. And the others will too.' Leilani nodded but she seemed unsure and her eyes were slick with tears.

'It'll be okay, Leilani,' said Chloe, stepping closer, 'I promise.' She had no idea what made her say that last part. How could she promise?

'Thank you, Miss Chloe.'

'It's just Chloe,' she replied gently but Leilani only shrugged and shook her head. Chloe clearly wasn't going to win this one—not right now, anyway. 'I'll go and get the others to help look for Audrey.'

As Chloe left the kitchen, Archer asked, 'Last time, did you find her on the property?' Chloe paused just outside the door to listen to Leilani's reply and it sent shivers down her spine. 'Yes but ... she was sitting on the clifftop, on the other side of the fence.' *Oh my god.*

'Where do I find a torch—sorry, a flashlight?' Archer asked as Chloe hurried to gather the others.

Chapter Nineteen

LUCY

The others cleared out quickly but Lucy was rooted to the spot. She'd been seething with anger only moments ago but that had dissipated right after Audrey's departure.

Had Audrey's emotional outburst been her fault? Perhaps she'd read more into the Will–Audrey team-up than she should have, simply because Audrey had flirted with Will the previous night. Perhaps their pairing truly was innocuous and she was just being paranoid. Besides, with all Audrey's help with the Christmas stockings that day, Lucy had thought they might even become friends.

Gah! It was all just so confusing.

Will approached with the care that one might a wounded bull. 'Hey, Lucy ...' She looked up at him. 'Hey ...' He gently clasped her arms and ran his hands down their length, his hands slipping into hers. 'Are you okay?'

She shook her head slightly, eyes locked onto his and glossing with tears. Wordlessly, he pulled her into a hug—one of his (often longed-for) Will hugs. Her breath shuddered, caught between a sigh and a sob. 'What's going on, Lucy?' he asked gently as his arms tightened around her.

What *was* going on? Was this all just a manifestation of the pent-up angst she'd been feeling for months? There were too many questions tumbling through her mind and, in that moment, she longed to be back in her flat on her own so she could properly sift through them and make sense of everything.

All she knew for sure was that Audrey had pushed her buttons and now she was on the precipice of telling Will what was really going on. What if he thought it was all too much and ended it? 'Gah!'—*another* question!

Will pulled back. 'I get the sense that there's a lot in that "gah",' he said and she hid her face. She hadn't meant to express her frustration out loud. 'Lucy?' His fingers found her chin and he lifted it. 'She's just a young girl.' Right, so he *did* know Audrey was making a play for him.

'She's in her twenties.'

'*Early* twenties.'

'She likes you.'

'Uh, yeah …' He pressed his lips together. 'I just figured that out.'

'Only just now?'

'What can I say? The man—'

'—waits patiently for a signal.' They shared a weak smile. On one of her visits to Colorado, they'd gone down the YouTube rabbit hole of funny advertisements and had stumbled upon an old Australian commercial for beer or something. With David Attenborough style commentary, a woman in a bar makes an overt play for a man who misses every signal as he 'waits patiently'.

Jules was right, Lucy realised. Will *had* been oblivious that Audrey was keen on him. Right at that moment, Chloe dramatically burst into the room. She seemed to be doing that a lot on this trip and any other time, Lucy might have laughed. 'Guys, Audrey's missing.'

'What?' they asked at once.

'Yeah, Leilani couldn't find her in her bungalow or the art studio or a bunch of other places she's already looked.'

'We'll help look for her,' said Will, releasing Lucy from his embrace.

'Oh, yes, of course,' said Lucy, shoving aside her cacophony of discordant feelings.

'Will you guys tell Jules and Matt? And somebody needs to search the top floor.' Lucy rarely saw Chloe flustered like this and felt a nervous twinge ripple through her.

'Is there something you're not saying?' she asked.

'Just … Archer's gone to check the cliff—the one just past the fence line. You know … just beyond the pool.'

'Why?' She and Will traded concerned glances.

'That's where she was found last time.'

'Last time?' asked Will.

Chloe nodded. 'The morning after she went missing. Now go! And call out if you find her.'

Will grabbed Lucy's hand and they hurried upstairs to alert the others.

'That's the last guest room,' said Jules. 'At least, I *think* it is—this place is huge.'

'No, I think you're right,' said Lucy. 'And we've checked the yoga studio. That *is* all the rooms up here, isn't it?'

'Don't ask me. Since we've been here, I've worn a path between our suite, the kitchen, and the gym but that's about it.'

'Let's check in with the others,' said Lucy, running ahead and scurrying down the stairs, Jules following closely behind her. They entered the lounge but it was empty.

'Chloe!' called Lucy. No response. 'Will?'

'They must be outside.'

'Do you know where they keep the torches?' asked Lucy. 'Or should we search the ground floor?'

'Again? I'm pretty sure it's been covered—twice. Maybe we should be calling the police.'

Lucy looked at her horrified, that gnawing feeling in her stomach intensifying. 'Really?'

'Well, if she's gone off before—*and* put herself in danger ...' Jules shrugged then huffed out a sigh. 'What do you think?'

'It's all my fault!' blurted Lucy.

'What? What is?'

'If I hadn't made such a fuss over the game thing and the teams ...'

'Hey! No. *None* of this is your fault. You were just calling her on her bullshit.'

'That's what I mean! Why did I have to do that? I mean, she's harmless really. Will's not going to—'

'Of course not, but that doesn't mean she wasn't being a brat. She knew what she was doing. And even if the whole "teams" thing hadn't happened, she's clearly got a lot going on—the breakup with that YouTube guy, and Leilani said she's pretty much estranged from her parents. Then, here we are with *my* dad—all "happy family" ... Something had to give. You did nothing wrong, Lucy. Even if she's having a hard time, that's no excuse to make a play for someone else's boyfriend.'

Lucy flopped onto the nearest sofa. 'Really?' she asked hopefully.

'Yes!' Jules sat next to her and gave her one of those Jules looks—a 'what's really going on?' look.

'What?' asked Lucy feebly—she knew full well.

'Are you going to tell me?'

Despite the situation, Lucy snorted out a laugh at her accurate reading of Jules' facial expression, but her wry smile vanished immediately. It was one thing to confide in her about Audrey but Jules was Will's big sister. Lucy was hardly going to moan to her about his investment—or lack of—in their relationship, especially after what happened last year. Jules had been less than pleased to discover that Lucy and Will had got together. What if she took Lucy's worries as criticism of Will?

'Luce?'

'It's nothing, really.' Lucy wished she was a much better liar.

'Bullshit.' Lucy laughed softly again—Jules could always see through her. But dare she risk telling her the truth? 'You missing your folks? Is that it?' asked Jules, her voice softening.

An out! Lucy sighed heavily for effect but was surprised when the tears came. 'Yes,' she said—she really did miss them, especially two days before Christmas. Jules reached over to squeeze her shoulder. 'Do you ever just wish for a magical place where all your loved ones could be together?'

'Like Kauai?' asked Jules, a cheeky smile stretching across her face.

'Well, no. I mean, most of *your* loved ones are here right now …' Jules shrugged in acknowledgment. 'But I mean more like, we all live our lives in our hometowns, but those hometowns are all the same place.'

'Yeah, that does sound like it requires magical intervention,' Jules agreed.

'It's just that no matter where I am, I always miss someone.'

'I totally get that, Luce.' They were quiet for a while. 'Is this about missing Will?' she asked and Lucy's eyes flew to hers. Jules was dangerously close to the truth.

'Well, yes, of course, but also my parents and you girls. And Matt and Archer,' she hurriedly added.

Jules nodded solemnly. 'Look, it sucks when we're apart from our families or our closest friends, but that just makes the reunions all the sweeter, right? I mean, when Archer called about coming here, for me, it was a no-brainer. It was only when I talked to Matt and he agreed, *that's* when I felt it—how much I miss you all—you and Chloe and my dad and Will. And my mom. But it's hard to feel that every day, you know?' Lucy nodded. She did know because she *did* feel it every day. 'I mean, how would I function? So I just sorta push it aside, lock it away.'

Lucy *wished* she could do that. And yes, the pain she felt every time she and Will said goodbye did begin to dull after a while—weeks, usually—but it was always there. She wasn't sure she could do what Jules did—pretend it didn't exist at all.

'Have you talked to Will?' asked Jules. 'About how you're feeling?'

'Hello, you two.' Archer and Matt entered from the terrace, giving Lucy a reprieve from Jules' emotional examination. But only fleetingly—she knew Jules would ask again soon. She also realised that they'd been so wrapped up in their conversation, they'd completely abandoned the search for Audrey. Oh, she was a horrid, horrid person.

'No luck?' she asked, though it was rhetorical because they were alone.

'Hey!' said Chloe, bursting into the room, Leilani and Nate in tow. 'We've been back to the garage, all the bungalows, and the art studio. Nothing.'

'Well, at least she's not on the clifftop,' said Archer, his relief palpable.

'Would she have left here on foot?' Jules asked Leilani.

'You mean the property?' she responded and Jules nodded. 'I

...' Lucy noticed how her hands worried the hem of her top. 'I don't know.' Leilani's eyes filled with tears and Lucy crossed to her, reaching down to give her a hug.

'It will be all right,' she said. 'We'll find her.'

'Do you think we should call the police?' asked Jules. Lucy looked over at her, still stroking Leilani's back as she succumbed to tears.

'I think we're close to that, yes,' said Archer.

'Shit,' said Matt. 'Hey ...' He looked around the room. 'Where's Will?'

A phone pinged and Jules retrieved hers from her pocket. She read the message quickly, then looked up. 'It's Will. He's with her and she's safe.'

The collective sigh was an entity unto itself. Leilani shuddered in Lucy's arms and blew out a long breath and Lucy loosened her grip on her and stepped back. 'So, where are they?' she asked Jules.

'Uh ... I'll go,' she replied. Jules headed to the door, a slew of questions at her back. 'No, it's cool,' she said turning back to the room. She threw Matt a look, adding an unsubtle head jerk.

'I'll come with you,' he said and they left together.

As the others fell onto chairs and sofas around the room, Lucy remained standing. *What was all that about?* she wondered. Jules had acted very strangely after reading the message.

Lucy observed the others but they didn't seem perturbed by Jules' odd departure. Archer ran his hands over his face, then ruffled his hair as he expelled a heavy sigh. Chloe nestled in next to him and stared at the fireplace. And Nate looked like he could fall asleep in that club chair. Only Leilani was still buzzing about, obviously at a loose end and possibly too wired to sit.

'Hot chocolate?' she asked, almost manically.

The others looked up from their spots around the room, an air of exhaustion hovering over them, and offered a range of affirmative responses. When Leilani looked her way, Lucy smiled at her brightly. 'I'll help,' she said. At least it would give her something to do and perhaps it would assuage some of the guilt she felt about how the evening had played out.

Chapter Twenty

JULES

M att was hot on her heels as Jules rushed towards the pool area. Will's cryptic text had said:

The pool. She's safe. Help!

'Will?' she called out.

'Back here,' replied Will.

Jules and Matt rounded the corner of the mansion, nearly running into Will who was standing with his back to the pool, his eyes wide, and his lower lip locked between his teeth.

'What's going on?' Jules asked, clocking her brother's strange demeanour.

Will jerked a thumb over his shoulder and Jules peered around him as Will raised his hand to Matt, saying, 'You probably don't want to look, man.' But Jules looked. Audrey was floating on her back, her arms moving lazily through the water and completely naked.

'Are you fricking kidding me?' Jules said, her voice low and edged with anger.

'So she *is* here,' said Matt, baffled. 'But we checked the pool—twice.'

Jules dragged her eyes from Audrey—her casual late-night swim was an infuriating sight considering the worry she'd caused over the past hour—and turned back to Matt and Will. 'She was probably playing some sort of cat and mouse game, hiding when we got anywhere near her.'

'That's messed up,' said Matt, stroking his forehead as though he couldn't quite believe it.

'Yeah, she's definitely got issues,' Jules agreed.

'Well, yeah, but what do we do now?' asked Will.

'I'll handle this. You two go back inside. And don't—'

'Oh, hey, you guys. Hey, *Will*.'

Their heads swivelled in the direction of Audrey's voice and there she was, standing poolside, still naked and gently dabbing her long hair with a towel. 'Shit,' said Will, immediately dropping his gaze. 'I'm … I'm going back inside.'

Matt, who'd also looked away, placed a hand on Will's arm. 'Just don't say anything to Lucy about this. Or the others.'

'That's what I was going to say,' added Jules.

Will looked at them like they were idiots. 'Of *course* not. Geez.'

'She's safe and that's *all*, Will,' Jules asserted. If he slipped up, if Lucy got wind of this at all …

'Yeah, I get it, thanks.' He walked off in a huff but Jules knew he wasn't mad at *her*.

'Wait, Will, where are you going?' Audrey called after him.

'Oh, for fu—' Jules dropped her chin to her chest, incredulous. *What's with this chick?* 'Cool your fricking jets, *Audrey*,' she said loudly. She ignored the indignant 'hmph!' that shot back through the late-night air.

'Want me to stay?' asked Matt.

Jules lifted her head. 'Nah, I'll handle it.'

'You sure? I'll keep my eyes closed. I promise.' Jules shook her head at him as Matt's mouth stretched to a wide grin, his dimples making an appearance. He came closer. 'Besides, she's got nothing on you.'

'Yeah, yeah. Go on, get out of here.'

'Good luck,' he said over his shoulder.

'Good luck not pushing her back in the pool, you mean,' Jules muttered to herself. She turned towards Audrey who was still very naked and seemingly in no hurry to rectify that. 'You can put your clothes back on now,' said Jules drily, 'they're gone.'

Audrey's lips flattened into a line and she swung the large towel in an arc before wrapping it around herself just above her bust and tucking in the end. She perched on the nearest lounger, watching Jules with a lifted chin as if to say, 'Go on, tell me off, see if I care.'

Jules sighed as the anger ebbed away and in stepped irritation and bafflement. How the hell was she supposed to reconcile *this* Audrey with one who'd thrown a tantrum, then burst into tears, and run off into the night? She really had no idea what to say to this girl. *Lucy would*, she thought—ironic that the true empath amongst them was the one person Audrey should steer clear of till further notice. Or, more likely, forever.

'What's going on?' Chloe appeared at Jules' side, staring past her at Audrey. 'Jules?' she asked, looking at her expectantly. 'Everything okay?' Jules was relieved to have a reinforcement but no, everything was *not* okay.

'She's pissed because it was Will who found me.'

'I'm *pissed* because you were *naked*,' said Jules through gritted teeth.

'What the hell, Audrey?' said Chloe. She marched over to the sun lounger and glared down at her. '*And* we've been looking for you for over an hour. Leilani's been in there *crying*.'

At that, Audrey's defiant expression softened—but only for a second. 'I …'

'You what?' asked Chloe. 'You're sorry?' Audrey mumbled something unintelligible, then slumped, shoulders rounded, and picked at a fingernail. Jules wasn't buying it—this girl was clearly a master of manipulation and, surely, this was just another ploy to elicit sympathy?

Chloe glanced over and Jules just shrugged. This really wasn't her area. Sure, she had younger cousins—two of whom were girls—but neither Briony nor Bridget would pull a stunt like this. Chloe would need to take the lead here, which Jules hoped she'd conveyed with the shrug.

Chloe pursed her lips and looked back at Audrey. Maybe she was deciding between tough love and the 'there, there, it'll be okay' approach. If Jules had her way, it would be the 'don't let the door hit you on the ass as you leave' tactic—even if this was essentially *her* home.

'Were you *really* naked in front of Will?' Chloe asked Audrey. Jules assumed the little head jiggle was supposed to be a yes. 'Right, sooo … you were swimming in the nuddy and he happened to find you or …?'

Chloe was obviously giving Audrey an out and Jules watched her closely for any sign that she'd attempt to lie. This time, it was Audrey who shrugged. 'You might as well come clean, Audrey, 'cause Will'll tell us anyway,' prompted Jules.

With a quiet, almost childlike voice—apt because she was *acting* like a child—Audrey muttered, 'I stripped off and dived into the pool.'

'*After* Will found you?' ask Chloe.

'Yeah, so what?' came the reply, the defiance in her eyes kicking in again. This girl was a nightmare! Maybe they could ask Archer's friend to come and pick her up—like a naughty kid who's been suspended from school.

'Why would you do that? After we included you today—after all the effort you went to, helping out with the stockings …?

Lucy's been really nice to you today and then you go and do this?' Audrey shrugged again. 'Not cool, Audrey, not cool!' *Understatement of the century*, thought Jules.

'No one says "cool" anymore,' taunted Audrey. 'I mean how old *are* you?'

Jules' eyes widened, then swung back to Chloe—Audrey clearly had no idea who she was talking to and things were about to get *very* interesting.

'Right, so this is how things are going to play out,' said Chloe, her fists landing on her hips. 'First, *never* make a play for Will again. He's with Lucy. You *know* he's with Lucy, and if I see you even glance in his general direction, I'll—'

'You'll what?' sneered Audrey. Oh, you're playing with fire here, kiddo.

Chloe bent over and got in Audrey's face. 'I'll talk to Archer and he'll call Sean and *he'll* ask you to leave.'

'Who'll ask me to leave? Archer? 'Cause he can't—'

'Not Archer. Sean!'

Audrey appeared genuinely baffled. 'But Sean's my *stepmom*.'

'Wait, what?' said Chloe. Her eyes met Jules' and it was obvious that, like her, Chloe had assumed that Sean was a man.

'So, Sean's your stepmom?' asked Jules, even though she knew they hadn't misheard her. Then to Chloe she added, 'All this time I was thinking—'

'Yeah, me too.'

'I don't think I know any women named Sean,' added Jules.

'Well, there's Sean Young, that actress from the 80s.'

'Oh, yeah, I vaguely know who that is.'

In the aftermath of this revelation, they'd missed that Audrey had left the sun lounger and was gathering up her discarded clothes from beside the pool.

'Hey, you're not going anywhere,' said Chloe, 'not till we lay down some ground rules.'

Audrey stood, her dress and sandals clasped to her chest. 'Are you going to add "young lady" and send me to my room?'

Chloe threw up her hands in exasperation. 'I give up.'

'Good. See ya.'

'Not so fast,' said Jules stepping forward and blocking Audrey's path. 'Chloe's right—you stay away from my brother.' Audrey rolled her eyes and sighed dramatically. 'Seriously. *And* not a word of this to Lucy.'

'I wouldn't—'

'I don't buy that for a second,' said Jules, pointedly. Audrey stared at her, eyes wide, but Jules found it impossible to read the muddied emotions passing over her face. She was defiance, bravado, loneliness, and bitchiness all rolled up into one neat little LA-styled package. She was a mess.

Chloe, now playing the role of conciliator, stuck an arm out between them. 'Look, Audrey, why don't you go get some sleep and in the morning, we'll start fresh—forget all this ever happened.'

A frown scuttled across her face, her shoulders dropping in resignation. 'Okay, fine, whatever.'

'Just remember what we said—not a word to Lucy,' said Jules. 'She doesn't know you owe her an apology—even though you do—and it needs to stay that way. Got it?'

'I said *okay*.' Audrey pushed past Jules and headed towards her bungalow, the blackness of the night swallowing her up.

'Please tell me I was never that much of a pain in the arse,' said Chloe.

'What, like, *ever*?' teased Jules.

'Ha-ha.'

'No, you weren't. None of us were—even at that age.'

Chloe giggled. 'You sound like you're about to say, "Kids these days …"'

'Well, if the shoe fits! Seriously, though, if she so much as *thinks* about what she did when Lucy's around …'

'God, Jules, Lucy would be devasted.'

'I know. Hopefully my brother has enough sense to let it lie.'

'You mean, enough sense to *lie*.'

'Yeah, that too, I guess. Come on, we should get back.'

'So, what's *our* lie?' asked Chloe, hooking her arm through Jules'.

'How about "Audrey is my new favourite person"?'

'She's not that bad.'

'She's my least favourite person here.'

'Fair,' conceded Chloe.

'But you're still one of my dead-set faves, Chlo.'

'Aww, listen to you speaking Aussie! So proud,' she said, placing a hand over her heart.

'Yeah, yeah.'

Chapter Twenty-One

CHLOE

Chloe had accidentally disturbed a beehive while walking in the woods and was about to be set upon by a swarm of angry bees. That is, until the dream dissolved and reality took hold. She reached across the expanse of the enormous bed, feeling for Archer, and her eyes blinked open when she came up empty.

The intermittent buzzing that had permeated her dream was still at it and she spied the culprit on Archer's bedside table—his phone. 'Archer?' she called. Maybe he was in the bathroom. As she waited for a response, she looked to her own bedside table to check the time on her phone. 7:12am. He was probably in the gym. Old habits die hard, even when you're on holiday in Hawaii and even if it's Christmas Eve.

Christmas Eve! Chloe loved this day almost as much as Christmas itself. It was a day filled, not only with its own traditions, but with anticipation of what was to come, a feeling that had carried over from childhood—'Santa's coming!' morphing into something more adult, but no less potent.

Archer's phone finally stilled and Chloe let her eyelids flutter shut. Maybe just an hour more of sleep. The buzzing began again.

'Argh!' She flipped onto her stomach and commando crawled the width of the bed, snatching up his phone with annoyance. George, Archer's Publicity Manager, grinned at her from the screen. He was under strict instructions not to call unless it was an emergency. *Hmm. I wonder what constitutes a publicity emergency*, she thought. There weren't any wardrobe malfunctions in their recent history, so definitely not that. She accepted the call. 'Hello, George, what's up?'

'Chloe! Thank god I've got through. I was beginning to worry that you didn't have mobile coverage there.'

'Uh, no, we have coverage.' A bazillionaire like Sean had probably paid to have a tower erected right across the road. *Sean.* Chloe's mental picture of a middle-aged man had been obliterated by Audrey's big reveal last night.

'Oh, right, excellent. So, is Archer there?'

In a moment of perfect timing, in walked Archer, the sheen of sweat making his workout clothes cling in ways that made him even sexier than usual. 'Uh, yep, hang on, he just got back.' Archer crossed the room, looking at her quizzically, before leaning down for a quick kiss.

'Who's that?' he mouthed. 'George,' she mouthed back, handing him the phone. His face contorted in annoyance before he took the phone and lifted it to his ear. 'Hello, George,' he said with a sigh. As George's garbled voice spoke a mile a minute—Chloe could not make out even a single word—Archer's annoyance transformed into concern with just a tad of fury.

'I see,' he said finally. 'Any chance we can reach out to Harriet for assistance?' *Uh-oh.* Chloe only knew one Harriet. She was Madison Strumpet's agent (and full-time wrangler). Any time Madison got up to no good and it impacted Archer (or, more often, Chloe), Harriet had been on damage control. The publicity emergency was without a doubt Madison-related—*again*.

Chloe scooched up the bed and burrowed in amongst the

pillows as Archer sat heavily on the bed, coursing through a series of utterances—mostly 'mmm-hmm', 'oh dear', and 'ugh'. He ran a hand through his slightly damp hair and ended the call with, 'All right, George. Please keep us up to date.' He gently placed the phone on the bedside table and turned towards Chloe.

'How bad is it?' she asked with a hefty sense of trepidation. The very first time Chloe had been in Madison's sights, she'd been slathered all over the internet labelled as a 'skank'. There had been a few comparatively minor skirmishes in the past year, but based on Archer's reaction, Chloe girded herself for something not-so-minor.

'As yet, it's not terrible.'

'Oh, well, that puts me right at ease. Should we have pancakes for breakfast or eggs on toast?'

He smiled wearily. 'Madison is on Kauai,' he said simply.

'What? Why? And how did she ev—' He reached for her hand, calming and silencing her at once.

'Somehow, she must have got wind that we were here. Apparently, she was supposed to spend Christmas with her family in Indiana but she changed her plans at the last minute. She's staying at a wellness retreat on the other side of Lihue.'

'Okay, well, that doesn't mean she's going to come here. Maybe her being on the island has nothing to do with us. People travel to Hawaii all the time. Maybe she decided to fly here on a whim.' He tilted his head, donning a knowing smile. 'Well, shit.' When it came to Madison, Chloe had done her best to keep her head held high and ignore the slanderous things that she'd said about her. But there was a big difference between accepting that she was going to be tabloid fodder from time to time and worrying that Madison's tactics to get Archer back had escalated to the point that she might now be a physical threat.

'George has been trying to get on to Harriet so she can talk some sense into her, but Harriet is in Lapland for the holidays and so far, she's unreachable.'

'Wonderful.'

'Darling, we're safe here. This property is very secure and—'

'Sure, but we can't stay locked in here the whole time. And even if she doesn't show up, what if she's got someone watching us … What if I finally decide to let Matt teach me how to surf and we pile the surfboards into the Jeep and find this secluded beach where the surf is perfect and she's got someone following us and they—'

'Darling, *please*,' he interrupted. 'Like you said, it may be innocuous. Perhaps she'll see out her stay entirely at the retreat.'

'Or she may sneak in here and try to murder us in our beds.'

His lips flattened into a line. 'You, my darling, are rarely one to catastrophise.'

'No, I know. For today's performance, the part of Chloe will be played by Lucy.'

He chortled softly. 'Please, *please* don't let this ruin our Christmas.'

'I'll try.'

He landed a quick kiss. 'It may end up being a tempest in a teacup. Right, I'm taking a shower and eggs on toast, I think,' he said with a wink. He headed into the en suite, leaving her staring at its closed door.

The thing was, Chloe *wanted* to be the cool girlfriend—and not 'cool' as in 'Insta Influencer' cool—but chilled, calm, mature, adult. Her boyfriend was (THE) Archer Tate and at that moment—as with many others over the past year—she felt the entire weight of that name. (THE) Archer Tate was considered (by many) to be a public commodity—he belonged to the movie industry, the production companies, his fans, the media … He was a brand—just like Chanel or Kleenex or QANTAS.

He was Madison Strumpet's ex-boyfriend.

But he was also her love. Archer was a man, a *human being*.

Yes, he was bright, talented, resourceful, and funny. He was a genuinely beautiful person—inside more than out—but he also suffered from bouts of insecurity (like most people) and had the occasional super-moody, everybody-stand-clear-of-me days (like all people). He got the occasional hangover, burped and farted (though always discreetly and—if awake—followed by an apology), and sometimes got spinach or broccoli caught between those perfect teeth of his. He was a whole person—the good, the bad, and the not-so-ugly. And sometimes—this being one of them—Chloe just wanted the rest of the world to go away and leave them be. Madison included.

Chloe reached for her phone and tapped out a quick message to the girls on their WhatsApp group.

Madison on Kauai. ARGH! Meet me downstairs in five.

Then she slipped out of bed, threw a sweatshirt on over her summer PJs, and called out, 'Just heading downstairs,' before leaving the room.

'No fricking way,' said Jules.

'Way. *All* the ways, Jules,' said Chloe.

'Well, that's a bit rubbish,' said Lucy as she flicked on the kettle. 'Tea?' she asked over her shoulder. Chloe was momentarily distracted—not by the offer of tea, to which she replied, 'Yes, please,' on autopilot, but by Lucy's response to her news. Lucy was the most empathetic of the May Ladies—*and* the one who was prone to anxiety—so 'a bit rubbish' was not only an understatement, it was … well, a bit rubbish! Maybe Lucy was preoccupied with her own stuff—the concerns about her relationship and the more recent spanner in the works—(frigging) Audrey.

'Yeah, exactly, Luce—it is rubbish,' replied Chloe. 'I mean, how am I supposed to *relax* knowing that Madison Strumpet could be out there hiding in the bushes as we speak?'

'Do you really think she'd go that far?' asked Jules, measuring out coffee beans into the grinder. The (noisy) twenty seconds the machine took to grind the beans was enough for Chloe to ask herself that question—for real.

Would Archer's ex *really* do anything so extreme as to attempt to get inside the grounds? And even if she did manage to scale the high stone walls or the front gate without impaling herself on one of those metal spikes, then what? What could—or *would*—she actually do? Until then, her 'attacks' had been in the media—a slew of self-victimising 'look what she did to me, that home-wrecking skank' rants on Twitter and some 'interviews' in third-rate tabloid magazines. She wasn't *dangerous*.

Or was she?

'Chlo?' Jules had finished grinding her coffee and looked across the counter at her, and Lucy paused the business of making a pot of tea to regard her curiously.

'I don't know,' she said. 'I just want her to stop. Why won't she stop? It's been over a year!'

Lucy came around to her side and wrapped her up in a hug, resting her chin on Chloe's head. *This* was the Lucy she'd needed when she'd sent out the call. Lucy didn't even need to say anything—her support was salve enough. 'Thanks, Luce.'

'Of, course, lovely,' she said, going back to making tea.

'So, what's our game plan?' asked Jules, filling a cafetière with coffee grounds and hot water. 'Are we just on "Madison Watch" or you want to do something more proactive?' And *this* was one of the things that Chloe loved most about Jules—fierce loyalty, especially the variety that came with a game plan.

'I love you girls,' said Chloe. 'Sorry, that kinda came from nowhere.'

'Oh, lovely, you never need to apologise for that. We love you too.'

'Yeah, totally.' Jules shot her a smile.

Lucy poured tea through a strainer into two mugs, adding a generous slug of milk to Chloe's (just how she liked it) and a more modest measure to her own, and Jules pressed the cafetière's plunger, then poured coffee into a mug and topped it up with milk.

'Not exactly a flat white, hey, Jules?'

'Ha! Don't get me started. Moving to Melbourne's almost ruined me for normal coffee.'

'Almost?'

Jules held up her mug. 'A girl's gotta get her caffeine on somehow. *And* you woke me up.'

'Oops, sorry. It was an emergency.'

'Yeah, I got that part. And stop apologising. You're starting to sound like Lucy,' Jules teased.

'I'm ignoring that,' said Lucy. 'Shall we take these out to the terrace?' Lucy didn't wait for a response. She just picked up her tea and exited the kitchen by the external door.

Jules and Chloe exchanged a look. 'You know, sometimes Lucy surprises me,' said Jules with a smile.

'You mean, when she doesn't take any of our crap or when she "suggests" we do something and just expects us to follow her?'

'Ha! Yeah, both.'

'I can hear you,' Lucy called from the terrace. 'And hurry up! My tea's getting cold.'

'Uh-oh,' whispered Chloe, 'we're in trouble.' She jerked her head towards the door and retrieved her mug from the counter. 'Coming, Luce,' she said, Jules sniggering behind her.

Chapter Twenty-Two

LUCY

Helping Chloe with (yet another) Madison crisis was an excellent distraction from Lucy's own woes.

She'd had a fitful night's sleep, fraught with dreams in which she was a giant monster terrorising a small town. She didn't need a psychologist's help to work that one out. She'd woken before sunrise, her eyes gritty from lack of sleep, and had snuggled up to Will's broad back, hoping that the feel of him would set her at ease. Even when they rolled over, making her the little spoon, and Will had slung a strong arm around her waist in his sleep, she still hadn't felt any relief from the crippling remorse.

It *was* her fault that Audrey had run off and hidden last night. Thank god she'd shown up unharmed, but if anything had happened, anything serious … Lucy shivered despite the sunny morning and warmish air.

'You right there, Luce?' asked Chloe.

'Um, yes, just a goose walking over my grave.'

'And you say Aussie expressions are weird,' said Chloe with a laugh—now seeming more at ease than she had just minutes ago.

'Aussie expressions *are* weird,' Jules retorted. 'I could live there the rest of my life and still hear a new one every week.'

'Hilarious,' replied Chloe drily.

'Last week it was "he's a legend in his own lunchbox".'

'Oh, that's a good one.'

'Sure,' said Jules, pretending to agree. Lucy could divine its meaning from context but she agreed with Jules—it was an odd expression.

Jules took a sip from her coffee and tipped her face to the sun, her eyes closed and smiling serenely. That reminded Lucy—she hadn't put on any sunscreen yet and she shifted her chair so she was facing away from the sun entirely.

'Okay, so back on my thing,' said Chloe. 'Do you think we just go on "Madison Watch" like you said, Jules? I don't want you to feel like you can't leave the property or anything.'

'Well, good, because Matt and I are going hiking today.'

'Oh, that sounds lovely!' said Lucy. Maybe she and Will could tag along. It wasn't exactly snowshoeing to a remote cabin in the Colorado woods for a romantic getaway, but they hadn't explored much of the island yet. Well, *she* hadn't. Will had gone surfing—twice—but hiking was something they could do together.

'Yeah, we're really looking forward to some time alone, especially Matt.' *Oh*, thought Lucy, *of course*. 'It's a lot, you know, all of us here together, and Matt's even more of an introvert than I am.'

'Oh, absolutely,' agreed Lucy, hiding her disappointment. Perhaps she and Will could find something else to do today. They were in Hawaii, after all. And even though it was Christmas Eve and felt like the least Christmassy thing to do, it would be nice to see more of the island than this property—as lovely as it was. She'd suggest it when he came down for breakfast.

'But, yeah, Chlo,' said Jules. 'We all know what she looks like, so let's just keep our eyes peeled—'

'Weird *American* expression,' interjected Chloe cheekily.

'You trying to be annoying or are you just distracting yourself?'

'I'm being *hilarious*,' Chloe quipped.

'Uh-huh. *Anyway*, let's just be extra cautious, okay?'

'Right, and what do we do if we see her?'

'Well, if she comes here, we call the police and—'

'But what if you're out on your hike and you run into her?'

'Yeah, that's probably not going to happen.'

'But let's say it does.'

'But it's very unlikely, isn't it, Chloe?' interjected Lucy. Chloe seemed to be spiralling again and Lucy wanted to interrupt before she wound herself up any further. Jules sent a grateful look down the table. 'Look, worst case scenario is that Madison sees you out and about and makes a big scene—'

'Worst case scenario is that she causes a big scene and cameras capture it,' interjected Chloe.

'Hmm, fair,' Lucy agreed.

'So, you guys head out, do some sightseeing, but I probably shouldn't go anywhere. I'll just hole up here for the rest of the holiday.'

'But that's no fun,' said Lucy. Surely, it was overkill for Chloe to lock herself away? If they did run into that horrid woman, they could always bundle Chloe into the car or shield her in some other way.

Chloe shrugged, clearly aiming for nonchalance but falling short. 'I'll just pretend we're at a resort.'

'Why are you pretending you're at a resort?' Audrey had appeared from nowhere and Lucy jumped, clutching her chest with one hand.

'Geez, *Aud*,' said Chloe. 'Maybe announce yourself next time.' Lucy agreed—these 'popping out of shadows' episodes were wearing thin—but she stayed silent, scrutinising the younger woman from her spot at the other end of the table. Audrey *seemed* all right but she didn't know her well enough to be sure.

'It's Aud-*rey*,' the younger woman replied. She pulled out a chair, making herself at home, and looked at the others as though it was perfectly acceptable to interrupt their conversation. It irked Lucy that Audrey irked her. And, yes, she owed Audrey an apology, but she certainly didn't feel like giving it now after such an intrusive entrance. That irked her too.

But as Lucy sat in silence, her unease about her behaviour the night before returning, she caught Jules and Chloe exchanging a strange look. Something was going on.

'So, what are you up to today, Aud*rey*,' asked Chloe. Lucy may have been mistaken but she thought she heard a touch of acidity in Chloe's voice.

'Maybe I'll just hang out with you here, you know, by the *pool*.' Jules huffed out an annoyed sigh—something was definitely going on but Lucy felt she shouldn't ask in front of Audrey. 'And why are you pretending this is a resort? You never answered my question.'

Chloe locked eyes with Audrey. '*Because* there is someone on the island who I want to steer clear of.'

'Madison Strumpet,' Audrey said matter-of-factly. Lucy noted immediately that she had stated Madison's name, rather than posing it as a question. *Oh, god, had Audrey …?* Her eyes darted towards Chloe just in time to catch her mouth drop open.

'How did you know that?' asked Jules.

Audrey shrugged. 'Easy guess. She's Archer's ex, she hates Chloe, and I follow her on Insta. Here, look,' she said, retrieving her phone from the back pocket of her tight pink jeans shorts. She tapped on the screen a couple of times and held up a picture of Madison sitting on the beach in lotus position, her eyes closed. Lucy couldn't read the caption from where she was sitting but it was mostly hashtags. She could just imagine: #stalkingmyex #IHateChloe #TeamMadison #MadisonAndArcherForever. She swallowed a laugh, knowing it was both inappropriate *and* a nervous reaction to what was becoming a suffocatingly tense situation.

'Right,' said Jules, standing hastily. 'Just …' She shook her head quickly—either to dislodge a thought or talk herself out of saying something, Lucy wasn't quite sure. 'Just let us know if you see her, okay?'

Audrey perked up—perhaps she liked being thought of as useful. 'You got it.'

'I'm heading back in … gotta get ready for the day,' said Jules. Lucy glanced back at Chloe, whose mouth was set in a taut line. What weren't her best friends telling her? Well, whatever it was, they obviously weren't going to mention it in front of Audrey.

'I'll come with you,' Lucy said to Jules. She gulped the last of her now-tepid tea and followed her into the house.

'Thanks again for letting us come along,' said Will from the backseat.

'Oh, yes,' added Lucy, wrenching her eyes from the incredible scenery, 'thank you.'

'Yeah, no worries. Got to make the most of our time here, right?' Matt replied from the driver's seat.

'You know it, man,' Will agreed.

Lucy watched Jules for a reaction but could only see a sliver of her face, making it impossible to read her expression. Was she annoyed that Matt had invited her and Will to join them? Lucy hoped not—she also hoped she'd have time with Jules alone at some point. Her earlier attempt to get Jules' take on the Audrey situation had been thwarted. As soon as she'd crossed the threshold from the terrace into the kitchen, she'd come upon everyone else in the throes of eating breakfast—Nate, Leilani, Matt, Will, and Archer.

The smell of toast had made her stomach rumble, so she'd abandoned her quest in lieu of a plate of toast slathered in homemade pineapple preserve, a new favourite that had (forever) relegated Baxters rhubarb and ginger jam to second place. She'd have to ask Leilani for the recipe.

'Not much further …' said Matt, slowing the 4x4. Shortly after, the sat nav announced that they'd arrived and they turned down a driveway that led to an enormous car park, half-filled with cars and surrounded by thick jungle.

'Not too crowded,' said Jules. 'That's good. Apparently, some days, you're lucky to even get a parking spot.'

'It *is* Christmas Eve,' added Matt.

'Oh, yeah, good point,' Will and Jules replied in unison. Jules spun in her seat to share a smile with Will.

Lucy, who was glad they hadn't come all this way only to have to turn around again, felt the buzz of excitement building. Less than a week ago, she'd been meticulously packing for a snowy Christmas holiday and now, here she was, well out of her comfort zone (in a good way) and about to hike to a waterfall in Hawaii! What an adventure!

Matt eased the 4x4 into a spot next to a grimy forest-green hatchback, its rear bumper covered in peeling stickers, and they piled out, each stretching away the two-hour drive before shrugging into their daypacks.

Everything in Lucy's was borrowed—the swimsuit Jules had brought her from Melbourne, an Indian cotton towel Leilani had procured from her now-infamous linen store, and the water bottle she'd pilfered from the kitchen. Even the daypack and hiking boots were borrowed from the stash of equipment set aside for houseguests and, of course, the majority of her outfit came from Steph's wardrobe.

Leilani had also insisted on sending them off with enough food to cater for everyone in the car park—everything from (portable) fruit to mixed nuts to an assortment of muesli bars.

'Ready?' asked Will, grinning down at her.

'Ready!'

'This way,' said Jules, leading the way into the jungle.

'Coming in, Luce?' asked Jules. Lucy stood ankle deep in the freezing cold water, willing herself to take the plunge—*literally*. The rest of her party were already in the water—Jules treading water near the waterfall, Matt repeatedly diving under and emerging a few feet away, and Will traversing the breadth of the rockpool with strong overarm strokes. Most of the dozen or so other people there were also swimming.

'Um …' Stalling, she scanned the incredible setting—the tall narrow waterfall cascading several hundred feet into the rockpool like a bridal veil, the vibrant green foliage blanketing the rocky ground of the steep valley, boulders scattered haphazardly and smoother, smaller stones beneath her feet, and the brilliant blue of the sky above them. It had been quite the hike to get here—some parts of the trail arduous, even a little terrifying—but it was definitely worth it for the scenery alone. She didn't *need* to swim in a waterfall.

'Come on, babe—it's cold at first but you get used to it.' Will pushed his hair back from his face and grinned at her. Well, now she had to go in—she was powerless under the spell of that smile.

'Just dive in, Luce. Get it over with,' prompted Jules.

'Oh, come on, Lucy,' she muttered to herself, 'don't be such a muppet.' She strode into the water until it was over her knees then executed a shallow dive. The shock of the cold meant that she broke the surface feeling winded but Will was there in a shot, his arm wrapping around her waist, holding her as she steadied her breath.

'Can you stand up here?' he asked. She held tightly to Will, then stopped treading water and cautiously stretched her legs, reaching for the bottom of the rock pool. She was relieved when her toes made contact—just.

'Oh, yes.'

'But it's better to keep moving—it'll keep you warm. Come on.' He took off towards the waterfall, powering through the water, and Lucy followed, steadily breast-stroking along. Will slipped behind the waterfall, ducking around it from the left, and Lucy traced his path. The others were right—she *was* starting to get used to the temperature of the water.

'Hey,' he said when she'd made her way behind the watery curtain. 'Look!' He stood, half of his body popping out of the water. 'But you have to come a little closer to the rock face.' He held out his hand and Lucy swam towards him, her eyes locked onto the heavenly sight of Will's slick and muscular torso. She reached him and felt about for the rock he was standing on with her feet. It was a little slimy, but he grasped her hand and pulled her onto it, capturing her in a hug, then leaning down for a kiss.

Lucy slid her arms up his chest and hooked them over his shoulders. It was an incredible sensation, kissing his already wet lips, their slippery bodies pressed together, his hands slick against the small of her back, one of her most sensitive spots. Despite the chill of the water and the coolness of the shade behind the waterfall, Lucy felt the heat building inside her and she instantly wished that she and Will were there alone. She'd never been with someone out in *nature* but if he kept kissing her like that, if he kept stroking her skin exactly as he was, she might very well be tempted to chance it.

Will broke the kiss, panting slightly. 'Lucy ...' he said, his voice husky with desire. Lucy *loved* that tone in his voice. It typically signposted that she was about to be ravished. But she also heard hesitation *and* frustration.

'Probably best not to chance it,' she said with a cheeky smile. This was the version of herself that only Will ever saw—the supremely confident Lucy, the one who felt sexy and desired.

Will dropped his head back and groaned, voicing his frustration with an 'argh'.

'Hey, what are you two up to over there?' shouted Matt. 'You know we can see you, right? And I'm pretty sure this waterfall is rated "PG", not "R".'

A ripple of laughter—not just from Matt but from *strangers*—reached them as Will shouted back, 'Hilarious!' Ordinarily in a situation like this, Lucy would have been horribly embarrassed, but her eyes were locked onto Will and he was beaming at her with that smile again, so all else was forgotten. She reached up for another quick kiss.

'Race you back,' she said, breaking the spell. And even though there wasn't a hope in hell she'd ever beat Will in swimming—or any other sport, for that matter—it would still be fun to try. She turned and dived under the waterfall, coming out the other side and racing as fast as she could to the edge of the pool, the splash of Will's strokes behind her and closing in making her shriek with laughter. As expected, she didn't win the race, but when she waded out of the rock pool, he was waiting with her towel held wide. She stepped into his embrace and he cocooned her in both the towel and his arms. 'I love you, Lucy,' he cooed in her ear. In moments like these, it was easy to forget how it felt to sleep in an empty bed night after night during their months of separation and as Lucy snuggled into his embrace, she thought how brilliantly this day was turning out to be.

And it was Christmas Eve! This may not have been the Christmas she'd planned for, but there was something rather magical about Hawaii. And as soon as she made peace with Audrey—something she promised herself she would do that very day—then she could properly enjoy the Christmas festivities.

Chapter Twenty-Three

JULES

'Phoof, I'm beat,' said Jules, resting her head against the car seat. A long drive, four hours of hiking—two each way—and an hour at the waterfall had been incredible, but Jules was longing for a shower and maybe a power snooze.

'That was brilliant,' said Lucy from the backseat.

While Matt and Will agreed with Lucy, Jules turned to flash her a lazy grin. 'I wasn't sure you were coming in, Luce.'

'It was a long way to go just to stand on the rocks and watch,' she replied earnestly.

'Mmm, yeah.' Jules turned back around, fixing her eyes on the road to quell the surge of motion sickness. Matt was a good driver but these were winding roads and looking anywhere besides straight ahead was a no-go, she reminded herself.

'So, what's on for tonight?' she asked the others, distracting herself from the queasiness. 'Luce, what do you guys do on Christmas Eve?'

'Guys?' came the puzzled replied.

'Yeah, you, your mom, and your dad.'

'Oh, um … well, we just have dinner. Mum goes all out on

Christmas Day—full cooked breakfast, then a late Christmas lunch—so we usually have something light, then watch Christmas specials.'

'Oh, yeah,' Jules drawled. 'It's sorta weird how they do that, don't ya think?'

'How who does what?' asked Lucy, an edge in her voice.

'British TV shows.'

'You mean Christmas episodes?' asked Will. 'American shows have those, Jules.'

'Yeah, but British TV's like, "Here you go—six whole episodes *and* the season's over. Oh wait, let's add a Christmas special."'

'Not *all* British shows,' said Lucy. 'Lots of them have more than six episodes per season. And, besides, we *love* the Christmas specials. My family watches the *Vicar of Dibley* one, where Geraldine has three Christmas lunches, every year. It's brilliant, even if we have seen it a hundred times.'

Yep, Jules had definitely put Lucy on the defensive. Time to dial it back. 'You're totally right, Luce, sorry.' She chanced a glance in the backseat and Lucy was staring at her, brown eyes wide and her eyebrows raised. Jules fixed her eyes back on the road, smiling to herself. She'd been told off. By *Lucy*.

'Have *you* ever seen the *Vicar of Dibley* one?' Lucy asked.

'Uh, no, can't say that I have.'

'Right, well, that's something we could do after dinner tonight—educate Jules on the virtue of the English Christmas special!' Will chuckled behind her and Jules joined in.

———

'Hey, Matt,' Jules called out.

'Yeah?' he replied from the shower.

'Have you seen my grey hoodie? I can't remember if I packed it or not.'

Lucy had already installed herself in the living room, Christmas music blaring and the AC blasting just like it was last night. And the insipid fireplace—more for show than for warmth—was doing a crappy job of keeping up. What was the name of that goddess that Leilani had mentioned last night? Well, whatever her name was, she'd made herself at home downstairs and Jules hadn't come to Hawaii to freeze to death. If she'd wanted to be cold, she would have flown home to Colorado for the holidays. But even after going through her entire suitcase twice, she'd come up empty and was silently cursing her lackadaisical approach to packing.

'Um, can't remember. You can borrow one of mine if you like—second drawer, I think.'

'Thanks, hun!'

She opened the second drawer, noting Matt's neatly unpacked clothes—T-shirts in a perfect stack that anyone working at GAP would be proud of, three sweatshirts, also neatly folded and something that gave Jules pause—a velvet jewellery box. Was this his Christmas gift to her? But Matt knew her well enough by now to know that the closest Jules came to wearing jewellery was donning her Fitbit every morning.

She looked over her shoulder, tuning her ears to the sound of Matt lathering up all over—as he liked to do—and humming softly to himself as he rinsed off. She had at least a minute or two before he'd finish showering and a little peek would be okay, wouldn't it?

With another quick glance over her shoulder, she picked up the square velvet box. *Not a ring box, thank god,* she thought, so at least there was that. She eased open the spring-hinged lid and gasped. *Shit, shit, shit, shit, shit.* Not jewellery—worse! A key. And not just any key. Based on the keychain—made from an old wine barrel and on sale in the tasting room of Matt and Twoey's winery for $8.99—it was a key to Matt's place.

Jules snapped the box shut. 'Find it?' Matt asked from the bathroom.

Did I ever! thought Jules. 'Uh, yep, thanks!' She shoved the box back into place, grabbed a sweatshirt from the top of the pile, and slammed the drawer shut. As she raced out of the room, all she could think was that she needed to speak to Chloe—as soon as possible.

———————

'What's going on?' whispered Chloe. Jules had beckoned Chloe to join her outside on the terrace while the others were helping set the table and getting ready for Christmas Eve dinner. Leilani had been cooking all day and they were having a Hawaiian feast—ahi tuna poke, huli-huli chicken, lomi-lomi salmon, and roasted sweet potatoes. Jules' mouth was watering just from the aromas as they'd passed through the kitchen, but getting Chloe's advice was far more pressing than sneaking a pre-dinner bite—no matter how ravenous she was.

'It's about Matt.'

'Oh, everything okay?' Chloe's face clouded with concern so Jules got straight to the point.

'I think Matt's going to ask me to move in with him. For Christmas.'

'What? Sorry—' Chloe shook her head. 'He's asking you to move in with him for Christmas? But we're here for Christ—'

'No. I mean, yes, we're obviously here for Christmas. I meant as my gift. I found a key to his place in a gift box.'

'Ohhh, *right*. Way to ruin the surprise, Jules,' Chloe teased with a smile. 'Wait.' The smile fell away. 'Is that a problem? Why's that a problem?' she added, not waiting for Jules to respond.

'It's just … I've never lived with anyone before.'

'You live with Ash.'

'Yeah, and even that's a challenge sometimes. I mean, I had my own room growing up, a single dorm room in college, and then I moved into my own apartment. This is the first time in my life I've had to …'

'Share?'

'Sure, for want of a better word. Actually, I've been thinking of getting my own place in the city—not that Ash hasn't been amazing. I mean, I adore her. It's just …'

'You don't like sharing,' said Chloe.

'God, that makes me sound like a spoiled brat.' Jules folded herself into one of the Adirondack chairs that looked out at the view, leaning against its high back. Any other time, she would have relished the array of colours streaking the dusk sky but her growing feeling of ill-ease took precedence.

'You're not a brat,' said Chloe, taking the chair next to her.

'Then what's wrong with me?'

'You're not broken, Jules. You don't need to be fixed.'

'Yeah, right. I love Matt, Chlo.'

'I know you do.'

'And we already see each other quite a bit—most weekends I'm either down at the vineyard or he's up in the city. Sometimes we'll get together mid-week too. It's perfect as it is.'

'Maybe not for Matt, though.' Chloe's tone was gentle—kind even—but the words were like a punch to the gut.

'That's what I'm afraid of. I've made a lot of changes over the past year—and I needed to; I was totally in a rut—but next year … I thought I'd get my own place, keep dating Matt … and find my simpatico, you know?'

'I don't *know* know, 'cause—'

'Because your life is like a travelling circus.'

Chloe laughed. 'Not the most flattering portrayal, Jules, but okay. Anyway, I just meant that I have different priorities from you. Wherever Archer is, that's home for me.'

'You must be a little sick of LA,' said Jules with a wry smile.

'Oh, god, you have no idea. When you're in it, it's easy to forget how … I don't know, *weird* it all is, I guess. But even being away for a few days is enough to get perspective. I definitely need to spend some time in Australia in the New Year—reset, you know.'

'A reality check.'

'Yeah, that too. But back to you and Matt. You just need to be honest with him, Jules.'

'But it's in a fricking velvet box, Chlo! It's obviously a big deal to him. What do I say? "Great keychain, hun, pass the eggnog"?'

'Blech, I hate eggnog. No idea how you Americans drink that crap.'

Jules shook her head, unable not to smile. 'You're not helping.'

'Look, Matt is one of my closest friends, but you're my bestie—'

'Lucy too.'

'Yes, of course, Lucy too.'

'See? I'm not totally useless at sharing,' said Jules.

It was Chloe's turn to shake her head. 'Can I finish?'

'Please. But be quick—my stomach is rumbling like a mofo.'

'Yeah, I noticed that. I'm just too polite to mention it.'

'Ha-ha.'

'*Anyway*, I love you both. I love you *together*. So you've got to be honest with him, Jules.'

'Okay.'

'And don't screw it up.'

'What does *that* mean? That's terrible advice.'

Chloe shrugged. 'Matt may be one of my closest friends, but you probably know him better than I do, Jules.'

'Mmm, maybe.'

'What does your gut say? Besides that it's dinnertime?'

'My gut is nervous and confused and worried.'

'Worried that you'll lose him?' Chloe's green eyes locked onto hers and all Jules could do was nod. 'Then that might be your answer. If your fear of losing him is greater than your fear of moving in with him ...'

'There you are, you two!'

'Hey, Matt,' said Chloe, spinning around at the sound of his voice. *Oh, crap*, Jules thought. Had Matt heard any of their conversation?

'Leilani sent me out to find you. Dinner's ready.'

Jules leapt out of her seat. 'Thanks, hun. I'm *starving*.' He smiled, then headed back inside. 'Oh!' she said to Chloe. 'I forgot to ask—any sign of Madison today? She wasn't lurking in the bushes or anything, was she?'

'No, nothing like that—I was probably just being dramatic.'

'What? You?'

'Hilarious. Anyway, we just took it easy, had a quiet day.'

'Sounds good.'

'Yeah.' Chloe smiled but Jules could tell it was still on her mind—or something else was.

'So, should we ...?' asked Jules, pointing inside. Chloe went on ahead, Jules following, and her thoughts returning to her thing. God, she *really* hoped Matt had been out of earshot when Chloe said that stuff about her fear.

And which *was* more terrifying? Living with Matt, or losing him?

Chapter Twenty-Four

CHLOE

Chloe could quite happily spend the rest of her life eating Hawaiian food, she decided as she helped herself to more huli-huli chicken—its sweetness, tang, smokiness, and spiciness converging to make the perfect dish. And what a Christmas Eve feast! Leilani seemed genuinely pleased with the moans of pleasure doing the rounds of the dining table like a culinary Mexican wave.

'Leilani,' said Archer, 'you simply must share your recipes with me. This is the best poke I've ever had.'

Leilani's face flushed as she donned a shy smile and waved off the compliment. 'Oh, it's just the mahi mahi—we have the best tuna in the world. Hard to go wrong there.'

'You're being modest and I wasn't exaggerating.'

'It's really good, Leilani,' said Jules and there was general agreement from the others, including Chloe, whose mouth was full. Even Audrey was eating with gusto, seemingly unaffected by the drama (or was that trauma?) of last night. Chloe was just about to ask Will to pass the salmon when a voice rang out around the room.

'Well, isn't this terrific sight?'

All heads swivelled in the direction of the voice and there stood a tall fifty-something woman with cropped silver hair and a winsome smile. 'Sean!' Audrey leapt out of her seat and flung herself at the new arrival who hugged her tightly, saying, 'Hey, peanut.' Right, so this was the infamous Sean. What a nice surprise, especially for Audrey, whose façade of bravado and nonchalance had fallen away the second she'd seen her stepmother in the doorway.

Archer laid his napkin on the table and stood, smiling broadly, but what caught Chloe's eye was Leilani's reaction. She also stood, only very slowly and her face was a picture of … Was it shame? That couldn't be right. Leilani swallowed hard, her eyes boring into the table, and Chloe was torn between watching her and observing Sean reunite with her stepdaughter, then Archer.

'You made it,' said Archer, wrapping Sean up in an affectionate hug. So, he'd known Sean was coming. Why hadn't he mentioned it to her, Chloe wondered, both curious and slightly miffed.

'Honestly, it was a no-brainer.' She stepped back and held out her hands. 'Work through Christmas—alone—or take a five-hour flight and spend it with you all. Hi, everyone,' she said, smiling at them in a way that was both charming and disarming. 'Sorry to burst in on your dinner like this.'

'No, thank *you* for letting us stay here!' said Matt, rising and holding out his hand. 'Hi, I'm Matt.'

'Hi, Matt, great to meet you,' she replied, taking his hand. Matt flashed her one of his broad double-dimpled grins and Sean reciprocated.

'And, of course, the rest of the introductions,' said Archer. While Audrey clasped Sean's hand as though she was afraid Sean would disappear if she didn't, Archer went around the table and introduced everyone in turn. As Chloe had come to learn early in their relationship, Archer had a special way of bringing people together, evidenced by his thoughtful explanations of who they all were to each other. 'This is Lucy and Jules, Chloe's oldest and dearest friends—they met here in Hawaii aged eleven, if you can believe that. And they've been friends all these years.'

Lucy waved from her place at the table and Jules replied, 'Hi, Sean. Wow, it's … it's amazing to meet you,' like she was fangirling. *Was* she fangirling? As far as Chloe knew, Sean was a Hollywood executive—why would that mean anything to Jules?

'Great to meet you too.'

'And this is Will, Jules' brother and Lucy's boyfriend—he's brilliant at just about any sport you can imagine—' Will took the compliment with a modest shrug. 'And you've met Matt, who's not only an old friend of Chloe's *and* Jules' boyfriend, he makes the most incredible Pinot Noir.'

'Oh, I love me a good Pinot,' said Sean. 'And I'm totally spoiled living so close to Napa.'

'Well, I brought a case with me …' said Matt.

Sean raised her hand. 'I'm in.'

'And this is Nate, Jules and Will's dad—'

Sean interjected. 'Glad to see I'm not the only grown-up here.'

Nate laughed good-naturedly. 'Me too. Now I have an excuse to skip the surfing lessons with my son. Secret grown-ups' business,' he said, tapping the side of his nose.

'Oh, I surf,' quipped Sean.

Nate guffawed. 'Of course you do. More fool me.'

Chloe looked back and forth between them, *sure* she was witnessing flirtatious banter. She glanced at Jules who looked back at her, eyes wide. Chloe knew then that she hadn't imagined the frisson between Sean and Nate—*and* that Jules seemed quite tickled by it.

'You standing up yet?' asked Sean.

'Not even close,' replied Nate, shaking his head.

'I can get you there—guaranteed,' Sean said with a smirk.

Jules coughed out a laugh, then tried to disguise it as an actual cough, and Chloe's eyebrows shot up involuntarily. This was some expert-level, almost lascivious, flirting. *Impressive*. Now she *definitely* had to debrief with Jules later. Archer continued. 'And, of course, the lovely Leilani has been looking after us brilliantly.'

The Jules–Sean–Nate thing was immediately forgotten as Chloe looked over at Leilani; she appeared to want to disappear into the floor. 'Leilani, one of your masterful spreads, I can see,' said Sean.

Leilani's eyes shot up for a sec, a wan smile appearing on her face. 'Uh, yes, Ms Sean. I will just go and get you a place setting.' She scurried away, practically sprinting towards the kitchen. *Weird*, thought Chloe.

'And this, Sean, is my darling Chloe,' he said, gesturing towards her.

Chloe got up, walked over, and stuck out her hand. 'Hi, Sean, so nice to meet you.'

'Oh, no, sweetheart, *you* get a hug.' Sean reached down to envelop her in a spice-fragranced hug and Chloe knew instantly why Audrey had clung to her since her arrival *and* why she was giving Chloe the stink-eye behind Sean's back. There was something magical about Sean's hug, even her presence. 'I've heard so much about you,' Sean whispered. Chloe tightened her grip in reply, as she'd heard almost nothing about Sean. 'And you make him really happy.' Okay, that made her feel a little uncomfortable. Clearly Archer and Sean were closer than Chloe had realised—*and* he'd known she was coming.

Chloe released Sean and stepped back, smiling brightly. 'Thanks,' she said for want of something better. 'I'm just gonna help Leilani in the kitchen.'

'Oh, sure,' Sean replied. Nate had retrieved one of the extra dining chairs from against the wall and the others were making room for Sean's place at the table when Chloe threw a 'come with me immediately' look at Jules.

'Do you know who that is?' whispered Jules as they headed down the hallway to the kitchen.

'The woman flirting with your dad? *Yeah*, it's Sean—*the* Sean—the one who owns the house.'

Jules placed a hand on her forearm and came to a halt. 'That's Sean Alessi,' said Jules. Chloe, having no idea why that name should mean anything to her, looked at Jules blankly. 'The tech billionaire?'

'Oh, wow.'

'You have no idea who that is, do you?'

'Nope.'

Jules sighed impatiently and moved closer. '*She* is one half of the husband–wife team that founded Infinity.'

'You mean like the search engine?'

'Not *like* the search engine—the *actual* search engine.'

'Holy shit.'

Jules grinned. 'Yeah! And she was the brains—it's her site score algorithm that started it all.'

'Wow, that's really impressive.'

'Uh, yeah, Chlo. She's basically my hero—she's the reason I wanted to become a programmer.'

'Oh! So *that's* why you started acting weird in there.'

'I wasn't weird. Was I? Shit, was I weird in front of Sean Alessi?'

Jules' eyes pleaded with her and Chloe did the only thing she could to set Jules' mind at ease: lie. 'She wouldn't have noticed. It's just 'cause I know you so well. You were fine—*normal* even.'

'You're lying.'

'Just a little,' replied Chloe. 'Maybe it'll be less weird between you when she marries your dad.'

'Whatever.' Jules added an eyeroll.

'Oh, and Audrey will be your stepsister.'

'Ugh.'

Chloe barked out a laugh. 'Come on, let's go see what's up with Leilani.'

'What do you mean?' Jules asked.

'You were probably too starstruck to notice but Sean's arrival really freaked Leilani out.'

'Oh, that's ...'

'Not good. Now, come on,' she said, waving for Jules to follow her. They rounded the corner and bumped right into Leilani.

'Oh, sorry Miss Chloe.'

'Leilani, enough with the "Miss Chloe" stuff. It's just Chloe, okay?'

'Okay.'

Leilani made to move past them but Chloe held out her hand and Leilani stayed put. 'Are you okay?' she asked the older woman. 'You seem a little ...'

'Freaked out, according to Chloe,' finished Jules. Chloe shot her a 'Geez, Jules' look but Jules just shrugged, unapologetic about her propensity to blurt out the truth. Though, Chloe was one to talk.

Chloe turned back to Leilani, whose eyes were now filled with such a complex array of emotions, Chloe was a little flummoxed. 'What is it?' Leilani shook her head. 'You can tell us.'

'It's just ... I wasn't expecting Ms Sean and ...' Her mouth drooped into a frown.

'And?' prodded Chloe. They'd only been there a few days but she'd never seen Leilani like this—this larger-than-life woman, unsettled and worried. It was as though her personality had shrunk in Sean's presence.

'I was at the table—with *guests*.'

'*Ooh, right*,' drawled Chloe.

'And that's unusual?' asked Jules. Leilani nodded vigorously.

'But you're like family, aren't you? That's what Audrey said,' prompted Chloe.

'To her, yes, I am Mama Leilani, but it's not my place to join the guests. I know better.'

'But you're our mama too, now, Leilani. And I asked you to join us,' said Chloe. 'It just wouldn't feel right with you not at the table, especially when you've prepared most of the meals.' There was a glimmer of acknowledgement in the slight shrug of the woman's shoulder so Chloe pressed on. 'I can talk to her if you want—tell her it's my doing.'

'That's if she's even worried about it,' interjected Jules. 'She may not care as much as you think.'

Leilani's features morphed as she chewed over the offer, her face finally settling into a weak smile. 'If you wouldn't mind, yes, I think that would be good. I don't want her thinking I'm taking advantage.'

Chloe reached out, hugging Leilani quickly, then letting go. 'Of course. I'll seek her out after dinner, okay?'

Leilani nodded and held out the items for Sean's place-setting. 'Would you mind?'

'You're not going to come back in?' asked Jules.

'No, I shouldn't.'

Jules and Chloe glanced at each other—it was clear they'd have to honour Leilani's wishes. 'Sure,' said Chloe, taking the tray that held a plate, a napkin, a wine glass, and cutlery. She may not like this situation—and she hoped she'd *never* make someone in her employ feel like Leilani obviously did—but this was Sean's home and she'd have to find a way to broach the topic carefully. *And* there was the matter of Archer keeping Sean's arrival from her. Or maybe he just forgot.

Hmm, it was going to be an interesting Christmas Eve, that was for sure.

Chapter Twenty-Five

LUCY

Sean's arrival had been quite the disruption, Lucy thought as she pushed food around her plate. She'd suddenly lost her appetite, too concerned about Leilani, who had dashed out of the room, obviously mortified to have been caught at the dinner table with *guests*. If Chloe and Jules hadn't gone after her, Lucy would have.

And Jules! She'd been so starstruck by Sean—utterly tongue-tied. Lucy had never seen her like that. Though, she could understand Jules' reaction. As soon as she'd clapped eyes on her, Lucy had known immediately who Sean was—one didn't spend a decent portion of their working life in San Francisco and *not* know about Sean Alessi. But it hadn't occurred to Lucy till then that the Sean who'd so generously allowed them to stay in their home was *the* Sean Alessi. And for some reason she'd thought that 'Mystery Sean' was a man.

She watched the others curiously as Sean settled in at the table next to Nate. Audrey's countenance had completely transformed in her presence, so that was something to be thankful for. Archer and Sean clearly had a long history of friendship together, falling right into a conversational sympatico as they caught up. Though not as starstruck as Jules, Will's eyes were riveted on Sean, and Nate's eyes creased at the corners in amusement as they conversed.

Lucy tried to catch Matt's eye across the table but he, too, seemed to be hanging on Sean's every word. 'Here you go,' announced Chloe coming back into the dining room bearing a tray. Jules followed closely, taking her place at the table. Leilani was nowhere to be seen, but Lucy wasn't surprised. She just hoped that Leilani was all right—surely Jules and Chloe had been able to set her at ease.

'Oh, thank you. What a sweetheart you are.' Sean grabbed the items from the tray and arranged her place setting herself, something that Lucy noted with interest. And as Chloe sat down, Sean craned her neck to see down the hallway. 'Where's Leilani?' she asked, turning back around.

Jules and Chloe shared an 'uh-oh' look. 'Um ...' uttered Jules.

'I'm not sure she's coming back to the table,' Chloe replied.

'Oh, that's too bad. Is she not feeling well?' asked Sean.

There was a tense silence during which several glances were exchanged, then Lucy witnessed the realisation on Sean's open book of a face. 'Oh, I think I understand.' Sean stood. 'Matt, I'd love to try your Pinot, if you don't mind pouring me a glass. I'll be right back—I'm just going to ...' she trailed off but Lucy understood immediately. Sean was going to coax Leilani back to the table!

Lucy stood and reached for her plate. 'I'd be happy to make you a plate, Sean,' she offered.

'Oh, that would be terrific,' she said, handing it over. 'I barely ate on the flight, knowing that I had Leilani's cooking to look forward to.' She scanned the length of the table, eyeing the various serving platters and bowls. 'Just some of everything,' she said, waving a hand. 'Now, please excuse me, everyone.'

As Lucy made her way down the table, serving up small portions of each dish, conversation started up again. And by the time she set a loaded plate at Sean's place, then made her way back to her own, Leilani had re-joined them, sliding quietly into her chair and resuming her meal. Sean had only taken one bite when she called out down the table. 'Leilani, this salmon is extraordinary.' She shook her head, seemingly lost for words, and Leilani smiled shyly.

'Wait till you try it with the Pinot,' said Nate, casting her a rather intriguing sideways look. Wait a minute. Was Will's dad *flirting*? Lucy wondered. Sean raised her eyebrows, lifted her glass to her lips, sipped, swallowed, then *licked her lips*—all while locking eyes with Nate.

Lucy had watched enough romcoms to know that not only was *Nate* flirting but Sean was reciprocating. She clamped a hand over her mouth to stifle a gleeful giggle. It wasn't so much that she found the situation amusing, more that she *adored* Will's dad and wouldn't it be *wonderful* if he and Sean …

Her thought was interrupted by a loud clap. 'I know!' said Audrey from the other end of the table, practically bouncing in her seat with excitement. 'Why don't we play games after dinner?' She looked around the table hopefully. 'I've already planned everything. You know, from last night, and now that you're here, Sean, I can run it and Leilani can keep score and you and Nate can be a team!'

Sean shrugged, looking at the others. 'Sounds fun. What does everyone else think?'

A few things occurred to Lucy in quick succession. Audrey *must* have picked up on whatever was transpiring between Nate and Sean and was playing matchmaker but wouldn't playing parlour games just remind them all of the (terrible) night before? Lucy would also have to give up that Christmas special she'd promised herself (and Jules). But lastly, with Audrey assuming the role of gamemaster, surely Lucy would be paired with Will this time? That would be worth skipping *The Vicar of Dibley* for.

She caught Will's eye across the table. He pointed a finger at her, then back at himself, and mouthed, 'We've got this.' Lucy grinned, her unease dissipating. Perhaps a series of parlour games was the perfect way to get their Christmas back on track.

'Fair warning,' said Jules, 'Matt is ridiculously good at this game. We play it all the time back home and he almost always wins.'

'It's not almost always,' said Matt modestly.

'Hun, you're a "Celebrity Heads" savant.' Matt shook his head vigorously and laughed. 'Though half the time I have no idea who the so-called celebrities even are,' added Jules.

'Everyone knows who Donald Bradman is.' Matt looked to the others for support but was met with head shakes and shrugs. Lucy thought the named sounded vaguely familiar but couldn't place it. 'The Mighty Don?' Matt incredulously asked the blank faces around him. 'Come on, seriously? How 'bout the best batsman the world's ever seen?'

'Told ya, hun,' taunted Jules.

'Okay!' interjected Audrey, '*Anyway*, let's start.' She circled the room affixing stickers to their heads. 'There are ten people, so the first person to guess which celebrity they are gets ten points, the next person, nine points, and so on. The last person only gets one point.'

Audrey pressed a sticker onto Archer's forehead and when she moved aside and Lucy could read the name, she coughed out a laugh. *How clever of you, Audrey*, she thought. Archer sent her a scrunched-nose smile across the room, giving her a nostalgic glimpse of the boy she'd once had an enormous crush on. Sometimes it struck her that Alan Tate, the boy she'd grown up with, was now Archer Tate, famous film star. Most of the time, however, he was just Archer, her best friend's boyfriend—and soon-to-be fiancé!

Audrey worked her way around to Lucy and peeled the sticker off the sheet, catching Lucy's eye as she pressed it onto her forehead. Her neutral expression was difficult to read but this was as close as they'd been since Lucy had erupted at her the night before, so Lucy smiled up at her and said, 'Thank you, Audrey.'

Audrey made an odd face and moved on to Matt. But what did Lucy expect? She hadn't yet apologised to Audrey; it had been a rather full day and there hadn't been an appropriate time. At least, that's what she'd told herself to assuage the niggling guilt she felt.

'Okay,' Audrey said, addressing the group. 'We'll start with you, Archer. You get one "yes or no" question, then we move on to you, Chloe. And then we just keep going around till the second-last person guesses correctly.'

Matt raised his hand. 'What if the answer's both yes and no?'

'Like, what do you mean?'

'Okay, so let's say I think I'm Casper the Ghost and I ask, "Am I dead?" Well, technically he's dead 'cause he's a ghost, but he's also alive, because he's a character in the cartoon.'

There were a few murmurs of agreement and Lucy could tell that Audrey was getting frustrated. 'You're not Casper. No one is. Let's just start and if we have to make any rulings, Leilani and I will think about it then, okay?'

'Sounds good!' said Sean, clapping her hands together. Lucy was grateful for the intervention, which appeared to appease Audrey.

'Right,' said Archer, 'Am I female?' to which everybody in the room replied, 'No!'

Jules had been right about Matt. He'd guessed 'Justin Bieber' in the fourth round of questions, winning ten points for him and Jules. The rounds continued and Lucy surprised herself by claiming seven points for her and Will with 'Megan Markle'. They were now down to Sean, who turned out to be *terrible* at guessing and was so far from 'Elon Musk' it wasn't funny, and poor Archer!

'Am I famous for playing a sport?' he asked.

'No!' called out (most of) the others before Matt interjected with, 'Hang about, this is one of the grey areas I was talking about. It's kind of "yes".' He must have been referring to Archer's baseball film where he played a major league pitcher.

'It's not a yes,' drawled Audrey. 'That's *not* what he's famous for!'

'Okay, fine,' conceded Matt.

Archer had watched this exchange intently and right as Sean began her question with, 'Am I—' Archer bellowed, 'Oh! Wait a minute!' All eyes landed on him, including Sean's. 'Am I me? I'm me, aren't I?' He caught Lucy's eye and she nodded at him with a wide but close-lipped smile. He peeled the sticker from his forehead to confirm, then threw his head back and laughed loudly. 'Oh, that's brilliant. Well done, Audrey.'

Audrey groaned as though she'd been defeated but the others applauded Archer's two points, peals of laughter filling the room and Chloe patting Archer on the leg. 'Good job, babe. You got us two points!'

Will looked over at Lucy to share the joke, and she lifted her hand to her heaving chest as she tried to breathe through the laughter. What a fun evening this had turned out to be—and they'd just added thirteen points to their tally. On impulse, she turned and pressed her lips to Will's, draping an arm around his neck to pull him closer. It wasn't often that Lucy initiated a 'public snog', especially around their friends. Perhaps frolicking at the waterfall today had been some sort of turning point for her.

'Get a room, you two,' teased Chloe. Lucy gave Chloe a sly side-eye as she slowly pulled away from Will, then lifted her chin in Chloe's direction in mock indignation. A moment later, she dissolved into giggles, feeling her cheeks flame with embarrassment. Right, so less of a turning point and more of a slight bend in the road.

'Hey, where'd you go?' Will said low in her ear as he scooched his chair closer to hers.

Lucy smothered her embarrassed laughter and locked eyes with him again, the rest of the room and everybody in it falling away. When Will looked at her like that, Lucy was practically (and willingly) helpless. She gulped, then caught herself wetting her lower lip with her tongue. 'Want to forfeit? Maybe head upstairs?' he asked quietly.

Will's final two words were drowned out by Audrey's cry of, 'Okay, score check before the last game!' but Lucy had heard him and was very much tempted. That is, until Audrey announced that Will and Lucy were in a tie for equal first with Jules and Matt.

'Oh!' she exclaimed, startling Will. 'We could win!' She looked about at the others, the romantic Will-and-Lucy bubble dissipating in an instant, and Will chuckled softly beside her. 'What's the final game?' she asked Audrey.

Annoyance scuttled across Audrey's face, making a small dent in Lucy's enthusiasm and reminding her that she still needed to make amends there. 'It's Christmas trivia,' replied Audrey.

Lucy instantly forgot about the Audrey situation *and* Will's seductive offer. Her mouth and eyes wide, she nudged Will. 'We are going to win this!' she whispered.

'Trivia?' said Jules from across the room. 'Oh, I suck at that. I'm out.' She raised her hands in defeat, then reached for a Christmas cookie from the platter on the coffee table and bit Rudolph's nose off.

Several of the others goaded Jules into continuing to play,

including Matt, but Lucy's voice was loudest. 'You've got to finish the tournament, Jules; otherwise it won't feel like much of a victory when we win!'

'Ha!' laughed Jules, her hand covering her mouth. 'You crack me up, Luce.'

'What? I'm being serious.' Lucy looked to Will for support.

'Don't be so sure of winning.' Chloe pointed back and forth between her and Archer. 'We know Christmas stuff too, Luce,' she sing-songed. 'And we're only two points behind.'

Lucy met her adversary's eye, her lips pursing. *Surely* she knew more about Christmas than even Chloe. She glanced over at Archer, who adeptly arched one eyebrow at her, then turned back to Will. 'Ready to beat the others?'

'Sure, let's go,' he replied, resting his arm on the back of her chair. To Audrey, he said, 'Bring it.'

Audrey rolled her eyes as she turned the page of her notebook. Perhaps she hadn't known when she'd suggested a games tournament that it would have such high stakes. *More fool her*, thought Lucy.

'Right, so just to be clear, there are no actual prizes for the winning team,' said Audrey, her tone that of a nursery teacher.

'I don't know about that,' said Sean. 'I can think of something for the winning team, if you like?' *A brand-new car?* wondered Lucy. What *did* a billionaire offer up as a prize? Lucy began running through possible prizes in her head—a thoroughbred horse, a seaside bungalow, a flight in Sean's private jet?

'How about …' said Sean, her forefinger to her bottom lip. *A small island in the Pacific?* thought Lucy. 'I know! The winning team is absolved from doing dishes for the rest of the holidays!'

'I'm back in,' said Jules, raising her hand like she was in school.

It was a decent prize, Lucy concluded, though she didn't really mind doing dishes. She glanced at Leilani, whose expression was unreadable.

'Okay, question one—oh, and the first person to answer correctly gets the point. Just call it out,' instructed Audrey. Lucy sat up straighter. 'Question one: in the song "The Twelve Days of Christmas", what is given on the seventh day?'

'Seven swans a swimming!' shouted Lucy.

Chapter Twenty-Six

JULES

'God, I'm beat,' said Jules, flopping onto the bed.

'How beat?' asked Matt. He leant against the doorway to the en suite, his eyebrows raised invitingly.

Jules looked over at him and had a quick discussion with herself. It *was* sorta early to go to sleep—just after 10:30—and the way Matt was watching her ... that would typically have a lot more sway. But her exhaustion made the decision for her and she used all her remaining energy to prop herself up on her elbows and reply, 'Too beat for that.'

'Bummer,' he replied.

She sank back again and stared at the ceiling, muttering, 'Yeah, bummer,' to herself right as her stomach made a loud gurgling sound. She patted it gently. 'Ugh, and I ate *way* too many cookies.' As if agreeing with her, her stomach gurgled again. Any second now, a baby alien would burst out of it, snarling and vicious. She snorted out a half-hearted laugh at the thought.

Matt popped his head back into the room, his electric toothbrush going and his mouth full of toothpaste. 'Hmm?' he asked.

'Nothing,' she called out so he could hear her over the hum of the toothbrush. 'Just talking to myself.' He gave her a thumbs-up and went back into the bathroom. Did she even have the energy to brush her teeth? Jules wondered. Why was she so exhausted?

She counted back to their arrival. Was it really only three days ago that they'd landed in Kauai? *Jetlag!* she mentally declared, allowing her eyes to drift shut. By the time Matt climbed into bed, Jules was almost asleep. 'Hun,' he said quietly, 'do you want to get ready for bed?'

Jules groaned. What she wanted was a twelve-hour coma-like sleep. She dragged herself from the siren song of sleep and plodded to the bathroom. She half-assed brushing her teeth, splashed some water on her face, and plodded back to the bed, slipping out of her clothes and crawling into bed in her underwear.

'Well, that's just cruel,' said Matt.

'Hmm?' She rolled over to face him and was met with a gentle smile.

'Never mind, hun.' He kissed her lightly on the lips and turned out the lights. Jules snuggled into her pillow and just as she was on the cusp of sleep, her mind played a wretched trick by tossing up the image of a small hinged box bearing a brass key. Jules' eyes sprang open and her stomach wrenched again, but this time it had nothing to do with too many cookies and everything to do with Matt's (thoughtful but terrifying) Christmas present.

Chloe

'That was a big night, huh?' Chloe asked, keeping her tone light, even though she was somewhat miffed. Why hadn't Archer told her that Sean was coming? It wasn't like him to forget something that significant. But it also wasn't like him to keep something from her, she reminded herself. As soon as he'd heard about Madison being on Kauai, he had shared the news. It was unlikely he'd deliberately been duplicitous about Sean. Wasn't it?

As she removed her earrings, placing them in a catch-all on the dressing table, Archer came up behind her and slipped his arms around her waist, nuzzling her neck with his chin. He sighed deeply, his breath tickling her skin.

'You okay?' she asked, patting one of his hands with hers.

'Mmm,' he murmured. 'Just feeling it, I think.'

'Feeling it?'

Archer sighed again. 'I know it's Christmas tomorrow and it's been great fun having everyone here together, but part of me just wants to curl up in bed and wake up in a week's time.'

Chloe frowned. This conversation had gone in a vastly different direction than she'd anticipated. She'd planned to broach the topic of Sean's unexpected arrival but that could wait. Something was up with him.

She turned around, pinning him with a scrutinising look. 'Are you okay?'

His eyes narrowed slightly as he tipped his head to the side, locking eyes with her. 'I'm fine, my love,' he said quietly. 'And I'm reminded yet again how fortunate I am to have found you.' Chloe's breath caught in her throat and she raised a hand to his face, cupping his cheek. 'I love you, Chloe,' he said, his brows furrowing.

'I know,' she replied, 'I love you too.' He wrapped her up in his arms and she rested her head against his chest, running her hands up and down his back.

'Chloe, darling?' he asked.

'Yes?'

'Will you ...?' His voice trailed off

'Will I what?' she asked after an uncomfortably long silence.

She pulled away from him and he smiled brightly at her, confusing her further. 'Never mind. I'm absolutely shattered. How about we get an early night—be bright-eyed and bushy-tailed for Christmas?'

Chloe found herself nodding involuntarily and she watched, perplexed, as Archer headed into the en suite and closed the door. What on earth was up with him? He'd been the life of the party all night, but then he'd said that thing about wanting to sleep for a week.

It then occurred to her that Audrey's appearance had also been a surprise, that Archer had known she'd be staying there but had failed to mention it. Maybe he *was* just being forgetful. Understandable, really. Their lives had been a blur over the past few months—editing the film, marketing it, a slew of promotional events … He must be exhausted, the poor guy.

But something else niggled at her. She scoured her mind for the elusive thought as her eyes drank in the smattering of stars that painted the inky sky beyond the large picture window. *Oh, god*, she thought, *it's not Madison, is it? Maybe he's more worried about her than he's letting on.* The realisation did little to dampen her uneasiness. How were they supposed to enjoy Christmas when his ex-girlfriend was only a few miles away? His unstable and tenacious ex-girlfriend who would think nothing of disrupting their Christmas celebrations.

'Crap,' she said quietly to herself.

Archer

That was twice he'd nearly proposed on the spur of the moment. Why was he suddenly being so impulsive? He leant against the bathroom vanity and stared at himself in the mirror. 'Archer Tate,' he whispered, 'do not mess this up. This proposal must be special, not something you blurt out after a boozy night of parlour games.'

He expelled an audible breath, noticing the tinge of blue under his eyes. He'd meant what he'd said about falling into bed and waking up in a week's time—partly, in any case. He knew what Christmas meant to Chloe, especially sharing it with Jules, Lucy, and the others, so of course he'd rally.

But there was no denying that the year had taken its toll—as brilliant as most of it had been—and now he was feeling the brunt of it. He was looking forward to the next few months when they'd finally get the chance to properly decompress.

He ran the tap then splashed some water on his face. It was only when he was patting it dry that he had a sickening thought. They hadn't seen hide nor hair of Madison that day, so there was every chance, especially considering her propensity for drama, that she'd try to derail their Christmas celebrations. He'd have a quick chat with Sean in the morning about the property's security measures.

Lucy

'That was brilliant!' said Lucy loudly, entering their room.

'Shh, babe, I think the others might be asleep.' He closed the door quietly behind them.

Lucy glanced at her watch. 'But it's only 10:42! Aren't we supposed to stay up all night and try to catch Father Christmas in the act?' Hmm, she *may* have had a little more wine than she realised.

'You still believe in Santa?' he teased.

'I believe in the magic of Christmas,' she stated matter-of-factly.

As Will approached, she slid her arms around his neck. 'I believe in the magic of you,' he said, dipping his head to kiss her. Lucy giggled through the kiss and he abruptly pulled away. 'Are you laughing at me?'

Lucy pressed her lips together to quell her laughter. 'Possibly.'

'Too cheesy?' He smirked.

'Like camembert wrapped in brie then smothered in melted gruyere.'

'You had fun tonight,' he said, smiling down at her.

'I did.'

'So you're no longer disappointed?' he asked.

She pulled away, tipping her head to the left. 'How do you mean? What do I have to be disappointed about?'

'Just … well, it's hardly the Christmas you had in mind when you got on the plane.'

'The plane?'

'From London.'

'Oh!' she exclaimed. 'Right. I thought you meant from Denver and by then I'd reconciled myself to a hot Christmas instead of a white one. But no, definitely not what I'd hoped for when I left home.' She pressed her fingers to her mouth. 'Sorry,' she said through them, 'that came out wrong. I just meant—' She dropped her hand. 'Will?'

'Mmm?'

'I'm a wee bit tipsy.'

'Really? You could've fooled me.'

'Oi!' She swatted him playfully, then slumped against him.

He chuckled as he trailed his hands up and down her back and eventually they came to rest at her waist, his laughter subsiding. Lucy took a deep breath and closed her eyes, snuggling into the crook of Will's shoulder. She'd been full of beans only moments ago, only now she felt knackered. It was like a switch had been flicked.

'Will?'

'Uh-huh?'

'I feel bad that I upset Audrey last night.'

'Really?'

She nodded, her cheek rubbing against his chest. 'And I

promised myself I'd apologise to her today but I just couldn't find the right time and … and now I feel bad about that too.'

'Hey.' He gently pulled back and she lifted her chin to meet his eye. 'You don't have to feel bad about that. She's clearly got stuff going on, stuff that has nothing to do with you.'

'Do you really think so?'

'Yeah, totally. Babe, we had such a fun night—and it's *Christmas*. Please don't let Audrey get under your skin. Especially not after the stunt she pulled last night.'

'But she was *upset*. It's understandable that she ran off.'

'Well, yeah, but that doesn't mean she has to go and— Shit, never mind.'

'What? She has to go and what? Am I missing something?'

'It doesn't matter,' he said, breaking their embrace and going to his side of the bed. He kicked off his shoes and unzipped his jeans, then pulled his T-shirt off over his head.

Lucy's fuzzy mind instantly cleared, then homed in on what was being left unsaid. 'Will? What aren't you telling me?' He turned towards her, his indecision whether to tell her whatever it was written all over his face. He bit his lower lip. 'Oh, for goodness' sake, Will, just tell me.'

'When I found Audrey out by the pool, she took off all her clothes.'

Lucy couldn't have been more surprised if he'd said she'd morphed into a mermaid. 'What?'

'She took off her clothes, then jumped in the pool. I turned around as soon as I realised what she was doing, I promise. Then I texted Jules and she and Matt came out, then Chloe, and they told Audrey off and that's all that happened. I promise.'

Lucy wasn't sure what to address first—that Audrey had made yet another play for Will, that he'd kept it from her until then, or that her best friends had known and hadn't mentioned it to her. Each thought fought for domination but Lucy settled on the one that played into her biggest fears about being in a long-distance relationship.

'I understand perfectly, Will. A pretty girl stripped herself naked in front of you but you didn't see a thing.'

'I *didn't*—maybe her boobs but only because I was too stunned to move for a second. Then I turned around. Even when she called out to me.' She eyed him warily. Was it was going to be like this forever? Women throwing themselves at Will without a thought for her or their relationship? 'I'm really sorry, babe, I … I swear, I didn't encourage her in any way.'

Lucy's cheeks flamed but not from embarrassment this time. That little trollop. How *dare* she insinuate herself into their relationship. How dare she disregard everything they had. As she felt the fury building inside her, Lucy realised that Audrey wasn't a threat to their relationship—she never had been. Deep down, Lucy knew that Will would never cheat on her, no matter who threw themselves at him. No, her concerns about their relationship had nothing to do with anybody else.

'You don't have anything to apologise for, Will,' she said after some (moderate) introspection.

'Really?'

'Of course! I believe you, Will. And I'm glad you told me.'

He sighed, clearly relieved. 'I wasn't sure if I should tell you but I didn't want you feeling guilty about Audrey when she's the one …'

'When she's the one who owes me an apology,' said Lucy.

'Exactly.'

'And you.'

'And me what?'

'Audrey needs to apologise to us both. It doesn't matter that she's heartbroken, you just don't *do* that. It's completely unacceptable. And it may be Christmas tomorrow, but I'll be having a word with that little …' Lucy couldn't think of a word bad enough to encapsulate her fury. 'Trollop' was far too mild, she realised.

'Hey.' Will traversed the room, his unzipped jeans hanging low on his hips. By the time he reached her, Lucy's mind finally caught up to her eyes. Goodness, he was gorgeous—so much so that she was torn between having her way with Will and figuring out exactly what to say to Audrey when she saw her tomorrow—on *Christmas Day*. 'It'll be okay,' he said softly. He dipped his head for another kiss, this one starting gently but quickly heating up and, as Lucy lost herself in Will's kiss, in his embrace, she let herself forget all about that little …

She'd think of the word later.

Chapter Twenty-Seven

JULES

Jules yawned loudly, stretching her legs down the length of the bed and her arms overhead. She rolled her neck from side to side until she achieved that satisfying 'pop' then slowly opened her eyes. Matt, who was playing on his phone, glanced over.

'Sleep well?' he asked, his mouth quirking in amusement.

'Like the dead.'

'You must have needed it.'

'Mmm-hmm.' She yawned again, then reached for her bottle of water and downed a few glugs. Her head fell back onto the pillow. 'What time is it?'

'Nearly nine.'

'Oh, wow. I slept, like, ten hours!' she exclaimed, completely forgetting that it had taken her a little longer to get to sleep last night than usual.

'Like I said, you must've needed it.' He rolled onto his side to face her, and it was only then that Jules noticed he was above the covers and fully dressed.

'You're already dressed.'

'Yep, and merry Christmas, by the way.'

He was leaning across, lips puckered for a kiss, when Jules sat bolt upright. 'Shit, we're late for Christmas. I totally spaced.' She flung back the covers and leapt out of bed. 'The girls are gonna kill me.'

Matt snickered from the bed as she went into the en suite. 'I doubt they'll *kill* you. But you may want to get a move on,' he called out. 'Your dad's dishing up brekkie any minute now.'

Jules popped her out the doorway. 'Oh, that's right!' She grinned at Matt who shook his head at her. 'Dad's Christmas breakfasts are the stuff of dreams!'

'Yeah, you've mentioned that once or twice,' he replied.

'Yeah, yeah. I'll be quick, I promise.'

She slipped out of her pyjamas, scooped her hair up into a messy bun and ran the shower, turning the setting to 'revitalise'. Not long after, when the strong stream of water was nice and hot—'lava mode', Matt called it—she stepped under it, letting it sluice away any remaining grogginess. *Coffee, then pancakes, then bacon and eggs*, she thought, mentally making her breakfast order. Maybe even a cinnamon roll.

She wasn't exactly sure what Lucy and Chloe had planned after breakfast, but no doubt it would involve the stockings they'd spent all that time on and exchanging presents. She and Will had kicked in together to get their dad a four-day adventure package in New Mexico—hiking, rafting, camping. He was going to *love* it. For Will, she'd cheated, getting something from his Amazon wish list—some sort of bracket for his car to make it easier to haul his snowboarding gear.

Matt had been a little trickier. She'd spent months trying to come up with something—even consulting with Chloe and Ash, his oldest friends—and she'd finally settled on what she hoped was the perfect gift.

At the thought of Matt's gift for her, however, her stomach

soured. She turned off the shower, shoving the thought aside. As she dried off, she decided she'd deal with it when it happened, sure she could fake enthusiasm till they had time alone to properly discuss it.

'Are you coming, hun?' called Matt.

She stuck her head out of the en suite again. 'Five minutes. Meet me down there?'

He crossed to her and kissed her lightly on the lips. 'I'll save you some pancakes.'

'You'd better!' she called to his back. He grinned at her cheekily, then closed their bedroom door.

———

'These are your best yet, Dad,' Jules said, her mouth full of buttery, syrup-covered ricotta pancakes.

'Same recipe as always, sweetheart,' he replied. Jules shrugged, not quite willing to agree. Maybe they seemed fluffier and more delicious than ever because she hadn't had them for the better part of a year.

Leilani had graciously given her dad free rein in the kitchen that morning—and he must have been up super early to get so much done already—but she was keeping a close eye on proceedings, continually following him around to clear away a dirty spoon or wipe the benchtops. 'Leilani,' said Sean, 'it looks like Nate has everything under control. Why don't you come join us?'

Half of them were seated at the breakfast bar like Jules—prime position to get the first pancakes off the griddle, she'd figured—and half were sitting at the kitchen table. 'I've saved you a seat, Leilani,' added Audrey, tapping the chair next to her like she was summoning a dog. Jules took another bite, clocking Leilani's expression but unable to decipher it. She watched closely as Leilani slid quietly into the chair next to Audrey, returning Audrey's grin with a wan smile. Chloe was right—*something* was up with her—and it started when Sean arrived the night before.

'So, I hear that the rest of the day is pretty much planned out?' asked Sean. 'Mind if I crash the party?'

Jules expected Lucy to chime in—of all of them, she loved Christmas the most *and* she and Chloe had been planning stuff since they'd arrived—but when she looked over, Lucy sat glumly at the other end of the breakfast bar, her shoulders slumped. *Geez, why's everyone in such a mood this morning?* Jules wondered.

'Sure,' said Chloe from the table. 'We're doing stockings first—you know, play Christmas music, crack open the bubbly, eat loads of Christmas cookies—then presents and ... Oh!' Chloe stopped talking abruptly, her green eyes wide with realisation.

'Hey, please don't even *worry* about something for me,' said Sean. 'Just being here—getting out of the chaos of San Fran, spending time with Audrey—that's present enough.'

Jules noticed Lucy watching their exchange, then Lucy's eyes met hers. Lucy pressed her lips together and tapped the side of her head, signalling that she had an idea. Jules motioned between her and Lucy, pointed over her shoulder at Chloe, then out to the terrace and Lucy nodded.

While they were silently arranging to meet up outside after breakfast, Sean and Chloe engaged in at least three rounds of 'Are you sure?' and 'Yes, of course!' before Archer interrupted with his own reassurance. Only then did Chloe back down. Jules knew how much Chloe hated not being prepared for something, a trait that pre-dated her career in event management, and may have been heightened since she'd become a film producer. She hoped Lucy's plan was a good one.

'All right, we don't have a lot of time, so I'll talk fast,' said Lucy. The others were either helping clean up after breakfast—much to Leilani's dismay—or had headed to the living room. Jules could already hear the faint strains of Christmas music from that part of the mansion.

'So, what's going on?' asked Chloe.

'Well, I've got two extra Christmas stockings, remember? Ones I brought from home. And I thought we could redistribute—'

'What?' Chloe interrupted, seemingly confused. 'No, I mean, what's going on with *you*, Lucy?'

'What do you mean?' replied Lucy.

'You barely said two words at breakfast and you seem really down,' Jules replied.

'That,' added Chloe, hooking a thumb in Jules' direction.

'Oh, right. I suppose I'm just missing Mum and Dad is all—*and* I went and left Mum's Christmas cake in Colorado like a muppet, so I don't even have that. But it's silly to be gloomy, because we're *all* here together, even your dad, Jules, and it's *so* beautiful—I mean, I *should* be grateful and I don't know what's wrong with me but ...'

She was whipping herself into a state and Jules placed a calming hand on her shoulder. 'It's totally understandable, Luce. I mean, it's awesome that my dad's here but I still miss my mom and my stepdad—even my aunt and uncle and all the cousins.'

'Me too,' said Chloe. 'My mum and dad, I mean. And Drew. I'm not sure when we'll all be together again, let alone for Christmas. I guess this is what we've all signed up for.'

'How do you mean?' asked Lucy.

'Just, you know, Jules and I live away from home now and you and Will are doing long-distance ...'

Lucy's expression soured and she stared down at the ground. 'Anything else on your mind, Luce?' asked Jules.

She looked up, first at Chloe, then at Jules. 'Why didn't you tell me about Audrey stripping down naked in front of Will?' Jules blew out a raspberry while Chloe bit her bottom lip. 'Did you think I wouldn't be able to handle it?'

'No!' they replied together.

'Not at all, Luce. Look, Will was totally mortified …'

'He was,' agreed Chloe. 'Like, beet red, frantic—practically hyperventilating.'

'Well, he was a little more chill than that, Chlo.'

'But *really* upset,' said Chloe.

'Yeah, he was nearly as pissed off as I was.'

'Will said that you told her off—both of you,' Lucy said, her expression transforming into a smirk.

Jules picked up her cue. 'I totally chewed her out.'

'And I tore her a new one,' said Chloe.

'What?' asked Lucy. 'A new one?'

'Arsehole,' said Chloe, matter-of-factly.

'What a charming expression, Chloe,' said Jules.

'What? It's Aussie. Surely you've heard that one by now?' she asked Jules.

'Uh, nope. Can't say I have. Can we get back to everything else, please?' Chloe spread her hands out motioning to 'go for it'. 'Recapping,' said Jules, 'Lucy's missing her folks—me too, you too,' she added, pointing to Chloe. 'Audrey's a conniving little witch and we need to keep an eye on her …'

'Agreed!' said Chloe.

'Definitely,' agreed Lucy.

'*And* Luce has an extra stocking for Sean. That about it?'

'Oh, and Madison is on the island,' said Lucy.

'Don't remind me.' Chloe huffed. She'd been secretly keeping an eye on the tabloids to see what heinous things Madison was saying about her now. So far, there was nothing, which made Chloe even more nervous about her showing up in person.

'Does that cover everything?' asked Jules.

'And Matt wants you to move in with him.'

'What?!' Lucy asked, her head swivelling in Jules' direction. 'He does? That's wonderful!'

'Yeah … uh … yeah.' Jules offered a weak smile.

'Jules! You've said yes, haven't you?' asked Lucy. Jules clocked the excitement on Lucy's face—the total opposite to her own reaction.

'Uh, he hasn't actually asked me yet, but I *think* that's what he's giving me for Christmas—a key to his place.'

Lucy reached down and grasped her hand. 'Oh, I'm so happy for you.'

Jules didn't want to burst Lucy's bubble, so she smiled. 'Thanks.' She glanced over at Chloe, who raised her eyebrows at her.

'Right,' said Chloe. She clapped her hands, indicating that she was taking charge. 'Luce, we've got your back where Audrey's concerned and Will loves you and you have nothing to worry about. We're all still on Madison Watch—super frigging fun. Hel-*lo*! Who doesn't want to spend their Christmas worried about the clingy ex-girlfriend showing up? Jules, you and Matt, you'll figure it out, so we just need to sort out a Christmas stocking for Sean. And I think that's about it.'

'Why do Jules and Matt need to sort things out?' asked Lucy.

'Doesn't matter,' said Chloe. 'Never mind,' replied Jules, talking over Chloe.

'All right,' said Lucy, dragging out every syllable—her tell for it *not* being all right. She shook her head, as though dislodging something. 'How about this? I go get a stocking from our room, you both get the others outside to … I don't know, look at the view or something and I'll' —she waved her hands about— 'redistribute, like I said.'

'Redistribute?' asked Jules.

'Stocking fillers.'

'Oh, right.'

'We may not have a present for Sean, but *everybody* gets a stocking on Christmas,' Lucy declared.

'Let's do it!'

Chloe led the way back into the mansion, followed by Lucy, then Jules.

Let's do it. Should she simply apply the same 'logic' when Matt asked her to move in?

Maybe …

Chapter Twenty-Eight

CHLOE

Corralling Christmas revellers out of the house, especially ones who had eaten their fill of a massive breakfast and just wanted to lounge about on couches and digest, proved to be more difficult than it should have been.

'Why?' whined Audrey. Chloe resisted the urge to lob a heart-shaped cookie at her.

'Because ... because ... um ... photos! It's perfect out on the terrace for Christmas photos!' The idea was genius, if Chloe did say so herself. She looked around at the others, grinning maniacally to drum up enthusiasm. Even Archer seemed a little hesitant. She turned to Jules for support.

'Come on guys, how often do you spend Christmas on Kauai?!' Jules prodded.

As they shuffled out the door, Will turned to Chloe and asked, 'What about Dad and Leilani? They're still in the kitchen cleaning up.'

'Good thinking, Will. I'll go get them ...'

'And where's Lucy?' he called after her.

Chloe decided that she could get away with not answering

under the guise of being too far down the hallway. She burst into the kitchen just in time to catch Nate and Leilani standing in a spotless kitchen and mid-conversation. 'Oh, sorry. I didn't mean to interrupt.'

'No problem, sweetheart. We were just talking about Leilani's plans for Christmas dinner. I'm trying to convince her to let me help.' Chloe didn't know if she'd be able to eat another bite—she'd devoured an enormous stack of pancakes and she *may* have snuck a Christmas cookie or two. Well, four.

'Um, great!' she exclaimed, ramping up the faux enthusiasm. 'So, the others are outside on the terrace so we can take Christmas photos.' They gave her odd looks, staying exactly where they were. Maybe it hadn't been the genius idea she'd thought—she hadn't anticipated this much reticence. 'Okay, look, Lucy didn't want Sean to go without a Christmas stocking, so she's doing her thing in the living room and I needed to get everyone outside.'

Nate barked out a laugh. 'Ah-ha, a scheme! Totally happy to play along.' He headed towards the door and Chloe followed. 'You coming?' he asked Leilani.

She shook her head. 'No, no, Mr Nate, you go on ahead.'

Chloe hated to see the woman so out of sorts, especially considering how much she'd endeared herself to them all in just a few days. 'Do you mind telling the others that I'll be right there?' she asked Nate. 'Oh, me *and* Lucy,' she added as an afterthought. 'Make up some excuse, I guess ...'

'Sure thing—I'll play my part.' After he'd left, Chloe crossed to the breakfast bar, pulled out a stool, and slid onto it.

Leilani pretended to busy herself, lining up the tea towels on the oven door rail. *She's a terrible actor*, Chloe thought, now far more in tune with that kind of thing having spent the better part of a year around dozens of them. 'Hey, Leilani, do you want to come sit?' Her back to Chloe, Leilani's shoulders rose and fell with her heavy sigh. She left her pointless task and joined Chloe at the breakfast bar.

'Are you okay?' asked Chloe.

Leilani manufactured a smile and replied, 'Of course.' *A waaay worse actor than I thought.*

'Hmm, I don't buy it. Do you want to talk about it?' Leilani stared hard at the counter in front of her, her hands fidgeting in her lap. 'It's just that you've been so bubbly, so full of life this whole time, but as soon as Sean arrived … it's like someone popped you with a pin and you're deflating before our eyes.' Leilani nodded in acknowledgement, her eyebrows raised in resignation. 'Is it Sean? Don't you guys get along?'

'Oh no, it's nothing like that. Ms Sean, she's very good to me. She treats me like one of the family.' It wasn't the first time Chloe had heard the 'one of the family' thing, but she reckoned there was still a line between 'family member' and 'employee', even if it was barely noticeable.

'Well, then, what is it?' Leilani exhaled slowly. 'You can trust me but if you don't want to tell me, it's okay.'

'You know how Ms Sean arrived out of the blue?'

'Yeah, totally.' Chloe knew exactly how surprising it had been—it had thrown her for a loop too, but mostly because of Archer's (glaring) omission which she *still* hadn't asked him about.

'Well, she's never done that before and …' Her antsy hands got even antsier.

'Believe me, Leilani, she didn't mind that you were at the table with us—she even invited you back.'

'No, it's not that.'

'Then what?' prompted Chloe, placing a hand gently on Leilani's forearm.

'What if she wants to sell?' asked Leilani in a hoarse whisper.

'Wait? You mean sell this house?' Chloe had imagined several outcomes of her talk with Leilani but none of them were Sean selling the property. 'Why would she want to do that?'

'Because—'

'Sorry, quick follow-up question: why do you *think* she wants to do that? Not because you were eating dinner with us, surely?'

'No, but ... you don't understand.'

'I really don't. But I want to.'

'This is the first time Ms Sean has been here this year.'

'Wow, really?' If Chloe owned this property, she'd be here all the time!

'Yes, and with it just being me here, I've worried for a long time that she would decide it wasn't worth keeping it.'

'But what about Audrey? Doesn't she visit?'

'First time for her in a *long* time. Nearly two years, I think. I've missed her.' Chloe couldn't imagine anyone missing Audrey, brat that she was most of the time, but perhaps she hadn't always been like that.

'Hmm. I can see now why you might be worried. But Sean seems to love this place. And it's not like she needs the money.' Chloe put her fingers to her mouth. 'Sorry, that was kind of crass.' To her delight, Leilani actually *smiled*. Chloe nudged her with her elbow. 'Do you think that maybe you're imagining it? Catastrophising, even?'

'Mmm, maybe.'

'Just talk to her. She'll probably be mortified to find out that you're worrying like this. This place is your home, right?' Leilani nodded. 'Then be brave. Find a time to talk to her *and*, if on the off chance she does want to sell, then at least you'll know, right? Knowing is better than not knowing.'

Now all Chloe had to do was take her own advice and talk to Archer about why he was being so secretive. Between Lucy, Leilani, and Archer ... God, so much going on. This was supposed to be a *holiday*—and it was *Christmas*, for crying out loud.

'There, you are, darling,' said Archer, startling them both—talk about surprise appearances! 'Sorry,' he said, 'it's just that we're waiting on you for the photographs.'

'Oh, right. And Lucy?' she asked.

'She's out on the terrace.'

'Right! Of course. Um …' She turned back towards Leilani. 'Come on, let's go take Christmas photos!'

'Oh, no—'

'None of that. This is a family Christmas—well, pretty much, anyway—and you're family. You said so yourself.'

'Absolutely,' agreed Archer. 'Besides, Sean asked me specifically to make sure you joined us.'

Leilani perked up at that. 'Really?'

'I wouldn't lie to you, Leilani,' he said, donning a conspiratorial smile. *No, just to me*, thought Chloe. She bit her top lip to stop the words escaping her mouth. They *really* needed to have a talk. *After presents*, she promised herself.

Leilani, her mood noticeably brighter, slid off the stool and removed her apron, then smoothed her bright floral muu muu. 'Let's not keep the others waiting,' she said, leading the way.

As they followed her outside, Archer slid an arm around Chloe, his strong hand resting firmly on her waist. When she looked up at him, he was smiling at her so adoringly it was easy to imagine that there was nothing at all to worry about—not his forgetfulness (or worse, potential lies), not Madison making an unwelcomed appearance, not a single thing that could mar their celebrations.

Chapter Twenty-Nine

LUCY

I t may have been sunny and twenty-six degrees outside, but the lounge was such a festive feast for the eyes (and ears) that Lucy could almost pretend she was somewhere snowy—or at least somewhere wintery—and most of it was Chloe and Jules' doing. After photographs, they'd bustled about staging the perfect Christmassy scene.

The flames in the fireplace were flickering—albeit on the lowest setting—they'd switched the Christmas music to Michael Bublé, who was crooning 'Let It Snow' (if only), Archer had, on Chloe's instruction, opened two bottles of fizz and was doling out glasses, and a platter of Jules' beautifully decorated Christmas cookies sat on the large coffee table. They'd also sent her to her room to change into her Christmas jumper. Lucy just loved her fellow May Ladies.

She even felt enough of the Christmas spirit to wish Audrey a happy Christmas as she held out her stocking. Audrey mumbled something in return, but Lucy brushed off her rudeness, handing out the next stocking, which Sean graciously received with a warm smile. 'You really didn't need to do this but thank you, Lucy. That's very thoughtful of you.'

'Well, thank you again for having us, and sorry it's got an "L" on it—that was mine, you see, but I ended up using the one I brought with me.' She motioned towards the mantelpiece where the last stocking hung, its familiar form lifting her spirits even more. Never mind that she now knew what was inside.

'Oh, how beautiful,' said Sean. 'I do love a traditional Christmas, I'll admit.' She half-sighed, half-groaned. 'It's been years since I've really celebrated.' Of Audrey, she asked, 'Remember when your dad and I took you skiing in Breckenridge for the holidays? What year was that?'

'2012,' said Audrey through a mouthful of cookie.

'That long ago? Really?' Audrey nodded and reached for another cookie. At this rate, there would be none left for the rest of them. 'See?' she said to Lucy. 'That was the last real Christmas I had and Audrey was a little girl at the time.' They both accepted glasses of fizz from Archer with thanks, and Sean lifted hers to tap Lucy's. 'Cheers.'

'Cheers.' Lucy took a sip. 'Did you know that Will's family are from there? Breckenridge?' she asked, nodding her head towards Will. 'Well, they have a holiday cabin nearby. I went there for Christmas last year.'

'No kidding? That's uncanny.'

'Will even taught me to ski.' Will appeared at Lucy's side and slung an arm around her shoulders.

'She was a quick study.'

Lucy laughed. 'That's, ahh … generous, but thank you.'

'You were!'

'I tumbled down the hill on my first run,' she told Sean.

'Oh, we all do that. It's part of the fun,' she replied.

Lucy looked up at Will. 'It *was* actually fun once I figured out how to stay upright.'

'I was proud of you.' He pulled her close and kissed the side of her head.

'So, tell me,' said Sean, 'I'm still not a hundred per cent clear how you're all connected. Except, you, Chloe, and Jules—you've been friends since you were kids?'

'Yes,' said Lucy, 'best friends since we were children—aged eleven, actually. We all met when our families travelled to Maui at the same time. We're the May Ladies.' Sean cocked her head in interest. 'At that age, we wanted a *name*, you see, and we discovered that we were all born in May—hence the May Ladies.'

'Ah,' Sean replied, nodding, 'that's sweet.'

'And we stayed friends—*best* friends—all these years. Anyway …' she said, taking another sip of fizz—goodness, it was going down well, 'we've been travelling together on our May Ladies trips since we were in our early twenties.'

'Audrey's age,' interjected Sean.

Lucy hadn't thought of that, but she was right. 'Er, yes, exactly. Anyway, *last* year—'

'Last year,' interrupted Will, 'Lucy came to Colorado.' He squeezed her shoulder as he smiled down at her and she basked in his adoration. *This*, she thought. This was the feeling that made those long months apart worth it. Most of the time, anyway.

'And Jules went to Melbourne where Chloe's from,' she said to Sean, 'and Chloe went to Oxfordshire, where my parents live.'

'Oh, of course—that's how Archer met Chloe. And that led to the whole Eloise Capel film. God, what a fantastic story—you swapping Christmases like that.'

'It *was* incredible, though I was a little overwhelmed at first.'

'My family can be a lot,' said Will. 'For Christmas, it's usually Dad, my mom, my stepdad, and my mom's sister and her whole family.'

'They're all *lovely*, though,' added Lucy.

'Oh, totally. But rowdy as hell.'

'So, quite different from what you grew up with, Lucy?' asked Sean.

'Quite.' She giggled. It *had* been different but also wonderful, especially the falling in love part. She leant into Will and he held her tighter.

'And Jules?' asked Sean. 'What about her and Matt—are they a Christmas romance too?'

'Uh-huh,' replied Will.

'Now *that* could be a movie—all three couples meeting at Christmas, all the connections between you ... You know, I have a friend at Hallmark,' Sean said with raised eyebrows.

Lucy's eyes widened. 'You do?' She placed a hand over her heart. 'I absolutely *adore* the Hallmark Christmas films. Well, any Christmas film, really.'

'Just say the word ...'

'I know you're joking' —Sean smiled— 'but I could easily be tempted. Who would play us, do you think?' Lucy asked Will.

He shook his head. 'That's all you, babe.'

'You know that I've planned a mini film festival for this afternoon, don't you?' she asked Sean. 'We're using your cinema. I hope you don't mind.'

'No, it's great that someone's using it. What's on the bill?'

'Well, we're starting with *The Holiday*—'

'Oh, that's a favourite,' said Sean.

'Yes, for me too. It's also *apt*, considering ...' She circled both forefingers in the air indicating the others.

'Oh, for sure. And then?'

'Well, we may only have time for two films before we sit down to Christmas lunch ...' She caught the confusion on Sean's face. 'It's really Christmas dinner, isn't it? I'm not sure why we call it lunch at home, but anyway ... I figured we could vote on the next film—either *While You Were Sleeping* or *White Christmas*—'

'Or *Elf*!' called out Jules, who had obviously been

eavesdropping. Lucy didn't *love* Elf but she'd committed to voting so she mentally added *Elf* to the ballot.

'Or that.'

'Sounds fun. And did you see the popcorn machine?' asked Sean.

'Honestly?'

Sean moved closer. 'Honestly. Actually, on second thought, we might not want to spoil our appetites.'

'Oh, good point. Tomorrow then—we can do another double bill!' she added excitedly. 'What other films should we put on the ballot?' she asked the others.

'What about *Die Hard*?' Chloe shouted from across the room. Lucy grimaced—*Die Hard* was hardly a Christmas film.

Will cleared his throat. 'Oh, I forgot that you like that film,' said Lucy. 'Sorry.'

'It's not that … just, tomorrow …' He sucked in air through his teeth. 'Remember, I was going to take Dad surfing?'

'Oh,' said Lucy. She'd forgotten that was the plan.

'That's right,' said Sean. 'You're teaching your dad how to surf. Hey, Nate,' she called out. Nate lifted his chin, indicating he was listening. 'You still up for surfing tomorrow?'

'Well, I promised my son, so … let's go with yes.'

'Mind if I tag along?' she asked.

'Not at all.'

'Fantastic. I *think* it's like riding a bike. At least I hope so!' They shared a laugh and Lucy looked between them. There was some sort of spark there, she was sure of it. And Nate was so lovely and he truly deserved to have someone special … And why not Sean? You'd never know from talking to her that she was one of the most notorious people on the planet. There were no airs and graces—she was just a down to earth, lovely woman.

'And don't forget your promise to get me up— Oh! *Standing*

up, I mean, *standing*,' Nate added quickly. His head shook with embarrassment and Sean grinned.

'I'll do my best, but it's been a while and I'm a little out of practice,' she said, causing Nate to erupt with laughter. *Ooh, forget 'sparks'—it's more like a firework going off in here*, thought Lucy. She looked over at Jules, but she was deep in conversation with Matt, then turned and caught Will's eye. He was smiling and Lucy wondered if he was thinking what she was—how fab it would be to have another Christmas romance amongst them!

'So, are we doing stockings anytime soon?' moaned Audrey, ruining the mood.

Lucy's lips pursed in exasperation. What would Jules say? Oh yes: 'Read the room!' Lucy doubted that Audrey could read a room if her life depended on it. Excusing herself from Sean and Will, she crossed to the mantelpiece to retrieve her stocking.

'Hello, everybody,' she said loudly. Conversations died down, all eyes alighting on her, and Lucy swallowed hard. Yes, this room held some of her most favourite people in the world but that didn't mean she was wholly comfortable commanding their attention. She donned a 'fake it till you make it' smile, and held aloft her glass of fizz. 'Um, happy Christmas!'

Almost everybody returned the toast, including Chloe who bellowed, 'And to you, Luce.' The hold-out was Audrey, who grimaced at her impatiently. *Ignore her*, Lucy told herself, *she's just a sourpuss—a grinchy, moody sourpuss*. The thought buoyed her considerably and, glancing at Will, she got an extra boost of confidence from his proud, beaming smile. 'So,' she said to the whole room, 'some of you may know that Christmas is my favourite time of the year.'

'No way, Luce, you never mentioned that,' heckled Jules.

'Ha-ha, very funny.' Lucy pretended offence but the banter killed off the last of her nerves and she proceeded. 'You also know that this wasn't what I had planned for Christmas. *But*, if I can't be home in Oxfordshire with my parents, or in Colorado, then there's no place else I'd rather be than here on this paradisiacal island with my dear friends, my darling Will and his dad, *and* our new friends,' she said, nodding her head at Sean, then Leilani. She wasn't about to add Audrey to that list as nobody, including Audrey, would believe her. 'Again, happy Christmas, and I hope you like your stocking fillers!' She raised her glass again, then took a sip.

'Hear, hear!' added Chloe, talking over a chorus of 'Cheers'. She and Lucy swapped smiles, Chloe adding a cheeky nose scrunch before she sipped some fizz, then turned to say something to Archer. Lucy looked over at Jules next, who sent her a warm smile. She loved them so much.

'Nice toast, babe,' said Will as he approached—another person who made Lucy's heart sing.

'Thank you. I hadn't planned on that, but makes it a bit more of an occasion, don't you think?'

He stooped to kiss her. 'Definitely,' he said, locking his eyes onto hers. Goodness, her heart wasn't just singing, it was *racing* under his intense stare. 'Come on,' he said, 'I've saved you a spot.' He led them to a sofa on the opposite side of the room from Audrey—a deliberate choice, she guessed—and she nestled in beside him, setting her glass on an end table. Lucy watched closely as Will dug into his Christmas stocking and pulled out the first gift: a dancing hula girl for his dashboard.

'It's just something silly. You don't have to put it in your car if you don't want to.'

He beamed. 'No, it's great. And it will remind me of you when you're back in England.' At that thought, Lucy's stomach churned with unease, despite the warmth in Will's eyes. Oblivious, he returned to his stocking, this time pulling out a cellophane packet of dried pineapple. 'Oh, these look *good*. Is it okay to open them now?'

'How can you still be hungry?' Lucy asked, incredulous.

'I'm a growing boy,' Will declared.

'Hardly,' she said laughing. 'You're a grown man.'

'I'm a *growing* man,' he retorted low in her ear. 'Want to cut out of here soon?'

'William Nathan Reinhardt,' she hissed, feigning shock, 'you are being very naughty.'

'It's deliberate.' She shook her head, succumbing to giggles. In the back of her mind, Lucy was aware that she'd gone from dread and longing to amusement and affection in a mere moment—a familiar marker of their relationship. She really was going to have to raise this with Will—and before she flew back to London—but not today. Not on Christmas.

She lifted her chin, determined to brush aside not only Will's poorly timed seduction, but her own niggling doubts. 'Can we at least finish stockings and presents?'

He gave her a teasing side-eye. 'Sure, babe.' Lucy expelled a tiny sigh of relief. 'Are you going to do yours?' he asked, indicating her stocking.

'Oh, yes, quite right.' She delved into her own, even though she now knew everything it contained. She pulled out a fridge magnet with a photograph of the Nā Pali Coast on it and regarded the beautiful scene. Hopefully, they'd get a chance to see it while they were on Kauai.

'Oh, wow, how cool.' Will held up a bottle of beer from Kauai Island Brewing, a boutique brewery on the island. 'We should check it out this week, huh?' he asked as his eyes scanned the bottle's back label.

'Of course.' Lucy had accompanied Will to many a brewery and distillery on her visits to Colorado. She'd half-anticipated that he might want to visit this one.

'You did a great job on the stockings, Luce,' he said.

'Oh, thank you, but it was a joint effort. Chloe was in charge, really—and Audrey helped, of course,' she added magnanimously. She might not like Audrey, but credit where it was due. Lucy lifted her eyes and scanned the room, noticing Audrey watching closely as Sean emptied her stocking. The stepmother and stepdaughter shared a smile over a packet of chocolate-covered coffee beans. *She's not all bad*, thought Lucy.

Beside her, Will dug into the packet of dried pineapple, offering her some but she declined, still full from breakfast. Right then, Chloe's laugh pulled her attention. Archer was making a show of playing the miniature ukulele from his stocking—badly.

'Keep your day job, Archer,' Matt called out. More laughter filled the room as Archer raised his eyebrows and played into the attention, plucking out a tune that only slightly resembled 'White Christmas' (if one were especially forgiving).

'Hey, can you actually play?' asked Sean. 'The ukulele?' she added.

'Absolutely,' he replied. 'It's on my resume under special skills, along with juggling and roller-skating.'

'You can't juggle,' said Chloe.

'I can—it's just that I've yet to graduate from two balls to three.'

There was a beat of silence before the entire room, Lucy included, erupted into laughter. 'What?' asked Archer, looking to the others. 'Oh, never mind.'

Between Archer and Nate, the innuendos were certainly abundant that morning and Lucy knew that no matter how many more Christmases were to come over her lifetime, this one would always be memorable.

Chapter Thirty

JULES

'Keep your day job, Archer,' teased Matt.

'Hey,' said Jules, poking him in the ribs with her elbow.

'He knows I'm just taking the piss,' Matt assured her quietly. He was probably right. They *had* formed a fast friendship, Matt and Archer, and the good-natured ribbing often went both ways. They were like that with Will too and Jules had to admit that she loved their little sixsome. This trip may have been last-minute and she didn't *love* being surrounded by a lot of people for days on end but even her dad was here and so far, the trip had been a net positive.

If Jules didn't think about the other thing. *Shit*, she thought, *after stockings come presents*. She wondered if she could fake a headache and escape to their room or something. Nah, that wouldn't work. Matt would just follow her and do all the super sweet Matt things he did when she got of one her semi-regular tension headaches: pour her a huge glass of water for her pain meds, give her a neck rub, then send Dex over to give her doggie kisses while he made dinner or put on a load of laundry or whatever other chore needed doing. Sometimes, if it was really bad, he'd run her a bath. No doggie kisses today, though, so another reason to skip a fake headache.

'Hey, can you actually play?' Sean asked Archer. 'The ukulele?' He replied that he could and Jules clocked the look that passed between Sean and Leilani. Leilani leapt up, then disappeared from the room while Chloe declared, 'You can't juggle!'

'I can—it's just that I've yet to graduate from two balls to three.'

Oh my god, thought Jules. She was going to lose it. She glanced at Matt, who, after a beat of silence, laughed loudly. The others, including Jules, joined in at Archer's expense—even Audrey was smirking.

'What?' asked Archer, looking to the others. 'Oh, never mind.'

'S'okay, Arch,' Matt called out, 'I can be the fluffer while you juggle the balls.'

'Bahahaha,' laughed Chloe loudly.

'Matt!' Jules nudged him in the ribs again as she tried stifling her own laughter. God! Her *dad* was in the room. She slid her eyes in his direction, mortified, but he was laughing as loudly as the others and Jules gave over to it, joining back in. Poor Chloe was doubled over, holding her stomach with one hand and wiping under her eyes with the other, saying, 'phoo' on repeat as she tried to recover.

By the time Leilani returned to the living room bearing a real ukulele, the laughter had subsided a little, but the mood in the room remained cheery. 'Here, Mr Archer,' said Leilani, handing the instrument over the back of the couch.

'Oh, thank you!' said Archer, taking the ukulele. 'I may do a little better with this one. *Or* do *you* play, Leilani?' He held it out for her to take back but she vigorously shook her head and returned to her spot on a small club chair near the fireplace.

Jules watched Archer with interest as she sipped some more champagne. *God, this stuff is good*. She turned and squinted at the empty bottle on the bar. *Oh, no wonder.* It was Dom Perignon—another reminder that she was in the presence of the (extremely wealthy) and (oh-my-god-I'm-totally-fangirling) Sean Alessi. Jules still hadn't had any one-on-one time with Sean, but she'd try to wangle some before they headed back to Melbourne—or Sean flew back to San Fran. Crap—she might need to get a move on. When you were under the same roof as the woman who had inspired your entire career, you needed to tell her, even if you came off like a dork.

As Archer tuned the small instrument, Jules' attention landed on Leilani, who had quietly resumed pulling small gifts and trinkets out of her stocking, each one eliciting a slight smile. Jules was glad she'd agreed to join their Christmas celebrations; she was a nice woman and Sean's arrival had clearly thrown her for a loop. Jules wasn't sure what was going on there but Chloe had said she was on it, so Jules was deferring to her.

Besides, she had her own thing going on.

Archer began playing and singing 'All I Want for Christmas Is You' and (unfortunately) Chloe joined in. They sang to each other duet style—Archer, man of many talents, sounding a lot like Ed Sheeran and Chloe sounding more like a squawking parrot operating a blender than a human being.

Matt shook with laughter beside her. 'Don't say a word,' she jokingly warned.

'You know that Chloe thinks she's a good singer, don't ya?' he whispered.

'Mmm-hmm. It's come up a few times over the years. Super painful karaoke in New York comes to mind,' she replied, her voice low.

'It's a good thing we love her.' Jules sniggered. So far, this part of Christmas had turned out to be a lot of fun—far more than she'd anticipated. She glanced over at Lucy—this was mostly her brainchild—and was glad to see her grinning as she tipped her head to hear something Will was saying, then laughed heartily. Maybe they were making fun of Chloe's singing too.

Sometimes it hit Jules that two of her favourite people—her brother and one of her best friends—had fallen in love. This one of those times—it *was* awesome, if a little surreal. She wondered if Chloe felt that way when she saw her and Matt together.

Archer and Chloe finished their song, Chloe standing up and extending her arms on the final (wobbly) note. The room erupted into applause. 'Bravo!' cried Sean.

'We should go on tour,' Chloe said to Archer.

'No!' shouted Jules and Lucy at once. They locked eyes and dissolved into more laughter.

'Hey! I can sing,' Chloe replied indignantly.

'You can sing just about as well as I can juggle, darling.'

Chloe had no words for that and was left gawping, her eyes wide. She backhanded him in the leg and plopped onto the couch, pretending to be pissed. Jules had seen that exact look on her face dozens of times but, surely, Chloe knew she was a terrible singer? Maybe deep down—like, *way* deep down.

'I think it must be time for presents,' Chloe declared, her chin lifted. Jules steadied her breath. *Here it comes*. She was about to drink more champagne, but she set the glass down instead. She'd need to have her wits about her.

'Darling, you do know that you are brilliant at a million other things,' Archer said, going with the 'sweet talking' method of placating Chloe.

'Ha! Easy for you to say. You, who are *actually* brilliant at a million other things.' Jules watched the exchange closely. Was Chloe really upset? She was probably the most confident person Jules had ever met. A second later, Chloe's hurt façade fell away and, eyes twinkling, she stuck her tongue out at Archer, who laughed. Chloe gave him a quick kiss, then headed over to the Christmas tree.

'Luce, do you mind if I play Father Christmas?' she asked. 'Since you did stockings?'

'No, not at all.' Lucy snuggled closer to Will, who rested a hand on her thigh. *Don't look*, Jules told herself. There was being happy for them both and there was getting a glimpse into their intimacy. *Uh, no thanks.*

Chloe loaded up her arms with presents from under the tree and began randomly handing them out. Knowing her best friends, there would be something for everyone—except maybe Sean—but she'd already said she didn't expect anything. What did you get a billionaire for Christmas, anyway?

'Leilani, wait!' cried Chloe as she tried to sneak out of the living room. 'This is for you.' Leilani smiled shyly and accepted the stiff white envelope from Chloe. 'It's from all of us. Merry Christmas.'

'Thank you,' Leilani replied quietly and Jules was again struck by how different her demeanour was from the larger-than-life woman who'd greeted them a few days ago.

When all the gifts under the tree had been handed out and Chloe had returned to her place next to Archer, Jules was confused. Where was the velvet jewellery box? Did Matt have it in his pocket? Oh, god, was he going to spring it on her like he was proposing or something?

'Matt!' Sean called from across the room, startling Jules. She held up a bottle of Matt's Pinot, 'This is super sweet—thank you.' There was a tag tied around its neck and Sean's eyes scanned the message. 'Oh!' She looked back at Matt. 'A case, really? You don't need to do that.'

'Happy to,' he replied, waving off her gratitude. 'I'll organise it when I get back—just let me know where to send it.'

'I will and thank you.'

Jules watched the scene unfold with wonder. Her boyfriend was sending a case of wine to *Sean Alessi*! God, she'd been so far up her own ass about the key thing, she hadn't even realised Matt was doing that. He was so thoughtful!

I am a massive shit, she told herself. *Matt wants me to move in with him and I want a place of my own. Massive. Fricking. Shit.*

'Hun?' Jules was pulled from her self-deriding thoughts and pasted on a smile for Matt.

'Mmm?' He was holding something out, a scroll with a red ribbon tied around it. She eyed it with a head tilt and looked back at Matt.

He was smiling, his dark brown eyes watching her. 'It's your Christmas present.'

Confused, but unable to confess why without giving away that she knew about the key, Jules took the scroll, slid the ribbon off, and unfurled the piece of paper. It was a photo of a deep sandy cove, surrounded by tall rocky cliffs with a natural arch worn through the rock at one end and low sloping greenery along the bottom of the cliffs. Jules knew exactly where that was. It was Honopu Beach on the Nā Pali Coast, one of the places on her travel bucket list. She and Matt had even talked about going there while they were on Kauai but she'd been so swept up in the whirlwind of the last few days, she'd forgotten.

She look back at Matt inquisitively. 'We're going. Just you and me. Two nights away. Hiking in and camping.' Jules got chills and goosebumps prickled her limbs. It was amazing—the ultimate gift. And *not* a key to his house.

'I love it.' She leant over and kissed him hard and fast on the lips. 'Thank you.'

'You're welcome, hun. Another bucket list item to tick off, eh?' That he knew that, that he *saw* her and really understood what would make this trip even more special than it already was ... *this* was why she loved him so much.

'Now, my present from you,' he said, tapping the present in his lap.

'It's just … it's just a little something.' She felt foolish about it now, wishing she could take it back and replace it with something more thoughtful, something more of the calibre of his gift.

'I'm sure I'll love it,' he said, his impatient fingers ripping at the paper and tugging on the ribbon she'd (probably) tied too tightly. Under the paper was a box and Matt slipped his fingers under the lid to lift it. Jules held her breath, capturing her bottom lip between her teeth as his eyes drank in the gift.

'Oh, wow. Jules …'

'Really? You like it?'

He nodded, his lips pressed together, heavy breaths escaping his nose like he was trying not to cry. That's when she noticed the unshed tears. She'd hoped he would like it—a framed photograph of Matt, Twoey, and Dexter the dog standing on the edge of the concrete slab that had become their winery's tasting room, marking it forever with their footprints. They were filthy from the workday—*covered* in dirt. Matt and Twoey had their arms slung around each other's shoulders and all three of them were grinning at the camera, even Dex.

'You just looked so happy, so proud … I wanted you to have something to remember it by,' she said. 'Especially, as they laid the floor over your footprints.'

'I don't even remember you taking this.'

'It was a big day,' she replied.

He looked up then. 'Thank you, hun. It's brilliant.'

Jules went in for another kiss, a gentler one that lingered. And, as they rested their foreheads together, taking time for themselves and blocking out revelry around them, she almost allowed herself to forget about the conversation that loomed.

Almost.

Chapter Thirty-One

CHLOE

C hloe was thrilled with how Christmas morning was turning out. They'd had Nate's yummy breakfast—she couldn't remember the last time she'd had pancakes that good—the stockings had been a hit—thanks in large part to Lucy and yes, all right, Audrey—the champagne was flowing, just as it would be back home in Melbourne, and now everyone was opening presents!

The only thing tainting the festivities—and not a small thing—was Leilani. Chloe would look for an opportunity to speak to Sean as soon as possible. But first! 'I don't think I can wait any longer,' she said to Archer. 'Open it.' In his lap was sitting an A4 envelope. His mouth twitched with mirth and his eyes danced with excitement. It had been almost impossible to figure out what to get him, just as it had been for his birthday in July.

For that, she'd booked them a weekend away from the film set—a massive accomplishment considering that, till then, he'd been working long hours every day for more than a month. She'd had to conspire with his AD (Assistant Director), the DoP (Director of Photography)—it had only taken Chloe a few days to get across the filmset lingo, thank god!—and Fi, Archer's close friend and the film's producer. But he had relented and they'd enjoyed cosying up at a beautiful and rather lux B&B in Cornwall before he'd eagerly driven them back to London to be on set first thing that Monday morning.

This gift was vastly different.

He carefully slid his thumbnail under the seal and peeled it back. When he slid out the piece of paper, confusion marred his handsome features for a second before he lifted his eyes to meet hers. They were filled with curiosity. 'I can't tell what it is,' he said. His eyes dropped back to the page and with his fingertip he traced the lines. 'A *C* and an *A*—and it's a clever design, entwining them like this but ... Is it a monogram? For us?'

'Um, no. It's the design for my tattoo.'

His eyes flew to hers. 'Seriously?'

Chloe nodded vigorously. 'As soon as we get back to LA. I've got the appointment booked and everything.'

'So ... where?'

'It's this cool place in Venice—a woman named Victoria. She normally does way more complicated desi—'

'No, sorry, darling, I meant where are you getting it? Where on your body?'

'Oh! I dunno. I haven't decided yet but I'm leaning towards my shoulder, just here,' she said, tapping the top of her right shoulder blade. 'And not too big or anything.' She closed her thumb and forefinger into a loop. 'About like this.'

Archer was looking at her so intently that her stomach lurched. Maybe he didn't like the idea. Was it dumb? Had she come across like some sort of Archer Tate groupie? For the first time since they'd assured each other of their love and commitment nearly a year ago, she felt the stab of doubt.

'It's' —*Oh, god*, she thought— 'absolutely perfect.'

Chloe blew out a breath. 'Really? Oh, thank god!'

He chortled. 'Did you think I wouldn't like it?'

'Only for a second—you were acting all weird.'

He chorlted again, his familiar self-deprecating laugh. 'Good thing I usually have directors telling me how to react, isn't it?'

'Um, yeah. I mean, hel-*lo*?'

He closed the small distance between them and kissed her tenderly, his lips moving gently against hers. 'I love it,' he said, his face only centimetres from hers. 'So much so, that I'll get one too.'

Chloe tucked her chin in surprise. 'Seriously?' He smiled and nodded, his eyebrows waggling. 'Where?'

'It's this place in Venice Beach …'

'Ha-ha. Hilarious.'

'I like to think so,' he replied matter-of-factly before his smile returned. 'How about in the same spot? On my shoulder blade?'

'I approve.'

'Excellent!' He pulled her close for a quick smack of a kiss.

'Now my present,' she said, standing to retrieve the medium-sized box from the coffee table. She grabbed one of Jules' Christmas cookies while she was up, stuffing the reindeer's antler into her mouth and holding the cookie between her teeth. Back on the couch, she laid the box in her lap and took a bite of the cookie. 'Oh god, these are good,' she mumbled with her mouth full. Archer's mouth quirked in amusement as she stuffed the other half into her mouth, her cheeks bulging.

Chloe was not one to stand on ceremony—what was the point in unwrapping a present so carefully you could reuse the paper? Though she did take a second to admire how prettily the box was wrapped—Archer's assistant, Anya, had done a great job—before ripping the paper. She dropped large pieces of it to the floor, revealing a plain white cardboard box.

She flicked a glance at Archer, then opened the hinged lid. Nestled on a bed of crumpled tissue paper was an array of items that flooded her with nostalgia. It was a taste of home—literally.

One by one, she removed each item and placed them on the couch next to her: a cellophane bag of Jaffas (her favourite lollies), a packet of TimTams (the dark-chocolate mint ones), Twisties! (chicken-flavoured, not the cheese), Burger Rings, and two more bags of lollies (Red Rippers and Clinkers) … When she looked back at Archer, his eyes were lit up with glee. 'So, for Christmas you're giving me diabetes?' she teased.

'Keep going.'

With all her favourite Aussie junk food now set beside her, she explored the folds of the crinkled paper, finding a Myki Card—now that was just weird. Why was he giving her a public transit card for Melbourne? She also discovered three more cards—memberships cards for ACMI (the Australian Centre for Moving Images), the National Gallery of Victoria, and the Melbourne Museum—and a fridge magnet of a Melbourne tram.

First, how the hell did he get all of this? Second, why was he tormenting her with stuff from home?

'Oh!' she blurted, finally understanding. Her mouth agape, she looked back at Archer who was smiling at her broadly. 'Really?'

'Yes, my darling.'

Chloe flung her arms around his neck and, her tears coming easily, he held her while she happy cried.

'What's happening over there?' Jules called from the other side of the room.

Chloe pulled away from Archer and dragged her fingers under her nose. 'We're going to Melbourne!'

'No way!' Jules replied excitedly.

'It's true,' Archer confirmed. 'And look, there's one more thing in here.' He rummaged in the tissue paper and pulled out a document that had been lying flat at the bottom of the box. 'Look.'

Chloe did as he'd instructed, her eyes scanning the document before, disbelieving, she met Archer's eye. 'This is a six-month lease.'

He nodded at her. 'It is. And if you'd rather look for a place together, we can do that. I just wanted to show you how committed I am to taking you back to Melbourne.' Chloe read the address on the lease, mentally perusing the map of Melbourne.

'I know where this is—well, the neighbourhood, anyway. It's on Port Phillip Bay,' she said.

'Not exactly the beach as we've come to know it, but by the water, yes.'

'And only a little ways from Docklands,' piped in Jules. 'Chlo! We're going to get to see each other all the time.'

'Yes!' Chloe replied, brimming with elation. 'Oh, Archer, this is the *best*! It's … I have no words.'

'And *there's* the present for the rest of us, Archer,' teased Matt.

'Ha-ha,' Chloe retorted. Just then, she caught sight of Lucy's face. 'Luce? You okay?'

'Of course!' she replied brightly. 'I'm so happy for you. Melbourne will be brilliant.'

Chloe was unconvinced but had no time to dig deeper because Archer's phone chimed in his pocket with the Facetime ringtone. 'That must be Mum and Dad,' he said as he took it out and unlocked it. Chloe scooched closer, ready to wish them a merry Christmas, only it wasn't his parents calling. It was Madison.

'Oh, for fuck's sake,' Archer muttered. It was unusual for him to bust out profanity but other than swearing, he seemed paralysed by the surprise caller and Chloe reached across and declined the call, her heart pounding in her chest.

I'll say, 'for fuck's sake'. What the hell does she want? Chloe thought, catching Lucy's hasty exit out of the corner of her eye. But it barely registered in the aftermath of Madison's intrusive call.

Chapter Thirty-Two

SEAN

I t was a little ironic that she'd flown here to get away from the drama unfolding in her company. Straight from the frying pan into the fire, she realised.

She knew from Archer that Audrey had been behaving like a five-year-old—well, older than that, considering her foray into inappropriate nudity, though it wasn't the first time she'd been in trouble for that. She looked across the room to where her stepdaughter pretended to be absorbed by the contents of her Instagram feed—scroll, stop, tap, scroll, stop, tap, her expression unchanged at each photo or meme.

Sean loved Audrey—*fiercely*. She'd become her stepmother at a formative age for Audrey, initially coaxing smiles out of a shy, sad little girl, aware that she cared more for Audrey than either of the girl's parents did. Sean frequently witnessed their (almost always cruel) disappointment in their daughter—disappointment that she wasn't as bright or cheery or as talented as they'd thought their child would be. The child of a brilliant man and a supermodel should have been extraordinary.

In Sean's eyes, however, Audrey *was* extraordinary. She was capable of boundless love—*unconditional* love—though Sean suspected *she* was the only person who had ever received it. Well, perhaps Leilani too. That was why she'd suggested Kauai after Audrey's breakup with Bugs. She'd thought that time with Leilani would have been salve for the heart.

Speaking of …

'I'll get back to Christmas dinner,' said Leilani, excusing herself.

'Thank you, Leilani,' Sean called at her back as she hurried out of the room. God, something was going on with her too.

There also seemed to be a *lot* going on with Archer and his friends, including Archer's inquiry that morning about the property's security, which she'd assured him was second-to-none. Now Lucy had suddenly excused herself, followed by Will, and immediately following that phone call, Archer and Chloe had begun speaking frantically in hushed tones. 'Anything I can do to help?' she offered.

'Er, thank you, but probably not,' Archer replied. His lips turned white with tension and his frown was Shakespearean. 'Will you excuse us, everybody? Just for a moment.' Typical Archer—always polite, even when shit was going down. And based on their reaction to that call, shit was definitely going down.

This place was drama central. She expelled a long, loud breath, knowing that no matter how much she wanted to turn the jet around—that day, if possible—she'd have to rally and help where she could. It just wasn't in her nature to walk away when she could be of use, even if she was (more than) a little out of her element.

'That was a heavy sigh,' said Nate quietly. She looked over to where he sat, his expression warm and open and sitting comfortably on his handsome face. She'd liked Nate immediately, trusting her sixth sense about people, a sense she'd honed after three decades in the tech industry. It was essentially her superpower. She was also attracted to him, she admitted to herself, their flirtatious banter feeling both familiar—*oh, right, I do remember how to flirt*—and exciting.

She ran one hand through her cropped hair. 'You caught me,' she said with a smile. 'It's just—'

'Hey, Dad?' Jules asked from across the room. 'Sorry to interrupt, but we're gonna head out to the pool. Just chill there for a bit.'

'Okay, sweetheart. I'll come get you if, uh … everything … you know.'

'Yep.' She and Matt got up and left, Matt raising a hand in Sean and Nate's direction. He was a good guy, too. And a *great* winemaker.

She looked towards Audrey, whose eyes met hers. 'Audrey, did you want to—'

Audrey didn't let her finish. 'Nope. I'll be in the bungalow.' She left the room so fast, there was a breeze in her wake.

'Hence the heavy sigh, huh?' asked Nate.

'You're a father …'

'I am, proudly.'

'You should be proud. Your kids seem great.'

'Thanks.' There was that smile again—it was very appealing, how his eyes crinkled at the corners and the smile commandeered his whole face.

'So, how do you know when to interfere or not?' she asked.

'Interfere?'

'No, that's not the right word. Maybe, step in?'

'Ahh.'

'It's just that when Audrey was younger, her problems were …'

'Something you could fix?' he asked, finishing her thought.

'Yes, exactly! I felt more useful then. She'd get herself into some trouble—acting out against her dad or her mom, mostly—and I could be there for her. But now she's a young woman and ...'

'I get it. I think it's the hardest part of being a parent, when they transition from being your child to being your *adult* child.'

'But I'm not even her mom.'

'Look, I haven't known you for long.' He looked at his watch, sucking air through his teeth as he calculated the hours and making her snicker. 'Yep, as I suspected, *just* over eighteen hours ...' He returned his gaze to her. 'Doesn't matter. I could see right away how much that girl loves you. And how much you love her.'

Tears pricked her eyes, surprising her. It wasn't often that her emotions rose to the surface. She blinked them away, not quite prepared to let Nate *that* far in. Maybe when she knew him better. Maybe. 'So, what do I do about Audrey?' she asked.

'Just talk to her. Actually, no, that's not quite right. *Listen* to her.'

'Right.' It was good advice—and deceptively simple-sounding.

'It's more complicated than it sounds,' he added.

She smiled. 'I was just thinking that.'

'You know, when Jules was that age, that's when Steph and I—sorry, her mom and I—that's when we divorced. Will took it hard but Jules ... she was ... *devasted*. And compounding that, she and her long-term boyfriend broke up right after. It was a really shitty time for our family.' He paused and scratched his head, frowning a little.

'I'm sorry to hear that.'

'Thank you. And I know how hard your divorce must have been for you too.'

'I appreciate that. A lot of people like to pretend that they didn't hear about it in the news every day for months on end.'

'Well, there's that, yes, but there's also Audrey. You two are close—that must have been a really hard time for her, not knowing if she was going to lose the only parent who really cared about her.'

'How did you …?'

'Again, I won't pretend …' He was obviously alluding to the media shitstorm about Audrey's custody. She'd had no legal right to custody of Dieter's (then) thirteen-year-old daughter but she'd fought for it as hard as she could, throwing every resource, every connection into the midst. In the end, he'd won—just to spite her and to the (gross and heartless) detriment of Audrey's wellbeing. At least she'd been allowed visitation rights, a small win in the scheme of things.

'Excuse me, Sean,' said Chloe, appearing just behind the couch.

'Oh, hey, is everything okay?' Sean asked, turning around.

Chloe's face bore none of the brightness it had less than fifteen minutes before; in fact, she seemed to be seething with frustration—anger even. She gestured wildly behind her. 'Archer's upstairs trying to get hold of Harriet Cummings—that's Madison's agent—manager—whatever. *Wrangler* is probably more accurate.'

Sean blinked at her. 'So that was Madison on the phone just now?'

'Ah yep! Turns out you can block a person's phone number and you can redirect their emails straight to spam, but they can still Facetime you!' she said, getting more agitated by the second.

'Do you want to sit down?' Sean asked.

'Yes, please, sweetheart, come sit by me.' Nate moved down to the end of the couch and Chloe accepted their invitation, dropping onto it between them.

'So, what can I do to help?' asked Sean.

'Help?' Chloe seemed confused.

'Didn't you come in to ask me something?'

'Oh, right! Yes.' She shook her head, waving her hand in the direction of upstairs. 'But not about that crap. It's about Leilani.'

'Leilani?' Sean should have been relieved—Chloe might have some insight into what was going on with Leilani—but her words had the opposite effect and Sean began feeling the weight of her responsibilities piling up, responsibilities that were *way* out of her wheelhouse. People and emotions and relationships. If she were good at handling those things, she'd probably still be married to Dieter. *On second thought, maybe not. That man is an asshole*, she thought, giving herself a (small) break.

'Yeah,' continued Chloe. 'Look, I don't know her very well but when we got here, she was larger than life—exuberant, helpful, *bossy* even ... like me, but tenfold, you know? But now she's totally ... I don't know ... different—*flat*.'

'I have noticed that she doesn't seem herself.'

'Yeah, right? And it's just since you got here.' Sean typically appreciated a straight talker but Chloe's words stung. Personal relationships may not be her forte, but she cared about Leilani—deeply. She hated thinking that she was the reason the poor woman was upset.

'She thinks you're going to sell this place.'

'What?' Sean frowned with incredulity. 'I'm not. Why does she think that?'

'Look, it's something to do with you not coming here very often but that's all I know. You need to talk to her,' added Chloe, right as Sean leapt up and said, 'I need to talk to her.'

'Snap, you owe me a Coke,' Chloe mumbled without even a trace of humour. 'Okay,' she said, standing, 'back to Archer—see if he's had any luck with Harriet.'

Something twigged for Sean. 'You know, you're a lot like me,' she said to Chloe.

'I'm not sure what you mean.'

'You're a fixer,' said Sean.

'Oh, right. Yeah, that's me. Can't stand it when people are all, you know, discombobulated.'

Sean snorted a breathy laugh. 'Great word. With me, it's usually a business conundrum or some tech problem to solve. Still not great at the people stuff.'

'You'll only get better at it if you try,' replied Chloe.

Sean was sure Chloe hadn't meant to come off as condescending and her mouth twitched as she smothered the smile. 'Good advice—thanks.' Chloe seemed pleased, then left the room as hastily as she'd entered it. 'Nate, you good here on your own for a bit?'

'I'll be right here,' he said smiling. There was something particularly comforting about the way he'd said that—and that smile! As Sean made her way to the kitchen to reassure Leilani that she'd never sell—this was her forever home for as long as she wanted to stay—Sean felt the stirring of a long-forgotten feeling. Butterflies.

Chapter Thirty-Three

LUCY

Well, she'd told herself this would be a Christmas to remember!

Only she hadn't anticipated the (extremely) disappointing news about Chloe and Archer not returning to London. *Is it unfair that I feel this way?* she asked herself as she shot up the stairs, tears threatening. *Don't cry, Lucy, don't cry. You should be happy for Chloe, not sad for yourself.* She could hear Will hot on her heels but didn't stop until she was safely ensconced in their room. As soon as she crossed the threshold, she spun around and practically crashed into him, her arms wrapping tightly about his waist as he cocooned her in his. Despite trying to talk herself out of it, the tears came easily then and she boo-hooed into his chest for a good minute as he stroked her back and cooed reassurances.

Eventually, she pulled away, dropping her chin and sniffling loudly. 'Sorry,' she said, breaking free from his embrace and going into the bathroom to splash water on her face. As she patted it dry, Will waited in the doorway, his concern obvious.

'So you didn't expect this, huh?'

As Lucy shook her head in reply, she looked into her own eyes in the mirror above the vanity. Dare she tell Will the rest of it? That Chloe and Archer's news was simply the nail in her coffin of loneliness? *That's a bit maudlin, even for you, Lucy,* she chastised. No, it wouldn't do to wallow, and it certainly wouldn't do to ruin the rest of Christmas by confronting Will with her concerns about their relationship. Surely, if she pulled herself together, they could get their Christmas back on track? She hadn't even opened her present from Will yet.

She blew her nose as delicately as she could—it was always a little embarrassing to do that in front of someone, let alone *Will*—then donned a bright smile and turned to him. 'I'm just being silly is all. I feel better now. Should we go back downstairs?'

'Are you sure?' He was clearly unconvinced but Lucy didn't want to impact their (till then, perfect) Christmas any more than she already had.

'Absolutely,' she said, grinning even wider. 'See? All better.'

His eyebrows knitted together. 'Why do I get the feeling there's something you're not telling me?'

Uh-oh. She gulped, her smile falling away. 'Well, there *is* something.'

'What is it?'

'I'm …' she whispered, her heart racing. Will came closer, watching her intently. 'I'm … *desperate* to open your Christmas present to me,' she said, hurrying past him and heading to the door of the bedroom. 'Come on!' she called over her shoulder. She was relieved that he didn't press her—and that she'd been able to hold her tongue. Now she just needed to make things right with Chloe. But, when they entered the lounge, it was almost empty. Only Nate and Sean were left. 'Where are the others?' she asked.

'Hey, you two,' said Nate. 'Everyone's dispersed, I'm afraid. Just us old folk.' He and Sean seemed tickled by that.

'You're hardly old,' Lucy said.

'Ha!' he laughed. *Just like Jules*, Lucy thought. If it were possible, it endeared the lovely man to her even more.

'So, anyway …' he began, redirecting the conversation, '… Leilani's making Christmas dinner—I'm going to try and sneak in later, help out while she isn't looking.'

'Yeah, good luck with that,' teased Sean.

'I'm making headway there, believe me,' he retorted. 'And Audrey *was* in her bungalow, but Sean went to get her and now she's with Leilani. *And …?*'

'Archer and Chloe,' Sean prompted.

'Right, they're upstairs dealing with their thing—oh, that happened right as you left. It's something to do with Madison.'

'Madison Strumpet?' Lucy blurted. 'Sorry, of *course* it's her.' She expelled a frustrated groan. Poor Chloe. When was the whole Madison thing ever going to end?!

'Yep,' confirmed Nate. 'Sean's been filling me in on *that* whole situation—geez. And who else?' he asked Sean.

'And Jules and Matt are out by the pool,' Sean replied.

'Oh, right—forgot my own daughter.' He chuckled at himself. 'So, that's everybody. But more importantly, how are you, sweetheart?' he asked her. 'I get the sense that Chloe and Archer's news … well, it seemed like it may have stung a little.'

'It's all right—honestly, I'm very happy for Chloe. I know how much she's been missing Melbourne. It's just that everything's been a bit topsy-turvy over the past few days and I think I got a bit overwhelmed.'

'That's totally understandable,' said Sean. 'Nate said you didn't even know about the change of plans till you landed in Denver.'

'Er, no, I didn't.' Will shifted next to her and cleared his throat. 'It's all right, though, Will,' she said reaching for his hand.

'Did you two want to join us?' Sean asked, indicating the sofa opposite them. 'We're just finishing up the champagne, talking about this and that ...'

As Lucy properly took in the cosy scene—Nate and Sean holding half-empty glasses of champagne, how their bodies were angled towards each other, and *especially* the way they'd played off each other to explain the whereabouts of the others—she realised something. 'Actually, we just came in to get this,' she said, crossing to where they'd been sitting and picking up Will's gift. She caught his eye and as subtly as she could, jerked her head towards the glass door that led to the terrace.

'Oh, yeah,' said Will, picking up her cue, 'we're just gonna head out ... see what Jules and Matt are up to ... so, catch ya later.' With wide eyes, he turned towards Lucy and they beelined for the door. Only when it was closed behind them and they'd moved out of sight of Nate and Sean, did Lucy allow the giggle to break free. 'So, Sean and my dad ... is something going on there?'

'Oh, absolutely.'

'Hmm.'

'You're not upset about that, are you? I mean, your dad, he's such a lovely man and—'

'No, no, I mean, yeah, he is and no, I'm not upset about it. Except, if they ever get married then Audrey will be my stepsister.'

Lucy rolled her eyes. 'First of all, it may be jumping the gun to start planning a wedding—they only just met.'

'Yeah, okay, I'll give you that,' he replied.

'And second, technically, I don't think you'd be related to Audrey at all. She's *Sean's* stepdaughter—she wouldn't be your dad's. So, therefore, she wouldn't be your stepsister. Not officially, anyway—although, she and Sean are rather close so you might see a bit more of her than you'd like.'

'You're very cute when you're being logical, did you know that?'

'Cute?'

'Adorable.'

'Adorable? Really?'

'How about as sexy as hell?' he asked, his voice rumbling with desire. He stepped closer and Lucy bit her lower lip, her heart starting to race again but for a very different reason this time. What a rollercoaster of emotions, all in a matter of minutes! Will stopped his advances as a shadow of realisation crossed his face. He stepped back and disappointment coursed through her.

'What is it?' she asked.

'Just checking myself. You're upset and ...'

'And?'

'And here I am lusting after you. Not great timing—sorry 'bout that.'

'Now it's you who doesn't need to apologise.'

'Lucy ...' He huffed out a little sigh, his frown descending again.

'What, Will?' she said.

'You've sorta been up and down since ... well, since I broke the news about coming here. I mean, ten minutes ago you were crying and ... I'm just worried about you is all.'

Lucy felt the weight of everything churning inside her and dropped into the nearest chair. 'That's what the girls said the other day.'

'That they're worried about you?'

'The bit about being up and down. What I said in there—about everything feeling topsy-turvy ... well, that's true.'

'Wait, everything?' he prompted.

She fiddled with the ribbon that was wrapped around the small box in her lap. 'Well, not everything. Work's been good—mostly—though I'm not sure I'll ever get used to travelling all the bloody time.' Oops, that came out as far harsher than she'd meant it to.

Will knelt in front of her. 'You *could* think of it as a perk. It means we get to see each other.' *Argh*, Lucy screamed in her mind. *Why don't you come visit me?* She had hoped her Christmas present would have been enough of a hint to make him see how lopsided things were between them. For months, he'd been talking about the possibility of working with some British distillers and brewers, perhaps expanding his business into the UK. Based on that—and with more than a little self-interest—she'd secured the domain name for a UK-based division of his company: BUTIQ.co.uk.

He'd called it 'awesome' but why had she even bothered if he was so dim about everything?

'Hey.' He reached up and stroked her cheek with the back of his large, strong fingers. 'I love you, Lucy. You know that, right?'

Her eyes met his. She *knew* Will loved her—she'd never *really* doubted that, not deep down. But how did she tell him that it wasn't enough, that she wanted more from their relationship, without losing him? Simple. She wouldn't. She nodded her reply and he smiled. 'So, are you gonna open that?' he asked, indicating the box.

'Of course.' She concentrated on unwrapping the present in a way that would preserve the paper—it was just so pretty, with its tiny alpine cabins dotted about a snowy scene. Underneath was a small gold box and when she lifted the lid, she gasped. 'Oh, Will,' she whispered.

'Did you want to put it on? I can help,' he offered.

'Yes, please.' Will took the delicate gold chain out of the box, undid the clasp with his thumbnail, and attempted to secure it behind Lucy's neck, fumbling the first two times. Being this close to him, feeling the warmth radiating from his body and inhaling that special combination of smells that made up Will's scent, right down to the fabric softener he used, elicited the most wondrous feeling.

This was what it felt like to be loved by a man she adored *and* happened to fancy the pants off of. She needed to revel in this feeling, rather than focusing on what was lacking in their relationship. Because, if she really thought about it, it was just geography.

Will sat back on his haunches and smiled at her. 'It looks amazing,' he said.

She reached up for the charm that sat just below her collar bones, her fingertips tracing the contours of the beautiful doe. It was just like the one they'd seen the day they'd gone to the hunting cabin in the woods, the day that they'd made love for the first time.

'I love it,' she said. 'Thank you, Will.'

'That was one of the best days of my life,' he said quietly.

'One of?' she teased.

'Definitely top three,' he countered.

'Three?!'

'Okay, okay, top *two*. It's right up there with the day I skied my first triple black-diamond run without falling.'

'Oh, in that case, I can see why it's such a difficult decision for you.' He grinned at her. God, she adored that smile.

'It's gonna be okay, babe,' he said, his smile softening. Lucy wasn't sure exactly what he was referring to—perhaps the situation with Chloe and Archer—but whatever it was, she hoped he was right.

'Hey,' he said brightly, 'I have an idea.'

Chapter Thirty-Four

AUDREY

Audrey slipped into the kitchen via the external door and looked around. Seeing that Leilani was alone, she sighed with relief.

When Sean had knocked on her bungalow door a few minutes ago, urging her to come back to the main house, Audrey had said 'no'. 'Besides, no one cares if I'm there or not,' she'd added glumly, even if it was mostly her fault she wasn't welcome.

'That's not true,' Sean had replied. '*I* care and you know Leilani does.' At the mention of her 'mama', Audrey had softened. 'Why don't you head to the kitchen, see if she needs your help?' Sean had asked. They were the magic words and Audrey had felt her mood lift a little. Now, seeing Leilani in her element, elbow-deep in a large silver bowl and humming softly to herself, Audrey was glad she'd come.

'Hi. Can I help?' she asked.

Leilani turned around, her face lighting up as soon as she saw who it was. 'Hello, my little chick. I don't need any help but I'd love you to keep me company.'

Audrey pulled out a stool at the breakfast bar and climbed

onto it. A smoky aroma filled the air and when Leilani brought the bowl over, setting it opposite Audrey, she saw why. 'You're making kalua?! Oh my god—that's, like, totally my favourite!'

Leilani winked at her. 'It won't be *true* kalua because I'm cooking it on the barbecue, not in a pit, but I promise it will be delicious.'

'Well, yeah! So, what else is on the menu?'

Leilani nodded towards a piece of paper on the counter and Audrey spun it around so she could read it. 'Oh my god, this looks amazing,' she said, her eyes scanning the list. 'It's also a *lot*, Leilani.'

'It's a little bit of something for each person—some Hawaiian dishes, some English, some Australian, mashed potatoes and gravy for the Coloradans ... Everyone gets a taste of their Christmas.' She smiled proudly.

'You're so generous, Leilani.' Audrey felt a pang deep within—shame, embarrassment, something else she couldn't quite put her finger on ... Whatever it was, she didn't like it. But she didn't like a lot of things about herself lately.

Leilani waved her off with a smile. 'Just being Mama for my chicks.'

Audrey brushed aside her self-loathing and returned to the list. 'Hey, what's a pavlova? Is that some sort of side dish?'

'It's like a meringue. About this big,' she added, holding her hands ten inches apart. 'And we will decorate it with cream and fresh fruit.'

'Oh, wow. So, we're having pavlova *and* a steamed plum pudding for dessert? That's it, I'm helping.' She slid off the stool and crossed to the pantry where she took an apron off its hook and put it on, wrapping the tie twice around her waist and securing it with a bow. 'What's first?'

Leilani shook her head. 'You really don't need to. I can manage.'

'Leilani,' she said firmly, pointing at the handwritten menu, 'this is a lot for one person. *And* I want to do something to help make it up to—' She cut herself off, not quite ready to say aloud that she needed to make amends with the others.

She'd known it was wrong to flirt with Will—even on that first night. She'd seen him with his arm around Lucy before she'd interrupted dinner; she knew they were a couple. But he was hot and the youngest guy here and part of her wanted to prove that she could get any guy she wanted, now that she was single—*again*. But what she did at the pool last night … *Ugh! What the hell was I thinking*? Now Chloe and Jules hated her too. And Lucy … she'd been super snarky to Lucy that morning. She couldn't help it—Lucy being nice to her just made her feel worse about herself. *Why am I such a cow?* had been playing on a loop inside her head since last night.

As these thoughts tumbled through her mind, Leilani regarded her thoughtfully, her expression shifting towards sympathy, which somehow made Audrey feel worse. 'All right, little chick, you can help. How about you tackle the pavlova. Here's the recipe.' Leilani washed her hands, then scrolled on her iPad, propping it up in front of Audrey. 'You start by separating ten eggs. We just need the whites, so make sure there's no yolk in them at all.'

'Like, none?' Audrey asked, grateful for something to concentrate on besides her shitty behaviour.

'If you get *any* yolk in the mix—even just a little bit—it won't fluff up like it's supposed to.'

'Got it. So, I should probably separate each egg into a small bowl first, then add it to the mixing bowl, right?'

'Good idea, little chick!'

Audrey went back to the pantry and returned with a well-used KitchenAid. When she was a kid, she'd *loved* coming into the kitchen and seeing it on the benchtop. It meant Leilani was cooking up one of her treats—cookies and cakes mostly, but sometimes it was something a little more exotic. She'd always let Audrey help, adding a cup of this or that to the mix, often trusting her to crack the eggs or frost the cupcakes, and she always got to lick the bowl.

Flooded with happy memories, Audrey got to work. It had been so long since she'd baked anything, she couldn't even remember what it had been. There was just never any reason to bake in LA. Her friends were all super obsessed with their weight—don't eat carbs, go to spin fifty million times a week, do not even *look* at a cupcake or you'll get fat. Their self-punishing mantras were never-ending and there was no way she could show up at a friend's place with a plate of cupcakes or cookies. They'd be horrified. Not to mention that Bugs was always telling her she was fat—'chunky', he'd called her. *Shit*, she thought, *I don't want to think about that loser*.

She took a deep breath. 'Okay, Audrey,' she said to herself, 'what next?' Hopefully, concentrating on the recipe would also keep her mind off her shitty ex and his—gulp—scuzzy new girlfriend. Audrey blinked away the tears that filled her eyes and sniffled. *Why* had she looked at his Insta feed that morning? He was such an asshole. They only broke up, like, two minutes ago and he goes and posts a pic of him with *her*, mugging for the camera wearing stupid Santa hats—#mybaby #MerryChristmasBaby #newlove. *Give me a fricking break!*

'Everything okay over there?'

Audrey looked down to where Leilani was transferring the salted pork to a large roasting dish and covering it with foil. 'Bugs has a new girlfriend,' she said quietly. She looked back at the bowl of egg whites, realising that she'd accidentally allowed some yolk to taint the mix. 'Fuck. I can't do *anything* right.' This time when the tears came, her body shook with the sobs.

'Hey, little chick.' Leilani was beside her in an instant, and Audrey fell heavily into her arms, fully succumbing to the tears and allowing herself a good cry. What felt like minutes later, the sobs subsided and she stepped back, trying to calm her ragged breathing. 'Here.' Leilani handed over several tissues she'd retrieved from her pocket. 'They're clean.' Audrey nodded her thanks and blew her nose. 'Why don't you go splash some water on your face.'

She nodded again and headed to the powder room next door to the kitchen. When she looked at herself in the mirror above the sink, her skin was all blotchy and her eyes were puffy—she looked like crap. She ran the tap and splashed water on her face a few times, then patted it dry with a hand towel, then licked her lips and wiped under her eyes where her mascara had run. 'Don't be such a little bitch,' she whispered to herself—words she'd heard from Bugs so often she'd begun saying them to herself, checking herself whenever she was being weak or whiny or was asking too much.

There was a gentle knock at the door. 'Audrey? Are you okay?'

She shook her hair back and lifted her chin, then opened the door. Leilani took her hand and patted it between her own. 'Come on, I'll show you how to get the yolk out of the whites.' Audrey nodded, not trusting her own voice.

An hour later, she bobbed down in front of the oven and turned on the oven light. 'Hey, Leilani, look!'

Leilani joined her. 'Oh, wow. It looks just like the photo in the recipe.'

Audrey grinned at her. 'I know! Chloe and Matt are gonna love it.'

'So, we need to turn off the oven and leave it open a crack so it can cool down slowly.' Audrey turned the knob to 'off' and Leilani grabbed a wooden spoon out of the drawer and used its handle to prop open the oven door.

'How long will that take?'

'Oh, a long time—hours.'

'Okay.'

'You did a good job with the fruit too,' said Leilani, admiring the carefully cut up fruit Audrey had been working on. The pineapple was cut into thin slices, cored and edged with a cool pattern, the kiwis were cut into wedges—slivers, really—their fuzzy skin removed, and she'd painstakingly made each of the strawberries into a rose. 'I love your little roses!'

Audrey grinned. 'Thanks. I watched a video on YouTube. So, what's next?'

'You can get to work on those,' she said, nodding towards a huge bowl of potatoes. 'Peeled perfectly, no eyes, no blemishes. We're going to make the smoothest, silkiest mashed potatoes they've ever had.'

As Audrey ran the peeler over two dozen potatoes, inspecting each one as she went and cutting out any eyes or blemishes, it occurred to her that she liked this feeling—being helpful, especially the sense of accomplishment. She'd felt it the other day too, when she'd made all those Christmas stockings, each one a distinct design, and then had helped shop for stocking stuffers—or *fillers*, as Lucy called them. Whatever they were called, Chloe and Lucy seemed really happy with how the stockings had turned out and that's all that mattered.

Audrey felt another pang when she thought about Lucy. She seemed like a really nice person. And it wasn't like Audrey believed Will would ever leave Lucy for *her*! *Ha! As if!* Lucy was so pretty and so nice and she was … she was just a boring, ugly girl who didn't have a job and had no idea what the hell she wanted to do.

Something twigged in her mind and she reached for the menu, her eyes scanning the list. 'Hey, Leilani, which of these dishes is for the English people?'

'The plum pudding—that's on the stove—and the pigs in blankets and glazed carrots.'

Audrey scrunched her nose. 'Glazed carrots?'

Leilani arched an eyebrow at her. 'You know, people who didn't grow up eating poi make that same face.'

'I love poi!'

'Exactly.'

'Okay, so when I finish these potatoes, I'll make the glazed carrots—*and* the pigs in blankets.'

'Good girl,' said Leilani, winking. 'And thank you.'

'No problem.' Audrey just hoped that helping Leilani with the Christmas feast would be a good way to make it up to the others, *especially* Lucy.

Chapter Thirty-Five

CHLOE

C hloe caught Archer's eye as she entered the bedroom. 'Any luck?' she mouthed.

He shook his head. 'All right, George, thank you. And sorry to bother you with this so late—and on Christmas. Will do. And to you too.'

He ended the call, the hand holding his phone dropping by his side in defeat. Chloe knew that look. She'd only seen it a few times before—once when they'd failed to borrow the exact model of car that Eloise Capel had driven on a solo trip across Europe—and it pained her to see it now, especially on Christmas Day.

'Come sit,' she said, heading towards the bed. He followed sullenly and plopped down next to her. 'Look, since we discovered she was on Kauai, we haven't seen hide nor hair of her, to borrow one of your favourite expressions.' Usually Archer would find it amusing when she parroted him, but there wasn't even the hint of a smile at that. This was worse than she'd thought—or maybe he knew something she didn't. That would explain the unease she'd felt about him being forgetful (or

253

secretive). Maybe he *was* hiding something from her but, even if it was to protect her, he needed to spill. And now.

'Archer, what is it? What aren't you telling me?' she prodded gently. When his eyes met hers, she could only describe the look in them as panic, which elicited a hefty dose of her own. 'What?' she whispered, her stomach suddenly in knots.

'I think I need to speak to her,' he said, his gaze landing in his lap.

'Uh, no. That's not a good idea.' Not only wasn't it a good idea, it was far from what she'd imagined him saying.

'She'll never leave us alone,' he insisted.

'Maybe not—actually, if the past is anything to go by, *probably* not—but talking to her will just make it worse. It'll fuel the fire.' He sighed. She wasn't getting through to him. 'What did George say?'

'Happy Christmas.'

'Don't be obtuse. You know what I mean.'

'He said that he still hasn't got hold of Harriet but that there wasn't anything of note on Madison's feeds.'

'And she hasn't been blabbing about us to the media or anything?'

'No.'

'Right, so essentially nothing to report?' she asked rhetorically.

'Exactly.'

'In that case, there's nothing we can do. Well, there *is*.' He looked back at her, his eyes alive with curiosity. 'We can stop letting the spectre of Madison Bloody Strumpet loom over our relationship—stop giving her *any* power over us. It's been a *year* of this shit and I think we need to resign ourselves to the fact that she will always be there lurking in the background. At least till she's moved on to some other poor bastard.' He smiled at that, which encouraged Chloe to ask the next question. 'Is that all?'

'How do you mean?'

Chloe wracked her brain for when things had begun to feel 'off' with him, the chronology of events troubling her. Was it before or after they'd got the news about her being on Kauai that Archer had started acting odd? She might as well just come out with it.

'Is it just the Madison stuff?'

He blinked at her and she wasn't sure how to take that. They'd been together a year now, and once they'd got over the initial hurdles, she'd always felt secure in their relationship. How else would she have had the guts to quit her job and move across the world to start a whole new life?

But now …

'Yes,' he said, adopting a broad smile and giving her hand a reassuring. 'It's just the Madison matter. But you're right. We can't let it rule our lives. I mean, I thoroughly enjoyed our time alone yesterday,' he said, alluding to several hours of lovemaking while the others hiked to a waterfall, 'but we shouldn't sequester ourselves away because she happens to be on the same island!'

'Too bloody right! So, what did you have in mind?'

'I'm not sure yet. Some kind of day trip, an adventure. I'll have a think—'

'Noodle on it,' she interjected.

'Exactly. I'll noodle on it and plan something lovely for us. How does that sound?' he asked.

'Sounds great. Just, um …'

'What?'

'Just not, like, climbing a mountain or anything, okay? That's more Jules' thing, you know?'

'Oh, I know, my love. So, a not-too-adventurous adventure of some kind?' he asked, his eyes sparkling with mirth.

'Exactly!' She leant closer and kissed him. 'Thank you for getting me,' she added.

The mood between them shifted, as did Archer's gaze. 'You

really are the most extraordinary woman,' he said, his voice a raspy whisper.

Chloe's playfulness fell away as she slowly moved towards him and touched her lips again to his. He closed his eyes, so she did too, luxuriating in the exquisiteness of how his lips moved against hers, how his hand lightly caressed the small of her back shooting tingles up her spine, and, mostly, how it felt to be loved by this wonderful man.

It's all going to be okay, she thought as he gently laid her on the bed.

Jules

Jules was in her favourite spot on the property—leaning against the terrace railing near the pool where she could wistfully stare out at the bluest water she'd ever seen. Mexico, San Diego, the Mediterranean—they all paled in comparison. And, sure, she lived near the coast in Melbourne—just a couple of miles away—but that was Port Phillip Bay and it tended to be a murky greyish-blue, even on the sunniest days. 'Do you think there's any chance we can cut out of here today instead?' she asked Matt.

'I know you don't mean that,' he replied.

She tore her eyes away from the view. 'Don't I?'

Matt clasped her hand. 'No. You love your dad and Will. You love Chloe and Lucy ...'

'I love you more,' she said, her mind a half-second behind her mouth.

Matt tilted his head, his eyes narrowing and his mouth quirking. 'Do you now?'

'Yep, *you* are my favourite person,' she replied, speaking the truth. It might just make her stance on their living situation and her hope of putting him off—just for a year or so—a little less of a blow.

'I'll take that as a compliment.'

'It's the *highest* compliment. I don't know if you've worked this out yet but I don't like people much.'

He broke into a smile. 'Oh, I know that. People are constantly asking me why you don't like them.'

'Constantly, huh?'

'Pretty much daily.'

She smiled wryly to herself. 'So a no-go on cutting out of Christmas, huh?'

'What, and miss the movie marathon?'

'Ugh.'

He jostled her with his shoulder. 'You weren't this much of a Scrooge last Chrissy,' he said.

'There wasn't this much drama last Christmas,' she replied.

'Hang about. Are you forgetting that' —he counted off on his fingers— 'you left your luggage on the shuttle bus, they wouldn't give it to you without photo ID but your ID was in your bag, *and* it took *hours* for the people at the bus company to finally see sense?'

'Well, yeah, that was a bit dram—'

'Oh, I'm not done. *Then* there was the whole Ash and Davo thing, where we had to pretend it wasn't weird that we were all having Christmas together when they'd broken up six months before but "secretly"' —he did the air quotes— 'wanted to get back together. *And*,' he said, forefinger on his pinkie, 'I fell off a horse and had to go to hospital.'

'Oh, I definitely remember that part—you scared me half to death.'

'It was just a fall.'

'Into the path of a deadly snake!'

'Fair enough. So you were saying something about not much drama …'

'Okay, you win. There was a tonne of drama last Christmas. I just hate drama!' she added dramatically.

Matt cackled with laughter. 'Maybe it's you. Maybe you're a drama magnet.'

'Hey!'

'Jokes. Just jokes!'

'I'll "just jokes" you,' she said, digging into his side where he was ticklish.

'Stop! I'm sorry! I'm sorry,' he said, barely getting the words out.

'You will be.'

'Oh, is that right?' Jules giggled as Matt overpowered her, scooping her up in his arms and threatening to throw her in the pool. 'No, please don't. I'm wearing my good bra!'

He set her down, keeping her captured within his embrace. 'You're trouble, you are.'

'I am not. I'm a good girl—you can ask my dad,' she said, looping her arms around his waist.

'Oh, I am *not* having that conversation with your dad.'

'He likes you, you know.'

'Well, yeah, *hello*?' Matt held out his hands, his immodest expression making Jules laugh again.

'I like him too. And Will. Maybe next year, we should go to Colorado so I can meet the rest of your family.'

'You want to meet my mom?'

'For sure. And your stepdad and the famous Auntie Jackie.'

'You can go a little while longer without meeting Aunt Jackie. Besides, they live up in Seattle.'

'Detour? I love Seattle.'

'Mmm, maybe.'

'We could visit some wineries, make it partly a work trip … write it off on taxes …'

'Ha! Ulterior motive. I knew it.' He shrugged, unbothered by the allegation. Actually, it wasn't a bad idea. Maybe they could escape the dreary Melbourne winter and head to Colorado during the northern summer—and okay, yes, Seattle. Although, Seattle didn't really have a summer if her cousins' complaints were anything to go by. Briony, the eldest, used to beg to come down to Colorado when school finished—'to escape the grey skies,' she'd say.

'What's going on in there?'

'In my head?' she replied.

'Yep.'

'Just planning our trip to Colorado next summer—*northern summer*, I mean. And fair warning, we make crappy wine.'

'Yeah, you've said.'

'Good beer, though—Will can hook us up.'

'That's if he's even there.'

'Huh?'

'Aww, shit. I don't know if I was supposed to say anything. Just pretend like I haven't told you.'

'Haven't told me what? You're not making—'

'Hey, guys,' Will called out. *Uncanny timing, brother*, thought Jules.

'Don't say anything, *please*,' Matt whispered to her. 'Hey, you two, how's it going?' As Will and Lucy approached, Matt dropped his hands from Jules' waist and she turned to greet them, eyeing her brother curiously.

Why wouldn't he be in Colorado next summer? What the hell was going on and why hadn't he told *her*?

Lucy

'So?' asked Will. 'Good idea? Bad idea?'

'I love it,' Lucy replied. 'And you're right, if Chloe and Archer aren't coming back to London anytime soon, we should maximise our time together.'

'Great,' he said, leaping up.

'Wait,' Lucy said as she stood. 'Do you think it's rude to leave the others here?'

'Well, I'm guessing there's no way Leilani will want to come and my dad and Sean seem pretty … uh …'

'Right.' Lucy took a deep breath, dreading his response to the next question. 'And Audrey?' Will raised his eyebrows and cocked his head at her, making her giggle. 'I was just asking. It's the polite thing to do.'

'Yeah sure, but I don't think we should invite Audrey. Besides, this is about the six of us, not some misguided girl who keeps acting like a b—'

'You keep calling her a girl,' said Lucy, interrupting, 'but she's a grown-up.'

'That makes it worse. She'll be fine here with Leilani.' He paused, his gaze penetrating. 'You know, you're a truly good person,' he said gently.

'Hardly. If you only knew all the horrible things I think.'

'That's what makes you a good person. Most people have those kinds of thoughts—I sure do—but the difference between you and most people is that you would never act on them. You're kind.'

Lucy thought Will was overplaying how good she was, especially when she reminded herself of how curt she'd been to Audrey only a couple of nights ago—*and* how she'd reacted selfishly to Chloe and Archer moving to Melbourne. But she also knew she wouldn't convince him otherwise.

'Should we go find the others?' she asked, deflecting.

Will didn't answer right away and the machinations behind his eyes indicated that he wanted to say something else. He didn't though. 'Sure. Let's head out to the pool first—find Jules and Matt.'

They rounded the corner and the first thing Lucy noticed was how cosy they looked—*and* deep in conversation. Lucy stopped and was about to ask Will to hang back when he called out, 'Hey, guys,' interrupting them.

'Hey, you two, how's it going?' replied Matt.

Will turned and tugged at her hand. 'You coming, Luce?'

'Er, yes, of course.' They skirted the edge of the pool, joining the other couple, and Lucy wished they had hung back after all. Jules' face looked like thunder.

'Sorry to bother you,' Lucy said, wanting to smooth things over. It was (mostly) lovely all of them being here together, but she did understand Jules wanting time alone with her boyfriend.

Jules adopted an unconvincing smile, confirming Lucy's suspicions. 'What are you two up to?' she asked. 'Oh, and hey, Luce, are you okay?'

Lucy adopted a smile of her own, hers coming fairly easily in comparison with Jules' grimace. 'Much better now. We were just about to ask you—'

'Oh, yeah, the Christmas movies,' Jules interjected, not seeming particularly enthusiastic. It was a good thing Will had had a better idea than wasting such a pretty day sitting inside in the dark.

'Actually, we wanted to invite you to the beach,' Lucy said.

'The beach? Hell, yeah, I'm in,' said Matt. Lucy knew from Jules that Matt would *sleep* at the beach if he could. He was as keen on surfing as Will was but, unlike Will, wasn't landlocked most of the year so went all the time.

'What do you think, Jules?' asked Lucy.

'Are you sure you want to give up your Christmas movies to go to the beach?' she replied.

'Absolutely. We can watch those any time.'

'Yeah,' added Will, 'but how often are all six of us together? We thought we could ask Chloe and Archer and make an afternoon of it.'

'Hey, we could go back to that beach. You know, that one—'

'—with the awesome breakers?' finished Will.

'Yeah, that surf was unbelievable,' said Matt.

'Oh, for sure, man. Although, it's afternoon ...'

'Yeah. True, but worth a look, eh?'

Lucy watched the exchange with fascination, not fully understanding the shorthand between Will and Matt, but *loving* that they got along so well. She supposed they were almost like brothers-in-law, even though none of them were married—*yet*. She knew Jules wasn't keen on marriage but *she* wanted to get married one day. Hopefully it would be to Will. Perhaps they should live in the same country first. As these thoughts flew through her mind with lightning speed, she realised that Jules was poking her arm. She looked over and Jules was signalling towards their boyfriends. They'd now gone off on a whole tangent of surf talk, Lucy only understanding every third word.

'How long do you think they can go on like that?' stage-whispered Jules.

'Hey! I heard that,' Will said to his sister.

'You were meant to, surf geek,' taunted Jules.

'Yeah, you betcha I'm a surf geek. That's not an insult, you know?'

'I'll have to try harder next time,' retorted Jules drily.

'Okay, *okay*—geez, you two,' said Matt, raising his hands and standing between them. '*I'm* getting a flashback to your childhood and I wasn't even there!'

'So!' said Lucy, aiming to get their plans back on track, 'it's a yes to the beach! Excellent. So, we just need to round up Chloe and Archer and get ready.'

'So, uh ... who's gonna go knock on their door?' asked Jules.

Lucy laughed. 'You make it sound scary.'

'It's just ... well, you know ... they had that whole Madison thing— Hold on, that happened after you went upstairs.'

'Yeah, we know about that,' said Will. 'Dad filled us in.'

'Okay. But even so, they've been up there a *really* long time, *aaand* …' Jules said cryptically, drawing out the 'and'.

Lucy frowned at her, confused. 'Just finish a sentence, *please*, Jules,' she insisted. It was extremely frustrating being updated piecemeal like this.

'They're probably bonking,' supplied Matt, matter-of-factly.

Lucy's cheeks flamed and it had nothing to do with the midday sun bearing down on them. 'Right, I see.'

'Mmm-hmm. So, you can knock on their door if you like,' Jules said with a smirk.

'Perhaps we should just wait for them to come down,' Lucy replied, sensibly.

'Screw that, man,' said Will, 'we're wasting daylight. I'll go.' He turned and jogged away before the others could say anything.

Chapter Thirty-Six

CHLOE

'Turn it up, please. We can't hear it in the back,' she called to the front of the four-wheel-drive.

'How's that?' Archer shouted from the driver's seat.

It was *marginally* better. But with her and Jules squashed in the very back in the 'kiddie seats', the windows down because Will had insisted on 'fresh air', and listening to local radio, which cut out every time they neared another mountain (so every thirty seconds), Chloe could barely hear even hear it. Still, she knew Ed Sheeran's song by heart and filled in the missing bits in her head as she sang along.

Jules leant across, practically shouting in her ear to be heard above everything else. 'Do you know anything about Will?'

As Jules sat back, Chloe looked over, confused. 'Yeah, he's about six-three, he's thirty, and he's your brother,' she replied, hoping she was talking loud enough to be heard by Jules, but not the others.

'Smart ass.' Chloe shook her head and shrugged to indicate she had no idea what Jules was even talking about. Jules came closer again. 'Matt let it slip that Will might not be in Colorado this summer. You know anything about that?'

Chloe vaguely knew something about something but as far as she could tell, it was early days and there was nothing set in stone yet. And, even though Jules was one of her best friends, wasn't it better not to say anything till Will had figured it all out? 'Um, no, not really.'

'"Not really" as in you *do* know something?'

'"Not really" as in I'm not sure there's anything to tell. Why don't you ask Will?'

'I'll do that.' Jules sat back again, clearly ticked off, but Chloe just looked out the window and started singing to herself again.

'Holy shit, this beach is ...' Chloe mentally scrolled through several adjectives—beautiful, intense, scary-as-hell-and-there's-no-way-you're-ever-getting-me-in-that-water—before settling on, '... unbelievable.' And she meant it. It was a far cry from the wide white sandy beaches in LA with their volleyball nets and brightly painted lifeguard stands. This beach, its yellow sand surrounded by ragged black rocks, lush greenery, and trees, had no lifeguards, no *toilets* even, and was about as 'back to nature' as beaches came.

'Right?' asked Matt, his eyes focused on the sets of (huge and terrifying) waves crashing on the sand. 'She's a beauty,' he added, almost sighing.

'Are you really going surfing in that?' Lucy asked Will, panicked. 'Those waves are enormous!' Chloe was on Lucy's side, especially as she wasn't sure if Archer's surfing skills were on par with this place.

Will approached Lucy. 'It's fine, babe. I've surfed way bigger waves than these.' Lucy seemed even more horrified by that revelation. 'I'll be careful, I promise. And we'll stick to the breaks in the middle. Just there.' He extended one arm but Chloe didn't see much of a difference between those waves and the ones at the far right of the beach. Lucy looked to her for support but she felt helpless too.

'If you want to swim, you can head over there,' said Matt, pointing towards an inlet where a river met the ocean.

'Sounds good, hun,' replied Jules. She gave him a quick kiss before flicking a beach towel into the air and letting it float onto the sand. She climbed onto it and stretched out, tipping her head upwards and inhaling deeply. Right, so Jules was unconcerned—and that was her brother and her boyfriend going out there.

The guys were getting ready, stepping into their wetsuits—Archer's borrowed from the house—and waxing their boards, all with one eye on the water.

'So?' asked Chloe, approaching Archer. 'What do you think?'

He looked up from his surfboard, also borrowed, and grinned at her but the smile disappeared as soon as he saw her expression. 'Are you worried, darling?'

'A little.'

He smiled reassuringly. 'I'm probably not as good as Will or Matt, but I do know what I'm doing. Quite a bit of down time in Los Angeles, remember?' Yes, but Chloe hadn't known he was surfing waves like this! If she had, her concerns would have come up before. 'Besides,' he continued, 'it was ages ago that Keanu taught me how—*years*, in fact—and I've had lots of practice since then.' Chloe nodded, wishing away her unease. But it didn't budge and she peered up at him, her eyes pleading with him to be careful. 'I'll be careful, I promise,' he said, reading her thoughts like he did sometimes. He dropped a kiss onto her lips, then looked to the others. 'Ready?' he asked.

'Hell, yeah,' replied Will.

'Let's do it,' said Matt, and all three trotted down to the water, comically leapt through the breakers with their knees high, and landed on their boards, arms paddling.

'They'll be fine,' said Jules reassuringly.

Chloe looked over at Lucy, who was chewing on her lower lip, her hand pressed to her chest in that self-soothing way she used to stem an oncoming panic attack. Geez, she was in far worse shape than Chloe. 'It'll be okay, Luce,' Chloe said, the words allaying her own fears. 'Will's a good surfer and a strong swimmer.'

'Exactly,' agreed Jules.

Lucy nodded, her fear for Will (and likely the others) still evident on her face, but at least she stopped staring out at the surf and began busying herself with laying out her towel and settling in. Soon enough, the three of them were lying back, side by side, propped up on their elbows so they could watch the guys, and with Mariah's Christmas album playing softly on a portable speaker.

'So, what's the latest on Madison?' Lucy asked from the other side of Jules. Chloe figured she was only asking to keep her panic at bay.

'We're going with "no news is good news",' she replied.

'Is it?' asked Jules.

'I hope so,' said Chloe. It was all very well and good to tell Archer they needed to let it go, but that didn't mean she could turn off her worries like she was turning off a tap—*or* her frustration and anger and all the other emotions that seemed to pile up whenever that woman was in their lives, even peripherally.

'Well, that sounds sensible,' said Lucy. 'You can't keep hiding yourself away forever.'

'Especially when you're on vacation,' added Jules. 'That just gives her more power over you.'

'Exactly,' Lucy agreed.

'Hey, Luce?' Chloe sat up and looked over at her. 'I didn't

know about Archer's present, I promise. I was just as surprised as you were.'

Lucy

'I know. And you *must* be missing your family and your Melbourne friends. Please don't think I begrudge you going home. It's just—' Oops. She'd been about to say that missing Chloe ever since she'd moved away from London had only compounded her loneliness but she had yet to share her relationship woes with Jules.

'I get it,' said Chloe, coming to her rescue yet again.

Lucy stared out at the water, contemplating. It was time to trust Jules with her true feelings, she realised. It might turn out that Jules' first loyalty was to Will—and that would be fine, Lucy told herself, even if she was lying—but it was no use bottling it up any longer. She was struggling and something needed to change. It was also time to ease the burden that Chloe had borne alone for many months as the only person Lucy confided in.

'Jules?' Jules' gaze lingered on the surf a moment longer, then she turned towards Lucy with a slight smile. 'There's something I haven't told you—about me and Will.'

Jules pushed her palms into the sand and sat up taller. 'Is everything okay? I told him that he'd better be good to you—'

'No, no, nothing like that. He is—he's very good to me.'

'There's a "but".'

Lucy pressed her lips together and gathered her thoughts. How in all these months of fretting about it had she never planned what she'd say to Jules when the time came? She drew in a deep breath before beginning. 'I knew when Will and I first got together that we'd have to see each other long distance. I mean, we *all* knew that, didn't we? You fall in love with someone who lives across the world … that means a long-distance relationship. But then, Chloe, you and Archer were practically joined at the hip almost immediately and, Jules, you moved to Melbourne in April. You've had more than half the year with Matt. But with me and Will …'

Jules reached over and laid a hand on Lucy's leg, all the encouragement she needed to finish her thought. 'Well, it's been a little one-sided.'

'It's been totally one-sided, Luce,' Chloe added. 'You only ever see each other when *you* go to Colorado.' Jules turned to look at Chloe, then back at her, and Lucy expelled a slow breath as she tried—and failed—to soothe her churning stomach.

'I guess I hadn't given that any thought,' Jules said. 'What an asshole.'

'What?' Lucy screeched. Oh god, this was going poorly. 'Will's not— He's not an arsehole, not at all.'

Jules raised her hand. 'No, sorry, Luce. I meant that *I'm* the asshole.'

'Oh. Right. Well, I don't think you are one either. I just … it's been hard—*very* hard at times. I mean, sometimes it's months before we see each other again and … I'm … I'm lonely.'

'Oh, Luce, why didn't you say anything? It was dumb of me not to ask, but you could have told me.'

'I haven't wanted to bother you with it. I didn't want to put you in the middle.'

'Luce, you're my best friend.'

'*Co*-best friend,' Chloe reminded them.

'Seriously?' Jules threw over her shoulder. 'What are you? Five?'

'And a half!' Chloe stuck out her chin and blinked her large green eyes at them, breaking the tension a little and making Lucy smile, if only briefly.

'Anyway,' said Jules, turning back to Lucy, 'you could have told me. It's not like you two are fighting or anything—you're not going to put me in the middle just 'cause you're in a shitty situation.'

'Are you sure?'

'Think of it this way: Matt's one of Chloe's closest friends, and you and Archer have known each other since forever … the six of us, we're all intertwined. That doesn't mean we can't tell each other stuff.' She threw a look over her shoulder at Chloe.

'I told you, I don't know anything,' said Chloe.

'Know anything about what?' Lucy asked them.

'Nothing,' they said at the same time. Well, that was just confusing—*and* contradictory.

'So, back to you, Luce—'

'Just a moment. You just said that we can tell each other anything,' she said pointedly, pinning each of them with a stern frown, 'so what's this "nothing" that you're not telling me.'

'You know more than I do,' Jules said to Chloe, gesturing for her to go ahead.

'Hardly.'

'Jules?' Lucy asked.

Jules

Matt's voice was faint but loud enough to draw their attention and all three of them turned to watch him as he rode the crest of a near-perfect wave.

An out! thought Jules. Whatever Will's news was, she didn't know enough about it to spill to Lucy—she barely knew there was anything to tell. And ironically, she *didn't* want to get caught in the middle of this—whatever it was.

'Woo-hoo!' she bellowed at Matt, her hands cupped around her mouth. Even from the beach, she could see the white of his smile. He was grinning so broadly, she could almost make out his dimples too. She loved seeing him like this—he was like fun and freedom and good living personified.

On impulse, she got up and jogged down to the water's edge, striding into the white foam. 'Come on!' she called to the girls over her shoulder, her arms waving wildly. She turned back in time to catch the remnants of Matt's wave, clapping and woo-hooing as he wended his way to shore. 'That was awesome!' she exclaimed as he got closer.

He grinned, standing in the shallows and hooking his board under his arm, then came in for a kiss. 'This beach is intense, eh? Reminds me of Torquay.'

'Totally.'

He offered his board. 'You wanna ride?'

'Ha! Yeah, I don't think *this* is where I want to learn. Maybe St Kilda's more my speed,' she said, referring to a beach on the bay back in Melbourne.

'There's no surf in St Kilda!'

'Exactly.'

'Having fun?' Chloe was knee-deep in the water a little ways off.

'Totes ma goat. Just trying to get Jules to have a go.'

'Yeah, good luck with that,' teased Chloe.

'Hey! I like to go *in* the water …' Jules retorted. 'I just don't want to ride it on a piece of plastic.'

'Ouch, hun.' He tipped his head towards his board. 'She's *fibreglass*, not plastic.'

'Oh, brother,' said Jules, and Chloe and Matt shared a laugh at her expense.

'Okay, time to get back out there. Kiss?' Jules obliged, licking the saltwater from her lips as he turned, made his way through the small breakers, and paddled back out.

Jules waded closer to Chloe, and they were soon joined by

Lucy who held out a shell she'd found. 'It's pretty,' said Jules, glad Lucy wasn't going to press her on the Will thing.

'There are loads of them, right close to the water. I'm going to collect some more.'

Lucy wandered off, her head down as she hugged the water's edge and headed south along the beach while Jules and Chloe stayed put, their feet sinking into the sand as the water pulled at their shins, first in one direction, then the other. A few seconds later, Chloe shielded her eyes with her hand as she watched the waves and Jules followed her line of sight. Will was riding a huge wave, making it look easy to wind up and down its face. 'God, he's really good,' said Chloe.

'Yeah, you'd never know he only took it up a few years ago.'

'Natural athlete, I guess,' said Chloe. 'Oh, look, Archer's caught one.' She extended her arm and they both watched as Archer, who seemed a little less adventurous than Matt or her brother, rode a mid-sized wave further down the beach. He finished his run inelegantly by tumbling off his board into the foamy breakers, not far from where Lucy was.

'Well, he can't be great at everything, I guess,' Jules said with a laugh.

'Hey!' Chloe backhanded her lightly.

Lucy had waded in to meet Archer, reaching out for him when he stumbled and nearly falling in herself. Their laughter carried back to Jules and Chloe on the breeze. 'I really do feel like an asshole about the whole Lucy–Will thing, you know.'

'I know. I did try getting her to talk to you—'

'I should have asked.' She turned to Chloe. 'Do you think I should say something to Will?'

'I don't know that Lucy would like that. I think that's what she meant by not putting you in the middle.'

'Mmm, maybe. Oh!' she exclaimed, realising the connection. 'That must be it!'

'What must be what?' asked Chloe.

'Matt said something about Will not being around if we go to Colorado next summer.'

'Ohhh.'

'So, you thinking what I'm thinking?'

'Maybe?' Chloe posed it as a question.

'Why did you say, "Ohhh," if you have no idea what I'm talking about?'

'Oi, don't be so snippy.'

Jules bared her teeth in apology. 'Sorry.'

'It's okay. Anyway, it's just that I heard Will and Archer talking the other day. I think *that* was something about Will going to the UK.'

'For a visit?'

'That's the part I'm not sure about.' She shrugged. 'I wasn't really paying attention.'

'Why does Matt know, do you think?'

'*Jules*. I. Have. No. Idea.'

'Now who's being snippy?' Jules retorted.

'Look, I'll ask Archer. You ask Matt—'

'I did but he won't tell me.'

'Hey, here's a novel idea, why don't you ask your brother what's going on?'

'Yeah, maybe. I mean, he should have already told me.'

'And you're wondering why Lucy didn't want to tell you her thing,' mocked Chloe.

Something caught Jules' attention out of the corner of her eye. 'What was that?' she asked, squinting into the bushes that surrounded the sandy cove.

'What was what?' Chloe asked, looking in the same direction.

'I saw a glint or something.' She kept her eyes trained on where she'd seen it but there was nothing there now, just leaves rustling gently in the afternoon breeze. 'Huh, never mind. Seeing things, I guess.'

'Must be old age.'

'I'm one week older than you.'

'A lot can happen in a week,' Chloe quipped.

Lucy

'Hello, Mum. Hello, Dad!'

'Hello, love, and happy Boxing Day!' said her mum brightly.

'Yes, happy Boxing Day,' her dad added with a smile.

Lucy had thought that calling her parents would be the proverbial icing on the Christmas cake. But after a topsy-turvy day that had (mostly) come good by the end, missing their Christmas entirely just made her feel blue. She revisited her vow to herself. No matter what happened in the next three-hundred-and-sixty-four days, she was absolutely spending Christmas with them in Penham next year! On her own, if need be.

'So, tell us about your Hawaiian Christmas, Lucy,' prompted her mum.

'I'll say my goodbyes, love,' said her dad, his face already half out of frame.

'Oh right, bye, Dad!' She waved vigorously at the screen, and he returned the wave with a pained smile.

Her mum moved her face even closer to the screen. 'Just his morning constitutional, love,' she said.

'Oh!' Lucy shook her head, unable to stop the giggle that burst forth.

'Sorry, love, probably a bit TMI, as you used to say.'

'No, it's fine—it's something normal at least.'

'What's going on, Lucy?' her mum asked, staring at her intently.

'Shall I just give you the digest?'

'You can tell me however much you like, you know that. What's the place that you're staying at like?'

'Enormous.' Her mum giggled. 'And very beautiful. Actually, do you remember that resort we stayed at in Tenerife when I was about eight?'

'Goodness, you have a good memory—vaguely, love. Is it like that?'

'It has that feeling—tropical, luxurious …'

Her mum laughed again. 'I don't have clear memories of that place, but your judgement about the level of luxury *may* be a little off. We didn't have much money back then.'

'Oh, I suppose you're right,' she replied, simultaneously scouring her mind for mental pictures. 'In any case, it's lovely, if not a little too … *rich*, I think is the best word. I don't know that I could live here. It's certainly not very "homey".'

'But it's been good seeing everybody?'

'Absolutely. That's been the best part, of course.' She smiled broadly, then told her mum all about their afternoon at the beach.

'And how did the Christmas cake turn out?' her mum asked, inelegantly changing the subject.

'Sorry, Mum, I actually left it at Will's in all the rush.'

'Oh, well …' Her mum paused a moment, then waved it off. 'Not to worry. You'll have it when you get back to Colorado then. No doubt it will be extra tasty by then.'

Or all dried out by then, Lucy thought but dared not say aloud. She didn't want to make her mum feel bad—or to feel any worse about herself for it leaving it behind.

Will came into their room, weaving a little from that evening's festivities. Leilani had put on an *incredible* Christmas feast, a menu that included dishes from all their homelands, with some Hawaiian touches, which Lucy thought was especially considerate.

Lucy had loaded her plate with some of everything, but would easily declare the slow-roasted pork as her favourite. Just utterly divine—smoky, juicy, and so *flavourful*. She'd have asked Leilani for the recipe if it didn't have to be roasted for most of the day! As well as the menu, the other surprise had been Audrey. Leilani had ensured they all knew how much she'd contributed to the meal and if that (beautiful *and* delicious) pavlova was anything to go by, Audrey was quite the cook.

When Lucy had thanked her for contributing to the lovely meal—those glazed carrots were heavenly—Audrey had even *smiled*, then said, 'You're welcome. I'm really glad you enjoyed it.' It wasn't quite an apology but hopefully a turning point—they still had another week or so together.

'Hi!' Will whispered loudly. 'You still talking to your mom?'

'Yes, I am. Want to come and say hello?'

Will crossed the room, Lucy catching the shake of his head as though he was attempting to clear his foggy mine. 'Hi, Mrs Browning. Merry Christmas!'

Lucy didn't bother correcting him—Americans didn't celebrate Boxing Day—and neither did her mum. 'Happy Christmas to you, too, Will. And I've told you before, love, it's Susan.'

'Sorry—Susan.' They shared a smile.

'Lucy mentioned you've been to the beach today. Quite a departure from your usual Christmas activities, I imagine.'

'Oh, for sure. We went to this great surf beach.'

'Oh, are you learning to surf, Lucy?'

'Um, definitely not,' Lucy replied. 'I'm strictly a spectator. But the beach was lovely and I'll be bringing home lots of shells.'

'So, Will, I imagine that you'll be heading our way for Christmas next year?'

'Oh!' Will appeared to be caught off-guard. Lucy was too, for that matter.

'Mum, that's a whole year away! We're not sure what our plans are for Christmas.'

'Not to worry. You've got plenty of time to plan, of course. And you'd be most welcome, Will. We'd love to have you.'

'Uh, thanks Mrs— sorry, Susan.' He hooked his thumb in the direction of the en suite. 'I'm going to get ready for bed, but so nice talking to you.'

'And you, Will.'

Once Will had closed the door of the en suite, Lucy's smile fell away. '*Mum*, why did you say that?'

'Oh, love, I just hope you know that relationships should be … well, *equal*, is all.'

'I know that, Mum.' Of course she did and, as an accountant, Lucy had a deep-seated love of balance and all things that added up. But a relationship wasn't a scorecard where, if the tallies didn't match up, there was a problem.

Or was it? Bollocks! That's *exactly* what she'd been feeling all this time, the inequity of it all. Her romantic balance sheet wasn't balancing!

'Have I upset you, love? Oh, I have, haven't I?'

'No, it's all right, Mum. Just a big day is all—and I'm probably still a little jetlagged.'

'Well, if you're sure.'

Lucy forced a smile. 'Absolutely. I love you.'

'I love you too. Bye now.'

'Bye.'

Lucy hung up and laid the phone in her lap, expelling a loud breath. 'This is just going to keep bubbling to the surface, Lucy,' she said to herself. Resentment—for that's what it was—didn't dissolve if left alone; it compounded.

'Sorry, what was that?' asked Will as he emerged from the en suite.

'Nothing.' She smiled what she hoped was convincingly and went to get ready for bed.

Chapter Thirty-Seven

JULES

'Not *quite* what I had in mind,' Matt purred in her ear.

'I know! And to think, we were going to slum it.' When she looked back at Matt, her wayward ponytail whipped in the wind and smacked him in the face. 'Sorry,' she said with a laugh. She captured it and twisted it into a bun—far more manageable, especially for a ride on the bow of a silent yacht.

'I hate to admit it,' he said, 'but this is *far* better than what I had planned.'

'I *love* your present,' she reassured him.

'You love that we're gonna get some time by ourselves.'

'Yeah, true—best present ever.' They shared a smile.

Jules rested against Matt, keeping her knees soft to ride the rise and fall of the yacht, and inhaled deeply. 'God, I love the briny air,' she said, almost to herself.

'*I'm* blown away by the scenery,' he replied.

'Well, yeah, there's that too.'

'We wouldn't have got this if we'd hiked in.'

'No, I guess not.'

Last night, during that amazing Christmas dinner, Sean had

got wind of Matt and Jules' plan to hike in to Honopu Beach. She'd then *insisted* on organising a ride for them so they could 'maximise their time on the beach'. That made some sense, as there were only two ways onto that beach—a day's hike in or arrive by boat. They'd had a quick and silent conversation across the table—looks, nods, head tilts, and shrugs—before accepting. In Jules' mind it was a no-brainer—arriving by boat, they'd get two days on the beach, instead of one.

Little had they known that by her 'friend's boat' Sean meant a multi-million-dollar silent yacht—a sleek and luxurious vessel that ran entirely on solar power. Jules was mildly jealous that the others were spending the day aboard—and the night too, if they wanted. For some reason, Jock—the yacht's owner and captain, and (apparently) fellow billionaire—had leapt at the chance to schlep Sean and her friends around the day after Christmas.

And now they were 'all aboard' and making their way to the Nā Pali Coast, including Audrey—also on Sean's insistence. Jules was starting to see the power of Sean's gentle but targeted resolve, admiring how she got her way without eliciting resentment or conflict. Maybe Sean was secretly a Jedi.

'Oh, wow!' Jules exclaimed involuntarily. 'Matt, look!'

'I'm looking.'

The yacht slowed, drawing level with a pair of sandy coves, one much smaller than the other and both cutting into the steep mountains behind them. Jules had seen pictures of Honopu Beach but nothing could prepare her for its magnificence.

'It's like they were created by a giant with an ice cream scoop,' Matt said.

'Ha! Yeah, I can see that.' The sand of both coves was white and smooth, a vast contrast to the rising rock faces which were mottled with red and grey rock and dotted with patches of green before they rose steeply into the volcanic mountain range. The water close to the shore was vibrant aqua, white foam smashing against the base of the rock promontories either side of the coves, but gently lapping at the sand. The most incredible sight was the archway cut into the promontory between the two coves, carved by millions of years of water. It was so fricking beautiful, Jules got tears in her eyes.

And there was not another person on the beach. They'd have it completely to themselves.

'What do you reckon?' asked Matt.

She hugged him tightly, her gaze still fixed on the view. 'This is the best present I've ever gotten. Thank you.'

He grinned. 'We're not even there yet.'

'Doesn't matter,' she said quietly.

'Excuse me.' One of the crew members, a young Hawaiian guy dressed in crisp navy-coloured shorts and a polo shirt, was waiting to speak to them. Jules dropped her arms from around Matt and smiled at him as Matt turned around. 'Sorry, I didn't mean to interrupt …'

'Nah, it's all good, mate,' said Matt.

'We're preparing the tender now, so we'll be able to take you in about ten minutes. Just meet us at the stern when you're ready.' He smiled politely, then left.

Jules turned back to Matt and squealed with unbridled excitement, her shoulders rising to meet her ears.

'Wow, a squeal. Don't usually get those from you.'

'Well, you do, just not in public,' she quipped. Matt sniggered, then grabbed her hand and led her inside to get their bags.

Lucy

'Have an absolutely *brilliant* time!' Lucy said, waving vigorously at Jules and Matt, who were standing in the small boat below. The back of it was practically brimming with camping equipment—Lucy was sure that giant silver box was a stove—and she wondered if this is what Matt had in mind when he'd planned to take Jules camping. *Glamping*, more like.

The others said their goodbyes as well, then they raced towards shore, Jules' hair breaking free from its bun and flowing in a blonde stream behind her.

'We can moor here for a while,' said Jock, their captain. 'Swim off the boat, have some lunch. It's a great spot.' It *was* a lovely spot—and luxuriating on a yacht was a far better way to spend Boxing Day than watching the men surf (again)—but shouldn't they move further along first? It would hardly be romantic for Jules and Matt with a great hulking yacht moored just offshore and their friends within shouting distance. Archer seemed to be on the same wavelength.

'Do you think we should give them a little privacy?' he asked, cocking his head towards shore. 'Perhaps find somewhere else further along the coast?'

'Oh, yeah, great point. We'll head off as soon as Cory returns with the tender.' Poor Cory was going to be a while, as he'd have to help Jules and Matt unload it and cart the equipment up the beach. Jock disappeared inside the yacht, most likely to scout out another place to anchor, and the rest of their party dispersed, Audrey murmuring about changing into her bikini, leaving Lucy and Will alone at the stern.

Their skipper, who'd met them at the marina that morning, was an affable man, slight of build, lean and wiry, with a thick head of silver hair and a face that had seen more than its share of sunshine. It was incredibly generous of him to bring Jules and Matt to this beach—not to mention, hosting the rest of them for the day. She'd overheard Sean tell Chloe that he didn't have any family in Hawaii, so had leapt at the chance for some company.

It was sad to think of people alone during the holidays. If they hadn't all descended on Kauai, Leilani would have had a solo Christmas and, apparently, Jock was in a similar situation. Had she known a friend of Sean's was spending Christmas alone, she would have insisted on including him. Especially as he seemed so lovely. Lucy also felt for the crew, having to work on Boxing Day. That's why she'd insinuated herself into the galley to make tea and coffee for everybody as soon as they'd left the marina. One of the crewmembers had tried to shoo her out, but she'd insisted. She'd even helped clean up afterwards.

'Penny for your thoughts?' Will stepped closer, his strong hand finding the nape of her neck, his fingers then entwining in her hair and playing with her spiral curls. All else was forgotten for a moment—even the darker thoughts that had raised their (ugly) heads last night—and she sighed with pleasure. 'Actually, I'll give you a whole dollar for *those* thoughts,' he added.

She turned slightly, her eyes narrowing. 'Cheeky.'

'It's pretty here, huh?' he asked, turning to the view.

'It's absolutely beautiful,' she replied. Her eyes swept along the coastline, taking in the incredible colour of the water and the brilliant blue of the sky—especially how they contrasted against the vibrant greenery that covered the mountains like sheaths of velvet. Kauai was rather spectacular.

'Hey, there's something I've been wanting to talk to you about,' said Will. It was a total non sequitur and threw Lucy for a loop. *Not here and not now*, she thought (somewhat annoyed), even though she had no way of knowing what he wanted to say—just that from his tone, it was something important.

'What's that?' she asked, hoping she'd sounded unconcerned—*breezy*, even, like she didn't have a care in the world—while inside her stomach was spasming and her breathing had turned shallow and raspy.

'Hey, everyone! Get up here! Quick!' Chloe's gleeful shout from the bow of the yacht was a welcome interruption and Lucy rushed towards the sound without waiting to see if Will had followed. She arrived at the bow as the others emerged from the cabin and Chloe turned towards them, a broad smile on her face. 'Dolphins! Look! A whole pod!'

Lucy had never seen dolphins in real life before. Chloe and Jules had seen them on a sunset sail off the coast of Mexico once, but Lucy had been in the loo. By the time she'd arrived back on deck, they'd swum away.

She took a spot at the railing next to Chloe, her eyes scanning the water. 'Oh my goodness, *look*. There are so many!' she exclaimed. The pod of ten or twelve dolphins—it was hard to count them as they moved too fast—seemed to be playing, darting about under the water, then leaping into the air and spinning. Lucy laughed when two dolphins spun at once, like they'd rehearsed some kind of maritime ballet.

'Aren't they incredible?' Will asked, coming to stand behind her and slipping his arms around her waist.

'Amazing!' She craned her neck to kiss him with a quick smack, then turned back to the show. Everybody was on deck now, 'oohing' and 'ahhing', even Audrey, who Lucy noticed had changed into a teeny tiny bikini.

She focused back on the dolphins. 'Why do they spin like that?' she wondered aloud.

Jock, who stood at the railing next to her, explained. 'These are spinner dolphins.'

'Oh, perfectly named then,' she interjected.

'Absolutely. Supposedly they do that to communicate—some marine biologists say they're trying to shake parasites off their skin. *I* think they're just showing off.'

Lucy grinned at him then turned back to watch some more. 'They do look rather pleased with themselves.' Out of the corner of her eye, she noticed Audrey filming them with her phone. 'That will make a great reel for Instagram,' she said to the younger woman.

Audrey flicked her a glance and shrugged slightly. Lucy wasn't sure how to read that reaction. And she really didn't like being at odds with anybody, but perhaps Audrey *was* a lost cause, running hot and cold the way she did. *And why would I want to be friends with her anyway?* Lucy asked herself. Why indeed! Surely it wasn't expected to befriend the woman who had stripped naked in front of your boyfriend—on purpose! She needed to give herself permission to *not* make friends with Audrey, no matter how much it pained her, nor how encouraged she'd been by their exchange the night before at dinner.

'Do you think we can talk later?' asked Will. Although he *was* saving her from falling down the rabbit hole of self-rebuke and people pleasing, Lucy did not want to have a serious conversation on the yacht. First, it wasn't *that* large and how could they be assured of privacy? And second … her stomach lurched and it had nothing to do with the increasing ocean swell.

She patted his hands reassuringly. 'Of course,' she replied—just like the people pleaser she was.

Chloe

'Seriously, how cool was that?' Chloe and Archer were stretched out on side-by-side sun loungers, Chloe sipping ice water and keeping an eye out for more dolphins and Archer lying perfectly still with his eyes closed behind the dark lenses of his sunglasses.

Chloe didn't expect a response—he was probably meditating—but he did reply. 'Just wonderful, darling,' he said eventually in a very relaxed voice.

She was glad that he was (finally) relaxing. She couldn't actually remember the last time they'd lounged around together doing absolutely nothing. And sex didn't count—at least not the way they did it. She sniggered softly to herself.

'What's funny?' he said lazily.

'Nothing. I'm going to grab something to drink—something a

bit more "I'm on holidays and it's Boxing Day" than water. Want anything?'

'Mm-mm,' he replied.

Chloe stood, swinging her sarong around her and tying it in a knot above her boobs. She liked how her bikini showed off her curves but she was hardly going to strut around a stranger's yacht without covering up. She wasn't a twenty-something from LA (like Audrey).

Her eyes took a little time to adjust when she entered the cabin. *Cabin*—what an inadequate word to describe the palatial interior of the yacht. On this deck alone was an enormous galley where two crewmembers were cooking lunch, a salon that would easily seat fifteen people comfortably on those lux-looking couches, a dining table set for twelve, and an actual bar. She headed straight to it, happy to help herself, but Cory (the cute crewmember) appeared an instant later, asking, 'What can I get you?'

'Uh, I can get it myself. I know you're busy with lunch,' she said.

He shook his head. 'All part of the service.'

'In that case, I'd love a white wine. Anything you've got will be fine.' She had her preferences, of course—more of a Chardy than a Grigio girl—but, not expecting a huge choice on a *yacht*, she would take whatever was on offer.

Cory began rattling off choices and when he got to the fifth one, Chloe interrupted. 'Sorry, just … do you have, like, a full cellar on board or what?'

'Not *like* a full cellar—an actual cellar,' he replied with a charming smile. He peeked under the bar. 'Though I've only got … four bottles of white wine up here.'

'I'll have Chardonnay, thanks.'

'Coming right up.' Cory retrieved the bottle from the wine fridge, then placed a globe-shaped wine glass on the bar and poured.

'Oh, you've read my mind,' said Sean, joining them at the bar.

'Apparently, he's got a whole bunch of others if you don't want a Chardy.'

'A Chard— Oh, right. No, that's perfect.' To Cory, she said, 'I'll have what she's having,' then sat on a bar stool.

Since Sean was having her wine inside, Chloe climbed up onto the stool next to her, having to use the footrest to hoist herself up. Being petite had its perks but sometimes it was a pain in the bum. 'Thank you again for organising this,' she said to Sean.

'Oh, no problem. You know, this trip was so last-minute, I didn't get a chance to really plan anything. But Jock's a good guy and I'm really glad we were able to make today work.'

Cory slid two glasses across the bar with a smile. 'Thank you,' they said in tandem and with a nod, he returned to the galley.

'Cheers,' said Sean, holding up her glass.

'Cheers.' Chloe took a sip. 'Oh, that's good.'

'Mmm.'

'I haven't had a chance to talk to you since yesterday. How'd it go?'

'You mean with Leilani?'

'Yeah. I mean, she was a lot brighter at dinner last night and it seems like she's back to her usual cheery self today—sorry, I hardly know her. It's just from what I've noticed,' said Chloe.

'No, no, it's totally fine. And you were right. She was really scared that I'd sell and she'd lose her home. But I reassured her. I told her that she's got a place to live for as long as she needs it.'

'It's really lovely of you.'

Sean shook her head. 'Not so much lovely as ... well, it's gratitude, to be honest. During the divorce, this was where I holed up, here on Kauai. God, that was brutal. It nearly destroyed me. Dieter was a *total* asshole—dragging my name through the mud, lying about me, trying to steal my IP and claim it as his own. Just the absolute worst version of himself. I didn't even recognise the man I'd married.

'And there beside me the whole time was Leilani. Not so much as my confidante, though there were some particularly low times when she really looked after me, but she was just *there*. She created this *home*, this safe place for me to be … for me to be myself, you know? *And* Audrey. She was away at boarding school most of the time, but she came to stay when she could. And it was just the three of us. Our little family.'

'I could tell she was someone special the second I met her,' said Chloe.

'She is—she's the best. It pained me what you said yesterday. But that's on me. I haven't been here much lately and I haven't connected with her as often as I should. I'm going to be better at that.'

'New Year's Resolution?' Chloe asked with a smile.

'Can you believe we're just days from a brand-new year?'

'Nope, not at all. This time last year I'd only just met Archer and *so* much has happened since then.'

'Bit of a wild ride, huh?'

Chloe grinned. 'You have no idea. Oh … sorry, that was dumb. Of course *you* would have an idea. You're Sean Alessi.'

Sean shook her head. 'She's just a persona. A bit like Archer Tate. Really, I'm just Sean.'

'And he's just a guy called Alan from a small village in Oxfordshire.'

'Wait, *Alan*?'

'Oh shit, didn't you know that?'

'I didn't, but I won't say a word, I promise.'

'Chloe, darling.'

Sean looked over Chloe's shoulder then back at Chloe, placing her fingertip against her lips. 'Yes?' replied Chloe, spinning on her stool and flashing Archer a big smile.

'Do you know where Lucy got to?'

'Um, I think she's up on the fly bridge with Will. Why?'

He sighed heavily. 'It's this,' he said, holding out his phone. She took it, *seeing* what was on the screen but unable to parse it. 'I'm *so* sorry, my love. I've already got George onto it and I promise we'll fix it.'

'What is it?' asked Sean, looking over Chloe's shoulder. 'Oh, fuck. When was this?'

'Yesterday,' whispered Chloe, her breath having been knocked out of her. It was impossible to reconcile the words blaring from the screen with the photo of Lucy and Archer together in the surf:

ARCHER DUMPS CHLOE FOR MYSTERY REDHEAD

Chapter Thirty-Eight

LUCY

Lucy (literally) couldn't believe her eyes. She kept staring at Archer's phone screen, hoping that something would click into place and it would all start to make sense. 'But … *why*?' was all she managed to say after several (heavily pregnant) moments.

'They're paparazzi, Luce,' said Chloe. 'They don't need a reason. They just want to sell photos.'

'Chloe's right, I'm afraid. They're horrid people—*mongrels* without morals or empathy. As are the editors who publish this tripe.'

'But how did they even know where we were? Were they following us? Well, *you*?'

'It seems so, yes.' Archer and Chloe exchanged a loaded look.

'Oh! Was this Madison's doing, do you think?'

'Probably. She just won't leave us alone! And now's she's targeted you, Luce! Why can't she ju—'

'Darling, it's no use getting all riled up again.' Chloe blew out a raspberry—clearly exasperated—and plopped onto the nearest seat, her chin in her hands. 'I'm very, *very* sorry you've been dragged into this, Lucy,' Archer added.

'Me too,' added Chloe quietly. Lucy couldn't ever remember seeing her so defeated.

'It's not *your* fault,' she asserted. 'Neither of you need to apologise.'

'At least let us commiserate then,' Archer replied.

Lucy nodded. 'Right, of course. So, what happens now?'

'So, now,' said Archer, pocketing his phone, 'we hand over to George, my Publicity Manager. Actually, I've spoken to him already and he's preparing a statement that we'll issue—to *explain*.'

'Explain?'

'How it happened that you and I were on the beach together—and seemingly alone even though that's far from the truth.'

'Oh, I see. That makes sense.'

'Actually, we were also thinking …' said Chloe, perking up. 'What if we were to get a photo of the four of us together?'

'What do you mean? To publish?' asked Lucy. She didn't particularly like the sound of that. It was one thing to be friends with one of the most famous men in the world; it was another thing entirely to actively seek the public eye.

'Um, kind of—' Chloe began.

'It would only be for Instagram,' Archer interjected. 'We're proposing that we post a photograph of the four of us and caption it with something like "lifelong friends", "spending Christmas together", "Boxing Day fun"—something like that. What do you think?' What Lucy thought was that it didn't sound any better—Archer had several million followers on Instagram!

She looked up at Will to see what he thought of all this. 'I'm in, but it's your call, babe,' he said gently.

'Do you really think it will help?' she asked Archer.

'I do, yes.'

Lucy sighed. 'All right then. If it will help.'

'Excellent—and thank you. I'm so very sorry about all this.'

'I know.'

'Right, so …' Archer looked around the flybridge, then walked to the railing and peered over. 'Down on the stern, I think. With the coast in the background.' He looked to the others for approval.

'Come on,' said Chloe, leading the way downstairs, 'let's get our happy snap, send it to George, and hopefully, by then, it will be time for lunch! I'm starving!'

'That's the spirit, darling,' said Archer, following close behind.

'You know,' said Will, taking Lucy's hand, 'even though this whole situation sucks, there is *one* good thing to come of it.'

Lucy dropped her head to the side, her brow creased into a disbelieving frown. 'Oh, really? And what's that, I wonder?'

'You look awesome in that photo, babe.' Lucy tutted and made a move towards the stairs. 'No wait,' he said pulling her back to him. 'I'm serious. You look … I don't know … happy—free. *Alive* even.'

'Oh,' she replied, her posture softening. 'Well, I suppose there is that.'

'You're beautiful, Luce. If Archer wasn't with Chloe, he'd be *lucky* to have you. *I'm* lucky to have you,' he said, his voice nearing a whisper as he came in for a kiss. Lucy succumbed, sinking into it as Will's arms enveloped her.

'Oi, you two. Hurry up!' Chloe shouted from the deck below.

Lucy and Will broke their kiss with gentle laughter.

'Be right there, Little Miss Impatient!' Lucy shouted back.

Archer

'So, will that do the trick?' he asked George.

'Well, it definitely won't hurt,' George replied, his voice sounding tinny on the speakerphone. Archer met Chloe's eye and they shared a pallid smile. 'I'll get this out straight away. And,

Chloe, I'll tag your account as well. You should probably comment.'

'Okay, sure. No worries.'

'Er, Archer, could I speak with you privately before we end the call?'

Chloe made a face—surprise mingled with annoyance. 'Sorry, darling,' Archer mouthed.

'Bye, George,' she said, hastily leaving the cabin and closing the door behind her.

'Goodbye, Chloe!'

'She's gone.'

'Oh. Apologies for that. It's just … the proposal.'

Archer snatched up the phone and took it off speakerphone in case Chloe could hear them through the door. He raised it to his ear. 'It hasn't happened yet,' he hissed.

'So you're still planning it for New Year's Eve then?'

'Yes. Unless some other disaster befalls us. This has been a bit of a week,' he said, huffing out a sigh. 'Wait a moment, why are you bringing it up?'

'It's just … have you considered how it will look? You proposing to Chloe immediately after being caught with another woman?'

'But I haven't *been* caught with another woman.' He paused. 'I'm sorry, George. This isn't your fault and I shouldn't take it out on you.'

'Not at all. It's certainly within my purview to keep an eye on these things and I'm sorry if I've failed you in any way.'

'You haven't failed me, George. How could either of us have predicted this turn of events?'

'Mmm. You're right, I suppose.'

They were both quiet for a while, then Archer asked the question he didn't want to ask. 'Do you really think I should hold off on the proposal? Wait till all this blows over?'

'I don't *like* to think that, but, well, it's a consideration.'

'Right, I see.' There was a light tap at the door. 'I think Chloe wants me. I should go.'

'I'll keep you informed. And do ensure she comments on that post, won't you? It will go out in the next few minutes.'

'Will do.' They rang off and Archer crossed the cabin to open the door. 'You can come ba— Oh, sorry, I was expecting Chloe.'

'She's on the fly deck with the others,' replied Sean. 'One of the crew is mixing up a pitcher of margaritas.'

'I could use something a little stiffer than that.' He ran a hand through his hair. 'Don't suppose Jock would be willing to break out the good scotch.'

'Jock's a billionaire, Arch—all he has is the good stuff.' They shared a wry laugh. 'Look, before you go back out there, I just wanted to see if there's anything *I* can do.'

'Thank you for the offer. However, I'm not sure there's anything more we can do besides damage control—and George is already seeing to that.'

'Right.' Sean scrunched her nose. 'Sorry I can't be of any more help. I hate it when I can't offer a solution.'

'You being a good friend to me—and to Chloe—is enough, believe me.'

'She's pretty amazing, Archer.'

'I think so too, which is exactly why I'm planning to propose to her,' he whispered.

'You are?' she whispered back. 'Oh my god. That's fantastic, Archer! When?'

'New Year's Eve. Or at least that was the plan.'

'Why would that change?' she asked.

'George is concerned how it might look—in light of today's headline, that is.'

'Oh god, Arch, if I worried about everything that's been said about me, I'd wouldn't be able to get out of bed in the morning.'

He regarded her for a moment. 'You know what? You are absolutely right. Thank you. I shall stick to the plan.'

She grinned at him. 'Great, now what do you need from me?'

'From you?'

'To help with the proposal? Oh! You know who's great at organising things? Audrey!'

'Ah.'

'Look, I know she can be a little … uh …'

'Challenging?' he suggested.

'Yes, at times. She means well, though.'

'Does she really?'

Sean laughed. 'She's a good kid—at heart, anyway. I'm hoping I can help her turn things around this time. I've sort of dropped the ball in the last couple of years.'

'How so?'

'By being an absent parent. The reality is, Leilani and I are all she has when it comes to family. Dieter's just an ass—always will be—and Marika … I couldn't even tell you where in the world she is. I doubt Audrey could either.'

'Audrey is lucky to have you.'

'I just need to be a better mom to her. She's lost her way of late—in a way, I have too. That's the real reason I came to Kauai for Christmas—to spend time with Audrey, see if we can help each other out.'

He smiled at her encouragingly. 'Should we go and join the others? I think I *would* like a margarita after all.'

'Sure, let's go.' She left the cabin first and Archer followed. 'And I'm telling you,' she said softly over her shoulder, 'Audrey's got chops when it comes to this kind of thing.'

He hadn't exactly warmed to the girl, but Archer only had five days to finish planning the perfect proposal—including choreography for the dance. He might have no other option but to take Sean's word for it.

Chapter Thirty-Nine

JULES

'That's *got* to be everything,' Jules said, plonking onto a camping chair, exhausted.

Matt was rummaging around in one of the large chests that had been brought to shore on the tender. 'Yep, looks like it.'

'Come sit.' She patted the chair next to hers, both positioned so they could look out at the ocean.

'Before I do …' he said, disappearing into the enormous tent. She heard the small fridge door close and he reappeared holding two craft beers.

'Ahh, good idea.'

'Oops, hang about—not twist tops.' He disappeared again, returning with a bottle opener.

'Seriously?'

'They've obviously thought of everything.'

'Yeah, but who has this much camping gear just lying around waiting to be used?'

'Bazillionaires, I s'pose.'

'Mmm. It would take me a *month* to plan all this.'

'Oh, yeah, for sure. I mean, that's how long it took me.'

'You dork.' They grinned at each other, then she held out her bottle. 'To glamping it up.'

'To glamping it up.' They clinked bottle necks and sipped in silence for a while.

'Why do you think they're still out there?' Jules asked, eyeing the yacht. She'd figured that once the tender got back, they would have sailed off by now.

'Wait here.'

He disappeared back inside and Jules laughed. 'What are you coming back with now? A telescope?'

'Nah, just these.' He stepped through the tent flap and held out a pair of binoculars.

'Of *course*,' she said dryly, 'I never leave home without my binoculars.'

'Hey, if you don't want 'em …'

'No, gimme.' She took them, then set her bottle on the low table in front of them and raised the binoculars to her eyes, twisting the knobs until the image came into focus.

'What can you see?'

'They're all looking at something in Lucy's hand—a phone, I think.' She watched a little while longer. 'And now it looks like they're having an intense conversation—but it's mostly Archer and Lucy. Huh, that's weird.'

'Do you want to call them? There's a satellite phone.' Jules dropped the binoculars into her lap and stared at him. 'It's the last gadget, I promise.'

Jules shrugged. 'I suppose it makes sense. We should have a way to contact them in case of an emergency.'

'Yeah, exactly. So, what do ya reckon? Is this an emergency?'

'I meant, in case *we* have an emergency.'

'I know. Now who's the dork?'

'Ha!' Jules laughed. She went back to spying on her friends.

'Wait, now they're at the stern and Sean's taking a picture of them.'

'Of who?'

'Lucy, Will, Chloe, and Archer. Hmm. It must be okay, whatever it is.' She replaced the covers on the lenses and set the binoculars on the table, retrieving her beer and taking a sip.

'*Aaand*, they're on the move.' Matt waved, even though it was highly unlikely they could see him. The yacht disappeared around the northern promontory and Matt turned towards her. 'Alone at last.'

She grinned. 'I thought they'd never leave.'

Matt inhaled deeply, tipping his head to the midday sun, and Jules did the same. The air was briny, sure, but it also smelled earthy, *fresh*. She turned in her chair, looking away from the water at the lush greenery behind them, then through the natural archway. She knew there was a waterfall just on the other side but she couldn't see it from her current vantage point.

'What are you looking for?' he asked.

'That waterfall. It's supposed to be really pretty and it's just through there. Want to go check it out?' she asked.

'Maybe after—we can use it as nature's shower.'

'After what?' He waggled his eyebrows at her and she smiled. 'I've always wanted to do it on the beach but *you* have never been game.'

'That's because you only bring it up when there are dozens of people around,' she replied, dissolving into laughter.

He held his hands out wide. 'No one here now. Not a single soul.'

Jules bit her lip, instantly hungry for him. She placed her beer back on the table, then stood and pulled off her T-shirt. Matt's eyes widened before he broke into a slow smile. She slipped her shorts over her hips and shimmied till they fell on the sand, then she stepped out of them. Her eyes locked on his, she reached

SANDY BARKER

behind her to unclasp her bra, taking her time and enjoying Matt's gaze skimming the length of her body.

At the last second, just as her bra fell away, she covered herself with one arm. 'Hey, no fair!' Laughing she ran towards the water, her feet barely getting wet before he was upon her, grabbing her from behind and spinning her around. 'Oh no you don't. Where do you think you're going?' She collapsed against him, giggling as his lips nuzzled her neck.

She turned to face him. 'I'm staying right here,' she said, her voice thick with lust and he kissed her, his lips possessive and his kisses, his *touches*, lighting her up inside. She was exactly where she wanted to be.

———

'God, that was so refreshing.' Jules squeezed the excess water out of her hair, then ran her hands down her torso and limbs to sluice away the water clinging to her skin.

'We have towels,' teased Matt.

'The sunshine will dry me,' she replied, slipping into her flip-flops and making her way back to camp along the shaded path. Matt followed, a damp towel slung around his neck and the dry one over his arm. As her feet hit the soft sand, she glanced back at him, admiring how gorgeous he looked with his shiny black curls slicked back from his face. Actually, he was gorgeous when his curls were dry and framing his face too. He was gorgeous, period.

'Stop staring, you'll give me a complex,' he said, shaking his head. She turned back around, her eyes focusing on the horizon. It must be mid-afternoon by now—though it didn't really matter what the time was. They had the rest of today, all of tomorrow, and then the following morning before Jock would swing back to pick them up. Matt caught up and walked by her side.

'What do you reckon we have an early tea? Get a fire going, cook up some of the tuna that's in the fridge?'

'Oh god, yes, I'm *starving*. We sorta skipped lunch, huh?'

'For a good reason,' he said with a smile.

'A very good reason but we may have to bust out some snacks before dinner. I don't think I can make it that long—god, I've been *ravenous* since we got to Hawaii. I want to eat *all* the things.'

'Holiday mode, do you reckon?'

'Yeah, it must be.'

'Well, how 'bout you organise some nibblies and something to drink and I'll organise tea?'

'Deal.' When they got back to camp, they set about their assigned tasks. Matt began by digging a shallow firepit in the sand, then laying out the pre-cut logs and briquettes that had come with the camping equipment. Jules shook her head again in mild disbelief—if they'd hiked in, they would have had to forage in the scrub for kindling and dried wood. She supposed that glamping had its advantages—one of them being that you got to enjoy the perks of camping without all the labour.

She rooted around in the hamper and dug out some nuts and crackers, then chose a round of brie from the (ridiculous) selection of cheeses in the small fridge. There were two bottles of wine—a Shiraz in the hamper and a Chardonnay chilling—but beer felt more her speed and she opened two more bottles.

By the time she was setting out their snacks on the small table, the flames from the fire were a foot high. 'We'll let that burn hot for a while, then when it reduces to coals, I'll put the fish on. How does that sound?' he asked.

It seemed rhetorical, but she answered anyway. 'Sounds great. You gonna come hang out with me now?'

'For sure!' He settled into his chair and helped himself to cheese and crackers, then sat back munching. He took a pull from his beer.

'How's the serenity?' she asked, attempting an Aussie accent. She'd wanted to mimic the cast of *The Castle*, one of Matt's favourite movies, but when he started choking because he was coughing and laughing at the same time, she knew she'd 'made a dog's dinner of it', as he'd say.

'You okay?'

He nodded. 'Just ...' He coughed loudly again and she patted him hard between his shoulder blades. 'Thanks, I think I'm right. Sorry I messed up your moment.'

'Want me to say the line again?' she asked. 'I know it's your favourite.'

'Yeah, that and "Tell him he's dreamin'!"'

'How about, "What do you call this, love? Chicken. You could sell that in a shop!"' Matt began laughing so hard, he wasn't making any sound except for an intermittent wheeze. 'Are you laughing at the lines or my accent?'

'Both,' he managed before succumbing to more laughter.

'Figures,' she replied. 'You try to fit in, you try to assimilate ...'

His laughter subsided and the mood shifted when Matt picked up her hand. 'You do fit in, hun.' They shared a look, Matt's near-black eyes boring into hers. 'I love you, Jules,' he said quietly.

'I love you too.'

He watched her for a second, then leapt up, breaking the spell. 'Wait right here.'

She snorted. '*Please* say you're not bringing out another camping gadget! I thought you said that was everything.'

He reappeared by her side, one hand behind his back. 'Nothing to do with camping. It's just something I've been wanting to give you, but I've been waiting for the perfect time.' He held out his hand and in it was the velvet jewellery box. *Oh fuck*, she thought. When he hadn't given it to her yesterday, for Christmas, she'd pushed it to the back of her mind. *Now—here*—there was nothing to divert his attention. They were all alone, exactly as she'd wished for, and she had nowhere to hide.

'Open it,' he said, moving it closer to her.

'I already know what's in it,' she blurted.

'What?' He sounded surprised but she didn't dare look at him.

'I'm sorry, but I peeked already. I found it in your drawer back at the mansion.'

'Oh-kay.' Something about his tone made her look up but his expression made her wince. He met her eye. 'And?'

'And …' She breathed out through her nose, her brows kitting together.

'Right.' The tip of his tongue pressed against his top lip—his thinking face. 'So, I take it you're not happy about it.'

'It's a sweet gesture.'

'It's not a gesture, Jules, it's the key to my bloody house. *Our* house … if you'd just say yes.'

She stood, grabbing for his free hand but it was limp in hers and he wouldn't look her in the eye. 'Matt, please. You know I love you. I do. And I'm *in* love with you and I've never loved anyone this intensely before. I love *us* b—'

'But you don't want us to live together,' he replied acerbically.

'Maybe, just … just not yet. I mean, we practically spend every night together already.'

'It's not every night, Jules. It's a couple of nights a week, maybe three, sometimes four … but that's not what I want. I want us to be a family—you, me, and Dex.'

'I love that dog. You know I do.'

'That's great, Jules, but I want us to live together. I want us to share a home.'

'Can't we just keep things the way they are for a while?'

'Really? 'Cause you seem more than ready to move out of Ash's flat.'

'Exactly. I was thinking I'd get a place of my own. I've always had my own place—ever since I got out of college and—'

'So? Where do I factor into that?'

'What do you mean, where do you factor? I moved across the *world*, Matt.'

'You've always said that was for you, that you needed to shake up your life, do something different, live in a new place! You must have said that a dozen times.'

'I would never have chosen Melbourne if it weren't for you,' she said, looking at the sand, her voice barely audible. *Oh, wow.* Her truth had been there all along, only she hadn't wanted to admit it—not to Matt and certainly not to herself. If she'd admitted it, then she'd be vulnerable—open to getting hurt again. But the truth always had a way of coming out, didn't it? And now, here it was, staring her in the face.

'Sorry?' he said, his tone softening around its edges.

She tore her eyes from the sand and looked him straight in the eye. 'You're the reason I moved to Melbourne,' she said, her voice catching as tears slicked her eyes. 'I'm so sorry, Matt.' A fat tear slashed onto her face.

'Hey,' he said, stepping closer. He reached for the tops of her arms and held them loosely.

'I'm so, so sorry,' she repeated, her head shaking.

'What are you saying sorry for, Jules?'

He gulped then and she realised that he must be imagining the worst. She had to set him straight and took a steadying breath. 'No, no, not that—just … for not letting you in, I guess. You don't deserve that.'

'Oh, right, okay.' He breathed a ragged sigh—relief, she supposed.

'I do want us to be together, Matt.'

'Just not at the vineyard.'

'I don't know. This is a lot, you know?'

'You had to know this was coming, Jules—even before you snooped around my drawer.' It was just like him to lighten the mood and she paid his weak humour with a small smile.

'I guess. I've just ... Can you give me some time? To *really* think it through?' she asked, hopeful.

'Yeah, sure.'

'You mean it?'

'Yeah—'course.'

It was her turn to expel a sigh of relief and she fell into his arms, hugging him tightly as they swayed back and forth for a while. 'I reckon the fire's about ready. Should we tell the chef to put the fish on?'

'Ha!' she said, leaning back. She sniffled and ran the back of her hand under her nose.

'There're tissues in the tent.'

'Of course there are. It's like the Tardis in there.' She paused, her hands clasped loosely around his neck. 'I do love you.'

'I know.' He pecked her on the nose, then left to retrieve a box of tissues from the Tardis.

Chapter Forty

CHLOE

The minibus taking them home from the marina was going off. The driver, a good-natured, sixty-something surfer dude, was playing The Beach Boys at top volume and everyone was bopping in their seats and singing along, even Audrey, who was reading the lyrics from her phone. And Chloe, tiddly on margaritas, was delightedly sing-shouting from the back of the minibus, murdering one song after the other and not caring whose ears might be bleeding.

It had been an awesome afternoon—one of the most fun Boxing Days she'd ever had. Well, once they'd dealt with the 'Boxing Day Blip', as Archer had jokingly called it. But Chloe was happy to let all that fracas recede into the background, perhaps to be unpacked and examined another time. Or not. Either way, they had another week in Hawaii and she wanted to make the most of it. And that meant forgetting all about Madison (Bloody) Strumpet and her paparazzi goon squad.

'Little Deuce Coupe' began but Chloe didn't know enough of the words to sustain her special brand of singing, so she sat back against the seat, tapping one foot, and looked out the window.

God, Kauai was beautiful, especially at dusk. No wonder photographers called this time of day 'magic hour'.

When she and Archer had changed their Christmas plans, there was part of her that had been a little worried. Had her memories from that family trip all those years ago conflated with the sweeping shots of Hawaiian scenery she'd seen in movies like *Jumanji* and *Jurassic Park*? Was her idea of the island state little more than a fabrication of her imagination?

The simple answer was 'no'. There had been many times during their stay that a bend in the road revealed such epic scenery, it seemed almost unreal, like a CG rendering. Today was no exception and as she was on the land side of the minibus, rather than the ocean side, she became transfixed by how steeply the mountains rose and how majestic they were with their lush blankets of green.

'It seems to be working.' Chloe turned at the sound of Lucy's voice to find her standing in the aisle, gripping the seat in front with one hand and holding out her phone with the other.

Chloe took Lucy's phone, scrolling through the (already) hundreds of comments on the latest @ArcherTate (blue checkmark) Instagram post. Next, she backed out of Instagram and tapped on the Twitter icon. The hashtag #Tatims (the celebrity name they'd been lumped with nearly a year ago) was trending. As was #Archlo and #Charcher. *How do you even say that one?* Chloe hoped that neither of those two stuck.

'That all seems rather positive, darling, don't you think?' Archer asked, reading over her shoulder.

Chloe nodded her agreement and handed the phone back to Lucy. 'What do you think, Luce?' Lucy gathered her hair in one hand and draped it over her left shoulder, then twirled the ends. To the uninformed observer, this might have been a sign of confidence, but Chloe knew better.

'I'm not sure, to be honest. Do you think it'll be all right?' she asked, a smidge of concern in her brown eyes.

Chloe rushed to reassure her. 'Luce, I *promise*.' She looked at Archer. '*We* promise that this will all blow over soon. It always does,' she added, lying (a little) to her best friend.

'Absolutely,' agree Archer. 'And, Lucy, again, I'm so very sorry you've been caught up in this at all.' He reached up and clasped her forearm and Lucy appeared to relax.

'Thank you. It's just a little … er … strange is all—to be swept up in it, I mean.'

'I completely understand,' said Archer. 'At times, it's still strange for me too—for both of us.' He and Lucy swapped smiles, then Lucy returned to her seat next to Will. 'I meant that, you know,' he said to Chloe. 'That it will all blow over soon. But I feel awful that poor Lucy has been dragged into this.'

'I know you do.'

He kissed the side of her head and pulled her close. 'Thank you, my darling, for understanding.'

Chloe had just nestled back into her seat, one hand resting on Archer's thigh in reassurance, when Sean bellowed, 'Archer?' from the front of the minibus. 'You're gonna wanna see this.'

Archer shot Chloe a baffled look, then carefully made his way down the aisle. 'Whoa,' said the driver, as he pulled into the driveway. He flipped a switch on the dash and the music stopped abruptly, throwing the inside of the minibus into an eerie silence.

'Park up but keep the door shut,' Sean ordered, her voice low, and her gaze fixed out the windscreen.

'You got it, man.'

306

Archer

Archer *should* have been mentally prepared but as he surveyed the scene outside Sean's property, it was almost unimaginable. All he could manage was to utter, 'Oh, god.'

'What do you want me to do?' asked Sean.

It took him a moment to respond, such was the impact of the tableau outside the wrought-iron gate. He hadn't seen this many paparazzi in one place since … he couldn't remember when.

'I actually don't know.'

'Holy shit.' Chloe was standing behind him in the aisle, her head poking out around him and her eyes fixed on the melee outside the bus. As the minibus came to a complete stop, the swarm of paparazzi surrounded them, angling for the best photograph.

Archer looked at Chloe, then Sean. 'I really don't know what to do here,' he said, feeling more helpless than he'd ever felt before. Perhaps they should just drive away? But no doubt the bastards would wait it out and it wasn't like they could drive around indefinitely.

'Archer, is that your new girlfriend?' The deep voice, muffled by the bus windows, had a knock-on effect and the others joined in, questions and accusations flying. Lucy emitted a shriek and when Archer turned around, Will was attempting to shield her from the cameras.

'Fuck,' said Archer, his palm rubbing his forehead. 'Fuck, fuck, fuck.' It wasn't like him to swear but sometimes only the mouthfeel of a good swear word could truly express what you were feeling. He'd only even been ambushed like this a couple of times before; typically, the paparazzi were inconspicuous, like when they'd capture the photograph of him and Lucy on the beach. This? This was … 'Now what?' he asked helplessly.

'I'll go,' said Chloe and Sean at once. They eyed each other for a moment, then broke into matching smiles.

'So what, we owe each other another Coke?' quipped Chloe. *How can she be so calm and collected?* Archer wondered—especially since he was very close to losing his mind.

'How about we both go?' Sean asked Chloe.

'Fuck it, I'm game. S'cuse me, babe.'

Archer was reluctant to let Chloe leave the safety of the minibus. But she was her own woman and Sean would be there to back her up.

On their signal, the driver opened the door and Chloe and Sean stepped off the bus, Archer lingering in the doorway and blinking at the bright flashes of light. Was he *really* sending his girlfriend—and hopefully, very soon, his wife—into battle for him? He felt ill.

'Excuse me!' shouted Sean. 'You're on private property and you're going to have to leave.' There was a beat of silence, then a roar of raucous laughter.

'Good luck with that, honey,' taunted one of the photographers.

'Chloe! Chloe! How do you feel about Archer cheating on you?' The question came from a wiry man with slicked back hair as he shoved a microphone under Chloe's chin. Several others followed suit as Archer tried—and failed—to get her attention. *Never feed the beast*, he thought, remembering what George had told him many times before. But George wasn't there—they'd have to deal with this situation themselves.

Chloe laughed as though she didn't have a care in the world. 'If you're referring to that photo of him with at the beach one of my best friends, then you're barking up the wrong tree.'

'Woof, woof!' barked one of the paparazzi.

'Hilarious. You guys are wasting your time. There's nothing to see here—just some friends spending the holidays together. That's it. Surely, you've got better places to be?' Chloe shouted above the fray.

'How long has your best friend been screwing your boyfriend?' shouted someone from the back of the pack.

'Yeah! Have you confronted her yet?'

'Is that her hiding in the bus?'

'Archer! Let us meet your new girlfriend!'

'Oh, for fuck's sake!' Chloe said under her breath. She turned to Archer and rolled her eyes, exasperated.

'Can I?' he asked her, signalling that he wanted to swap places with her.

'Be my guest—see if *you* can shut the idiots up,' she replied, stepping aside.

'Police are on their way,' Sean said to him, her voice low.

Archer nodded tersely, then steeled himself to face the unfriendly crowd. He held up one hand and they quietened, shouted questions giving way to low murmurs.

'As Chloe has stated—and as we posted to Instagram earlier today—there is absolutely nothing going on between me and our friend, Lucy.' *Bollocks*. He realised his mistake too late and an instant later the questions came fast and thick.

'Is that the redhead's name?'

'What's her last name?'

'How long have you known her?'

'Have you and Chloe split amicably?'

'That's enough!' Archer shouted. This time, there was complete silence. 'I shall only say this once more. I am not in a relationship with anyone but Chloe Sims. I love Chloe. I have never cheated on her—and never will. Our relationship is as rock solid as ever.'

'Ha! Spoken like a true cheater!' called out an anonymous voice.

'I am not a cheater. In fact, I'm planning to propose, for god's sake!' Archer had never been this angry before but nevertheless, he'd let his emotions best him. And now Chloe—and soon, everyone else in the world—knew about the proposal.

Chloe

'What the …?' Several things happened in quick succession, each competing for Chloe's attention: sirens wailed, growing louder, then stopping abruptly as three police cars pulled up behind them; uniformed officers piled out of the police cars, shouting and pinning the paparazzi with powerful beams from their torches; the paparazzi scurried, dispersing like giant ants during a summer downpour; and Archer stood at the bottom of the minibus stairs, head in his hands and shaking it from side to side.

Had he really just announced to the paparazzi that he was going to propose?

Nate rushed past her and stepped off the minibus, pulling a shellshocked Archer aside and leaning in close to talk to him. Matt and Will followed and the four men formed a huddle as Chloe watched numbly from the front seat of the minibus.

'You've got to tell her, Audrey!' implored Jules from the back of the minibus. Shaken from her muddled thoughts, Chloe spun around to find Jules, Lucy, and Audrey looking her way.

'Tell me what?' she asked.

Audrey hesitated, grimacing at Lucy who shooed her encouragingly, then made her way up the short aisle, stopping in front of Chloe and Sean. 'What's up, peanut?' asked Sean. Just like Leilani's nickname for Audrey, 'little chick', 'peanut' didn't suit her either.

'Um…' she began. She bit her lip. 'I think it might be my fault they were here.'

Chloe could tell it had pained Audrey to admit that and, ordinarily, she'd give her kudos for coming forward but there was something more pressing. 'What did you do?' she asked warily.

Audrey's eyes widened, then flew back and forth between Chloe and Sean. 'It's okay, Audrey, you can tell us,' Sean prodded.

'It's just that ... Madison DMed me—the day before yesterday—and I ... I mean, I thought it was *cool*. I mean, she's *Madison Strumpet* ... And I—'

'You told her you were with Archer,' interjected Chloe. She couldn't listen to the girl stumble over her words for one more second *or* hear Madison's name again.

'She knew—she already knew that part. I *swear*.'

How? Chloe wondered. 'Even so, you should have blocked her,' she said to Audrey.

'I *know*, I'm sorry.'

'It's okay, peanut. We're fixing it, okay?'

Audrey nodded at Sean, now on the verge of tears, and Chloe reached over to squeeze her arm. 'It's okay.' It wasn't but she didn't feel like piling on—Audrey clearly had stuff going on and was already beating herself up. 'Thanks for telling us.'

Audrey slunk back to her seat at the rear of the bus. 'Well, that explains a lot,' said Sean.

'Really? Because I'm still stumped. How did Madison make the connection between Audrey and Archer? And more to the point, how did she know we were here?'

'Because she's wily,' Sean stated simply. 'I have no doubt she pays people to keep tabs on Archer *and* she knows that we're close. As soon as she found out Archer was heading to Kauai ... well, she would have two and two together—'

'And got four,' finished Chloe. If that were true, Madison was smarter than Chloe had given her credit for. Chloe mentally counted backwards along their timeline in Kauai. Madison *had* arrived after them. Chloe didn't follow Audrey *or* Madison on Insta—why would she?—so she had no idea what clues she'd used to find out where Archer would be over Christmas. Maybe Sean was right about the 'keeping tabs' part. Or worse, she still had a spy in Archer's team. Though George had assured them he'd cleaned house after that incident at the Ritz last year.

'Ms Alessi?' One of the officers, a man in his mid-forties with silver sideburns peeking out from under his hat, leant into the minibus.

'Hi, yes.' Sean stood and looked down at him from the top of the stairs.

'We've cleared them off and checked the perimeter. All clear.'

'Thank you.'

'One of cars will stay here overnight—keep an eye on things.'

'Are you sure? You don't—'

He raised a hand to interrupt her. 'Ma'am, please.'

Sean acquiesced. 'I'll be sure to send out some coffee and something to eat.'

'That's very kind.'

They exchanged a smile, he touched the brim of his hat and, with a nod, he left, issuing orders in his wake. Sean turned back to the rest of us. 'Well, I guess the excitement's over. We can head inside now.' Only for Chloe, the excitement wasn't over. Archer had told the paparazzi that he planned to propose. So, now what?

Outside, the gate started to roll back and Leilani ran towards them. 'Ms Sean, Ms Sean …' Sean stepped off the bus to meet her and the others piled out. As Chloe followed, she caught Nate squeezing Archer's shoulder, then he, Matt, and Will turned to walk up the driveway. Excited chatter, punctuated with 'oh my god' and 'I can't believe that', filled the night air.

Archer looked at her sheepishly and was just about to say something when Sean spun around and called out from the front of the pack. 'Hey, Archer?'

'Yes?'

'Tip the driver, will you. And *well*.'

Archer chortled good-naturedly as he dug into his pocket for his money clip. It was a welcome sound to Chloe who'd been worried he would self-flagellate for hours to come. He peeled off two hundred-dollar notes, stepped back onto the minibus, and pressed them into the driver's hand. 'Thank you. Sorry it was such a dramatic end to the night.'

'Oh, no worries, dude. It's the highlight of my week so far.'

Archer laughed and Chloe joined in, relieved that they could both find humour in the situation—and so soon afterwards. God, what a bizarro life they had. 'Thank you,' said Archer to the driver. 'And have a good night.'

'Drive safe,' Chloe called, as Archer joined her. They watched him drive away and, with the others already inside, they were finally alone.

'I really am very sorry,' he said, turning to her and taking both her hands in his.

'It's not your fault. Madison was clearly behind all this—she's been in contact with Audrey and—'

'No. Well, yes, but I mean about blurting out that I'm proposing. Believe me, that's not at *all* how I wanted to ask you.'

'Well, technically, you *didn't* ask me.'

'Sorry?'

She lifted her chin, and blinked at him, her lips disappearing between her teeth.

He grinned. 'You're absolutely right.' She returned the smile. 'God, I love you so much.' Archer dipped his head and captured Chloe's lips in a soft, sweet kiss.

'I love you too,' she said when the kiss ended. 'And I can't wait for my proposal!' At that, she ran up the driveway laughing, Archer close on her heels.

Chapter Forty-One

LUCY

'I am *beat*.' Will fell face first onto the enormous bed, kicking his shoes off, and they landed on the carpeted floor with dual thuds. 'Can we just stay in here tonight? In the room?' he asked, his voice muffled by a pillow.

Lucy giggled and headed towards the en suite, pausing at the doorway. 'I don't think there's anything planned. I suppose we could help ourselves to some Christmas leftovers then pop back up here for a quiet night, just the two of us.'

Will rolled over and propped himself up on one elbow, flashing his perfectly straight teeth. 'I knew there was a reason I loved you.'

'Only one?' she quipped. 'Hmm,' she added, pretending to be peeved. She went into the en suite and closed the door on Will's low rumble of a laugh. 'What a day,' she said to herself in the mirror. She'd done her best to keep out of the sun but the smattering of freckles that decorated her nose now had a pinkish background. 'Bollocks.' She turned on the cold tap and splashed some water on her face, then patted it dry and applied some moisturiser. Hopefully, by tomorrow the sunburn would have subsided. At least it didn't smart too much.

But her long curls bore the full brunt of a day spent out on the sea—beyond windswept, they were a mass of tangles and frizz. Not for the first time, her hair reminded her of Merida from *Brave*—only today it was a thousand times worse. Was there such a thing as hurricane-swept hair? If she'd ever wanted dreadlocks, now would be the time to start! She ran the tap again, wetting her fingers and trying to drag them through her mane to tame it.

'Ow.' It was no use. She wouldn't get anything through these locks till her hair was saturated with both water and conditioner. She eyed the shower but realised she was too tired even for that, then scooped up her hair, twisted it into an enormous bun and secured it with a scrunchie. Chloe had teased her about wearing scrunchies once. 'It's not 1995,' she'd said. But Chloe had a pin-straight, shoulder-length bob so she could be quiet.

'What are you doing in there?' she heard through the door.

'Mind your own business!' she yelled back. Wonderful. Will would probably think that meant she was pooping, but Lucy was too tired to care about that either. She took a final look in the mirror, assessing herself as presentable, and opened the door.

Will was still propped up on his elbow, only now he was shirtless and wearing a Cheshire cat grin. Lucy paused in the doorway. 'Your shirt's missing,' she said.

'Some guy came in and stole it.'

She slowly crossed the room, her eyes fixed on his. 'Some guy, you say?'

'Uh-huh.' He swung his legs around and sat on the edge of the bed, reaching for her. 'A big, mean, ugly, scary guy. I gave it to him to save you.'

'Save me?' When she got to the bed, he captured her hand and pulled her closer.

'Yep. He wanted this.' Will started unbuttoning what she was wearing from the top button.

'He wanted your mum's beach coverup?'

He stopped with one button half out of its buttonhole. 'Luce, please?'

'Sorry. It's very sexy. Keep going.' He reached for the next button but dropped his hands by his side. 'Did I kill the moment?' she asked.

'A little.'

She used her knee to press his thighs apart then moved closer to him. Reaching down to cup his face between her hands, she moved closer till her face was only a couple of inches from his. 'Sorry, you sexy, sexy man, you,' she whispered. She pressed her lips to his. The kiss began slowly, his full firm lips moving against hers and his hands coming to rest just above her hips, pulling her into him. Then he stood, their lips still connected and her chin lifted as he towered over her. In one swift movement, he hooked his arm around her waist, lifted her from the floor, spun her around and, bracing himself with his other arm, gently lowered her onto the bed—all while they kissed. Lucy gasped, inhaling the taste of him. His lips moved more fervently against hers, one hand roving her body and igniting every sense.

Everything else was forgotten—the accusatory headline, trying to make the most of the day when she'd been blindsided, the paparazzi at the front gate ... all of the day's woes and worries flew from her head and she existed only there and then with the man she loved.

'Oh, and some of this.' Will was passing containers of leftovers to her from the fridge.

'Have you left anything in there for the others?' she inquired cheekily. He gave her the side-eye from his vantage point. 'Apologies, my love. Please continue.' *He can do anything he likes after what he did to me upstairs,* she thought. *Lucy, you wanton woman!* She giggled to herself.

'Miss Lucy! I can help you.' Leilani had surreptitiously appeared in the kitchen and now Lucy felt like a child caught raiding the biscuit tin.

'Um, Will,' she said, prodding him in the bum. He turned around, his hands laden with even more food.

'Hey, Leilani. I hope you don't mind but we're just having some leftovers for dinner.' He froze right before he put them down. 'Oh, sorry, did you have something else in mind?'

'No, no, this is exactly what I had planned. Ms Sean said you'd have a big lunch on the boat so I— Here, let me.' She relieved Will of his load, placing it on the countertop, then began rummaging in the cupboards below, pulling out platters.

'Oh, you d—' Lucy tugged on Will's arm so he'd let Leilani be. Leilani truly was their mother hen and it might upset her if things weren't done just so—like guests helping themselves haphazardly to leftovers.

'Sit, sit!' the older woman instructed, indicating the kitchen table. 'I'll bring everything over.' Fortunately, a quick glance at Will showed that he got it and they moved to the table without protest.

'Oh, hey! Are we having leftovers?' said Chloe—as always, announcing her arrival loudly. 'Oh, thank god. I'm starving!' She reached across and stole a glazed carrot from its platter. Chloe must have been one of Leilani's favourites because she didn't even get told off.

'Where's Archer?' Will asked.

'On the phone with George. I swear, if I didn't know better, I'd be worried about those two running off together.'

'It's been quite a day,' said Lucy.

Chloe spun around. 'Said the mystery redhead.' She waggled her eyebrows and Will laughed.

'Oi, that's not funny,' Lucy said, scolding them both.

'Too soon?' quipped Chloe. 'Sorry, Luce.' She didn't seem particularly sorry.

'I know what we're missing,' said Will getting up from the table. 'Drinks!' Lucy suspected he was only busying himself to earn brownie points after laughing at Chloe's poor joke. 'Chloe, Luce?' he asked.

'Mmm, just water for me,' said Chloe.

'Me too,' added Lucy, whose mouth suddenly felt dry.

'Two boring waters coming up. Leilani, can I get you anything?' His question surprised her, Lucy could tell, but she refused his offer with a smile and shake of her head.

'How can you be so blasé about it all, Chloe?' Lucy asked.

She'd caught Chloe cramming a crusty piece of baked stuffing into her mouth and Chloe replied with her mouth full, her hand in front of her face—which was as far as Chloe's manners extended when she was ravenous, Lucy knew from vast experience. 'I don't know. I mean' —she swallowed— 'sometimes it gets to me, of course it does. But after that shitstorm last year—"Skank Gate" as I like to call it—I knew I'd have to learn to shake it off.'

'Like Taylor Swift.'

'And *not* like Taylor Swift,' Chloe retorted, talking over her.

'Why don't you like her?' asked Lucy. 'Everybody likes Tay Tay.'

'I don't mind her,' interjected Will with a shrug. He placed tall glasses of icy water in front of Chloe and Lucy.

'See?' Chloe rolled her eyes and something occurred to Lucy. 'Oh! Have you met her? Did something happen?'

'Lucy Browning, are you fangirling?' Chloe teased.

'Have you? Met her, I mean.'

'Hey, what's this?' Will called out, now deep within the

enormous pantry. He emerged with what looked very much like a Christmas cake.

'Oh!' said Leilani, rushing to take it from him. 'That's not ready yet!' Leilani appeared to be paralysed, standing stock still in the centre of the kitchen, holding the cake. Only her eyes moved as they darted between it and Lucy. After several (confusing) moments, she relaxed and set the cake on the countertop. 'Oh, Miss Lucy, I'm so sorry. I made this from your mother's recipe but I wanted to give it a couple more days to soak in the brandy before I served it.'

'What?' asked Lucy, even more confused.

'The brandy. I know it's supposed to be made months ahead but I thought it would be even better tomorrow or maybe the day after if I let it marinade a little longer.'

'Sorry ... you made my mum's cake?'

'Yes! And I asked her if I should add pineapple—you know, give it a little bit of "Hawaii"—and your mom ... she *loved* the idea. She's a really nice lady,' Leilani replied, a twinkle in her eye.

'But how did you ...?' Lucy looked over at Will, who clearly had no idea how this had happened, then at Chloe who clearly did.

Chloe raised her hand. 'It was me. Leilani and I called your mum to get the recipe.'

'Oh, that's ... that's so lovely.'

'You seemed pretty— Ooof.' Chloe's words were cut off as Lucy enveloped her in an enormous hug. Then she laughed and patted Lucy on the back.

'Thank you!' Lucy released Chloe and peered down at her lovely, *lovely* friend.

'You're welcome, Luce. We just wanted to make it up to you—coming here last-minute and leaving your mum's cake in Colorado.'

Lucy looked over at Leilani, tears prickling her eyes, then

rushed around the counter and wrapped her arms around her. Like Chloe, she laughed as she accepted Lucy's hug. *So this is what Mum meant when she asked how the cake had turned out!* Lucy realised. She stepped back and ran her fingers under each eye in turn. 'Can I be very cheeky?' she asked the older woman.

'What do you mean, chick?'

'Can we *please* have some tonight? I don't think I can wait till tomorrow.'

Leilani patted her on the arm. 'You got it.' She added a wink and Lucy grinned at her.

'What can't you wait for?' asked Archer as he entered the kitchen.

'Lucy's mum's Christmas cake that Leilani made,' replied Chloe. 'That cat's outta the bag.'

'Oh, right, though I'm not sure I could eat another thing—especially not after this evening's events.'

'Well, you only have to eat a sliver but it's compulsory, I'm afraid,' Lucy stated.

Archer raised his hands in defeat. 'A sliver it is.' His tone shifted and he added, 'It's the very least I can do.' He was looking at Lucy with such contrition … only none of the day's events had been his fault. It hit her then—*really* hit her—how difficult it must be for him. *And* Chloe. With all her worries and woes—some likely imagined or at least hyperbolised, she told herself—she would never change places with either of them. Not for all the pineapple in Hawaii.

———

'*Now* I'm stuffed.'

'I know. I thought yesterday was bad,' Lucy agreed. She and Will were lying side by side on their bed, holding hands.

'That cake was *so* good.'

'And so boozy,' she agreed.

'Oh, yeah. Maybe even more so than your mom's.'

'Do you remember telling me that you didn't like Christmas cake?' she asked.

'Uh-huh.' He squeezed her hand and she looked over, meeting his eye. 'I remember almost everything about last Christmas.'

'Almost? Why only almost?'

'That's just in case there's something I've forgotten—only how would I know, because I've forgotten it—and *you* remember it.'

'How much of that cake did you have again?' she teased.

'Just covering my ass.'

'And it's a very nice arse.'

'Thank you.' He paused. 'Hey, can I talk to you about that thing now?' He rolled onto his side, tucking his arm under his head.

'What thing is that?'

'See? Now *you've* forgotten. The human mind is fallible.'

The human mind was indeed fallible—until he reminded her, Lucy *had* forgotten that earlier, while they were on the yacht, he'd asked to speak to her about something. Her stomach launched into a series of somersaults as she wracked her brain for clues about what it could be.

It doesn't matter, Lucy, she admonished herself. Regardless of what Will had to say, Lucy knew she couldn't put it off any longer. It was all well and good to cocoon herself in a romantic, Christmassy bubble—run-in with the paparazzi notwithstanding—but it was time to stop procrastinating. She had to listen to what Will had to say, then tell him all the things she'd been shoving down deep for the better part of the past year. It was time for THE TALK.

Lucy sat up and crossed her legs. 'You have a weird look on your face,' he said. 'Everything okay?' He sat up as well, stuffing a pillow behind his back. 'Lucy?'

'Can I go first?' she blurted. Will paled, the colour draining from his face as though he were a cartoon character, but he nodded. Lucy swallowed the bile rising in her throat, then licked her parched lips. She reached for her water glass and took a sip.

'Wait,' Will said. 'Just … is something going on?'

'How do you mean?'

He gestured between them. 'This feels really weird all of a sudden and I'm a little scared of what you're gonna say.'

He was scared? Lucy was about to draw a line in the sand, one that would either change their relationship for the better—or … *Oh, god*. She couldn't even think of the 'or'. She steadied her breath. 'You know I love you …' she began.

'Oh, god,' he muttered, his gaze dropping to the duvet cover and a frown commandeering his face.

'Will, please, can I just get this out?'

'Sure, go ahead.'

This was already going terribly. Perhaps she should have waited—she was a little tiddly from the brandy-soaked Christmas cake and it had been quite the day … 'Should we talk about this tomorrow?' she asked.

'I have no idea, Lucy. All I know is that I wanted to share some good news with you and now we're having … whatever this is.'

'What's your news, then?'

'Uh-uh, nope. It's obviously much more important that you get your thing out first.'

Now Lucy frowned. 'Going terribly' was an understatement and her churning insides doubled their efforts. She and Will hadn't argued before—not really, minor tiffs on occasion, but nothing like this. The way he was looking at her, the cold tone in his voice … both filled her with dread. 'It's just that …'

'Please just *say* it.'

'It all feels very one-sided is all.'

He seemed confused, his head cocking to the side and his eyes narrowing. 'What feels one-sided? Our relationship?'

'Yes, well, no. I mean—' She sighed. To his credit, he didn't say anything. He just watched her silently, giving her time to get her thoughts in order so her words would make better sense. 'The only time we've seen each other this past year, besides coming here, has been in Colorado. It's always me who travels to see you and … *and* it kind of feels like you don't miss me as much when we're apart as I miss you. And I really miss you, Will.' Her voice caught but she continued. 'And I don't know how much longer I can see you every couple of months, and *only* for a week, then spend the bulk of my time feeling your absence *so acutely*. And once we're together again, once I'm ensconced in you, in *us*, it's *very* easy to forget how bad it is when we're apart. But then I'm back on that plane and the whole horrible, *horrible* cycle begins again. My work colleagues— at the end of the day they go home to their loved ones. Whereas *I* go home to a flat filled with plants I can barely keep alive. I'm lonely, Will. When I'm not with you, I'm lonely. And it's not that I *need* to have someone—that I *need* you. I don't! I'm an intelligent, capable woman, except when it comes to the plant thing, but other than that, I'm perfectly able to look after myself. This isn't about being independent. It's just—'

Before she knew what was happening, Will pressed his lips to hers, firmly and for several seconds, stopping her spiralling descent with a kiss. His hands cupped her face and when their lips parted, he pressed his forehead to hers. Eventually, her shallow, ragged breathing slowed and only then did she notice that tears were streaming down her face. Will pulled away slightly, his face only inches from hers, his hands still in place. 'Oh, Lucy. I'm so sorry I've put you through all that. And I know you don't *need* me, that you're all the things you said you are and so much more. Even if you are a plant murderer.'

Her resulting laugh resembled a hiccup, and she smiled

through her tears and sniffled. 'And you're right about the one-sided stuff,' he said dropping his hands from her face and reaching for hers, 'I've been aware of that, believe me, and that's why I've been working on something—something with Archer, actually.'

'With Archer?'

'Mmm-hmm. His buddy—his name is William, if you can believe it—anyway, William has this distillery in London making gin and he's been wanting to expand into other geos for a while now, to take his business to the next level. Archer connected us a while back and we've have been figuring out what a partnership could look like.'

'And what could it look like?' she asked, her heart filling with hope.

'It could look like— Actually, it *looks* like me moving to the UK to work with him on expanding into the North American and APAC markets.'

Lucy's mouth fell open. 'Are you serious?' she asked once she'd recovered her senses.

'Yeah!' He grinned at her. 'I was going to wait till I'd heard about my work visa before telling you but, apparently, everything in the UK shuts down over Christmas for, like, *ever* and I couldn't wait any longer. Besides, your Christmas present—the British domain name—it was *perfect*, Luce, and I was just dying to tell you.'

'You're moving to the UK?' she said, hoping that hearing the words out loud would help them sink in. It couldn't *possibly* be real.

'Uh-huh—visa pending, of course.'

'Right, yes, a visa …' she muttered, her gaze fixed on the duvet. *Is this really happening?*

'So, Luce?' Her gaze lifted and she met his eye. 'Good surprise?' he asked, hope adorning his face.

It *was* real, she realised at last. No more long-distance relationship! 'Yes, yes, absolutely!' Now she was grinning.

'Oh, thank god. I got really worried there for a second.'

Her smile fell away. 'I'm so sorry.'

'No, no, don't apologise …' He expelled a long breath replete with relief. 'Luce,' he said softly as he squeezed her hands in his, 'we're gonna live in the same city.'

Lucy could only nod, she was so choked with emotion, and the tears started flowing again. 'Hey … come 'ere.' Will pulled her close again, kissing the top of her head. Then Lucy wrapped her arms around him and held him tightly. It was a Christmas miracle and perhaps the best present she'd ever had.

Chapter Forty-Two

ARCHER

He'd never been so nervous in his life, which was laughable really. He'd presented awards at the BAFTAs, the Oscars, the Golden Globes, and (for some reason), the Grammys. He'd been nominated for all three acting awards a total of eight times (attending all the ceremonies) and had won the BAFTA for Best Actor in a Leading Role three years ago for his role as a Gulf War veteran, giving his acceptance speech to an audience of two thousand people in the auditorium and millions watching on television. He'd been invited to toss the coin at the FIFA World Cup and the women's final at Wimbledon. He'd even addressed the UN on climate change and had met Queen Elizabeth—*twice*.

But this was his first—and only ever—marriage proposal.

After spoiling the surprise on Boxing Day night, it had taken him two days to get over it and regroup. Thank god for Sean and Nate—and Matt, once he'd arrived back from the camping trip. All three had got in his ear at various times and talked him around and Matt had given him the idea for a new surprise, one that he was sure would blow Chloe away.

And only to console him, Archer was sure, Nate had even

promised to learn the dance. Though, Audrey was now in charge of that and, not only had she changed the song from The Righteous Brothers to Bruno Mars, her choreography was far more complicated than what he'd originally planned—just one more detail to worry about. He may have been a capable actor and he had a decent singing voice but 'double threat' was about the limit of his talents. He was a mediocre dancer at best and had been secretly practising the new choreography when Chloe wasn't about—mostly in the shower.

Now it was New Year's Eve and Archer's stomach was convulsing so much from nerves that he'd spent a good portion of the day in the loo.

'Pssst, Leilani.' He waved at her wildly, beckoning her to join him in the pantry.

She did, her eyes wide and blinking, silently asking why he was behaving like such an idiot. 'Yes?' she asked slowly.

'I'm ridiculous, I know.' She didn't disagree. 'I just want to make sure everything's perfect for tonight.'

'There you are!' Audrey joined them in the pantry, which was really more of a two-person space. She bore an iPad and an annoyed expression. 'You're supposed to be in the studio rehearsing with the other guys. It's the final run-through.'

'I was just—'

'Nope. Come on.' She waved him past.

'Oh,' he said spinning around, 'sorry, which studio? Art or—'

'*Yoga*, sheesh. It's on the schedule.'

'Got it. My apologies.' He scuttled out of the kitchen, Audrey moaning about him to Leilani at his back, and made a beeline for the yoga studio, slipping inside just as Will, Nate, and Matt struck the final pose. 'Sorry, everybody. Just a little discombobulated this afternoon.'

'It's all right, son,' said Nate, and not for the first time, Archer was glad to have his steady presence there.

'You're over here,' said Will pointing to the spot front and centre.

'I see, right.' He crossed to his place and stood, shaking out his arms, his nerves seeming to compound as the minutes ticked by.

'Let's go from the top,' said Will, running over to re-start the music. Seconds later, Bruno Mars' poppy tune blasted from the studio speakers. Thank goodness the room was soundproofed, lest Chloe was nearby and it ruined the surprise!

Audrey

'It's a good thing I'm here,' she said to Leilani, shaking her head as she watched Archer go. Leilani followed her out of the pantry and Audrey consulted her iPad again, muttering to herself. 'The fireworks guys are setting up …' She made a checkmark next to that item. 'Garden pruned and mowed this morning …' Another checkmark. 'Terrace cleaned, lights set up.' Two checkmarks. 'I'll light the candles and lamps just before … Oh, hey, Leilani, that guy Cory, the one who works on Jock's boat … he was supposed to come by to stock the bar while we were at the salon.'

'Been and gone hours ago,' Leilani replied, returning to a tray of mini blinis, her nimble fingers adding teensy sprigs of dill to each one.

'Awesome. And did he remember he's supposed to bring more ice with him when he comes at eight?'

'Uh-huh.'

'You know, I totally could have hired a caterer.'

Leilani gave her one of those looks that used to silence her immediately when she was a kid and in trouble. 'What have I told you?' she asked unnecessarily.

'Sorry. Um …' Audrey looked back at the iPad. 'Do you know where Sean is?'

'In her room, I think—*resting*.'

'Oh, right.' Just then, the buzzer for the gate blared from the control panel on the wall. 'Awesome—the DJ's here.' Audrey crossed the room and pressed the button to check who it was before she opened the gate. The grainy little screen revealed not one, but three people—two men and a woman. 'What the—?' she said to herself. 'Hello?' she called thought the intercom. 'Are you the—'

'I have some questions for Archer Tate.' 'So do I.' 'Me too!' 'Can I just have a couple of minutes—'

'Uh, he's busy!' Audrey shouted, turning off the video feed and the intercom by pushing every button on the panel.

'You might have locked us in for good doing that,' said Leilani from the other side of the kitchen.

'What do we do?'

'Nothing *to* do, little chick. You can't let them in.'

'Well, yeah, I know. But the DJ's due any minute now, the servers are coming soon, and Cory's coming back later. Plus there's Archer's surprise. How do we let in the people we want but keep the paparazzi out? Besides, you'd think they'd have given up by now—it's been a week!' Leilani pondered for a second but she must have come up empty, and (annoyingly) she just shrugged. 'Hmph,' Audrey said to herself as she stared at the tiled floor.

'Hey, you two, what's going on?' asked Sean, entering the kitchen. She yawned silently and ran her hands over her face.

'Oh, thank god you're here. There's a bunch of people outside—paparazzi—and I don't know what to do.'

Without being asked, Leilani poured Sean a glass of ice water and slid it across the bench to her. 'Thanks.' Leilani winked, then moved on to the next tray of hors d'oeuvres, squares of seared chilled mahi mahi topped with caviar and micro-greens. 'How many is a bunch?' Sean asked Audrey. 'As many as the other night?'

'No, thank god! It's just three at the moment.' Annoyingly, Sean smiled as though it wasn't a serious problem. 'But more might arrive—if word gets out,' added Audrey.

'Mmm, and speaking of that, how do you think word got out that we're hosting a party?'

'I don't know!' Audrey wailed. 'I thought I'd thought of everything, but how do you stop people you hire from spilling the beans?'

'In my experience? You can't—there's always someone.'

'Do you think it was the police?' Audrey asked, alarmed.

'Mmm, probably not,' Sean replied. 'Did you hire security?'

'I didn't think I needed to. It's just us and the people working the party. It's not like it's gonna get out of hand.'

'Well, you're right about that. I'll just be happy if I make it to midnight.'

'You're not *that* old.'

'Gee, thanks, Aud, but I meant because I'm still feeling the jetlag.'

'Oh, sorry.'

'Sometimes I think the smaller the time difference, the harder it is to get on the right time—even a week later. Anyway, back to your thing—security. I can call someone, if you like. It's late notice but …' She shrugged and Audrey mentally filled in the rest of the sentence. If you offered enough money, you could almost always get what you needed, even at the last minute.

Audrey had grown up hearing that constantly from her dad, but Sean rarely played the 'billionaire card', as she called it. And Audrey had never seen her be anything but respectful towards the people she employed—in her companies, at her properties, and even for one-off events like tonight.

'Do you mind? I think it'd be a good idea.'

'I'll make a few calls.'

Chloe

'What do you think?'

Jules, who was sitting on Chloe and Archer's bed popping peanut M&Ms into her mouth one after the other, mumbled, 'You look good,' around her mouthful.

Lucy, the romantic amongst them, stared at her wistfully. 'Oh, Chloe. You are absolutely stunning.' Chloe had worn this dress before on the red carpet. She'd packed it just in case and now she was glad she had. It was in a deep blueish-red silk, cut on the bias and held up by the thinnest of spaghetti straps. It draped impeccably over her petite but curvy frame and fell to just above her ankles with a handkerchief hem. She wore strappy silver sandals, a single silver bangle, and silver drop earrings. Her eye makeup was a touch of shimmer and lashings of mascara and her lips matched the colour of the dress.

'And this is just the proposal! Imagine what she'll go with when she's a bride!' teased Jules.

'Hey, you, back in your box.' Chloe pointed a finger at Jules, who pretended to cower behind a throw pillow.

'Eh, you look great and you know it.' Jules climbed off the bed and stretched her arms above her head. 'I should go get changed.'

'Oh, so you're not going with "casual yoga mum doing the school run" chic?'

'Yeah, yeah. Hilarious. Wait' —she paused at the doorway— 'Luce, what are you wearing?'

'Well, I've got exactly three options, all of which were borrowed from your mum's wardrobe and one of which I wore on Christmas night.'

'Oh, I love that dress. I thought it looked familiar.' Jules grinned at her.

'Well, probably not that one, then.'

Jules signalled for her to follow. 'Come to my room. I've got something—you'll look *great* in it.'

'Are you sure?'

'Yeah, totally.'

'All right. We'll see you down there, Chloe,' said Lucy.

'See you down there.'

'And, Chloe, you really do look divine.' Lucy flashed Chloe a smile and closed the bedroom door quietly behind her.

Save for being in the bathroom, Chloe couldn't remember the last time she'd been alone in the past nine days and she exhaled a long slow breath as she regarded herself in the full-length mirror once more. Whatever else happened that night—even if a swarm of bees attacked them on the dancefloor, or the party was crashed by a marauding band of pirates, or everyone got food poisoning (not that they would because, well, *Leilani*)—by the end of the night, she would be engaged to the most beautiful, thoughtful, brilliant man in the world (who also happened to be the sexiest man alive, as agreed by *People* magazine).

If only the others could be there—Ash, her gorgeous friend from Melbs, her parents, even her brother, Drew. Never mind. They'd just have to throw a massive Aussie-style engagement party when they moved to Melbourne—one with all her extended family, friends from her old job, friends from high school and uni—pretty much every person she'd ever met. The thought made her smile. They were moving to Melbourne! She hadn't realised until she'd opened Archer's Christmas present how much she missed her hometown. Well, she had, but then she'd either bury herself in work or just pretend she didn't feel the longing. It never really left her though.

She hoped that no matter where their jobs in the movie industry took them, they'd always keep Melbourne as their home base. Well, one of them, because London was home to Archer too. God, since the start of the year, she'd lived in three different countries! It was funny to think back to this time last year—all of them swapping Christmases and three budding romances. So much had happened in just fifty-two weeks. She glanced at the time on her phone. Two minutes until she'd promised to meet Archer at the bottom of the stairs—and she was never, ever late.

'It's showtime,' she said to her reflection.

Chapter Forty-Three

CHLOE

Chloe, who had spent ten years in the event management business, was highly impressed with what Audrey had managed to pull together in under a week. At first, Archer had wanted to keep their New Year's celebrations low-key but for some reason, he'd changed his mind and given Audrey the green light. And, somewhat surprisingly, the girl had a good eye and serious skills.

The enormous terrace and surrounding gardens were as pristine as always, but now glowed with the most gorgeous array of lights. There were floating floral and candle arrangements bobbing in the pool, tiki torches bordering the property, and hurricane lamps spilling warm light onto every flat surface in sight. And Chloe wasn't typically one to go with fairy lights—a little clichéd, if not totally passé—but the lighting guys had done a great job of using them to subtly highlight the trailing bougainvillea.

A DJ was playing a fun mix of new and retro dance music, Cory from the yacht, who was clearly a practised bartender, was mixing cocktails—Chloe's hibiscus margarita was going down a treat—Leilani had worked her magic in the kitchen and the food being passed around by two lovely servers—a high-school-aged brother and sister—was incredible and there were even whispers about fireworks at midnight.

'Isn't this awesome?' asked Jules, a mojito in one hand and an hors d'oeuvre in the other. 'I could seriously live off this tuna.' She popped it in her mouth and reached for another one before the server got away.

Melbourne must have been rubbing off on Jules because tonight's dress was more flowy and feminine than her usual style. It was essentially a sleeveless floral maxi dress, only the fabric was lux, the 'flowers' were more abstract than literal, and the neckline plunged nearly to her waist. If Chloe had a body like Jules—and was as tall as her—she'd have worn it in a heartbeat. She looked gorgeous.

Lucy did too, having borrowed Jules' ice-blue silk shift—similar in style to Chloe's dress, only in Jules' heels, Lucy was now over six feet tall. That colour looked stunning on her too. Jules had told Chloe how much convincing it had taken to get Lucy to even try it on, especially as she'd had to go braless. But Lucy, who had no idea how much of a knock-out she was, wouldn't have looked out of place on the red carpet. If Hallmark ever *did* make their story into a Christmas movie, Eleanor Tomlinson would be perfect to play her.

'It's absolutely divine,' said Lucy. 'It even *smells* like heaven, doesn't it?' She closed her eyes, inhaling deeply.

'Yeah, Audrey's done a great job,' said Chloe.

'What does she *do*, anyway?' asked Jules.

'You mean for a living?' Chloe asked.

'Uh-huh.'

'She's a personal shopper,' Chloe replied.

'For *gifts*,' added Lucy. 'She helps people choose the perfect gift.'

'Right,' acknowledged Jules. 'Any chance she'd be good at what you do?'

'Movie production?' asked Chloe, confused.

'Nah, your other job. When you were part of the little people.'

'Ha-ha. You're hilarious, Jules.'

'Seriously, though, Ash is always saying how understaffed they are and I think she's keen to take someone under her wing, mentor them—you know, pass the torch.'

'I'm so proud of her for getting that promotion,' said Chloe.

'Yeah, me too. I'm still recovering from the celebration.'

'Let me guess—a full-on, week-long festival.'

'I've been to destination weddings with less events. You'd think as an Event Planner—'

'Event *Manager*.'

'Sorry, Event *Manager* … anyway, you'd think Ash'd be over it—leave the planning to someone else.'

'Ha! Hardly. Ash is a planning freak.'

Jules laughed. 'That's what she calls you.'

'Oh, is that so?'

'Actually,' said Lucy, joining in, '*I'm* very proud of *you*, Chloe.'

'Why? How? What do you mean?'

'Well, you let Audrey take charge tonight. You didn't harp on at her with suggestions or explain the "best way" to do things … You didn't even offer to help. It's good of you to let her shine.'

'So you're Team Audrey now?' Jules asked Lucy.

'I'm … well, I still don't want her anywhere near Will but she's not all bad. And she's clearly worked hard on tonight. Credit where credit is due.'

'I guess so,' replied Jules. 'Hold on, you're very quiet all of a sudden, Chlo … *Oh!* You did butt in, didn't you?'

'Just a little but then … well, it was obvious she had everything under control so I backed off. Besides, it's doubtful we'll get an *actual* apology from Audrey, but Sean said this party is her way of saying sorry.'

'Oh!' exclaimed Lucy. 'That's so lovely.'

'Seriously, Luce? Now she's lovely?' Jules asked drily.

'It's a nice gesture is all. Like I said, she's not all bad.'

'Sure, okay,' Jules conceded. 'But are you still proud of Chloe? Now that you know she couldn't help herself?'

Lucy reached over and took Chloe's hand. 'Always. I'm proud of both of you. Oh, that doesn't come off as condescending, does it?'

'No, not at all,' said Chloe. 'Hell, I'm proud of all of us. Look at all the things we've accomplished this year!' They paused, exchanging knowing smiles that said everything words didn't. Chloe was suddenly overcome—she loved these two *so much*! They were her soul sisters—and that wasn't just the tequila talking.

'Hello, my beautiful darling angel.' Archer slipped an arm around Chloe's waist and nuzzled her neck. Jules smirked and Lucy looked away, sipping her bubbles and looking particularly interested in those floating candles. Chloe could always tell when Archer was tiddly on the verge of tipsy—one endearment turned into a slew of them and he became especially touchy-feely in front of others.

'Hello, my handsome soon-to-be fiancé,' she replied, leaning against him. At her words, Archer's whole countenance changed—he pulled away from her while his grip on her waist tightened and his intake of breath was so loud, she heard it. 'Sorry, babe, no pressure or anything,' she added, turning towards him. *Oh my god, the poor guy!* 'Um. Do you mind giving us a sec?' she said to Jules and Lucy. Both shook their heads, Jules clearly tickled and Lucy appearing (beyond) relieved as Jules steered her towards the buffet.

Chloe spun around. 'Hey, are you okay?' She placed her empty glass onto a passing tray, then looked back at him, concerned.

'Absolutely. Top notch. Superb even.'

'Did you want to add, "pip, pip, cheerio" or anything else?' She smiled at him, lacing her fingers with his but he still looked like a deer caught in headlights. 'Babe?'

'Mmm?'

'I promise I'll say yes.'

His expression was unreadable for a moment, then he looked over her shoulder and his eyes lit up. Chloe was about to turn around and see why when a pair of hands covered her eyes. 'Guess who?' The voice was so familiar—but so out of context—that she didn't reply. She tugged at the hands and spun around, her mouth falling open when she saw who it was.

'Drew?!' He looked like he'd stepped straight off the ski fields, his face tan except around his eyes, where his skin was pale—like a raccoon in reverse.

'Surprise, sis!' he said with a laugh as he wrapped her up in a hug. He rocked her from side to side a couple of times before releasing her. That's when she had an even bigger surprise.

'Mum! Dad! Wha— I can't believe it!'

'Hello, Chloe,' said her mum, leaning into her and kissing her left cheek.

Her dad, always the less reserved of her parents, hugged her tightly. 'Hi, love. Good to see you.'

'Good to see you, too, Dad,' she said, choking back tears and clinging to him. How were they even here? But a better question was how had she gone so long without seeing them, without going home to Melbourne to see her family? Yes, it had been a whirlwind of a year—an action-packed, extraordinarily busy year—but having her family with her on what might just be the most important night of her life to date? That was everything. It was Archer's doing, she knew that, and she was just about to thank him for the beautiful gesture when she heard, 'Ahem.'

Standing just off to the side, (impatiently) waiting her turn, was Ash. 'Oh my god!' Chloe squealed.

'I know!' Ash squealed back. Then they were hugging and jumping up and down at the same time. When they finally let go, Ash turned around and waved someone over. 'And look who I brought with me!'

'Davo! Come here, you big spunk rat.' Davo, big man that he was, swept Chloe up in a huge hug and she didn't even care that her feet were dangling off the ground. Eventually, he put her down and the first thing Chloe did was call the others over and commence the introductions. Jules and Matt helped because they knew everyone and Chloe found a brief eye in 'Hurricane Reunion' to pull Archer aside.

'You are the most incredible, most wonderful man,' she said, tears welling again. 'Thank you so much.'

He lightly trailed the back of his fingers down her cheek, a slight smile on his face. 'You are so welcome, my love.'

'How did you even ... *How*?'

'Lots of help. Sean, Nate, *Matt* ... once I stupidly ruined the surprise of the propos—'

'That wasn't your fault.'

'Even so, I wanted to do something special—extra special, I mean. I had to have *some* surprise up my sleeve. You're Chloe Bloody Sims, you know, and it's extremely difficult to organise things around you—both to your standard and without you finding out.'

She grinned at him. 'You may just be the perfect man.'

'Well, I seriously doubt *that*. All I want to be is worthy of you.' Archer's words struck hard and, not for the first time since they'd been together, Chloe saw a glimpse of the Archer Tate that very few people saw—the boy from the tiny hamlet in

Oxfordshire who'd left for drama school with an enormous amount of talent, high hopes, and more than his fair share of self-doubt. That boy had exceeded even his wildest dreams when it came to his career, but he was still in there and, at times, he poked his head out.

'Oh, Archer, you absolutely are.' She stood on tiptoes and smacked a loud kiss on his lips.

'Archer!' *Great timing, Mum—not!* thought Chloe.

'Mum.' Chloe reached for her hand.

'I just wanted to thank you again for flying us here,' she said to Archer, barely acknowledging that Chloe was there. 'It's such a treat to be back in Hawaii.'

'You are more than welcome. Thank *you* for agreeing to the change in plans.' She waved him off.

'Oh, that's right,' said Chloe, 'aren't you and Dad supposed to be on a cruise right now?'

'Oh, Chloe, as soon as Archer called us—and, Archer, you have to know that leaving in the middle of a cruise is a very big deal,' she admonished. His eyes flicked to Chloe's and their microsecond-long look spoke volumes—her apologising, him tickled. 'Anyway, as *soon* as he called us—and you know, your dad and Archer had already had their man-to-man talk *weeks* ago or was it longer?' she asked herself. '*Anyway*, after he told us how he'd botched the proposal, he practically *begged* us to come, didn't you? So we got on the plane. We just had to be here for you. For you both,' she said, including Archer.

'It's really good of you to come, Mum. I'm so glad you're here.'

'Wouldn't miss it, sweetheart. Besides, Archer's flying us directly to Auckland the day after tomorrow so we can re-join the cruise.'

'That's great, Mum.'

Her mum planted another cheek kiss, then made her excuses to go in search of a 'decent Sauv Blanc'. Apparently, she'd would *kill* for one. 'So,' Chloe said to Archer, 'the plane that brought them here?'

'Sean's private jet, yes.'

'Right. I thought so. It's good of Mum to endure such hardship.'

'She's a woman who's willing to make sacrifices.'

'Ah, yep. And she must love you to leave in the middle of a cruise.'

'It's that she loves *you*, I suspect, darling.'

'Can I steal her?' said Ash, hooking an arm around Chloe's neck.

'You may.' He winked at Chloe then left.

'Here.' Ash thrust a cocktail into Chloe's hand. 'You were dry and I'm looking out for my girl.'

'Oh, thanks,' she replied, slipping out of Ash's grasp. 'I'm going to sip, though, because I want to remember this night.' She regarded her friend. 'God, I've missed you.'

'Yeah. Me too.'

Chloe looked over to where Davo was chatting with Matt and Will. 'And that's going good?'

'I love him so much, Chlo,' said Ash staring wistfully in his direction. 'Who woulda thunk it, eh?' she asked, turning back to Chloe.

'Thunk what exactly?'

'Just … you and me and … our boys. We're all loved-up, eh?'

'Yeah, it's like Noah's Ark around here.'

'Matt's happy,' said Ash.

'Yeah, he and Jules are a good fit.'

'He said he asked Jules about moving down to the peninsula.'

'Yeah.'

'I hope she comes around. I mean, I love living with her—she's a cool chick but …'

'She just needs time,' said Chloe, feeling the pull of allegiance from both directions. 'And what about you two?' she asked, redirecting the conversation. 'Any plans to make it official?' Ash's lips disappeared between her teeth. 'Ashley?' Ash's eyes widened. 'No?!' Chloe whispered. 'Seriously?' Ash nodded vigorously. 'Oh my god!'

'But shhh,' said Ash, looking around.

'Why are we shushing? This is amazing news.'

'Because,' said Ash, grabbing Chloe's hand and looking her in the eye. 'Firstly, it only just happened on Boxing Day' —now Chloe's eyes widened— 'but we're waiting to announce it officially till after we tell our families in person—well, sorry, hang on. Callie and Thea know because, well ...'

'Callie and Thea,' finished Chloe.

'Exactly. And they are *so* sorry they couldn't be here, by the way, but Thea's *so* pregnant. I mean, like ...' She rounded her arms at full stretch in front of her. 'Anyway, forget all that. The other reason is that tonight is *your* night—yours and Archer's—and we don't want to take away from that.'

Chloe hugged Ash hard and fast. 'I won't say anything, I promise. Not even to Davo, 'cause—'

'I get it. It's a miracle he's kept his mouth shut this long and if you mention it, he's gonna tell anyone who'll listen.' They shared a smile.

'Promise me we can at least have a double engagement party—'

'Oh, I was gonna suggest a double wedding,' quipped Ash.

'Ha! Yeah, right,' said Chloe. 'Like you want *The Women's Weekly* at your frigging wedding.'

'Nooo. That's, uh ...' Ash held out her palm in Chloe's direction. 'That's *your* thing. Now that you're marrying a movie star!'

'He has to propose first!' Chloe said, laughing.

'Speaking of ... any indication when that's happening?'

'None.'

'Maybe he flew us all the way from Melbs just for a party,' she teased.

A second later, the music stopped and the sound of someone tapping on a microphone echoed across the terrace.

Chapter Forty-Four

JULES

Jules, who was way more ravenous than usual lately, had just bitten into a spicy shrimp when the music stopped and someone tapped on a microphone. 'This must be it,' said Lucy, excitedly bouncing next to her. Jules finished the shrimp and wiped her mouth on a cocktail napkin. She had no idea why she'd bothered with lipstick.

'Um, hello, everybody,' said Archer, his voice a little shaky.

'Oh, how sweet,' Lucy whispered. 'He's nervous.'

'Thank you so much for being here,' continued Archer. 'It's so lovely to see out the "old year", as it were, with all of us together. So, as you all know, tonight is not just New Year's Eve. It's a special night for another reason …'

Jules leant close to Lucy. 'Wow, Dad looks terrified.' She tried to catch his eye but he seemed miles away.

'Oh, he does! Poor love,' replied Lucy. 'Have you seen it?'

'The dance? Nope.'

'Chloe darling …' said Archer.

As he called to Chloe, his hand outstretched, Will stepped up.

'Hold on there, Archer, aren't you forgetting something?' he asked woodenly.

'Oh, right! Of course!' Archer replied—hands down, his worst acting ever.

'Oh, wow, this is already hilarious,' said Jules, losing it. She dug her phone out of her clutch, held it up, and pressed 'record'. Bruno Mars' song, 'Just the Way You Are', started blasting from the speakers and Will, Matt, her dad, and Archer stepped into formation.

Chloe shouted, 'Woo-hoo!' adding a loud two-fingered whistle. She'd tried to teach Jules how to do that so many times over the years, but Jules always ended up sounding like an asthmatic donkey.

The dance routine began and, just from the look of terror on her dad's face alone, Jules started laughing so hard she wished she had a Steadicam. Chloe, who was front and centre, bopped along, clapping and grinning, and Lucy beamed at Will, her eyes rivetted to him. Jules had to admit that her brother had some decent moves and her dad, now the routine had got going, was doing a decent job. Matt was great, but that wasn't surprising—he was a very sexy dancer. And all three were *way* better than poor Archer.

'Are they going to do the whole song, do you think?' asked Lucy. 'Isn't it about four minutes long?'

Jules hadn't kept up to date on the length of Bruno Mars' song so she shrugged. That's when she caught sight of Audrey off to the side, mouthing the words to the song and doing minuscule versions of the dance moves along with the guys. She nudged Lucy and nodded in Audrey's direction.

'Aww, bless, she must have choreographed it,' said Lucy.

'Mmm-hmm,' Jules replied. Lucy had really changed her tune about Audrey—even since the start of the night.

At the end of the chorus—the second iteration—the DJ faded

the music and the four men struck their final poses, Archer in front, as he'd been for the whole routine, but now kneeling.

'This is it,' said Lucy. 'Let's get closer!'

The small crowd applauded loudly, adding lots of shouts, whistles, and whoops, and all four men grinned broadly—Archer, no doubt, from relief. And as Jules and Lucy crept closer to a better vantage point, Jules clocked the look that her dad shot over to Sean. She glanced back and forth between them, realising that there was *definitely* something romantic going on. Sure, she'd witnessed them flirting the night Sean arrived, but when Will had mentioned something the other day, she'd shrugged it off. Oh, god, was she really so caught up in her own crap that she hadn't noticed what was happening with her dad? She'd find him later and ask him about it, ashamed that it had taken her this long.

Jules took her place next to Lucy, just behind Chloe, and started recording again, because what woman wouldn't want a record of her proposal? That's when she noticed, out of the corner of her eye, that the DJ was also filming on his phone. 'Take this,' she said to Lucy, handing it over. Lucy took it, obviously confused, but there was no time to explain. Jules headed straight for the DJ.

Chloe

She was clapping so hard, her palms were stinging, but she was so proud of Archer—and Matt and Will and Nate. How the hell had they pulled *that* off? She knew they'd snuck away a few times over the past few days—Audrey had explicitly made the yoga studio off limits—but Chloe hadn't expected *that*. 'Encore,' she shouted through the whistles and applause.

Eventually, the group hushed and Chloe was left smiling down at her love, who was kneeling before her, a light sheen of perspiration on his lip—more likely nerves than the rigour of the routine as he was super fit. He took a deep breath, confirming her suspicions, and she locked her eyes onto his, telegraphing, 'You've got this, babe.' He seemed to understand and visibly relaxed, but just a little.

He broke their eye contact to look around at their family and friends. 'I'm not sure why this is so nerve-wracking. I have it on good authority that my intended,' he said, 'will actually say yes.' There was supportive laughter and Nate stepped forward and laid a hand on Archer's shoulder, then whispered something before he stepped back.

Archer closed his eyes for a second, then opened them and looked up her again. 'My darling Chloe, from the moment you opened the door to me at my parents' home, nearly dropping that plate of biscuits you were carrying, I knew that my world had changed forever. People scoff at the idea of "love at first sight" but only the people who've never experienced it. What I hadn't understood until then was that another person could truly see *me*, could truly love *me*—not the man the world thinks they know, but *me*. You made me laugh that day and have every day since—mostly at myself …'

Titters of laughter cut into his words and surrounded her as tears filled her eyes. She blinked them away, not wanting to miss even a microsecond of this beautiful proposal for the blur of tears.

'The thing is, darling, I had no idea that was possible. I had begun to believe that I would spend my life without that kind of love, that it was only for other people, if it existed at all. But last Christmas, in a tiny village, I met a woman—a clever, sassy, funny, and very beautiful woman—who would open up to me a whole new way of seeing the world. You introduced me to people who would become close, trusted, and *treasured* friends' —he looked around at the others, smiling, and Chloe's heart swelled at being able to share this with them— 'as well as showing me what a true, epic love could really be. I'm very proud of what we've accomplished together over the past year, of who we've become—both as individuals and as a couple—and I can only wonder at what incredible lives we will live together.'

Chloe gulped and her lip trembled as her breath grew ragged from emotion. Her tears flowed freely now, trailing down her cheeks, but she didn't care. This was it.

'Chloe Evelyn Sims, it would be my greatest honour, my greatest joy, if you would agree to marry me.'

His expression bore such hope, such humility, that a sliver of her heart broke for him while the rest rejoiced. 'Yes!' Caught up in the moment, she launched herself at him with such force, it knocked him backwards, Chloe landing on top of him.

Horrified gasps surrounded them, then silence. Chloe looked at him, her eyes and mouth wide. 'Are you okay?'

He winced, then replied, 'I've conducted a mental scan and nothing seems to be broken.'

'Good.' She landed a vigorous kiss on his mouth and he returned it, wrapping her in his arms.

'Uh, do you want some help?'

Chloe broke the kiss and looked up at Nate's proffered hand. She took it and, as inelegantly as she'd landed on Archer, she climbed off him. Archer stood and slid one arm around her waist, addressing the group. 'It seems that's a yes!'

That set off more laughter and the evening soon became a blur of hugs, kisses, and—for Archer—hearty back slaps, as their loved ones congratulated the newly betrothed couple. 'Oh, Chloe, how wonderful,' said her mum. 'I can't believe my daughter is engaged to my favourite actor.'

Chloe glanced at Archer, who was, thankfully, deep in conversation with Nate, and replied, 'Since when has Archer been your favourite actor, Mum?'

'Since always.'

'So you don't remember that time you said, "Oh god, not another Archer Tate movie—why is he in *everything*?!"?'

Her mum feigned confusion, but Chloe would have bet a sizeable sum that she remembered. 'I never said anything like that. You must be thinking of your father.' *Sure, Mum.* 'Anyway, it's very exciting news. Oh! And I guess I'll have to choose something special for my mother-of-the-bride outfit.' She grinned and added a little shoulder shimmy.

'You most certainly will, Mum,' Chloe replied with a smile, despite there being no date set and knowing her mum was probably a Mumzilla in the making.

'And I need to ask you—who's that?' she asked, not-so-covertly pointing her pinkie in Audrey's direction.

'Oh, that's Audrey. She came with the house.' Her mum looked confused. 'She's Sean's stepdaughter.'

'Oh, right. She's very pretty.'

'I guess.'

'Do you think Drew thinks so?'

'What? You want to set Drew up with Audrey? I thought he has a girlfriend.'

Her face soured. 'Oh, that won't last long. She's …' Her mum shuddered, a gesture that spoke volumes.

'You never like his girlfriends.'

'That's because he has terrible taste.'

'Yeah, well, Audrey's kinda going through something right now, Mum, so maybe just … hold off?'

Her mum's lips drew into a taut line. 'Mmm, maybe.' Her expression softened. 'Anyway, Chloe, Archer is a good one—and only the best for my daughter. I truly am very happy for you.'

'Thank you, Mum. I'm really glad you could be here for it.'

Her mum gave her hand a quick squeeze, then left to congratulate Archer, her (new) favourite actor. 'Mum being weird?' asked her brother.

'No more than usual. How much of that did you hear?'

'Something about the blonde but not much else.' He looked over his shoulder. 'She's cute.'

'Steer clear. She just ended a serious relationship.' It was stretching the truth a little but she didn't want her circle of family and friends to get any more incestuous than it already was. And Audrey as a sister-in-law? Uh, no. A friend, maybe—*maybe*.

'Well, congratulations, sis,' said Drew, smothering her in a brotherly hug.

'Thanks, Drew,' she replied, her chin resting on his shoulder.

He stepped back, lifted his eyebrows, and walked straight over to Audrey. Chloe rolled her eyes.

'That was absolutely brilliant!' said Lucy, tears in her eyes. 'Congratulations, Chloe, I am beyond thrilled for you.' Chloe accepted Lucy's hug, breathing in her soft rose-scented perfume. It would be very hard to say goodbye to Lucy the day after tomorrow, especially as she had no idea when they'd be back in London. 'Oh,' said Lucy releasing her, 'we filmed the whole thing!' she said, nodding at Jules.

'Except the last part, right?' asked Chloe. It wasn't like her to get embarrassed but that could have been the least romantic way to say yes to a marriage proposal in the history of marriage proposals.

'Oh, no, I definitely got that part,' replied Lucy.

'Wonderful—Archer will be thrilled.'

'Internal use only, I promise,' said Jules. 'Hey, congrats.' She stepped closer and gave Chloe a quick squeeze.

'Thanks!' One huge advantage about moving to Melbourne was that she'd get to see Jules all the time. Chloe couldn't wait.

'And here,' said Jules, handing over an iPhone.

'It's a bit unusual for an engagement present, Jules,' Chloe joked.

'It belongs to the DJ. He was filming the proposal.'

'What?'

'Uh-huh. Look, we didn't want to worry you, but there was this situation earlier—some sort of leak about the party. Some people showed up—more paparazzi, Audrey said. Anyway, he must be our guy.' The three of them looked over at the DJ, who was—unsurprisingly—being asked to leave by a security guard. Sean glowered close by, her arms folded across her chest.

'Oh, wow. So, what do we do with this?' Chloe asked, holding up his phone.

'I already deleted the video,' said Jules with a shrug. 'I guess he can pick it up tomorrow along with his equipment.'

'But now we don't have a DJ,' said Lucy.

'I think we can manage, Luce. Besides, we can't let him stay.'

'Oh, right, of course.'

'Hey, Drew!' called out Chloe. Her brother looked up from his conversation with Audrey and Chloe signalled for him to come over. He appeared reluctant but came anyway. 'Drew was a DJ in high school,' she told the others as he made his way across the terrace.

'What's up?' he asked.

'You are. We need a DJ.'

'What happened to the—' He stopped speaking as soon as he saw what was happening. 'Wow, so … what'd he do?'

'He's a spy,' said Lucy dramatically. 'For the paparazzi!' Jules smirked, throwing Chloe a sideways glance.

'No shit? Cool. So, what do you wanna hear, sis? It's your party.'

'I don't know. Just something to dance to.'

'On it.'

'Your brother's so sweet,' said Lucy, watching him go.

'Don't get any ideas, Luce,' teased Jules. 'One brother should be enough for you.'

'Very funny. I didn't mean it like that.'

Jules' response was drowned out by a loud bang, followed by

'ooh's and 'ahh's. 'Holy shit, fireworks!' said Chloe. 'But it's not even midnight yet, is it?'

'Not quite, I don't think,' said Jules, her gaze lifting to the night sky.

A familiar presence came up behind Chloe, his arms circling her waist. He laid a soft kiss on her bare shoulder as she covered his hands with hers and sunk against him. 'One final surprise, my love,' he said, his voice low in her ear.

Several more bursts lit up the sky with golden cascading glimmers of light. 'Oh, I love these ones! They always remind me of champagne!' she exclaimed.

Archer's rumbling laugh rippled through her. 'I know, my love. That's why I chose them.'

She turned and looked at him, her chin raised for a kiss. He pressed his lips to hers. 'I love you,' she said.

'I love you too.'

She turned back around just in time to catch the next sequence of fireworks, multi-coloured sprays that filled the sky with rainbows. Matt had joined Jules, and Will arrived, slinging his arm around Lucy's shoulder, and the six of them stared up at the light-filled sky.

'Ten!' someone called out from behind them.

They joined in, excitedly exchanging glances with each other. 'Nine, eight, seven, six, five, four, three, two, one! Happy New Year!' There were kisses and hugs all around, laughter and cheers filling the night air.

What a perfect way to see out the year, thought Chloe—surrounded by her best friends and her family, and engaged to the man she loved.

Epilogue

ONE YEAR LATER

The May Ladies - Christmas Day

'Hello, loves! Happy Christmas.' Lucy was grinning from ear to ear. She'd been waiting all morning till it was a reasonable enough hour in Colorado to make the call.

'Merry Christmas,' said Jules through a yawn. Her hair was mussed, there were noticeable dark circles under her eyes, and she was wearing a long-sleeved pyjama top with reindeer on it. *Who bought her that?* Lucy wondered. Jules wasn't exactly what Lucy would have called 'a Christmas person', although perhaps that was different now.

'How's Felix?' ask Chloe. 'Is he there? I know it's only been a week but I miss his little feet.'

'His feet?' Jules asked. 'Don't you mean his face?'

'Well, yeah, I love his face too, but baby feet are *so cute*. I just want to bite them.'

'You want to bite my child?' asked Jules drolly. 'Pretty sure that would make you his evil aunt.'

'So, I'm the good auntie, then,' said Lucy. '*Is* he there, though? I want to see him!'

'Oh thanks, hun,' said Jules reaching out of frame.

'Ohhh!' exclaimed Lucy. 'He's got so big!' Felix's large brown eyes—exact replicas of his dad's, right down to the thick black lashes—blinked at the screen.

'And look at those feet—told ya they were cute,' said Chloe. 'Hi, Felix.' Felix cooed at the phone. 'See? He recognises me.' He reached for the phone and tried to drag it into his mouth.

'Or,' said Jules, wrestling her son for the phone, 'he has no idea who you are and is going through his oral fixation stage.'

'How does he like Colorado?' asked Lucy.

'He rates it three-point-five out of five. It loses points because it's cold and he takes after me.'

'Hey, you two! Merry Christmas!'

'Merry Christmas, Matty Matt,' said Chloe, more than a little tipsy. She blamed Callie. She and Thea may be parents now but Callie still drank like a fish—especially on Christmas, which, as she'd said about a hundred times throughout the day, was her 'favourite fucking day of the whole year'. Thea had gently reminded her that their anniversary and their daughter's birthday might be *slightly* more important. Callie had scoffed, then poured more sparkling. And Chloe was feeling it now.

'Hey, you. Did ya have a good Chrissie?' Matt asked.

'So good. We had everyone over here so Archer's spent the last three days in the kitchen. He even made a pav!'

'Aw, cool.'

'Oh, and Drew and Audrey came, but I think she's really missing Sean.'

'Did I hear my name?' Sean peered over Jules' shoulder into the screen and Felix reached for her from Jules' lap. Sean held out her forefinger for him to grasp and he took it, grinning a gummy grin at her, which she returned.

'Hey,' said Chloe to Sean, 'merry Christmas.'

'And to you! You have a good day?'

'It was great,' Chloe replied. 'But I was saying how Audrey's missing you—especially today I think.'

'Yeah, me too. I'm looking forward to my first visit to Melbourne—see where she's going to school, what her place is like. She said she's loving the part-time job at Ash's company.'

'Ha! Yeah, although it's not *Ash's* company ...'

'Does Ash know that?' Chloe laughed. To Jules, Sean asked, 'Want me to take him? Leave you girls to catch up?'

Jules handed over Felix with a grateful smile. 'Thank you.'

'No problem.' Sean held up his little hand. 'Bye, Aunt Chloe, bye, Aunt Lucy.'

'Goodbye, sweet boy,' said Lucy, waving at the screen. 'Oh, Jules, you and Matt have made the most beautiful child.'

'Yeah, we sorta like him too.'

'So, you're keeping him?' joked Chloe. ''Cause Archer and I will happily take him.'

'How about we take shifts? You get 1:00am till morning.'

'He'll start sleeping through the night soon, surely?' asked Lucy. 'He's only four months old.'

Jules yawned again and a giant red mug appeared over her shoulder. 'Thanks, Mom.' Steph blew them a kiss into the screen then disappeared. 'So, Luce, how's my brother behaving?'

Lucy looked off screen and smiled. 'He's lovely as always. And he completely spoiled me with presents.'

'You deserve it, Luce,' Will called from off screen.

Lucy smiled an uncharacteristically smug smile then schooled her face into a more 'Lucy' expression.

Chloe squinted at the screen. 'Hang on, that's not your parents' house. Where *are* you?'

'Across the road, at the Tates'.'

'Oh!' Chloe squinted at the screen, now recognising the guest room at her soon-to-be in-laws'. 'How come you're at Archer's parents' place?'

'Well, Mum and Dad's is only a two-up-two-down and my old room is far too small for both of us. And it's such a tiny village that there isn't anywhere local to stay. Apparently, Mrs Tate and Mum were talking …' she said, her face close to the phone and her voice barely above a whisper, 'and she offered to have us!'

'Wow. That's …' *Surprising*, is what Chloe wanted to say, especially since Cecily and Roger hadn't mentioned their houseguests when she and Archer had called them earlier. It was a weird thing to omit from the conversation.

'She's been lovely, *really*,' insisted Lucy.

'Of course she has!' Chloe replied with a slight pang of jealousy. She and Cecily shared a mutual respect but they were hardly chummy and the *last* word Chloe would use to describe her was 'lovely'. But she wouldn't say anything to Lucy. She was just glad that Lucy was having the Christmas she'd wanted, celebrating with her parents and Will at home in Penham. Just then, a wave of fatigue crashed over her and now it was her turn to yawn.

'We keeping you up, Chlo?' asked Jules.

She waved her hand in front of her face. 'I know I have no right to complain to *you*, Jules, but I'm absolutely knackered. I think I'm still on London time.'

'You've been in Melbourne for two weeks,' said Jules.

'Well, then, it was a big day!' retorted Chloe.

'All right, letting you off the hook,' teased Jules. 'And speaking of big days …'

'Oh, yes!' exclaimed Lucy. 'The countdown is on. I can't wait!'

Chloe broke into a smile. 'Me neither. Can you believe I'm getting married in three weeks?' She emitted a high pitched 'squee' and Jules winced—though, she really was excited about the wedding. They'd even bought Felix a little suit; he looked so cute in it.

'Breakfast is ready!' called her dad from the kitchen.

'I'd better go. Dad's serving up breakfast.'

'Oh my god, your dad's pancakes!' said Chloe, suddenly ravenous. Maybe she'd have some leftovers before going to bed.

'Yeah, they're pretty damned good,' agreed Jules.

'Oh,' said Lucy, 'just before you go, did Mum's Christmas cake arrive on time?'

'Oh, yeah,' said Jules. 'Sorry, I should have said—I'm blaming "mom brain". Anyway, we served it last night. Tell her thank you from all of us. That was really sweet of her.'

'I will.'

'Chlo, see you back in Melbourne next week. Lucy, see *you* in three weeks.' It was Lucy's turn to squee and Jules cracked up. 'Merry Christmas. Love you two.'

'Love you too,' said Chloe.

'See you soon! Love you!' Lucy waved at the screen as Jules left the call.

'I can't believe you finally get to come to Australia, Luce.'

'I know. Even if it wasn't for your wedding, it's an absolute dream come true.'

'Well, rest up before then. Audrey's planned an action-packed itinerary.'

'I don't doubt it,' Lucy replied with a proud smile. She really had come around on the girl—and it had nothing to do with the family connection now that Nate and Sean were together. She'd always wanted a little sister and now she had one, of sorts. 'Oh! Is Leilani able to make it?'

'Yes! I forgot to tell you. I had to make her promise not to lift a finger though. She practically offered to do the catering.'

'Oh, I heart her. I'm so glad she'll be there.'

'Us too. You have a great rest of your Christmas, Luce, and give your parents a hug for me.'

'Will do.' Lucy waved. 'Bye.'

'Bye! Love you.'

'Love you too.' She blew a kiss at the screen and they ended the call.

Acknowledgments

When I first had the kernel of an idea for *The Christmas Swap* back in 2019, all I knew was that I wanted to celebrate my favourite holiday and draw from some of the best Christmases I've ever had. I couldn't imagine at the time that I'd create a cast of characters I would come to love so much. But as I looked back on Christmases I'd experienced in the UK, the US, and Australia, homing in on some of my favourite (and most hilarious) festive escapades, so were born lifelong friends, Chloe, Lucy, and Jules—and their respective loves, Archer, Will, and Matt.

The inspiration for *The Christmas Trip* was simple—reunite the whole cast for a Christmas to remember, and Hawaii seemed like the perfect setting. I've travelled there before (Maui was one of the settings in A Sunset in Sydney), and I especially love the island of Kauai. What a stunning location.

It was a blast writing the May Ladies again and I'd like to thank the team at One More Chapter for indulging my fondness for all thing Christmas. Thank you, especially, to my editor Jennie Rothwell. Your feedback has helped elevate my writing and I appreciate all you've done to get this book over the line. It was great to finally meet you and the rest of the One More Chapter family during my recent trip to the UK.

Thank you, as always, to my (wonderful, insightful, and brilliant) champion of an agent, Lina Langlee of The North Literary Agency. Getting to see you in person, to celebrate our partnership and plan our future, was a great pleasure and a highlight of my mid-year European adventure. I am so grateful to have you in my corner and I'm very excited about what's to come.

I have so much gratitude for my writerly friends and colleagues. My fellow Renegades, Nina, Andie, and Fi—I genuinely couldn't do this (any of it) without our daily chats and your unwavering support. Thank you for reading my early drafts, for answering inane questions about 'the right vernacular', and for boosting my confidence the times it has ebbed. I love you to bits and (OMG) cannot believe I got to meet you in person, Nina! Next time, it will be the four of us! Thank you also to the #AusWrites squad for being my daily dose of writerly love, for supporting my journey, and for asking me to be part of such brilliant initiatives and experiences. Thanks especially to Jenna, Kate F & Kate M, Kevin, Darren & Veronica, Hayley & Maria, Kate A, Katya, Naomi, Mandy, and Belinda. Mwah!

Thank you to the leadership teams and volunteers at Australian Romance Writers, the Australian Romance Readers Association, and the Romance Novelists Association. What a (long anticipated) pleasure it was to attend the 2022 RNA Conference in the UK this year. Special mention for Anita, Kiley, Nina, Kathleen, Lynne, Sophie, the Lucys, Kate, Julie, Sheila, Pernille, Jules, Pia, Susan, and Ian—how lovely to see or meet you! Thank you, also, to the incredible romance-reading book blogging community, who continue to support and elevate our genre, especially Sue B, Anne W, and Rachel G.

A huge thanks to my partner, best friend, and love, Ben, and to my wonderful and supportive family—parents, Lee, Ray, and

Gail, sis, Victoria, brother-in-law, Mark, and nephew, Alexander. Thank you to my gorgeous extended family and the beautiful family of friends I've met along life's journey. Thank you all for decades of Christmassy inspiration and for instilling in me, not only a deep love for the holiday itself, but the knowledge that 'familial love' transcends time and distance.

Lastly, dear reader, thank you. I hope that wherever you are in the world, and no matter which holidays you celebrate, that you enjoy this read, and that you have a safe and joyous festive season and a very, very happy new year.

Sandy xxx

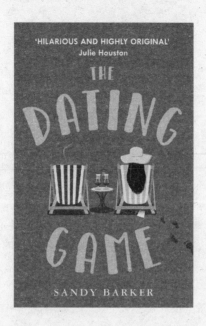

'HILARIOUS AND HIGHLY ORIGINAL'
Julie Houston

THE
DATING
GAME

SANDY BARKER

Once upon a time, twelve women joined the hottest reality TV show looking for love. Except one had a secret identity…

When a recap for *The Stag* – the must-watch dating show – goes viral, Abby's editor thinks she should be on set, writing the drama as it happens. The good news: the next season will be filmed in Sydney. Sun, sea and a glamorous trip abroad, this could be Abby's big break.

The bad news: the producers want her to be on the show. Abby can't think of anything worse, but her career depends on it, and when she meets gorgeous producer Jack, Abby begins to wonder if this job might not be so bad after all…

Extract from The Dating Game

'Okay, Abigail, time to sell off a little piece of your soul. Mama needs a new pair of shoes. Hah! Mama needs to pay her rent, more like.'

I don't often talk to myself out loud. All right, that's an abject lie, but sometimes I need a little pep talk, like when I sit down to write my columns for the online tabloid, Food for Your Mind—Hula Hoops and Jaffa Cakes, anyone? That's not its real name, of course, just a more accurate version of its actual name, which is (stupidly) Feed Your Mind. I'm not sure who came up with that, but it was pre-me and may indicate that they had loftier goals than photographs of celebs without makeup, gossip, and the trite tripe that I write, sarky recaps of reality television shows.

Last night was the premier of the latest season of The Stag, an archaic show about a single man seeking the love of his life—hah! more like fame, fortune, or someone to shag—amongst an array of women—the 'Does'—who are so homogenous and awful, they all blend into one fake-tanned blob.

It's rumoured that each season, the winning Doe gets her happily ever after *and* a hefty 'dowry' somewhere in the vicinity of

£50,000. If that's true, no wonder they clamber over the Stag like bargain hunters on Black Friday. It remains a rumour, however, as the Does are sworn to secrecy—and not just about the 'prize'. They film the show weeks in advance and every Doe, even those who are sent packing from Stag Manor after the first Pin Ritual, must remain tight lipped until the finale airs. I couldn't manage that for five minutes! Fortunately, I don't have to.

My mission, should I choose to accept it—and I do, because of that 'eking out an existence' thing—is to write witty recaps of each episode for our readers—far less taxing than keeping a slew of epic secrets. And my fans love my work, especially my recaps of *The Stag*. Sure, my posts about *Isle of Passion, The Incredible Chase,* and *I'm Super Famous, I Want Out!* go down a treat, but this is my opus, where I really get to sharpen my snarky, sarky teeth. *The Stag* has begun and hunting season is open! Brilliant—a tagline for my first post.

I do all this anonymously, of course. I am now somewhat famous—well, my alter-ego is. Apparently, Zoe Ball thinks I'm hilarious—*Zoe Ball!* So, not wanting to appear in my own online magazine, caught down at the local Tesco sans makeup and wearing last season's Lululemon knockoffs—the scandal!—I, Abigail (Abby) Jones, write my witty repartee under a much more exciting moniker. You see, I am *the* Anastasia Blabbergasted. It's quite a clever name, if I do say so myself.

And, besides my editor and my best friend, Lisa, no one knows. *No one*.

Right, enough of that, *Anastasia*. Time to stop faffing about and put that BA in Journalism to work!

The Stag Recap: Hunting Season is Open
by Anastasia Blabbergasted

Extract from The Dating Game

The Stag has begun and it's hunting season! Ah, Staggy, so good to have you back.

The producers have really upped their game this year with our delectable stag, Jameson (a good thing his father's favourite tipple wasn't Glenlivet!), aka Jaimie. If Henry Cavill and Alex Pettyfer had a love child, it would be this 6'5", chiselled, Greek-god-in-an-outdoor-adventurer's-body.

And this season's ~~Playboy Mansion~~ Stag Manor certainly is a step up from the last one—quite literally; did you see that imposing staircase?—with not one pool, but two! If the mercury cracks 22°C (all appendages crossed), we're bound to see some serious water action. Cue the barely there bikinis, sarky comments about cellulite and breast implants, and the montage sequence of splashing about and squealing, poolside posing, and a slick of spray-on tan floating on the surface of the pool—not to mention, many, *many* shots of those lovely Staggy abs!

So, the tried and tested format for the premiere is trotted out again (why mess with perfection?), with Jaimie waiting anxiously to meet and greet each Doe as they arrive in a limousine (nothing but the best for our girls). And how much does your heart twang for our little (big) Jaimie when he whispers to himself, 'I hope they like me,' just before the first Doe arrives? Aww, bless. Yes, this Staggy is straight out of a lusty romcom—even if he spells his name wrong (come on, the hint's right there in your name—it's 'Jamie', love).

Aside: Whoever designed that pathway from the limousine to Staggy is a maniacal sadist.

The brief: Nervous women wearing sky-high heels and floaty, drag-on-the-ground gowns will walk along this path at night-time. **The design:** Slippery flagstones surrounded by gravel. May the odds (of not slipping and falling) be ever in your favour!

Another aside: We all agree there's only one limousine, right? And that the Does are lined up on the other side waiting in turn to 'arrive'?

Thought so.

And what about our Does! In assembling ~~Jaimie's harem~~ this bevvy of beauties, the producers have obvs scoured Britain for the brightest, most gregarious, most altruistic, and socially-aware young women (Greta, Malala—watch out!). Sorry, just checked my research—that was for *Britain's Got OBEs*.

This season's casting call was for women who are constantly told how special they are, even if completely unremarkable, and were raised by parents who allowed talking back and slamming doors during their teen years. Vacuous celebrity hunters, influencers, wannabes, wannabe influencers, pouters, flouters, and BLTs (bossy little things) were also encouraged to audition.

The producers then assembled a cast *so* diverse, they've even included a natural redhead! I didn't know until I saw this season's premier that hair colour was a protected class. Thank you for enlightening us, Marie-Alice! (Love a double-barrelled first name, BTW—*super posh!*)

As usual, for your viewing pleasure, I have categorised members of the beauteous bevvy as follows:

- (potential) Brides
- Villains
- Dark Horses
- Miscellaneous
- Filler

Let's start with the last category: **Filler**

Do not bother to learn these Does' names; do not seek out their online profiles; do not become invested in them in any way whatsoever (even if you drew one of their names in a sweepstake), because they are just there to fill up spaces on those ridiculously long sofas. (Quick question: where do you buy those, or are they custom made for Stag Manor?) One by one, the Filler Does will be picked off in early episodes, tearily departing Stag Manor sans one of Jaimie's pins as if they've (actually) spent more than five minutes alone with him. Case in point: Byeeee **Cassie** and **Helen** (oops, I learnt their names, but let's not bother with the other four).

The Villains!
Ah, yes, the ones Jaimie will be ~~told~~ asked to keep around (until it becomes FAR TOO OBVS that the producers are doing that), just to up the drama.
This season's (wonder) Villains include:

- **Veronica** For the oldest Doe in the Manor, you sure do pout, shout, and carry on a lot – put your big-girl knickers on, Veronica—it's going to be a bumpy season!

- **Serena** In case you missed it (and really, how could you have?), Bond villainess, Serena, is a 'bossy little *thang*'. She described herself as 'the boss' so many times, I was able to decline the word in Latin by the time her meet and greet with Jaimie (or is that 'meet and *grate*'?) was over. Let's see … bossa, bossum, bossae, bossā

- **Donna** Is this girl a plant? Her acting is so bad, she's like a reject from a casting for *Emmerdale* extras. And I love a good swear, truly I do, but what's with using the F-word as a noun, adjective, *and* a verb, *Donna*? You'll definitely keep the censors busy.

- **Marie-Alice** (Or 'Marie Claire', as Serena calls her accidentally-but-really-on-purpose) is a #hotmess #trainwreck who will probably set feminism back 500,000 years. With all that airtime, the producers clearly love her, though Jaimie doesn't appear to be particularly impressed. And not that it *really* matters, but I'm not either.

Dark Horse

This season, the (only) one to watch is **Simone**! She doesn't seem to take herself—or this show—too seriously, and more than once she *may* have induced full-on snort laughter (don't judge me). Arriving at Stag Manor dressed as a llama?! Genius—the perfect way to stand out in a sea of pageant gowns. Not to mention that she's gorgeous, though seems to have no idea. Yes, our little (big) Jaimie's eyes lit up at the sight of Simone—a fascinating mix of mirth and lust—and she's my pick for Dark Horse. Or, rather, Dark *Llama*. Baaaa! (Llamas go 'baaaa', right?)

Miscellaneous

These are the (somewhat) odd Does who don't fit into any

Extract from The Dating Game

other category. They are *marginally* more interesting than the Filler Does, but definitely not Bride material:

- **Kerry** PLEASE CALM DOWN, KERRY! Nothing is *that* funny, love, not even Simone. And your laugh sounds like a donkey going through menopause—that will get old fast!
- **Natalie** Sweet, but she has one of those wide-eyed smiles that betrays she has no idea what's going on.
- **Daisy** No, Daisy, I'd bet *my* winged eyeliner that *you* will not get a one-on-one date—seriously, though, who bets on their eyeliner? Unborn child, absolutely, but *eyeliner*?

(potential) Brides

Only two that I can see: **Julia** and **Chloe**. These are the most real/lovely/I-would-be-friends-with-them-in-real-life Does of the lot. But as Julia is a mum of two and our little (big) Jaimie is a young man about town, how would that even *work*? Besides, did you *see* those fireworks between Jaimie and Chloe when they first met. I'm fairly certain I heard one of the crew bellow, 'Get a room!'

So, punters are already calling **Chloe** for the win! Huzzah.

But even if it is a(n almost) foregone conclusion, won't it be such fun to watch all the DRAMA unfold? Dah-duh-duhhhhh!

Til next time …

There, that should do it—£750 please. I know that may sound like a lot and it is considering it's for three hours of work—one for viewing and two for writing—but Feed Your Mind makes oodles of advertising money from Anastasia. She's a brand and she sells so aren't I entitled to my little piece?

The best weeks are when shows air concurrently. That keeps me busy, sure, but for someone who grew up in council housing, I like being able to put money away, build my nest egg. I'm not entirely sure what I'm saving for—perhaps the sense of security. My mum never had that chance when I was growing up. It was just the two of us and she worked three jobs and we lived payday to payday. I also give money to my mum, even though she tells me not to. I can't help it—I love my mum.

I live a modest existence. My one-bedroom flat is more of a bedsit, I only buy clothes and shoes from the sale section (more often than not, that's a *supermarket's* sale section), and I rarely splurge on anything—but it's enough. And with Anastasia bringing in my 'bread and butter', I have time for what I love to do—what I *trained* to do—which is proper writing.

I am constantly pitching to (real) magazines and news organisations, mostly deep dives into societal issues. I've had some pieces published—on average two or three a year—though sometimes it strikes me that I left university a decade ago and have little to show for it.

But I hold onto my dream, to have my own column in a real magazine and to write under my own name—*only* my name. Until then, I will don the moniker of Anastasia Blabbergasted, providing light entertainment to readers across Britain, and try not to think too much about how I am (probably) contributing to the degradation of society.

YOUR NUMBER ONE STOP

ONE MORE CHAPTER

FOR PAGETURNING BOOKS

One More Chapter is an
award-winning global
division of HarperCollins.

Sign up to our newsletter to get our
latest eBook deals and stay up to date
with our weekly Book Club!
<u>Subscribe here.</u>

Meet the team at
<u>www.onemorechapter.com</u>

Follow us!
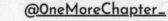 @OneMoreChapter_
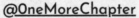 @OneMoreChapter
@onemorechapterhc

Do you write unputdownable fiction?
We love to hear from new voices.
Find out how to submit your novel at
<u>www.onemorechapter.com/submissions</u>